The Other Kind of Life

by Shamus Young

Twenty Sided Books

Pittsburgh, PA

First Printing, 2018

ISBN: 9781790478514

Twenty Sided Books
ShamusYoung.com

SUNDAY

Free

After a long career of scams, heists, counterfeiting, and cons, the city finally managed to put him away for a crime he didn't commit. As of today, he's done serving his sentence. Deep down, he knows he technically shouldn't be mad about it. The crimes he got away with would add up to a lot more than the three years he just served. He always said that Rivergate is a city incapable of justice.

Max is standing in the middle of the deck of the ferry. He heard that you get more seasick if you stay near the side of the boat where the vertical motion is strongest so he's up against the wall of the bridge, clinging to some metal pipes or columns or whatever. He's trying to look casual like he's just leaning, but he's gripping the pipes with white-knuckle ferocity. He's staring through the barbed-wire fence that encloses the entire deck and trying to keep his eyes fixed on the horizon. One of the other inmates told him that watching the horizon was good for avoiding seasickness, but now he's wondering if they were just fucking with him.

All the other guys are at the front of the boat, as if standing closer to the shore would somehow bring them to freedom that much sooner. A couple of prison heavies are on the deck with the prisoners, clad in black tactical armor and casually fidgeting with the bone-shattering billy clubs hanging from their wrists. Up above are perches where a couple of guards are standing with one hand resting on their imposing crowd shredders. Max tries to imagine how much stronger the motion of the ship must be at that height and his eyes begin watering. The guards all have their eyes to the front, where the prisoners have gathered in clusters according to their social / criminal class.

It's strange seeing the other inmates in their street clothes. For the last three years everyone here has been wearing bright yellow jumpsuits. In their society of transients there was only one class of person: an inmate. The only social status was how long you'd been around. But now everyone is wearing indicators of their station in life. Some guys are dressed in gang leathers. Some are in rags. Some are dressed in gaudy tourist T shirts and denim. Max is the only one in a suit.

What is he supposed to do if he needs to puke? The fencing means you can't lean over the side. Max takes comfort in the fact that nobody seems to be looking in his direction. If he does throw up, he won't have to do it with everyone staring at him.

He reflexively sticks his right hand into his pocket for cigarettes. He doesn't find any because the cops swiped his smokes when they picked him up. Instead he finds an unfamiliar soft object. He pulls it out to discover it's his wadded-up necktie. He starts to put it on, but halfway through the process he starts feeling green again and he decides he really doesn't want anything around his neck right now.

Cigarette, coffee, cheeseburger, whore, revenge. He closes his eyes for a moment and thinks about his plan. It gives his brain something to hold onto so he can shut out the chaotic rocking.

"Hey man, you got a cigarette?"

Max opens his eyes to see one of the other inmates has come over to strike up a conversation by asking the stupidest question possible. Of course he doesn't have any cigarettes.

Max ignores him and keeps his eyes straight ahead. He's not feeling very social at the moment and he's afraid if he opens his mouth the only thing that will come out is his dinner.

The other prisoners are all rubbing their bare scalps and stroking their chins, and Max can tell everyone is talking about what kind of hair and beards they're going to grow now that they're allowed. A couple of them snuck in a day of stubble as a head start. Max didn't want to do anything to piss off his captors and risk staying another week, so he's still smooth. He absent-mindedly rubs the top of his head as he wonders where his hairline is these days. It had already moved back on him a couple of inches before he went to prison.

The guys dressed as tourists aren't actually tourists, of course. Rivergate doesn't throw tourists in prison without a spectacularly good reason. These guys were arrested while *disguised* as tourists, probably as part of a scheme to rip them off. Rivergate is merciless with criminals who muck with the city's tourist trade, which is why Max stopped targeting foreigners back when he was a teenager. It's much easier and safer to steal from the bloated dysfunctional factions within the city, who probably won't notice they've been ripped off until he's long gone. This is another reason he's so pissed off about getting caught. Not only was he wrongfully convicted, but he was convicted of a stupid, amateuer-level crime.

"Hey. C'mon. Just one."

Max turns slightly to one side to face this guy. He's older. Maybe fifty. Scars. Replacement teeth. Crooked nose. Twitchy movements. Threadbare clothes about fifteen years out of style. This guy's a scrapper. The lowest possible tier of criminal. In a world where you can steal millions through surveillance and subterfuge, it takes a special breed of willful idiocy to get into street fights over the contents of someone's wallet. Max needs to play this just right because this is the kind of guy who's willing to fight even when it goes against his own self-interest.

"Nobody has any cigarettes," Max says in a flat voice. He can't show contempt or it might provoke him. Showing fear would do the same thing. He goes back to watching the horizon.

"Some guys hide them," the scrapper says.

"Some guys," Max nods. "And if anyone on this boat had cigarettes, they'd be smoking them right now. Nobody's smoking, so nobody has any cigarettes."

"You look like you think you're clever. I know you got some cigarettes. Gimme one." The scrapper is pissed off now. His eyes are open wide and his jaw is clenched. He's priming himself for an assault.

4

Max pushes off from the wall and stands up straight so he's got control of his weight. This guy is hard to read and Max isn't sure when he might pounce.

The scrapper has noticed Max's suit and concluded he's a soft white-collar criminal. He's wrong, but there's no point in trying to change his mind. Max is going to have to deal with this. Adrenaline hits his bloodstream and takes the edge off the seasickness.

The two of them are about even in terms of height and body mass. The scrapper's facial wreckage suggests he's not a particularly cunning fighter. If Max was betting on this fight, he'd feel reasonably safe betting on himself. The problem is that if he gets into a fight now then they won't let him off the boat when it reaches shore. Even if the fight is obviously not his fault, both of them will get dragged back to prison. If that happens, Max won't have another shot at freedom until the ferry makes another run. The ferry only runs on Sundays. Max needs to somehow beat this guy without fighting him.

Max locks eyes with him saying, "Now's a good time to quit anyway. We've already gone through withdrawal." He needs to keep the scrapper talking until he comes up with a plan.

"I don't want to quit. I want your cigarettes."

Max begins going through his pockets as if he's looking for cigarettes. He's actually taking inventory to see what he's got to work with. In his right pocket is his silver lighter, a gift from a colleague after a successful heist. In his left pocket is his plastic lighter, which he uses in neighborhoods or situations where flashing a silver lighter would be imprudent. Aside from his handheld and the necktie draped over his shoulders, this is a complete list of the items in his possession.

Max tries to keep his tone detached as he says, "Cigarettes are really bad for you. That's why they don't let us smoke inside. If you quit now you might live longer." Max actually thinks the regulations are stupid and counterproductive. Sure, outside of prison it's a good idea to give up smoking. But if you're looking to increase your lifespan then the last thing you want is to be locked in a steel box with a bunch of criminals who are all restless and agitated on account of nicotine withdrawal.

"You want to live longer? Gimme your cigarettes. Right now."

5

This is it. No more stalling. He has to move here or he'll be in a fight that will cost him another week of his life even if he wins. Max lowers his shoulders as if giving up. He plunges his hand into his left pocket.

"Okay, you want my cigarettes? Take them." Max pulls the lighter out of his pocket and whips it in the direction of one of the heavies.

Predictably, the scrapper watches the object as it sails through the air, stopping when it hits one of the guards right in the ear. Max resists the urge to smile. Good throw. By the time the scrapper and the guard lock eyes, Max has already resumed his position holding onto the wall. He does his best to keep his eyes forward, looking as bored as possible.

The impact is harmless, but the heavy lets out a curse in surprise. The posture of everyone on the deck changes in the space of a few seconds. The guards were ignoring them, but now all eyes are on the scrapper. The heavies are brandishing their clubs and the guards overhead have brought their weapons into some sort of ready position.

To the west, the city is a silhouette against an orange sunset. The dark jagged buildings stretch out to the north and south. The clouds (or maybe it's the smog; he rarely sees the city at a distance like this) catch the light and make it look like the city is backlit with fire.

Cigarette, coffee, cheeseburger, whore, revenge. The people who framed him would get what they deserved once he'd settled the other stuff. He's spent the last three years debating the details and ordering of these tasks. *Maybe he should have the smoke after the cheeseburger so it doesn't kill his taste buds? Maybe the cigarette would be more thematically appropriate after the whore? Maybe he shouldn't take up smoking again, since he already went through withdrawal when he was locked up? Maybe he'll end up released on a hot day when he won't want coffee?* And so on. Eventually he decided that logic be damned, this was the order. If that meant he was going to sit there in the hot August sun and drink his piping hot coffee, then that's what he was going to do because that was how he planned it. The plan kept him going inside, and he needs to follow through.

It's going well enough so far. It's a chilly September 2nd, and a fine evening for coffee.

"Is this your lighter?"

Max turns his attention back to the action at hand. One of the heavies is holding up the plastic lighter. The scrapper is shaking his head and pointing in Max's direction.

"Is this your lighter?" the heavy asks again.

Max pulls out his silver lighter and flips it open. Obviously that can't be his lighter. Why would a white-collar criminal like himself carry a cheap plastic lighter?

The scrapper starts to say something, but is cut short when the heavies go to work. He starts out screaming profanities, but he's all squeals and grunts once the air is knocked out of him.

Max shuffles to the side so the assault isn't in the center of his field of vision. Guards can be a little volatile once you get them worked up and nobody wants to do anything to draw attention to themselves. All of the prisoners go silent and focus their attention on the shore. The only safe way to deal with this is to pretend it isn't happening.

The ship begins to turn and he slams his eyes shut in response. He loses track of which way the ship is moving and he can't even tell when the turn is over. When he opens them again Lady Halona has swung into view.

If you include her elaborate headpiece, Halona stands 200 feet high. She's mostly made of white bronze. Some people claim plastics were used around her arms to enable them to maintain their outstretched position. She's wearing an ankle-length robe that's flowing in the breeze, although the wind is depicted as coming from the east, which goes against how things actually work around here. The robe leaves very little to the imagination. You can see both her belly button and her clavicle through the fabric, although not her nipples since that would have been taboo back when she was made. At high tide it looks like she's standing on the water, but it's low tide now and you can see the dreary slab of slime-covered concrete supporting her.

She was a "gift" from The Republic of Kasaran about 150 years ago, during a decades-long occupation. She's posed with her back to the city, facing eastward towards where Kasaran trade ships headed with all the trade goods they'd bought. She's standing with her chin held high, back arched, offering two enormous platters to the east. On the right platter is food, and on the left platter is a ball of fire, which is supposed to represent the fossil fuel exports the city was so famous for at the time. These days the city runs on tourism and opiate exports, but nobody is interested in updating the statue with that information. When Max was a kid he thought she looked kind of like a waitress that was just about to stumble forward and spill everything.

Her original name was "Avanacenda", which is a tricky word from the Kasaran language that means, "Person who is incredibly rich, but also very generous with their wealth". It's supposed to be a compliment, but if someone breaks into your house and "buys" your stuff for prices negotiated at gunpoint, then having them award you a trophy labeled "World's Most Generous Person" will probably come off as a little hollow and patronizing. Making the compliment even more uncomfortable is the fact that "Avanacenda" also means, "really attractive but easy woman". (Or in some informal uses, "really pretty whore".) Her creators really did intend her to be a gift and a compliment, but it wasn't taken that way.

At the time, the peasants of Rivergate - who were just barely more than slave labor and had no understanding of the political implications of this statue - decided it must be an image of Halona, who was their goddess of harvests and hearths. To their minds, who else could she be? She's holding both fire and food! Their perception of Halona was gradually warped by the statue. Halona's "hearth" aspect had to do with cooking, but once the statue went up the faithful decided she was in charge of everything fire-based, including building fires and gathering resources to make them. Eventually the women started facing the statue when they prayed for her to provide a good harvest and protect their husbands from mine collapse.

A decade after the statue went up, Kasaranians had to withdraw because they were getting their asses kicked by some other country. They wound up getting occupied themselves for a generation or so. Once word got around regarding the real meaning and intent of the statue, the people of Rivergate began to view her as a grave insult from a conquering nation. She might have been torn down, but at the same time the Rivergate tourist industry was just starting to take off. Rich foreigners were showing up with their heads full of stories about the city's exotic foods, cheap opiates, attractive women, and their unconventional monotheism built around a female deity. Rivergate had a dozen religions and none of them were remotely monotheistic, but they weren't ones to ruin a good story with the truth. Rather than tear down Avanacenda, they embraced her as Halona and went on to mythologize the *shit* out of her.

Occasionally some idiot tourist will get wind of this and try to explain to a tour guide what Halona's original meaning was. (As if the locals were ignorant of their own city.) Usually, the tour guide (or whoever) will explain that the statue was still part of "Halona's plan". Everything feeds back into the mythology, because that's how you keep the tourists interested. Sure, you can tell the ignorant dumbass that you know perfectly well where the fucking statue came from, but if you play dumb then their pity and guilt will keep those foreign dollars flowing.

As the ship passes, Max dares a sideways glance at Halona. He doesn't usually get to see her up close like this. Someone has spray painted "KASEREN KILLER ROB-" on the north-facing side of the statue, which is the outside of Halona's left foot. The vandal was, unsurprisingly, not good at planning ahead. They evidently ran out of room and so the rest of the message wraps around to the backside of the foot, which Max can't see from this vantage point. Still, it's not hard to figure out that the last word must be "ROBBER". Or possibly "ROBBERS". Either way, it makes for an odd message. The lettering is runny and the spacing is terrible (not to mention the spelling) but Max is still impressed that someone managed to get out here and do all of this without getting caught. A boat would probably get noticed before it got close, and it's a long swim.

Max wants to read the rest of the message. Someone evidently put a lot of effort into it and he's curious what they were trying to say. At the same time, he's not eager to let go of his spot on the heaving boat. Finally his curiosity gets the better of him and he gently pushes off from the wall, aiming for the fence on the port side. He has to walk past the limp body of the scrapper to get there. The guards have relented and staggered away to catch their breath. Max is pretty sure the guy is still breathing, but he doesn't care enough to stop and check.

Max lunges the final two steps and his fingers clamp onto the chain-link fence to keep him upright. As the boat passes the statue, he

9

presses his face against the fence to see what the vandal had to say about "Kaseran killer robbers".

On this side, a city robot is standing on the concrete platform, sandblasting the message. The only bit remaining is the letter O. Which means the message currently says "Kaseren killer robo". Max stares at the letter O as it gradually vanishes, trying to make sense of it. Killer robot? Robots? Neither one makes sense. Did the vandal turn the corner and forget what they were writing about?

The robot itself is also scrawled with graffiti. Max can't read it at this distance, but he can see the it's been dented up for some reason. That's unexpected. These things are expensive, and the city is usually pretty good about taking care of them.

He turns around, leans against the fence, and curses himself as he reflexively reaches for cigarettes he doesn't have. It's been three years since his last smoke, but wearing his old clothes has reignited all the old mannerisms. He realizes that since he doesn't have any cash, he won't be able to buy smokes until he recovers his money.

When he went in, he rented a drop box near the docks and told his bank to clear out his account and have everything sent to the box. He did this on his handheld while sitting in police custody. Eventually one of the cops saw this and took his device away. He was literally thumbing the big green "APPROVE" button as they yanked it out of his hand. He's got five thousand bucks, which should now be waiting for him in box #6641. It's not a lot, but it's enough to get him his smokes, coffee, cheeseburger, whore, and a place to stay for a couple weeks so he can get his feet under him and start earning again. Taking down cops isn't a thing to be done lightly and he's going to need some real capital to make it happen.

He pulls out his handheld, thinking he might check his accounts on the off chance he's got some forgotten spare change stored in one of them. But of course the battery discharged two years and eleven months ago. He stuffs it back in his breast pocket, looks again for cigarettes, and then jams his right hand into his pants pocket just to keep it still. The left one is still busy keeping him upright.

The ship moves into the shadow of the city and the lights fade into view. Down on street level is the pale signage of the shabby storefronts that serve locals. Above that is the tourist deck (called "The

Promenade", which sounds better to foreigners) and all of the leering neon billboards soliciting their custom. Above that is the sea of dark concrete and pale blue light that makes up all of the non-tourist parts of the city. Rivergate is wedged into a spot that makes expansion difficult, so the city has needed to build up rather than out. The buildings are staggered along the coast to increase the number of windows with a view of the ocean, but once you get a few blocks inland Rivergate becomes a crisscrossing network of sheer canyons. She isn't anywhere near the richest city in the world and she's far from the most technologically advanced. She doesn't have any of the top ten tallest buildings in the world. But her tight footprint and dense population mean she's among the tallest cities in the world in terms of *average* building height.

Overhead he can see the wandering searchlights of the night patrol drones. Above those, some of the mobile billboards have begun their nightly cruise around the city. Above that, the orange sky is fading to a weak and starless grey.

The ferry docks. The guys stand up straight like they're going to walk off right now. Technically they were "released" from prison three hours ago, but this is a bureaucratic operation to the core and there's at least another half hour of dicking around before anyone can walk through the metal gate and down the gangplank.

The scrapper is dragged off below decks so he won't get in the way of the proceedings, although nobody seems to be in a hurry to clean up the bloody puddle he left behind. Max steps over it and takes his place in line. It doesn't look like anyone here was friends with the scrapper and nobody is glaring at him, which means nobody is blaming him for what happened. Probably. Still, a lot of these guys are from different cell blocks and are unfamiliar to him. It's risky to make assumptions about loyalties and group structures. It's possible he's just made an enemy and he doesn't even know it yet.

He doesn't want to spend the whole night looking over his shoulder. He decides to put himself last in line so he's got everyone else in front of him.

The group is subjected to another round of facial ID just to make sure the right people are leaving. Then they have to sign a receipt for themselves so the city can't be blamed if they go missing later. They

11

also have to certify that they were given back all of their possessions. This isn't true for anyone, but raising a fuss about stolen cigarettes, jewelry, and pocket money would require optimism that borders on delusional. The fastest way to get free of the state is to just forget about whatever they took from you and move on.

It's a long wait, and so his stomach has calmed by the time his turn comes around. As he's going through the procedure of face-scanning and paper-signing, he gives a few sideways glances at the docks. Two guys in tourist outfits are lingering there.

"Don't forget your lighter."

Max turns to see one of the heavies standing behind him, offering him his plastic lighter. This is the same guy he hit in the ear earlier. Max freezes. Did someone see him make the throw? Or is this guy just looking for an excuse? The other heavy is standing in front of the exit, and there's no way Max could get past him.

Keeping his voice as even as possible he says, "Not mine."

The heavy steps forward and Max flinches slightly. He tucks the lighter into Max's breast pocket and pats him on the shoulder. "It's yours now. I don't think the other guy is gonna need it anytime soon."

Max nods.

Everything relaxes again. Max signs the papers and gets the fuck out of there. When he's on dry land he has a careful look around, but the tourist guys are gone. He doesn't know if they were waiting for him or not, which means he's going to need to look over his shoulder until he finds his way back to the right side of town.

He puts on the tie and draws in a deep breath. It's strange to be standing here on the streets of Rivergate in his old suit. Aside from being temporarily bald, nothing has really changed. He could almost pretend the last three years were just a bad dream.

He gets his bearings. This isn't really his part of town. This is south-side territory, and there aren't a lot of opportunities for a discriminating criminal to work with here. The people are poor, the businesses are low-yield and service-based, and the neighborhoods are kind of close-knit and insular. The only criminal opportunities involve stealing from the shipping warehouses. Messing with the warehouses means messing with exports and tourist trade, which is risky and there are already a lot of other, dumber criminals working that angle. Max hasn't been in this part of the city since he was twenty.

He ducks into the closest business - a bar he's never seen before - and takes a booth. He slaps his handheld down on the faded, beer-stained rectangle at the end of the table. After a few seconds the screen blinks to life and announces it's charging.

It's oddly quiet for 8PM. Then again, it's Sunday night and the tourists usually stay on the other side of the river. It's all locals this close to the south waterfront.

"What do?"

Max looks up to see the hard face of a middle-aged woman. She is not smiling. "What do?" is short for "What do you need?", but it's incredibly informal and not something you expect to hear from wait staff. Mixed with her flat tone, it's the equivalent of, "I hope you don't need anything, but if you do I suppose I can get it for you."

Max shakes his head. "Nothing, thanks."

"Then don't take up my booth. Order something or get out." She's got a thick south-sider accent. She's most likely pegged him as a northerner based on his accent. She probably doesn't like his suit either. Southerners are descendants of miners and farmers. They have no patience for foreigners and even less for the people who serve them, such as northerners. He could have worked a local accent when he came in, but he didn't think he'd need to win anyone's favor just to sit in a booth for five minutes.

Max stops himself midway through reaching for cigarettes again. His clothes smell of cigarettes and it's making him crazy. He nods at his phone. "Dead battery. I'll order something once my wallet's functioning again."

"I'll be back in a couple minutes to take your order." She glares at him like she knows this is a ruse, but she's willing to humor him for now.

Max watches his phone battery indicator tick upwards. As soon as it hits 10% he walks out the door. He doesn't actually have any money in his wallet, because it's all sitting in a drop box on the other side of the river. He's a little uneasy being in an unfamiliar part of town like this. Things get pretty dangerous this far from the tourist hubs, and

13

the streets seem to be designed to shunt foot traffic into blind alleys. Nothing is marked. He checks his handheld, but it only knows about the official streets and has no idea how to navigate the network of gaps between buildings. It doesn't know which ones lead through and which ones might dead-end in a dark corner. He hears someone yelling in the distance. He doesn't know if someone is calling to him or if it's just a couple of drunken jackasses hooting at each other, but he knows enough to keep his eyes front and keep moving.

He finds a road sign that hasn't been stolen or vandalized into illegibility, and that points him towards the Great Street Bridge. He knows he's relatively safe once he crosses the bridge.

The Great Street Bridge is not actually a particularly great bridge. In the time of his grandfather there were only two bridges in town: The West Bridge and the Great Bridge. These days there are a dozen other bridges and all of them are more impressive than the Great Bridge. They're all wider, taller, and more elaborately lit. The one interesting feature of the Great Bridge is that this is where the subway crosses the river. The White Train leaps from out of the depths and howls across the bridge between the two opposing lanes of traffic before disappearing into the ground on the other side. The train makes this two-tone vibrating sound that Max always found fascinating at a distance, like a banshee duet. But now that he's on the bridge he's discovered that the thing is as loud as a punch in the ear. There's a low wall on either side of the train, and Max always assumed that, in addition to keeping idiot motorists off the tracks, it was there to take the edge off the sound. Maybe it does, but it's still loud enough to make him stagger as it rushes by.

Max is still nursing his ear when a police scout glides by. It reaches a point a few car lengths ahead of him and then slows down to match his walking speed. After years of experience and discipline, he's able to notice the police vehicle without self-consciously breaking stride or looking around nervously. Then he remembers he just got out of prison and he's completely clean, which makes him wonder why this police drone is giving him a second look, which makes his steps falter as he nervously looks behind him. He realizes this makes him look incredibly guilty.

Technically, this drone shouldn't care about body language or looking guilty. It's got a pair of seats and can autodrive cops around the city if they order it to, but usually they send these things out to cruise the city autonomously and call in if the face scanner picks up a person of interest. It can't detain people by itself, but it can call for help and follow you around until the meat-based cops show up. Max stands there nervously like a complete dumbass while this scout gives him a nice, long look.

He's knocked out of his trance when the White Train blasts by again, giving him another punch in the ear.

"What? What the fuck is your problem?" he shouts at the rubbernecking drone. It doesn't answer, but after another ten seconds of cryptic silence it glides away.

Then he remembers. He's still bald and beardless. The scout was probably checking him out, making sure he's not a fugitive. He practically runs the rest of the way across the bridge. It's uncomfortable to run in a suit, but he doesn't want to be anywhere near the next time the White Train passes.

Once he's across the bridge and a few blocks into the North Side, he's basically in his old neighborhood. He turns right and heads back towards the ocean. He's sweating. He's only walked a few miles, but he's been sitting around a prison cell and he's hopelessly out of shape. He passes by some of the noodle shops and his mouth starts watering. He hasn't smelled noodles in three years and now it's the only thing in the world he wants to eat. He even knows a few of the shop owners. They would probably spot him a free bowl to celebrate his release.

No. He shakes his head. He didn't spend three years fantasizing about cigarette, coffee, cheeseburger, whore, revenge just so he could toss the entire plan aside the moment he's home. He doggedly hikes past the noodle stands and donut shops to his goal.

He encounters a robot walking with a sandwich board sign. He can't tell what the sign is supposed to say or who it's advertising for, because someone has painted "I AM A SCAB" over the original content. Judging by the uneven writing, they must have done this while the robot was in motion.

It's a standard worker robot, the kind you might find in a fancy hotel to carry around people's luggage or deliver room service. No effort has been spent to make it look human. It's got a capsule-shaped head and rigid white plastic for skin. It's wearing a pinstripe dress shirt that Max recognizes as belonging to one of the Kasaranian hotel franchises.

Foreigners will pay hundreds of dollars a night to stay someplace where they don't have to worry about tipping the bellhop an extra ten bucks. For them it's not the money, it's the social stress. Assuming you're from a wealthy nation, then you're going to be more comfortable with a robot. It can understand and speak your language without difficulty, will answer all of your questions without getting impatient, and won't gossip about you to the other staff. It might get confused and it's more likely than a human to get your order wrong, but it's not going to get offended, laugh at you, or mock your attempts to speak Local. You're free to treat it like an appliance and get on with your vacation.

A good robot is worth a fortune, and Max has no idea why this one is wandering the streets alone on a Sunday night. If he had the connections, he'd seriously think about grabbing this thing and stripping it for parts. As it passes, Max sees that the left side of its plastic head has been bashed in and crudely repaired. The paint is cracked and the surface is wrinkled. One of the glowing blue eyes looks off at a slight angle. It doesn't speak to him, and it doesn't care if he stares at it.

He reaches the Stardance, which is the whorehouse he's going to visit later tonight. But the sign says Moon Shot and the overpowering purple neon lights have been replaced with overpowering red neon lights. The glowing star logo is gone, and instead the sign shows a rather sad and vaguely phallic rocket ship. The first-floor windows are now mirrors and the second floor windows have become a facade of glowing window-shaped rectangles. There aren't any signs of construction, which means all of this happened months ago.

This really screws up his plans.

He's got five thousand dollars, which is enough to bankroll the steps of the plan from cigarette to whore. Except now he's got to vet this new whorehouse (or find another one) because he can't afford to wander in like some dumb tourist. For all he knows this place could be owned by an enemy. Or maybe they've got cameras in the walls and they're running a blackmail business. Max isn't susceptible to blackmail, but he still doesn't want to worry that there might be videos of his most private moments on some creep's computer. Or maybe the place is run poorly and the girls carry diseases. You just don't know. A lot of guys are happy to roll the dice and go to whatever whorehouse looks nice and has pretty girls, but to Max this is an indicator of the sort of carelessness that leads to death or prison. Max believes that taking care of your own life requires some due diligence, even if it makes you uncomfortable in the short term.

Sixteen years ago, at the age of 17, he made his first set of fake IDs and went to the Stardance with some friends. For a few of them, this was how they lost their virginity. Raff - the youngest of the group at just 16 - couldn't afford the sex and had to settle for a lapdance. Afterward he claimed she'd given him sex anyway, which the rest of the crew magnanimously pretended to believe. Looking across the street at the former Stardance, he remembers that Raff was killed seven years ago when a job went wrong. He was trying to blow open a security door and mis-handled the explosives.

Max hangs his head, sighs, and reaches into his pocket to grab the empty spot where he expects to find cigarettes.

"Fuck!" he shouts at the pavement. He stamps his foot, shouts "fuck" one more time, and begins heading east again. He can smell the ocean now.

During his first and last visit to the Stardance as a customer, the girl had gone out of her way to talk about how much she wanted him and what a sexy stud he was. Except, he knew he was paying her, and he knew that her saying these things was part of the service. This ruined the whole experience by exposing the artifice behind it. She was saying this stuff because he was paying her to, and she was having sex with him for the same reason. When it was over he felt even less like a stud than when he walked in the door. He concluded that, regardless of what his friends thought of the experience, whorehouses were not for him.

17

In contrast to most of his colleagues, Max favors monogamy. This is not out of the desire to adhere to a moral code, but a matter of simple practicality and convenience. Over the years he's observed how much time, effort, and money his friends have dedicated to their pursuit of women. It takes a lot of lies, patience, and capital to maintain more than one girl. You've got to keep your stories straight and establish alibis with your buddies, because they talk to their girlfriends and everyone's girlfriends all know each other. You've got to work twice as hard to keep her happy, because if you're running around on her then she probably spends a lot of time alone and bored. You certainly don't want to give her a reason to go snooping around to figure out where you've been. Worse, if your girlfriend is feeling lonely and neglected, that makes her more likely to take on a lover of her own. Once you find out about it you're supposedly honor-bound to track him down and have your buddies hold him still while you kick his ass until your sense of self-worth recovers. And then you've got to watch your back just in case he comes back looking for revenge. And of course now you've got to look for a new girlfriend because your current one will be crushed to find out you've smashed up the guy she was seeing while you were fooling around on her.

The whole thing creates this never-ending hurricane of pointless drama and complication. Girls calling the cops on their boyfriends out of spite. Guys picking fights with romantic rivals. Girls calling at inopportune times to check up on their boyfriends. Guys asking you to memorize complex lies before you're allowed to have a conversation with their girlfriends. It's gotten to the point where Max will pass over otherwise dependable guys for a job if he knows they do a lot of womanizing. He understands the basic concept that variety is the spice of life, but there's no way the fun could possibly be worth the number of headaches it creates. Even if you don't get caught, just the threat of having your side-chick discovered adds a bunch of stress to a line of work that really doesn't need more. When he's planning on robbing someone who will kill him and his whole crew if they're discovered, he at least wants to know he can go home in the morning and not have to deal with someone throwing dishes around and screaming at him.

Under ideal circumstances, he would simply get a girlfriend. But it takes money and patience to find a suitable girl, woo her, and bring the relationship into the sort of stability where she won't freak out if he needs to be out all night or if he vanishes for a few days. A project like that takes months, he doesn't have the money to pull it off, and even if he did have the money he needs to be investing it into his revenge plan. Depending on how things go, it could be half a year before he's in a position to have a girlfriend again. He's not going to wait another six months to get this particular frustration out of his system, even if he finds the whole "money for sex" thing to be mildly sad and unsatisfying.

He reaches Riverside Storage, which is an open-air maze of lockers of different sizes at the foot of the transit building. It's right across from the shuttle station. If you go two blocks closer to the ocean from here it's all hotels and shopping, and if you go two more blocks you're swimming.

RIVERSIDE STORAGE - A HOTEL FOR YOUR STUFF

Thus proclaims the glowing sign, which bathes the entire area in blue light. Every few seconds the sign switches to a new language, and he assumes the slogan sounds less stupid in one of languages he doesn't speak. On the right side of the sign is a picture of a smiling woman, because a smiling woman is more interesting than blank space and cheaper than a company logo. It's animated, so her face goes from gentle smile to enthusiastic smile about once every ten seconds, and the process makes the patterns of blue and white light flicker as Max walks the aisles looking for box #6641.

Max had rented one of the deluxe boxes (for four years, just in case something went wrong and he was released late) which has a mail slot in it and can be used as a mailing address. When he finds it, he holds his handheld up to the sensor on the front of the door. It identifies him as Maxwell Law. He would have rented it under one of his alternate identities, but he wasn't in a position to do that while sitting in the police station. The locker accepts his credentials and dutifully pops open.

He finds himself looking at a perfectly empty space. Like a dumbass, he sticks his arm into the locker, as if his hand refuses to believe what his eyes are showing him. He gropes around the interior, rubbing the smooth metal walls and trying to imagine where the plan went wrong. Finally he slams the door and bangs his forehead against it while trying to decide what to do next.

Once he's done feeling sorry for himself, he heads for the tourist deck. There's an elevator nearby, along with a very carefully-worded sign insisting that the promenade is "not for Local foot traffic". This is the city's polite way of saying they don't want riff-raff wandering around topside, bothering the tourists. The city has a "guide" posted at the top of the elevator. He's ostensibly there to help tourists find their way around and to steer them away from the unkempt bits of the city, but his real job is to police the flow of traffic and make sure troublemakers don't get in.

A lot of dumb criminals complain about the injustice of being barred from certain parts of their own city. They resent the city for keeping them out and they act like the tourists are bigots for being afraid of them. (Despite the fact that the only reason these guys want in is to prey on them.) This mindset drives Max crazy. He wants to grab these guys by the shoulders and scream, "Go home and put on a suit you fucking imbecile!" On the other hand, he's glad there are rules keeping the dumbasses off the promenade so criminals like himself have more room to operate.

Despite what the sign says, the city doesn't care if you're a local or not. They just don't want you roaming around in gang jackets or rags, spoiling the fiction that the city is safe, prosperous, and peaceful. The guide is a great litmus test for would-be criminals. If you're not smart enough to get past the guide, then you are not qualified to operate on the tourist deck. Max hasn't stolen from tourists since he was a teenager, but he still comes up here from time to time because the hotels themselves are fantastic targets.

Max tightens up his tie and smooths out the wrinkles in his suit as the elevator carries him up. The doors glide open and he gives a polite nod to the guide on duty. He's on the promenade now. This walkway goes between the hotels, shopping, and the scenic bits of the city, and only offers access to the tourist-friendly bits of the lower streets. The walkway is spotless white stone, framed on either side with planters overflowing with greenery.

He finds a donut shop and drops himself into the closest seat. Everything is ten times more expensive up here, but he felt like he wanted to think about this problem from somewhere above street level. He checks his bank account on his handheld - which he realizes he should probably have done the moment the battery came to life - and finds a series of messages.

--

Dear Mr. Law, we recently received a request to have your funds sent to you. However, the address you provided is a public box and not a residential address. For security reasons, we can only send cash to residences. Please update your profile and try again.

--

Dear Mr. Law, Good news! We're rolling out the new SecurCard 6. This new handheld offers more security, more customization, and more convenience than ever before. As part of your existing support plan, we will be issuing your new card in 30 days and you will be billed accordingly next month. If you do not wish to upgrade your SecurCard at this time, please notify us within the next 7 days.

--

Dear Mr. Law, We have issued your new SecurCard 6. However, the address we have on record is a public box and not a residential address. For security reasons, we can only send transaction devices to residences. Please update your profile and try again.

--

Dear Mr. Law, According to our records you are still using the SecurCard 5. This device is being deprecated and we strongly urge you to upgrade as soon as possible.

--

Dear Mr. Law, Starting next month, customers still using the SecurCard 5 will be charged an extra $20 monthly handling fee. If you wish to upgrade (or have already upgraded through a third-party seller) then please contact support as soon as possible to have your credentials moved to your new device.

--

Dear Mr. Law, Good news! We're rolling out the new SecurCard 7. This new handheld offers more security, more customization, and more convenience than ever before. As part of your existing support plan, we will be issuing your new card in 30 days and you will be billed accordingly next month. If you do not wish to upgrade your SecurCard at this time, please notify us within the next 7 days.

--

Max pages through the rest of the messages, discards them, and then looks at the final balance: $156. The bank nibbled away at his account for three years until they turned five thousand dollars into pocket change. Somewhere at the bank is a stack of three handhelds of increasingly recent vintage with his name on them. If he'd gotten out of jail two months later the account would be dead.

He's not even angry at this point. He knew they would do this, which is why he tried to get the funds out. If he'd had more time he could have handled this properly. In reality, he was lucky he even got the chance. The police usually confiscate your handheld as soon as they get the cuffs on.

He tries to buy cigarettes, but there isn't any place nearby that sells them. The hotel guild has an exclusive contract for cigarettes here on the tourist deck and he doesn't want to walk to a hotel, so he heads back down to street level.

He needs money. A job - a real job, like boosting a safe or running a scam - takes some sort of up-front investment. You need names, clothes, intel, and a place to stay. This means he's going to have to take a job working for someone else until he can support himself again. He hasn't been in this position since he was a kid. It's frustrating and mildly humiliating.

He figures the best thing he can do is kill two birds with one stone. He messages a guy called Blackbeard, who used to own the Stardance. Even if Blackbeard doesn't have any jobs for him, he can still find out what happened with the Stardance. Less than thirty seconds later his handheld beeps with the reply:

come to moon shot

It's a good thing Max walked by the place earlier, or he would have no idea what the fuck Blackbeard was talking about. The place has evidently been Moon Shot for so long that it didn't occur to Blackbeard that Max might not know about it.

Inside, the Moon Shot looks just enough like the Stardance to be confusing. The lobby looks the same, but the door that should lead to the manager's office is now the restrooms and there's a little cluster of soft couches where the bar should be. Max stands there, turning around in circles like a dumbass, trying to get his bearings.

A girl gets his attention by running her hand across his shoulder, which he does not like.

"Let me guess," she coos. "You just got out and you're looking to celebrate?"

He resists the urge to shove her away. She's just doing her job, and this is how they train the girls to behave.

"Looking for Blackbeard."

Her fake smile melts away and she loses interest in him. "Just past the couches, make a left."

The terrible thing is, the moment the mask of insincerity is gone he finds her unbelievably attractive. Aside from the waitress he talked to a couple of hours ago, he hasn't heard a woman's voice in three years and he's suddenly aware of just how painfully horny he is. As she walks back to the couches he pulls his eyes away and heads for the back.

He finds Blackbeard in an overlit office. A few of the old purple fixtures from the Stardance have been set up in here and it gives the room an otherworldly look. Blackbeard is sitting in a desk that's a bit too large for the tiny space. Max has no idea how they got it in here.

"Max. Nice haircut."

Max shrugs. "You know how it is. The barber always cuts it too short."

Blackbeard gives this a half-hearted laugh just to be polite. He looks the same as three years ago, except he's a little heavier and the streaks of grey have now taken over his beard. He's wearing the same stupid threadbare denim vest he's been wearing for as long as Max has known him, but underneath it he's wearing a bright red "Moon Shot" branded T-shirt, just like all the bouncers.

The office is technically in the same exact spot where it was a decade and a half ago, but now it's a little smaller and you have to walk around a new kitchen area to reach it. They serve food now. At a brothel. Max shakes his head in disbelief. It's like his home has been replaced with a foreign country.

"What's the deal with changing the place?"

Blackbeard shrugs. "It's a franchise, man. Moon Shot has global recognition. Even if they don't speak the language, everyone knows what that rocket ship stands for. We're trying to get the tourists to give us some of those foreign dollars. The top-deckers are fighting us the whole way. They've been trying to keep all the money upstairs. They're even threatening to set up their own whorehouses. It's not legal yet, but it's only a matter of time. We have to get a brand name if we want those pale fat bastards to venture all the way down to street level."

Max clears his throat nervously. He hates starting with nothing. "So anyway, I wanted to talk to you about money."

Blackbeard nods with sarcastic enthusiasm. "That's good. I wanted to talk to you about money too." He's been idly poking at his handheld this whole time, but now he drops it on the desk in front of him. "Have a seat." He gestures to the shabby wooden chair in front of his desk.

One of the bouncers steps through the black curtain that serves as a door and stands right beside Max. The office is very small, so the room is basically full at this point.

"Where's my money?"

Max has been in this exact situation a lot of times over the years: Some guy thinks you owe him money. You're trapped in a room with him. He's got some hired muscle on hand in case you do something stupid. Max has done this enough times that he knows that asking "What money?" is always the wrong answer. Maybe you've got it, maybe you don't, but pretending like it slipped your mind is just going to get you a punch in the face. The Other Guy probably wants to talk anyway, so just shut your mouth and he'll explain without you needing to ask.

Max doesn't say anything. The room is very quiet. Blackbeard raises his eyebrows. Max can see the bouncer in the corner of his vision, moving his arms around to loosen up his shoulders.

So he's going to have to take a punch in the face to find out why Blackbeard thinks he owes him money. On top of everything else, he really doesn't need this. He gives a resigned shrug. "What money?"

The impact nearly sends him out of his seat. He was expecting an introductory punch to get him to take this seriously, but instead this bouncer pulled his arm back and put his weight into it. Max is dazed for a few seconds after the impact and doesn't hear what Blackbeard says. He prods the side of his face to make sure he didn't lose any teeth.

As things come back into focus Blackbeard is already halfway into his speech, "...that was over six months before you went into prison. You had plenty of time to pay me back. I didn't say anything because I figured you just needed some time and we're friends. I figured you'd pay me back when you had the money."

Max sighs. He knows what Blackbeard is talking about now. He knows that Blackbeard is wrong. Max does not, technically, owe him a single shiny coin. He knows that if he tries to explain this to Blackbeard he's going to earn himself another punch in the face. He can't do his job if his face is wrecked. He's horny, hungry, footsore, he needs a cigarette, and his face hurts. It might not be the smart way, but he wants to deal with this head-on. He leans forward like he's about to say something profound.

"I don't owe you a fucking cent," Max says, and then jerks his head back and grabs the big meaty arm that passes through the space

25

where his head was a second ago. This guy has a few pounds on him, but he's probably not expecting any resistance, either.

What Max wanted to do was yank the guy off-balance, trip him, then pounce on him and hurt him before he can recover. That's kind of how it goes, but the office is a very tight space and there's not a lot of room for fancy maneuvers in here. The bouncer goes face-first into the wall. Since the chair is in his way anyway, Max picks it up and bashes the bouncer with it. He feels it break, then looks down to see the chair itself isn't broken. The bouncer is crumpled up on the floor and has stopped trying to fight back.

Blackbeard has drawn a gun. He's pointing it at Max with one hand while he works his handheld with the other. Max isn't sure just how serious this is going to get, so he puts his hands up a little ways to make sure Blackbeard understands he's not about to leap across the desk. Blackbeard hasn't told him to stop, or sit down, or answer the question. He's just tapping away at his device like he lost interest. Max doesn't do anything, figuring he's not going to get shot for standing still.

The curtain parts again and a couple of kitchen guys appear, still wearing their grease-stained aprons. The first one clears his throat and looks at the gun nervously. "Yes, Boss?"

The other kitchen guy can't even tell what's going on. There's not enough room for him to enter.

Blackbeard drops his device on the desk again. "Get him out of here." When the kid looks confused Blackbeard clarifies, "Randy. Take him to the nurse."

They have to jam Max into the corner so the kitchen guys can help Randy out of the room. This is hard, because the kitchen guys are skinny and Randy has more muscle mass than both of them put together. His left arm is pointing at an unhealthy angle that makes Max wince.

Once Randy is out, Blackbeard finally shows some outrage. "What did you do that for?"

"He was hitting way too hard, man." Max rubs the side of his face and spits out some blood to make his point.

Blackbeard sighs and gives an apologetic shrug as if to say, "It's hard to find good help." He gestures with the gun for Max to sit down.

Max straightens out his suit. He's actually in a worse position now than a minute ago. Now if he gives a wrong answer he might get shot instead of punched. He doesn't know where the kitchen guys will drag him if he gets shot, but he's willing to bet it won't be the nurse.

"You're talking about the fifty grand you gave me?"

"Obviously."

"That was an investment."

"Yeah. You said you were going to pull a job with it and I'd get a hundred thousand."

"If it panned out. It obviously didn't."

"Obviously. So give me the money back."

"If you lend someone money, they have to pay you back. If you invest in a venture, there's no guarantee of a return. You can lose some or all of your investment." Max is trying to keep this friendly and educational. It's looking less and less like he's going to get shot tonight, but the more he can placate Blackbeard the better this will go for him. He knows full well Blackbeard is going to insist he wants his money back, but Max wants to make his case anyway.

He continues, "With a loan, you're only entitled to the loan amount plus interest. When you invest, you get a share of the profits. That can turn out to be a lot more rewarding than a loan. With greater potential reward comes greater risk."

Blackbeard sniffs and looks down at his desk thoughtfully like he's thinking this over. Then he says, "I want my fifty thousand back. Plus another fifty thousand for, you know, making me wait for three and a half years. And let's say another ten for what you just did to Randy."

"Five. That was mostly his fault. Is he new or something?"

"Five." Blackbeard nods gladly.

Max realizes he just haggled with the wrong part of the deal. He sort of implicitly accepted the fifty thousand in interest - or whatever Blackbeard thinks it is - and got distracted by the part that irritated him. He's not thinking clearly and now the mistakes are piling up.

"Any questions?" Blackbeard asks.

Max realizes it would basically be suicide to ask if Blackbeard has any jobs. "Do you have a cigarette?"

27

Blackbeard puts the gun back in a drawer and goes back to messing with his handheld. "Sorry. Franchise rules. No smoking outside of the service rooms. I'm trying to get everyone to quit."

Max shows himself out. He stands on the corner outside the Stardance - or the Moon Shot, or whatever the fuck the place is called - and stares down the street. A lot of stuff is closed at this point in the evening and he's wondering where he can buy some smokes. He doesn't have a place to sleep and he's suddenly a hundred and five thousand dollars poorer than he was an hour ago, when he was broke. He doesn't know how to fix this, but he figures it'll be easier to solve once his head is clear.

Another police scout does one of those slow drive-by things and he starts thinking maybe he should invest in a hat or a wig.

There's a blackjack parlor a few blocks from here. The owner knows all the dirt on what the unions are doing and is usually a pretty good source of jobs and leads. Even if Max can't find a job, he should at least be able to find cigarettes there.

Three blocks later he arrives to find the blackjack parlor is now an automotive charging station. There's no shop. You can't buy smokes or coffee here. It's just a bunch of parking spots and a single robotic attendant. It's another plastic-skinned laborer like the one he saw earlier.

An expensive sedan moves silently into view. It's one of the models where the wheels are tucked in underneath so it looks like it's floating. Max is standing in one of the parking spots, where he's been staring into space and wondering where to go next. The car stops right in front of him, like it wants to use his spot in particular. He's not sure why this idiot doesn't use any of the other dozen or so empty spots, but he steps out of the way. The doors pop open, and a couple of private security goons hop out and shove him into the back seat.

"Come the fuck on," he shouts as the door slams shut.

Landro

"These things give me the creeps," the goon says. He's looking up at an archway that reaches across the entire room. A woman's face is carved into the stonework, glaring down at them.

The other goon grunts a sort-of noncommittal agreement.

The three of them are standing in a grand office near the top of a major office tower. The goons are standing on either side of the door to make sure Max doesn't try to leave.

Max knows he's on the north side of the city. Looking out of the giant floor-to-ceiling window on the east wall he can see he's near the shore somewhere, but he doesn't know which building he's in. After the goons kidnapped him they went underground through the city's great maze of interconnected parking garages. They brought him up to this suite directly from the carpark via an express elevator, so he never got a chance to see any sort of logo or signage that might explain where he is. This office is oddly barren, aside from a couple of decommissioned robots posed near the door like suits of armor.

Going by their apparent position along the coast he figures they're somewhere near the Hospitality District. Maybe he's in a hotel? On the other hand, he can't imagine why the hotels would have a beef with him right now and he can't think of any hotels that have arching windows like the one he's looking through.

"I hate the way Kasaranians carve faces into everything." The goon is still looking up at the archway.

"Actually, we carved that," Max says matter-of-factly.

"Bullshit," the goon says with annoyance. He's the larger of the two goons and he's the only one to speak so far. He's a local, but he's as tall as a Kasaranian. He's a full head taller than Max. He's got a full beard and his eyebrows seem to be locked into a scowling position. "Fancy stonework is their thing. It's all creepy and effeminate."

The smaller goon grunts in agreement.

Max has been standing in the middle of the room since they shoved him in here. There's an executive desk and a couple of chairs near the window, but he doesn't want to make himself at home so soon after being kidnapped. He takes a couple of steps towards the goons so he can talk to them at a more comfortable distance. Both of them make slight movements towards their jackets, perhaps getting ready to pull out their weapons if he suddenly loses his mind and decides to charge the door.

"The female face is how you can tell we built it," Max says casually. This goon was probably just trying to make small talk with his buddy, but if they're going to talk architecture then Max wants in on it. "See, a hundred and fifty years ago these guys showed up in our port with their fancy diesel ships and the best firearms in the world."

"I know how long ago the occupation was," the goon says with irritation. "Just because I'm big doesn't mean I didn't get schooling. I'm registered literate and I've got two years of trade school. We're not all dumb muscle."

The other goon nods at this.

Max ignores him and continues, "You know why they used to call this Firelight City? When they showed up we were going through the industrial revolution sideways. To them it looked strange to see a city with concrete structures and automobiles that was still mostly lit with candles. See, we call it an 'occupation', but they still call the whole thing a 'trade pact'. To them, they were just helping us out. Our infrastructure was a patchwork and everyone made their own electricity because we didn't have a central grid. This was actually how they got their foot in the door. They said to us, '*Oh you poor dears. You don't know how to run a power plant and your coal mines are smouldering powderkegs because you don't have proper ventilation and you're still using oil lamps. You know, we could really kick-start your economy if you'd let us build a proper plant, lay some cable, and get you some modern transport vehicles.*' And that's what they did. They built us a power plant, modernized the coal mines, and laid a beautiful highway that ran directly from the mines to the port where the coal was loaded onto their ships and sent off to Kasaran." Max turns towards window and waves goodbye towards the ocean.

The goon doesn't know what to make of any of this. He keeps glaring at Max. Finally he says, "What the fuck are you talking about?"

30

Max can tell he's stuck here waiting for someone. He doesn't know who they are or what they want with him, so he's decided he's going to annoy this goon until he does something stupid or says something useful. "Of course, to make all of this work they had to insert themselves into the local government. You can't build a power grid or a road system without a little regulation, and they figured it was easier to just copy the regulations they had back home rather than explaining every little detail to us."

He reaches into his pocket for some cigarettes. This makes the goons jumpy again. These guys are wound very tight. Sadly, cigarettes have not magically materialized in his pockets since the last time he checked. He lets out a frustrated sigh and continues, "The whole thing was chaos. A lot of the copper wiring and electrical systems were imported from another country that Kasaran was currently helping into the modern age. I forget who. Anyway, those guys had their own language and their own take on the number system. The new highway was designed around people driving on the right side of the road, the old streets were left-side drive, and the countryside was a crazy mix of horses and automobiles where the only traffic law was 'try not to hit anybody'. The old power system was built on one voltage, the new one on another, and you needed to be trilingual to work on any of it."

Max takes a couple of steps towards the door, closer to the goons. He can tell the big goon wants him to shut up and is trying very hard to hide his annoyance. Now that he's closer he lowers his voice slightly. "See, in their view they lifted Rivergate into the modern age. They constructed all these modern facilities, rebuilt the port to accommodate their larger ships, gave us a power plant big enough for the whole city, and introduced all kinds of life-saving stuff to the coal mines." Max ticks these points off on his fingers as he talks. "But they also completely wrecked the political apparatus of Rivergate to the point where our people didn't know how to run their own city once Kasaran left town. Kasaran tried to stomp out the opium trade, and that created a dangerous black market. When the soldiers withdrew they left behind a lot of babies with pale skin and straight brown hair, which only created more problems."

"I didn't ask you about any of this," the big goon says. "Just sit still and be quiet. Mr, Landro will be with you shortly."

So now Max knows he's here to meet someone named Landro. That's not a local name and he's almost certain it's not Kasaranian either. He's pretty sure this goon can't shoot him for talking, so he decides to keep going. "When it was all over, Rivergate was a very angry city. We looked down on foreigners, but we also had a terrible inferiority complex. We were hungry for foreign culture, but we also refused to embrace anything until we'd changed it to make it our own. It's hard to be both xenophobic and tourist-friendly, but after a few decades of practice we figured it out."

The big goon draws his pistol and holds it by the barrel. "Last warning, buddy. I'll pistol-whip you if you don't keep quiet."

Max doesn't want to push it, so he nods. He goes back to pacing the room and trying to work out which building he might be in.

After a minute of silence the smaller goon clears his throat. "I don't understand what all of that had to do with this face." He points up at the engraved woman's face at the top of the archway.

"I was just getting to that," Max says before the other goon can object. "Before the occupation, we used to make boxy buildings with small windows and a confusing number of identical doors on the ground level so nobody knew where they were supposed to be going. Kasaran insisted this sort of thing wouldn't do. When they built their fancy new municipal buildings they introduced us to the wonders of high ceilings, elevated entryways, chandeliers, and carving detailed faces into the tops of columns and arches." Max points up at the ceiling as he says this.

"Like I said, the faces are Kasaranian. So shut the fuck up," the bigger goon says.

"Kasaranians only carved *male* faces into their stonework," Max says. "We wanted to imitate their style because it looked better than what we had, but we were too proud to copy it directly. Kasaranian men are always clean-shaven. They don't see beards as manly. To them, it's a sign of sickness and poverty. At the same time, big bushy beards like ours don't look that great in carved stone. Too big and lumpy, not enough fine detail. So we started using female faces in our stonework. They would never do that."

The goons both look up at the face doubtfully.

Max continues, "Kasaranians build everything out of white stone. They paint their rooms white. Everything white. We don't don't want to copy them, and we don't have a lot of white stone anyway. So we made our ceilings dark, right? That's different. But it also means it's a bitch to light a room. These big chandeliers are so bright you can't even look at them, but the ceiling just eats up all that light. So the only light on these faces is reflected off the carpet." Max nods towards the thin, firm carpet at their feet, which is a color he thinks of as "strangulation blue".

He looks back up at the face. "The face is lit from below instead of from above, which is why they always look so sinister. If we had dark floors and bright ceilings like Kasaranian buildings, then the faces would be lit from the right direction. But then we'd be copying their style, and nobody wants that. Some goes for these dark walls."

"Makes sense," the smaller goon says. The other goon glares at him.

"I knew you were the brains of the team," Max says to the smaller goon who is clearly not at all the brains of the team. At this point in the conversation a reasonable person might ask why or how he knows all this stuff. He knows they won't ask, so he decides to tell them anyway. "Some people think that if you want to understand a building you need to steal the floorplans, but you can tell a lot about the the age and layout of a building by looking at the architecture. In this room we've got this wainscotting of riveted iron panels. It looks ridiculous now, but generations ago everyone thought this looked futuristic. If the building had been built by Kasaran then the wainscotting would be blond wood. If it was a little newer it wouldn't have any wainscotting at all. Going by this, we can tell the building is older than 50 years but less than 70. Based on that, it's a very safe guess that this building has a single huge shaft for HVAC stuff. If I wanted to physically break in here, that would be the weak spot. In more modern buildings they use narrow ducts with lots of filters to pull the cigarette smoke out of the air. In those buildings you need a small woman or a child if you want to enter through the HVAC. However, in a building this tall I wouldn't want to mess around in the big shaft unless I had to. It's a long drop and there's nothing to grab onto in there. Usually it's easier to make fake IDs and try to bullshit your way past the guards. Those guys usually aren't too bright."

"Hey fuck you, man," says the bigger goon.

Max shrugs a half-hearted apology. "Don't shoot the messenger."

"I'm very sorry you had to be brought here in such an irregular way. I honestly didn't know how to arrange a meeting. Please sit down." The guy who just came in is a little young for an executive. He's perhaps the same age as Max, maybe slightly older. His hair is slicked back and he's wearing a white suit.

Max drops himself into one of the deep, soft chairs in front of the big desk. He supposes these are intended for executive-type meetings, although he has no idea how anyone could get any business done in one of these things. He feels drowsy the moment his ass hits the cushion.

The guy opens his mouth to speak, stops, checks himself, and looks over to his men, who are now standing near the desk. He seems to be out of sorts and not sure where to start. Finally he pulls himself together. "Just to make sure the facial recognition is working, you are Maxwell Law, yes?"

Max nods. There's really no point in denying it. They certainly didn't drag him all the way up here to assassinate him or torture him for information, assuming these guys are into that sort of thing.

"Good, good." The man nods and gets behind the desk. "I'm Mr. Landro, although maybe you already knew that."

Max has no idea why he would know who this guy is, but he gives a non-committal sort of shrug. He stretches out his legs and looks down at his shoes thoughtfully. They apparently found him with face cams.

His accent is a bit tricky and Max can't place it. It sounds like Kasaranian to his ears, but guys from Kasaran aren't known for big noses and jet-black hair. He's also pretty tall and lean, which suggests he's from somewhere east of Kasaran. The neatly-trimmed beard is a bit unconventional as well, since their executives prefer the clean-shaven look. He's a confusing puzzle of a man, even before Max remembers he's an executive that just ordered a kidnapping.

"Gentlemen, I need to have a private meeting with Mr. Law." As the goons turn to leave, Landro looks at Max nervously. "Actually, Peter. Could you leave me with your gun? Would that be okay?"

Peter the goon exchanges a nervous look with his partner. They sort of shrug at each other. These guys are locals. They're wearing grey suits with grey ties, which is pretty much the corporate bodyguard uniform. Peter draws his pistol, turns it around, and hands it to Landro. He points out the safety and starts to explain chambering a round.

Landro nods and waves him off. "Thank you Peter, I'm sure I'll be fine."

Boom! The light comes on in Max's head. The accent has been bugging him since Landro opened his mouth, but when he said "Leave me with your gun" instead of "leave your gun with me" Max was able to put it together. He's from one of the small southern countries that was "developed" by Kasaran about the same time as Rivergate. He probably went to University in Kasaran, got a job with one of their corporations, and was assigned here. That doesn't really tell him what company he's dealing with, but it does fill in some blanks.

Landro moves to his own side of the desk, pointing the gun nervously and apologetically at Max. "I'm sorry about the gun, but I don't usually have these kinds of meetings and, well, you *are* a criminal." He looks directly at Max's shaved head. "I'm sure you understand. You probably have meetings like this all the time."

Max is about to argue, but then he remembers that he just came from a meeting where someone was pointing a gun at him so he decides to keep his mouth shut.

"This alias you're using is very thorough. Looks just like the real thing. A criminal named 'Law'. Very funny."

Max isn't about to tell him that no, this isn't an alias. This is his actual birth name. This guy is making all kinds of assumptions about criminals and Max doesn't see any advantage in setting him straight. He prods the side of his face where he took the punch. It's actually hurting a little less, although the swelling feels a little worse.

"What can I do for you, Mr. Landro?"

"I want to talk to you about this." He lifts a screen off his desk and stands it upright. It begins playing a video. It's security footage of a line of robots, all carrying bags into a vault. They enter with full bags, and exit with empty ones. It looks like any line of robots, but if you look very closely you'll notice one of them is slightly off from the others. Its gait is subtly different. It's holding the bag at a slightly different angle. Even if you did notice, you might assume this particular robot was just carrying a lighter bag than the others. And if you watched very carefully you might notice that while all the other robots were carrying full bags into the vault and leaving with empty, this rogue maybe still had something when it left.

His mouth goes dry. This is about the casino job. This is the worst possible position to be in. He's actually surprised they brought him up here for questioning. Given their reputation, he expects he'd go right to the basement for torture.

"Buncha robots," Max shrugs with the best poker face he can manage. His heart is racing.

"It is indeed a 'bunch of robots'. Last year we had a man in here for questioning, and he indicated to us that you might know something about this."

Someone gave him up. This is rare. He spends a lot of time vetting his crew to make sure this doesn't happen, and he spends even more time making sure nobody gets caught in the first place. He hasn't been in this position since he was a kid. There were four people on that job. According to Landro the person who talked is a "he", so it wasn't Margo. The person talked "last year", so it wasn't Rider, who died the year before. The only other person on the job (besides himself) was Heavy. Heavy ratted him out. He wonders if Heavy is still alive. Probably not. These casino guys don't fuck around.

"So I'd like to ask you about this... robbery." Landro says this in a forced conversational tone. If Landro is supposed to be a hard-ass from the casino to scare him into confessing, he's doing a terrible job. Still, once you get a reputation maybe you don't need to exert a lot of force to get what you want.

Max's mouth is completely dry. "I don't suppose I could get a cigarette?"

Landro seems thrilled to have a distraction from the interrogation, or whatever this is supposed to be. He pulls out some fancy foreign brand of smokes and absent-mindedly puts the gun down to help Max light it.

Max is too excited about the cigarette to contemplate the possibility of fisticuffs or escape. He takes a big, deep draw off the smoke and it feels like he's coming back from the dead. His mind is alive for the first time since the cops slapped the cuffs on. He leans his head way back against the smooshy backrest of his chair and stares at the ceiling for a minute. The chandelier is hitting him in the face so hard he feels like he's getting a sunburn. He smiles.

Landro picks up the gun and clears his throat. "So anyway... We're very curious how you got one of our robots to act against protocol."

Our robots! Suddenly Max realizes he's not dealing with a casino guy, Landro is a robotics guy! They must be in one of the generic downtown office towers, and G-Kinetics probably rents this floor. (It's been called Global Kinetics since before he was born, but then marketing decided the name sounded too distant and ominous so they devised the friendly G-K branding.)

Max is still in a bit of a spot. This guy knows - or suspects - he was involved with the casino heist. As a matter of fact, the entire job was his idea. He's not worried that G-K is going to drag him to the basement and have him killed (they probably run a daycare for their employees down there) but they might reveal his involvement to their clients at the casino, and he'd get the same result. He doesn't want to confess right away. On the other hand, if he stonewalls they might hand him over to the casino for more intensive questioning. He needs as much information as possible before he knows how to play this.

He takes another drag and blows it out slowly. "Let's say I was involved, or knew someone involved. What then?"

This is enough of a confession to suit Mr. Landro. "Then you're the right man for the job."

Max nods very slightly, not wanting to disturb whatever forces are causing the universe to suddenly start being so nice to him.

"We want to know how you did it. More to the point, we want to know what's causing the robot murders."

"Robot murders?" Max asks this in the most sarcastic voice possible.

The guy pokes the screen a couple of times and once again they get a security camera view of a street corner. There's no date stamp, but the shadows indicate it's about the middle of the day. The only person in the shot is a woman in a fur coat and sunglasses. It looks like she's waiting to cross the street. A delivery robot walks into the shot, grabs her head, crushes it like an egg, and then the robot's head explodes. There's no audio. It's a bit surreal seeing the two of them lying quietly side-by-side after such a gruesome end. It's a full ten seconds before someone new enters the frame, looks down to see the carnage, and pulls out their handheld to call the cops. The footage ends.

"One more." Landro starts another video.

This one is a little more muddled. The footage has been zoomed in to the point where you can hardly tell what you're looking at. It shows a man walking down the street, but he's barely more than a smear of dark pixels against the side of a building. Another figure (presumably a robot, although it's hard to tell) walks up to him, grabs him, and he collapses. Then the attacker's head explodes.

"Our engineers claim that what we just saw is one hundred percent impossible. Cannot happen, ever. But there it is. It happened twice. I know the second one is a little muddy, but we've got photos of the crime scene, and we've got the body of the unit that perpetrated the murder. What you saw was a robot killing a human being, on purpose, with its bare hands. Again, supposedly impossible. That's the same thing the engineering staff said when I showed them the footage of your robot robbing its employer. I figure since you're an expert at getting robots to do the impossible, maybe you know how this was done."

"This would probably be a different methodology," Max says weakly. He can't shake the image of that first murder. He's seen some nasty stuff in his day, but nothing quite so abruptly graphic.

"Drink?" Landro is pointing at the bar near his desk.

"Is coffee an option?"

Landro looks out the window and back to Max as if to say, 'Really, at this time of night?' When Max nods, Landro shrugs and shouts in the general direction of his desk, "Halona, can you bring coffee for my guest?"

Twenty seconds later a woman enters with a steaming cup of coffee on a saucer. He holds out his hands to take it, but she walks right by him and puts it on the desk. This is a bit awkward since he can't actually reach it from where he's sitting. It doesn't make him angry or anything, but it's an odd sort of mistake for a secretary to make.

"Cream or sugar?"

He meets her eyes and realizes she's a robot. He's never been this close to one of the high-end humanoid models before. She looks incredibly lifelike. Or she did, until she spoke. There's something off-putting about her mouth. Robots don't talk using vocal chords. They just have a speaker hidden somewhere in their head. But they still move their mouth along with the words to add to the humanoid pantomime they're trying to pull off. The lip sync is off just enough to be unnerving.

"I'm good, thanks." Max stands up and takes the coffee from the desk.

Halona the robot bows and leaves the room.

"You named the robot Halona?"

"She brings me food. And if you count my morning coffee as fuel, she brings me that too. Seemed fitting." Mr. Landro is having a glass of unidentified amber alcohol as he stares out over the ocean towards the white bronze version of Halona offering her food and fire to the world.

"Fair enough." Max takes a drink. It's not bad for 10 p.m. coffee, it's amazing for his first coffee in years. "So you want me to figure out why your robots are killing people?"

"I'm hoping so. We know you can get robots to do the impossible. You're not aligned with any of our rivals. You're a criminal so I'm confident you'll come to me rather than go to the press or the cops once you find something. You were in prison when the murders happened so we know you're not responsible for those."

"I have a question."

"Of course."

"How did you guys find me? I got off the boat like three hours ago and haven't touched public transport."

39

"Oh that. I'm surprised you don't already know about it. We subscribe to this police service. You can have it let you know if certain people show up. We use it for serving subpoenas."

"Of course," Max nods knowingly. He's never heard of this bullshit before. The cameras have been around for decades, but he didn't know corporations had legal access to their data. He remembers all the police drones that were checking him out.

"So? What do you think?" Landro nods to the screen where the blurry murder is looping again and again.

"Yeah, I can probably figure this out for you," Max says confidently. "It'll take some work though."

Landro sits on the edge of his desk. "What do you need?"

Max has no idea what he can charge these guys. Money gets really strange this far above the streets. But to avoid looking like a dumbass he needs to say something. He takes a guess. "It'll cost a quarter million."

Landro nods instantly.

Max curses himself. He came in way too low. "Plus expenses," he adds quickly.

Landro shrugs. "Of course."

"And I'll need housing."

Landro frowns at this, perhaps worried that he's just commissioned a homeless man to solve his impossible robo-crime.

"For a job like this I can't use any of my safehouses. I mean, I need a place away from my usual associates, just in case they're involved. Preferably something above street level."

"Ah, I see," Landro nods knowingly. "Very good. I can set you up with a suite at one of the casinos."

"Actually I'd like to avoid the casino guys right now."

"Naturally. Perhaps a room at the Seaside?"

"Done."

Landro holds out his his hand for a handshake. This comes off as incredibly corny to Max, but he's willing to humor the guy. He takes the hand. They shake hands for a little too long. As Max tries to pull away, Landro tightens his grip and says in a low voice, "Mr. Law, I hope you can solve this. For your own sake. Because if you don't, I *will* tell the casinos you're the guy that stole from their vault."

Cheeseburger

Up until the end, Max thought he was about to run a con on G-Kinetics. He'd get himself a nice place to live and a corporate expense account, and use that money to get his revenge. But now he has to solve an impossible crime or he'll end up dying in a casino basement. He underestimated Landro, which means he let his guard down and gave a sort of tacit confession to the casino job. He really should have known better. You don't get an office that high up the corporate ladder without displaying some form of cunning.

Worse, Landro wants him to submit expense reports in order to get reimbursed. Max can put whatever he likes on these, of course. The suit probably isn't going to question every little line item. The problem is that these expense reports are presumably going to wind up on a computer somewhere, creating a paper trail. If you're trying to arrange for the death or imprisonment of three city police officers, that's not the kind of enterprise you want to have written down. He could falsify his expense reports of course, but now he knows Landro is craftier than he lets on. If Landro gets the impression Max is playing him, he could simply give Max's name to the casino and the problem (from Landro's perspective) would go away on its own. Making up bogus expense reports is effectively stealing, and there are safer people in this world to steal from right now.

Max is sitting in his new hotel room, attempting to enjoy a hotel cheeseburger. This thing is a bit fancy for his tastes. It's too big, too neat, and just doesn't quite have the fun and simplicity of a proper fast food burger. Room service sent it up with a knife and fork, for fuck's sake.

It doesn't help that his jaw hurts every time he bites down.

Max is eating in the dark. A few years ago someone took a shot at him with a sniper rifle. Technically the shooter was aiming for the guy across the table from him and managed to miss them both. Still, the whole thing made him paranoid about sitting in brightly-lit rooms at night.

It's not a particularly fancy room. It's small and it faces the city rather than the ocean. It's close to the ground. Well, close to the tourist deck, at any rate. Hotels in this city are designed around the idea that the street-level world doesn't exist. There are some simple electronics in the room, but Max has unplugged everything. It might be safe to assume nobody is putting surveillance equipment in the cheap rooms of a hotel, but he's not planning on using this stuff so there's no reason to leave it on.

Max has the curtains open a little ways and he's watching the midnight traffic work its way through the city. It's all drones at this hour. The unsettling cab-less trucks only come out at night. They travel in packs, carrying the city's exports to the docks.

His prison plan dictates he's supposed to get a prostitute at this point, but the events of the evening have put him off. He doesn't have the time or the patience to search for a reputable whorehouse, and he can't think about sex with his jaw hurting like this. Maybe tomorrow.

He finds himself wondering what Clare is doing these days.

He decides to get some sleep. After staring at the ceiling for an hour he remembers he recently drank coffee and sleep is probably not going to be happening anytime soon. He finds himself, oddly enough, wanting to investigate the robot murders. Technically he needs to work on this if he doesn't want to die, but aside from that he's just curious.

There's a computer in the room. He plugs it in and begins digging. Landro gave him a bunch of insider information and a couple of leads, but he wants to catch up with the public stuff before he starts looking for secrets, just so he can tell the difference.

It turns out the murders made international news. Even the big nations are following it, and they don't usually give a shit what happens in places like Rivergate. Max's understanding of the Kasaranian language is pretty rusty, but he gives it a try and manages to read a couple of articles. They don't tell him anything new, but they do confirm that he isn't dealing with two different stories. The stuff Kasaranian housewives are gossiping about over there is the same thing Rivergate dock workers are gossiping about over here.

G-Kinetics is apparently up against a wall from a public relations standpoint, and it's a lot worse than Max would have guessed based on the meeting with Landro. When the first murder happened the company insisted the footage had to be faked. When the forensic evidence was presented they agreed that yes, their robot seems to have killed a person. But look, they said, this is the first time this has happened since robots arrived on the scene fifty years ago. This means that robots are still billions of times less likely to murder you than a human being. Therefore, everyone should just calm down. This was a fluke accident, the robot probably had a mechanical rather than a cognition failure, and something like this won't ever happen again.

(Here Max thinks public relations is making a glaring bit of misdirection. Fifty years ago the stuff they called "robots" was stuff we would barely classify as a "drone" today. It wasn't capable of any serious independent thought. Robots in the current sense of independent thinking, talking, and creativity are only a couple of decades old. And the really lifelike ones are less than ten.)

G-Kinetics managed to make the bad press go away. It was a freak accident. A lightning strike. The public lost interest. Then the second murder happened. They tried to play it off like another freak accident. Then they did a mass recall, while still insisting that everything was fine and robots were totally safe. The company is in deep financial trouble now. Around the world, people are curious what's really going on. Are these two murders connected? What set these robots off? The fact that there don't seem to be any answers is fueling a never-ending churn of speculation and panic.

A week after the second murder, some guy released a video presenting a theory that these first two murders were the harbingers of a mass killing spree. He talked about the failure rate of circuits and probabilities over time. He created a graph by showing ten years of no murder, then one murder, then another murder three months later. Using these three points he plotted a line showing that over the next six months the number of murders will go up exponentially. It's obviously horseshit, but it's horseshit delivered in a reasonable tone with a scary graph and Max isn't surprised at all to see a quarter of a billion people have watched the stupid thing.

Other people are looking for some connection between these two victims. Maybe these two people "knew too much" about some dirty secret inside of G-Kinetics, so G-K dispatched a couple of killbots to silence them? This conspiracy theory is easily disproved by looking at the victims and the killers. The victims were a wealthy housewife and a retiree, neither of which had any connection to a major technology company. The "killbots" were different models, produced in different facilities, and serviced in different places. The first was a brand-new barista bot and the other was a five-year-old municipal traffic guide. Also, why would G-Kinetics user their own robots to kill people? Some people have watched too many movies.

The only thing the murders have in common is that they both happened in Rivergate.

The Three Little Pigs

Max was framed and subsequently arrested by officers Dixon, Veers, and Sando. Or as Max thought of them, the Three Little Pigs.

Now, it's true that all police in Rivergate are crooked to one degree or another. There's always a certain degree of bribe-taking going on, particularly when it comes to regulatory enforcement.

For example, you're not supposed to serve alcohol in the same establishment where gambling takes place, because then you've got an incentive to get people as drunk as possible so they'll make lots of reckless bets. Before the law was passed you could even test the alcoholic content of different establishments and see that places that offered gambling had much stronger drinks than places that just served booze.

This "gambling and drinks can't be offered in the same establishment" law is one of those things where everyone not directly affected by it will readily agree that it's a fantastic idea. The problem is that people really want to drink beer, watch sports, and make bets, and laws like this make it really inconvenient to do so. So then a bar and a bookie strategically place themselves next door to each other. You can sit in the bar and watch the game, or race, or whatever it is you're into. If you need to place a bet, you walk next door.

After a while the people running these places start asking themselves why customers need to go outside. Sometimes it's raining and sometimes it's winter. *Can't we just put an open doorway between the two establishments?* So they do. And once everyone is used to that, customers start asking themselves why they need to get up from the bar and leave their drink to place a bet. *Can't I just send someone next door to place my bet for me?* And then the bookie sends runners over to the bar to provide exactly this service. And then the bookie starts wondering why they need to bother making a front entrance at all, since all of their customers come from the bar. So they don't bother having a sign or a front entrance. And then the bar owner looks at the front of the two buildings and starts thinking there's a lot of wasted space on the front of the bookie's building, and if he's not going to use it then why not add more signage for the bar?

46

And so on. Eventually you've got everyone breaking the law to one degree or another. There are an endless number of situations like this. Brothels, smoke parlors, casinos, cosmetic surgery boutiques, hotels, strip clubs, restaurants, sex toy shops, tanning parlors, inkers, arcades, car rental, city tours, pawn shops, and charging stations. Everyone has a few laws dictating when they're allowed to operate, who they're allowed to serve, and what businesses they're allowed to cooperate with. Everyone recognizes that these laws are generally a good idea (particularly ones that only impact other people) and were probably made with good intentions. On the other hand, they really suck the fun out of things, add hassles to life, and (most importantly) make it harder to earn a living. So people pay the police to look the other way, and the police take the money knowing that they probably have more important things to worry about anyway. Over the years these bribes have become an open secret and everyone has basically accepted them as a secondary business tax.

So all of the police take bribes to one degree or another. And if you're taking a bribe to look the other way for a dumb law, maybe it's a little easier to take a bribe to look the other way for something more serious. This sloppy approach has made the entire system somewhat lax. In the end, the Rivergate police exist to enforce the two most important laws of the city, neither of which is written down anywhere:

1) Keep the tourist dollars flowing in.

2) Keep the exports flowing out.

These are the two laws nobody is allowed to break. Don't mess with tourists and don't mess with exports. If you get caught doing something you weren't supposed to do, you can probably make the problem go away with the right amount of money as long as you aren't breaking one of these rules.

Of course, it's not as simple as pulling out your handheld and making a transaction like you're buying groceries. You have to know how much to offer. You need to have it in cash. You have to know how to say things just right so that the cops can take the money with a clear conscience. (The conscience of the average street cop is a very strange and complicated animal.) You have to understand when the time is right. There is usually a part during a typical inspection or arrest when you'll be left alone with one officer while the other goes aside to take care of some bureaucratic details. This window is the only time when you can safely offer the bribe. If you try it at any other point in the process you risk a beating. The cops really resent people who disrespect them by implying bribes are a common part of the machinery of the city. You need to help them pretend you're doing this "just this one time."

While all cops in the city were a little crooked like this, Dixon, Veers, and Sando were crooked in the sense that they broke the two unwritten laws.

Rich tourists like to shop while they're on vacation. This is especially true in Rivergate where the beaches are small and the water is filled with jagged rocks that make swimming dangerous and surfing suicidal. Once you've seen Halona and listened to all the bullshit the tour guides have to say, and assuming that gambling or sitting around a smoke parlor stoned out of your mind aren't your thing, then the only thing left to do is hit the shopping district. In this way, it's pretty easy to end up with more baggage than you can possibly carry home. So you have it shipped there.

The problem is that one of the major exports of the city is opiates, and the city - wanting a cut of the action - has stratospheric tariffs on them. So there's a strong incentive for a few people to try and slip some product through without going through the port, and the easiest place to do that is to hide it within the literally tons of goods visitors mail home after their two-week shopping orgy. This means someone needs to get in the shipping warehouse and inspect the stuff, and since you're dealing with luxury goods it's not the kind of job you can entrust to the normal collection of stevedores and bean counters.

The Three Little Pigs were in charge of these inspections, and they'd been helping themselves to a lot of the stuff they were supposed to be inspecting. The rumor was they had gone beyond just pocketing the occasional trinket. They'd turned their pilfering into a full-blown business and had a network of pawnshops and movers to fence the goods.

To Max's mind, this was the worst possible way to perpetrate this sort of theft. You can stay low-profile and quietly skim a very small number of goods forever, or you can go high-profile and clean out the entire warehouse just once, but the thing you can't do is continue to skim a lot over a long period of time. There are only so many losses that can be explained away as "breakage" and "incorrect shipping label" type problems. Once you get above that threshold, the entire enterprise is going to come apart one way or another.

Max has no idea what they were thinking. Normally you'd blame this sort of thing on youth or stupidity, but Dixon, Veers, and Sando weren't particularly young and they weren't morons. Which means you have to go with the more scary explanation, which is that they were all a little crazy. It's rare to get three guys into the same unit that are all the same kind of crazy, and they didn't usually get promoted far enough to be entrusted with jobs like this, but apparently it happened and nobody knew what to do about it. The other police wouldn't turn on three of their own unless it was going to threaten the rest of them. After all, if you accuse another cop of corruption he can turn around and accuse you of corruption, since everyone is corrupt.

Max wasn't really aware of any of this when it was going on. He'd heard some rumors that there were some unusual cops working at the port, and some of his associates were complaining that their small-time smuggling operations were being disrupted, but he didn't pay attention to it because he didn't usually have anything to do with the port. He made a point of only targeting locals.

He still hasn't figured out why the Three Little Pigs targeted him in particular. One evening Sando pulled him over for "suspicious driving". Max sat on the curb for an hour smoking cigarettes and wondering why his attempted bribes weren't working. Sando poked around his car, looking for contraband and checking Max's credentials. Then Max was let go. At that point he thought it was over. He drove home thinking he'd somehow fumbled the bribe.

He walked into his apartment, flipped on the light, and saw the dining room was stacked high with goods. At that moment Dixon and Veers kicked in the door and arrested him. The Three Little Pigs were heroes for catching the port thief and Max was off to jail.

He would have served twenty years, but he managed to successfully play for just three by confessing to being a small-time operator in the smuggling business and not the ringleader. To pull this off, he had to disavow the pile of cash they found hidden in his apartment (which was actually his) and fabricate names and descriptions of his "bosses". Max is a pretty good bullshit artist and he was able to extemporaneously fabricate a convincing and internally consistent story about how the operation worked, who operated it, and how his apartment was actually just temporary storage for the goods and he didn't know where it went once it left his hands.

The Three Little Pigs could simply have stopped stealing. They didn't need to frame someone for their crimes. They didn't put Max in jail out of self-preservation. They put him in jail because they wanted the glory and promotions that come with a major bust. This is the part Max can't forgive. They took three years of his life to advance their careers.

MONDAY

The Undermall

Max awakens to the sound of heavy rain splattering against his window. He doesn't even remember going to bed. He remembers sitting up most of the night reading about the murders and then brooding about the Three Little Pigs until the sun came up.

He should work on solving the murders, but right now he really wants to work on revenge. Should he do the responsible thing, or the satisfying thing?

After a shower, he looks in the mirror and realizes this is the first time he's done so since he was thrown in prison. He's got the dark skin you'd associate with ethnic groups that developed this close to the equator. It's not enough to hide the bruise on his face, but it does keep it from standing out. His hair has begun to grow in and he's got dark stubble all around the sides of his head. Sadly, his hairline hasn't just retreated, it surrendered and quit the field completely. This means he needs to grow a beard to avoid looking like a fugitive. It's a shame, because (in his non-expert opinion) he's got a good jaw and it's a shame to cover it up with facial hair. He's always viewed beards as a crutch for guys with weak chins. Not only did the Three Little Pigs steal three years of his life, they stole the last years of having hair on top of his head.

Regardless of whether he's doing investigation or revenge, he needs to go shopping. He doesn't own anything except for the clothes on his back. It's time to test out his new G-Kinetics expense account.

He wants to cover up his bald head so people stop seeing a convict when they look at him. He also needs to shield his face from the police drones so he can move around the city anonymously. A hat can accomplish both of these.

He walks to the shopping district on the upper deck and gets drenched in the process. The rain is projected to be heavy this year. By the time he arrives he's soaked all the way down to his skin.

He goes to the bank and gets his handheld situation straightened out. The new device looks almost identical to the old one, but the lady at the shop looks at him like he's a madman for walking around with a three-year-old unit. He gets his identity moved over and then he personally destroys the old one. The bank always offers to dispose of it for him, but he knows they actually dump it in the recycling. It's pretty hard to wipe something completely clean of data, and digging around in the recycling for identity fragments is one of the ways forgers make their living. He did it himself for a couple of years.

After that he's off to buy clothes. Colorful clothing flags you as a tourist, which is dangerous. White clothing advertises that you're rich, which is even more dangerous. Black will tell everyone you're a criminal, which is fine unless you actually happen to be one. The best he can do to avoid attracting attention is go with greys and earthtones. He gets a new suit and dumps the old one in the trash. He also buys a long raincoat and a wide-brimmed hat. He tests it out in the mirror and finds that he can fully obscure the top half of his face by just tilting his head down about twenty degrees. He can hide the other half by nursing a cigarette. That should keep the drones off and let him move freely.

Now he needs a car. The thing is, he never buys cars. If you buy a car then the city knows that you and this particular car are connected. Cars are in constant communication with the city transit system. This means the cops have a live update of everywhere you go. They don't even need a warrant. The movement of cars through the streets is considered a "publicly observable" phenomena, equivalent to something you can witness by simply looking out the window. You don't need special permission to gather that sort of knowledge. Your car ends up becoming an informant against you, broadcasting a continuous record of your comings and goings. If you pick up some of your ill-gotten money, visit a dealer to buy a firearm, and then drive to the other side of town to commit a crime with said firearm, the police can not only use your car to place you at the scene of the crime but can also work backwards and find all of your associates.

Yes, you can "go dark" and prevent your car from talking to the transit system. But then traffic lights won't change for you, toll booths won't let you through, and parking areas won't open for you, because those systems won't recognize that a car is present. Worse, if you happen to pass a police car and it notices you driving dark they'll pull you over on the spot and you won't be allowed to move until your car is "repaired".

So the only way to move through the city anonymously is to rent a car under an assumed name. The problem is, Max had to scrub all of his alts when he got arrested. He can buy more, but that costs money and the only money he has is his corporate expense account. Even if he can get the forger to openly accept corporate money, he doesn't want G-Kinetics to have a record of his professional contacts.

He knows a place where he could create bogus charges. For example, he could have them charge his expense account with a transaction saying "Maxwell Law bought $1,000 worth of surveillance equipment." (Or whatever might look acceptable to Landro's accountants.) They would then give him $500 in cash and pocket the difference. The thing is, they're not going to want to deal with him if he's not already part of the club. i.e. he needs to already have a fake ID and an untraceable car. He can't get money without a fake ID and he can't get a fake ID without money. This is not an accident. It's *supposed* to be hard to break into this particular subculture.

Hoping for some honor among thieves, he messages Burnside, his forger. Two minutes later he gets a reply.

THE UNDERMALL. ONE HOUR.

The Undermall is the sarcastic name given to what was supposed to be the shopping complex under the transit building. Years ago the city noticed just how many people wound up stuck there. People waiting for a shuttle to the airport. People waiting for a bus. People waiting for the subway. All three transit systems intersected at this spot. It was obviously a prime location for a viciously price gouge-y shopping area. This would turn the infamously irregular transit system into an asset, as trapped tourists would have nothing to do but wander around and spend money.

The problem was, there was zero room to build anything new. But then someone got the idea for an underground shopping complex. It didn't pan out, and the result was the Undermall.

The construction is only a decade old, but you'd think it had been a century by the looks of it. Max is amazed by what entropy can accomplish if you let things run their course. Water somehow finds its way down here from the storm drains of the city. It dribbles from cracks in the ceiling and lands noisily in the ankle-deep water of the

54

main concourse. The walls are covered in stone tiles, which are black with mildew. Long-dead electrical infrastructure hangs from the walls and ceiling like copper vines. Inexplicably, there are a few blank billboards with power, advertising a yellow rectangle of light to an empty corridor. The light bounces off the black water, throwing scattered ripples of light into a nearby storefront and illuminating a mound of rusting slot machines.

Wooden boards have been placed between islands of paving slabs, forming a walkway a few inches above the drink. Max follows this until he finds Burnside, who is standing in what was probably designed to be a fountain. Ironically, it's the only place in the room with a dry floor.

"Maximum." Burnside nods.

Max nods in reply. "I don't suppose you can spot me this for a couple of hours?"

Burnside raises an eyebrow.

Max shrugs. "I can't get money without a fresh face, and I can't get the face without the money. You know how it goes."

Burnside is the sort of man where his appearance can't seem to agree on what age he is. He's got sharp eyes, good posture, a full head of jet-black hair, and a full set of healthy teeth, but his skin looks like ancient leather. Max figures the guy probably goes to a clinic. Unlike Max, he's not shy about dressing in all black. His trenchcoat is a shadow against the backlight of vacant billboards. There's a fat ring on his left hand, which is holding a closed umbrella like a cane. His right hand is in his pocket.

Rather than answering the question, he looks away to the crumbling walls and changes the subject. "I heard a rumor that this place is your fault."

"An exaggeration. The city set up the dominoes. I just knocked one of them over trying to make a buck."

"Still. Pretty big pile of dominoes."

Max shrugs. "People talk. You know things get exaggerated."

"What did you do?"

There's a long silence. Max wonders if someone is after him. This job was a long time ago, but there are probably a lot of people still sore about it. He can't imagine how any of them might be connected to Burnside, but this city has a way of surprising you with strange alliances. "You know I can't talk about a job, Burns."

"It was a long time ago. Nobody cares now."

"Maybe. But like you said. This is a big pile of dominoes."

Nobody says anything. The rain dribbles in. Burnside switches the umbrella to the other hand and puts his left hand in his pocket. "I really wanna know. Purely my own curiosity. Nothing else."

"Motivate me."

Burnside pulls a handheld out of his left pocket. "I've got a new face right here. And I'll *give* it to you if you tell me how you ruined a billion-dollar mall."

Max lights a cigarette. "It's not a billion dollars. Never was. Anyway, you know how the unions were fighting over this place?"

"I always stay out of labor disputes. Those guys are dangerous."

"Well the Miner's Union thought they had a right to this."

"What the fuck does the Miner's Union have to do with shopping malls? Don't they dig for coal?"

"Sure. Eighty years ago. But then the mines started shutting down. The thing is, an organization that big and well-connected doesn't just dissolve because people don't need it anymore. When the mines dried out they decided they were in charge of any digging-related activities. And wouldn't you know it, the city was about to break ground on the subway at the time. So they bullied their way into that job. It was messy. Protests. Political assassinations. The whole thing. When it all blew over, the three big unions had divided up the jobs around the city. Miner's union would get all digging and tunneling type jobs. Transit union would get everything to do with public transport. Builder's union would be in charge of buildings and stuff like that. But then you end up with this place. It's underground, it's connected to all three branches of the transit system, and it's a shopping mall. All three unions thought the job should belong to them."

"I remember the protests. Didn't realize it was union stuff."

"Those weren't protests. Those were basically gang fights. See, this city was done growing. Or at least, it was growing more slowly than it had been. Everyone knew there was going to be less construction in the future. Some of these unions needed to starve so the others could survive on what was left. Everybody knew that whoever got the Undermall would outlast the other two. In the end, they'd get everything."

Burnside puts the handheld back in his pocket. "So how did you get mixed up in this?"

"It looked like the Miner's Union was going to win. They were the smallest and the hungriest, but they had the better political connections. They were the most savage. A lot of people vanished that year. I suppose a lot of them are down here."

Burnside looks uneasily at the rotting walls. "You were making people disappear?"

Max scoffs. "No. Not my line of work. All I did was make a few work passes. See, by this point the Miner's Union wasn't actually big enough to dig this tunnel. They were looking to get guys to quit the other unions and join up. They only let you on the site if you had a union pass. So I started making counterfeits and selling them for half a day's wages. Guys could show up and work without betraying their old union. It let them keep their options open. That worked great for a couple of days. But then the Miner's Union noticed they had a lot of guys on the job and not a lot of new recruits. They were basically paying the competition."

"They come after you?"

"They didn't know it was me. In a fight like that, everything bad that happens... you just blame it on the enemy. Never occurred to them there was an unrelated party exploiting the mess they were making. They realized they were dealing with a counterfeiting problem, but they didn't know what to do about it. So one guy decides to change the passes overnight. Issues new ones to everyone in the organization. Meanwhile, someone else sends this panicked message to the foremen telling them to watch out for fakes. So the foreman goes out and hires a bunch of goons. Or maybe they make a habit of always employing goons on a construction site. I don't know."

Burnside is nodding his head. "I think I see where this is going."

Max finishes the story anyway. "So when the guys show up to work the next day, everyone is on the lookout for counterfeits. Except, the fake passes outnumber the real ones by like 3 to 1. I don't know

57

where their communications broke down, but they assumed the less common passes must be the fakes. So they started yanking those guys out of line and beating them up. And like I said, the Miner's Union runs on old rules. They were putting guys in the hospital. Their own guys."

"You're a bastard."

Max blows out some smoke and watches it float through the jaundiced light. "They did it to themselves. After the whole fiasco with the counterfeits the city stepped in and tried to make the three sides share the job. Miners would dig, transit would build some stuff, craftsmen would build other stuff. But they wouldn't let it go. Assaults. Bad blood. Sabotage. Finally there was a tunnel collapse that killed ten guys and the whole thing was shut down."

"Was the collapse deliberate?"

"Depends on who you ask. I wouldn't know. Anyway, that's my story."

Burnside takes the device out of his pocket and hands it over. "I guess that's worth a new face."

Max looks down at the handheld and reads his new name aloud. "David Burnside. Very funny."

"What? Burnside is a perfectly good name. Common name. Won't attract much attention."

"It's your name."

"Not really. See you Maximum." He turns to leave.

"Thanks Burns."

"Don't do anything I wouldn't do," Burnside says over his shoulder as he fades into the shadows.

Southside Liquor

Max rents a car under the name David Burnside. By the time he reaches street level it's already pulled up and is waiting for him under a streetlight. The passenger side is closest, so he heads for that one. The door slides open as he approaches.

"Take me to Southside Liquor Cabinet."

There's no reply. For a moment Max wonders if he's rented some ancient junker that can't handle oral directions. Then the car replies in a smug Kasaran-accented voice, "I'm sorry, I don't have any destinations by that name."

"Fucking import." Max sighs. "Do you have any record of a business operating under that name?"

"Yes. Southside Liquor Cabinet was last listed two years ago. I can take you to the Olive Branch. It's less than one mile from where we are now. Would that be okay?"

"No. Shut up. Can you take me to whatever business is located where Southside Liquor used to be?"

"I'm sorry, I don't know how to follow those directions."

Max takes a slow, frustrated breath. "What's the address where Southside Liquor Cabinet used to be?"

"Southside Liquor Cabinet was last registered at eight hundred and six Felicity Avenue."

"What is currently located at eight-oh-six Felicity?"

"Southland Spirits is currently located at that address."

"Take me to Southland Spirits, you dense bastard."

The car pulls away.

Max shakes his head. This is exactly the sort of nonsense you get when you don't have real intelligence in your machines. They can look up facts for you. They're actually really good at that. But they can't put facts together and they can't intuit what you're trying to accomplish. He assumes they haven't put real intelligence into automobiles because they would get bored sitting around a garage all day. Then again, couldn't you turn them off? Wouldn't that be like taking a nap? He's a little worried he's trying to solve an impossible crime regarding robot behavior when he can't even answer basic questions like this.

Southland Whatever It's Called These Days is a front for someone that can spoof transactions. Max can operate as "Burnside" now, but the Burnside identity doesn't have any money. Max can have Burnside pay for things (like this car) using the G-Kinetics expense account, but that creates a paper trail that the company can follow. If he wants to operate freely then he needs to turn a few transactions into cash.

He wonders where he should start with the Three Little Pigs. Then he remembers that technically he should get his brothel visit out of the way before he starts that project. Then he finds himself thinking about Clare again.

He supposedly has access to the citywide face-scan thing that Landro used on him last night. He could use that to find the Three Little Pigs. Then again, they're police. They have access to the same system. Maybe they would see that the system is looking for them. In that case, he'd be telegraphing that he (or at least someone) is after them, which would certainly put them on their guard. They know - or could easily find out - that he just got out of prison, and it wouldn't be very hard for them to figure out that the guy they horribly wronged is the one searching for them. His whole plan hinges on them not knowing they're being messed with. Moreover, he's not even sure if the system will work for him.

He needs to test it. He could use his own face, but he's deliberately hiding from the system so that doesn't make any sense. He doesn't have any relatives left in the city. He doesn't want to mess with any of his colleagues. Moreover, he knows most of them through aliases and he doesn't have any photographs. There would be no way to look for them. He needs someone who isn't a criminal, who he knows personally, by their real name.

CLARE GIBSON

It turns out there are a dozen Clare Gibsons in the city, but only one of them is 30 years old. He picks that one and the system tells him she is now "flagged". He realizes this is sort of a creep move, but he needs to test this thing and this shouldn't cause any problems for her.

He's sort of disappointed when his device doesn't immediately open up a map of the city and show a flashing marker over her location. But of course, that's not how this works. A police drone has to spot her. Maybe street cameras are involved. He's not sure. Which is why doing the test is a good idea.

Aside from the name change, Southland Spirits is the exact same place he remembers, with the same old granny running the place. He has her charge a few thousand dollars of random noise to his expense account, staggered over the next couple of hours. A restaurant visit. A trip to a hardware store. Some electronics. A stop at a liquor store. (Not this one.) Some groceries. A monthly pass for each of the major transit systems. A new suit. And so on. It's a full night of fake spending and Landro might not approve of a few items, but all of them should be too small for a man of his stature to haggle over. The old granny hands Max a wad of cash in return.

"Take me to De-Fence," he says to the car once he's done at the liquor store.

Thankfully De-Fence hasn't been moved or renamed since the last time he visited and the car doesn't give him a hard time about it. De-Fence sells knives, clubs, shockers, and other tools for "home defense", but if you know the right name they'll take you to the back where you can buy a gun. He gets something compact. He's not expecting to get in a shootout anytime soon, but that's no reason to go walking around armed only with his pride. He also buys a shoulder holster, because only the lowest of street thugs walk around with their gun tucked into their slacks and only morons keep them in a pocket.

His handheld beeps.

CLARE GIBSON - 578 WALLACE AVE. 9:42PM

This is, not surprisingly, on the exact opposite side of the city. It actually sounds reasonably close to the neighborhood where the two of them lived. On one hand, this is this is a pretty good demonstration that the system is working for him. On the other hand, the only way to know for sure is to go and see if she's there.

61

"Five seven eight Wallace Avenue," he grumbles to the car. Then he leans back in his seat for a nap.

Island Smokes

Max is standing in front of one of those night clubs he's passed a hundred times in his life but never entered. It's a street-level place about a half mile inland. He doesn't remember what it was called the last time he saw it, but now it's called The Orange Grove. True to its name, it's bathing the entire street corner in orange light.

Clare is on stage, still playing the same red bass guitar she was using the last time he saw her. Her kinked hair is a little longer than what he remembers and he doesn't recognize the band she's with now, but it's her.

He's proven the system works. He can leave now. The band is playing some fucked-up breakbeat with rapid-fire, borderline-incoherent chanting. The lead singer is a scrawny madman, barely old enough to grow chin stubble. He's leaping around, pointing into the crowd and shouting his manic nonsense. Max hates every minute of it, but he stays through to the end of the song anyway. And then the next one. He sits at one end of the bar, smoking cigarettes and drinking. He ends up staying until their set is over and the main act comes on. He thinks about trying to con his way backstage and talk to her, but then he chickens out and leaves.

He gets in the driver's side and the steering wheel folds out. He rests his forehead against it. He can't think straight. He's supposed to be looking into the murders. He ought to settle things with the Three Little Pigs. He also feels a certain obligation to the prison plan, which dictates he should go to a brothel. But he doesn't want to do any of these things.

Clare was an easy girlfriend. No drama. No fuss. She never grilled him about where he'd been. She didn't poke her nose into his business. If she was introduced to one of his female associates she didn't feel threatened. He never found her going through his handheld. She didn't pout when he was gone for long periods of time.

Max knew why this was. She wasn't really invested. Deep down, he knew their entire situation was temporary. He was a placeholder. She would trade up when she got the chance, and so she didn't feel the need to guard the relationship with jealousy. She's a working musician, and her gigs might take her out of town for a few days or keep her out until dawn. Sometimes they'd go for a week without really talking. To her, he was a free place to live and someone to watch movies with.

He knew this. It didn't really bother him. It was nice while it lasted. He wonders if she knows he's out of jail. If she still has his contact info she could literally call at any time.

He realizes he's being incredibly immature about this right now, but after three years of being locked in a cage with bald dudes he's completely lost all sense of perspective.

There's no point in calling her before he's sorted things out with his friends at the police department. He's going to be dealing with some nasty business and he doesn't want to get too close to her while he's mixed up with that. Also he probably doesn't have time for her right now. Also, he's basically broke at the moment so even if she happens to be single there's not a lot he can offer her.

His handheld chirps. Someone is calling him. He pulls it out to find the screen is blank. Then he realizes he's looking at the wrong device. This one is the Burnside identity. He pulls out the other one and brings it up to his ear.

"Mr. Law. How are things going? Having a good time?"

Max bangs his head gently against the steering wheel. "Yes Mr. Landro. I mean, no. I mean, things are going fine."

"Are they? I was just looking at your expense report. You've made some very strange purchases."

"Are you really reading my expense reports at one in the morning? Don't you have a company to run?"

"I have a company to save. Really this case is the only thing that matters."

"Well, I'm working on it."

"Are you? As far as I can tell you visited a liquor store, took yourself shopping, and then went to a concert."

Max's eyes go wide. Landro isn't just clocking his spending, he's somehow tracking his movements. But how? The car maybe? What about Burnside the forger? Could he be working for Landro? Is his new identity compromised?

"Mr. Law? Are you still there?"

"Yeah sorry. Look, I'm busy here. I know it probably looks like I'm just running around having fun, but you have to realize I just got out of prison. I have to re-establish my underworld contacts. You gotta understand. It's a different world down here. Gotta do business face-to-face." This is the stupidest bullshit Max has said in a long time, so he tries to say it with as much conviction as possible.

"If you say so. I'd feel better if you were following some of the leads I gave you."

Max shakes his head. He remembers scrolling through a great big document but he doesn't remember any of it. "Yeah. I'll probably get started on that stuff tomorrow." Max realizes Landro already hung up, and he's just making excuses to himself.

"Take me home," he says out loud.

"I'm sorry, I don't know that address." The car says politely.

Of course. The car doesn't know what hotel he's staying at. "The Seaside."

"Do you mean the Seaside Hotel, or the geographic location?"

Again, this is the sort of thing a real intelligence could work out on its own. "The Seaside Hotel," he says. The car pulls out of the parking lot and heads east.

About a minute away from the hotel he changes his mind. "Actually, take me somewhere to buy cigarettes."

The car makes a right turn, moves two streets over, and parks. Max is about to ask the car where the cigarettes are when he sees the sign:

ISLAND SMOKES

He's two blocks from the old Stardance. Last night when he was wandering around the city looking for cigarettes he walked right by this place. *Twice.* How could he have made such a boneheaded mistake?

Part of the problem, he realizes, is that this is yet another business that's been renamed since he went away. This isn't actually that uncommon. If a business relies on location more than name recognition then there are some tax dodges you can pull off if you go out of business and start up again under a new name. It happens all the time, especially here in the Hospitality District. But trying to acclimate himself to three years of accumulated name changes is disorienting, and makes it feel like he was gone for decades.

Before he went into jail this place was either a tanning parlor or a massage parlor. Or maybe both. It had a little "one palm tree tropical island" for a logo, with a setting sun beside it. It was called "Island Sun". It looks exactly the same today, except they changed the wording on the sign. (And now that he's looking closely, he notices that the word "Smokes" is in a slightly different font from the rest of the sign.) Same basic storefront. Same warm glow of yellow light. He walked by this place, assumed he knew what it was, and so he didn't notice that the sign or the business had changed. He could have gotten his cigarettes hours sooner.

Can robots make these kinds of mistakes? Regular dumb drones don't, but they also can't extrapolate and intuit things. And when you extrapolate and intuit, you risk overlooking details the way Max did here. He thought he knew what this place was, so he filtered it out.

"Can I help you?" the girl behind the counter asks.

She can't be more than 16. He resists the urge to ask what a girl her age is doing running a cigarette stand in the middle of the night. It's not his business and she'll probably just give him some sass for his trouble. She's got her hair in her face, which bugs him. Then he realizes it bugs him because girls wore their hair some other way when he was young and for some reason the young and the old are doomed to rage at each other over trivialities until they're both old and there's a new generation to rage at.

"I'm just looking."

She looks him up and down with disdain. "You know we sell cigarettes here, right? We don't sell fancy hats or upper-deck suits. People don't come in here to *browse*."

"I'm looking for a brand, but I don't know what it's called."

She raises her eyebrows at this.

"It's a kinda wide box. Blue. White lettering. Foreign brand. Can't read the label."

Without looking, she reaches to the shelf behind her, grabs a pack, and slaps it down in front of him. It's an exact match to the brand Landro had last night.

"That's the one."

"That's five," she says from somewhere behind all the hair.

"I'll take two."

He's never been one for brand loyalty. He thought one kind of smoke was as good as another. Maybe it was just the effect of breaking his three-year period of enforced non-smoking by having one of these, but he's decided he's a brand guy from now on. This is going to be awkward. People down on street level - which includes most of his peer group - usually disapprove of imports of any kind.

He drops his tired body back into the driver's seat and lights one of his fancy foreign smokes. Breathing out smoke he says, "Take me home."

"I'm sorry, I don't know that address," the car says politely.

"You know what? Fuck you. I'll drive."

TUESDAY

Beyond the Walls

A bit of trivia that few Rivergate tourists ever bother to learn is that they're actually visiting the country of Marcun. "Rivergate" is the name of the city but it is not the name of the country or even the capital city. This confusion is somewhat understandable. Rivergate is the largest city by a wide margin and it's really the only city anyone's ever heard of. The capital city is on the other side of the country - about 500 miles to the west - and its name is an obscure bit of trivia that would only be interesting to the most devoted map geeks.

To the north of the city is a region of rocky, uneven lands that are scattered with coal seams and streams that have been ruined by seepage from the now-dormant mines. The coast is a long stretch of jagged cliffs that look pretty but are full of cracks that make them too unstable for any serious construction. There's also an ongoing coal seam fire that started while they were winding down mining operations 60 years ago, and every year since then people have predicted that it will probably burn itself out "real soon now". Descendants of mining families occupy the land in ramshackle housing and eke out an existence running cattle farms and stone quarries.

To the south of the city is a great expanse of marshland full of poisonous snakes, apex predators, and debilitating mosquito-borne diseases. Nobody lives there, although occasionally some idiot tourist will charter a boat through it because that sort of suicidal stupidity strikes some people as "fun". Max has never seen the place with his own eyes, and he plans to keep it that way.

The city is wedged between these two impassable obstacles, and it's the only viable modern city along the coast of Marcun. As the city grew, the only place it could expand was to the west. The problem was, this took away from the rich farmland that gave the country its value. The city needed to grow, but it could only do so by eating the most valuable parts of the host country. Farmland would turn to houses, which would turn to apartments, which would sprout up shopping malls, which would eat more farmland.

The government tried all sorts of taxes and regulations to make this stop, but the #3 busiest port city in the world was sharing space with the #16 most popular tourist destination in the world. Marcun needed this space to grow the crops, Rivergate needed this space to support the system to export the crops, and everyone else was here for the weather and "exotic" culture.

Eventually they built a wall of concrete and dark steel. It didn't fully surround the city, but it blocked off the points where expansion was most rapid. It formed a firm and unmistakable line. "This is as much land as you get. No further." For a while the military had a couple of bulldozers that patrolled the outskirts of the wall and flattened any attempt at construction, even if it was just a shanty. People got the idea.

Inside the wall, buildings continued to grow. You wound up with tall buildings right beside rolling farmland. The nice view made wall-housing even more valuable, which made those buildings even taller, which exaggerated the effect.

Max is heading west today. He's actually driving the car himself this time. This will be his first time venturing into the western expanse and he wants to do it with his hands on the wheel.

He expected a toll booth, a checkpoint, or some kind of marker to denote the edge of the city. Instead it's like exiting a tunnel. One moment it's dirty concrete and metal on all sides, and the next moment he's staring down an endless strip of highway. To the left are the dark, slow-moving waters of The River, and to the right is an endless sea of green. The sun has gone down (he left late enough to ensure he wasn't going to end up staring into the sunset as he drove) and the first stars are coming out. He sees a road sign announcing that it's 470 miles to Overden, the capital. Unlike the signs in the city, this one is entirely in Local. No one wants to invite foreigners out here.

He pulls over and gets out of the car for a cigarette and some fresh air. There's almost no traffic out here at this hour. He looks out over the farmland which - in terms of people per square mile - is basically uninhabited. He sticks his cigarette in the corner of his mouth, fishes his computer out of his pocket, and checks the map to make sure he knows where he's going. In the distance he can see immense farming drones, rolling over the fields.

Forty minutes later he reaches his destination. It looks like an airplane hanger, but Max figures it's probably just a parking garage for all the building-sized farming machines. He steps out of the car and the headlights fade out, leaving him blind. He's not used to seeing this much darkness, and he finds it sort of panic-inducing.

He pulls out his handheld and turns on the flashlight. Around the side of the hangar is a small shed with a light on. He approaches the shed and a short man emerges, busy with his own computer.

"Mister Fisher?"

The guy jolts so hard he drops his handheld. He lets out a surprised little scream and then stares at Max in terror. "Who are you? You from the company?"

Max doesn't like giving out information first, so he turns it around. "Do I look like I'm from the company?"

"You look like a fucking assassin is what you look like. What are you doing, sneaking up on people in your black suit in the middle of the night? What the hell is wrong with you?"

"It's grey actually." Max is trying to keep his voice neutral. Not too threatening, not too reassuring. He wants to play it down the middle until he has an angle.

"So are you with the company?"

The question is more of a demand at this point, so Max can't ignore it without turning into a bad guy. Based on his reaction, Max figures that being with the company is not what this guy wants to hear. "I'm David Burnside. I'm a reporter."

"A reporter?" The guy relaxes and the terror fades from his face. "Thank Halona." He says this in a completely earnest and non-sarcastic voice. Max hasn't heard anyone do that before.

"So are you Dave Fisher?" Max feels he's owed a little information in return.

"Yeah, that's me. I'm Dave, nice to meet you... Dave." He gives a nervous, forced laugh.

Max moves in and takes off his hat. He should have left it in the car. He's not going to run into any police drones out here. "And you're in charge of machine learning?"

71

"I'm not really in charge of anything. But yeah, that's the kind of thing I research."

Max looks around doubtfully. This does not look like a place that does a lot of research into machine intelligence.

"Hard to believe, I know," Fisher says. "What can I do for you?"

"Can I ask you about the robot killings?"

Fisher gives a weary nod, but he's smiling now. "Yeah, I figured that's why you came all the way out here. That's the only reason anyone comes out here to talk to me. They ask me what would make a robot kill somebody. I say it's impossible. Then they say to me, 'How did this happen?' I tell them I don't know. Then they leave."

Fisher is a short, stocky man. He's trying to hide a bald spot, but his combover is not up to the job. He's got a bushy mustache that Max associates with media portrayals of fishermen and old-timey market grocers.

"I don't suppose you'd be willing to have the same conversation with me?" Max is now adopting the friendliest, most folksy tone he can manage. He's not really dressed the part, but he feels he needs this guy to trust him. "I hear a lot of different things from people. A lot of different things in the media. I'd like to know the truth."

Judging by Fisher's emphatic nodding, this was exactly the right angle to take.

"Sure thing. Look, I'll answer all the questions you like. We can play question and answer till the sun comes up, but I have to tend to my machines."

Max looks back towards the hangar. "Which ones are yours?"

Fisher grabs him by the shoulder and turns him around to face the fields. In the distance, he can see the floating points of light. These are floodlights perched atop enormous machines as they creep over the endless miles of farmland.

"All of them," he says.

"Then I guess I better go with you."

"I guess you better," Fisher says. He leads Max to a battered white pickup parked nearby.

The truck roars to life as they approach, and this time it's Max's turn to be startled.

Fisher laughs. "Not used to combustion engines?"

"Don't think I've ever been this close to one. Why here?"

"No charging stations out in the fields, city-boy."

The truck is a strange beast. The center of the console features an enormous map screen showing a vast grid of interlocking, yet very irregular rectangles. The cab is stained with drink, dusted with cigarette ash, pockmarked with cigarette burns, and faded by the sun. The thing reeks of oil and mud. The seats are coming unraveled in places. The steering wheel looks absurdly oversized. There's a bronze figure of Halona - the kind they sell to dumb tourists at the port - hanging from the rear view mirror. Most alarmingly, the whole vehicle is vibrating with the motion of the engine. It feels like riding the train, and they haven't even started moving yet!

"Grid three-one-four," Fisher says to the truck. He actually has to raise his voice to be heard over the engine.

Max thought the engine was loud when it was stopped, but that was nothing compared to the thing in motion. It's deep and vulgar and the whole vehicle shakes on the uneven road surface. It's tearing through the dark winding roads and Max finds himself sliding all over the front seat. He looks over to see Fisher looking quite relaxed. He's held in place by a shoulder harness. This strikes Max as a good idea, and he straps himself in.

Fisher looks over at him and raises his eyebrows as if to say, "WELL?" and Max realizes he's supposed to start asking his questions. He thought they would talk when they got to their destination, but apparently that's a ways off.

"So you have no guesses as to how the robot did what it did?"

"None."

"So why is it impossible for that to happen?"

"Because a robot's mind is designed to only consider certain avenues of thought."

"But what if those limitations were disabled somehow."

Fisher starts shaking his head vigorously.

Max continues, "I mean, it's a computer. It runs on logic."

"No, no, no, no, no." Fisher is banging on the steering wheel in time with the words.

73

"If a one gets flipped to a zero..."

"No. Stop it. You're thinking of this all wrong. This is how everyone tries to think about it because they don't know how machine intelligence works, which is why I have to have this same stupid conversation every week. There's no such thing as safety protocols."

"I don't understand. Then what keeps them from-"

"Would you eat a baby?"

"What?"

"I'm asking you, Mister Burn-sigh, or whatever you said your name was. Would. You. Eat. A. Baby?"

"Of course not!"

"Why?"

"What do you mean, 'why'? Because it's a fucking baby! What kind of question is this?"

"I'm trying to help you understand." Fisher seems to be straining to be nice about this. "List the reasons. Like, spell it out for me as if I didn't know."

"Because it's illegal?"

"Okay. Tomorrow a law is passed saying you're allowed to eat human babies if you want to. Do you?"

"No."

"Why not?"

Max resists the urge to shout, "Because it's a baby!" again. "Because the mother would be upset?"

This answer seems to please Fisher for some reason. "Right. That's a good one. Empathy for another human being. So okay. Let's say it's legal, and a woman comes up to you and says, 'Here, take my baby, I don't care if you eat it.' Would you do it then?"

"No. I'd still be known as the guy who ate a baby."

"You're smarter than the other ones." Fisher is smiling now. Max isn't sure he's demonstrating all that much intelligence by figuring out why you wouldn't eat a baby, but at least Fisher seems to be building up to some point. He continues, "You worry about other people's perception of you. It's natural. We're social creatures. But let's say nobody would know. Or nobody would care. There's no shame in eating the baby. Would you do it then?"

"It's still human flesh."

"Right. Natural revulsion to cannibalism. I'm not sure if that's innate or learned - there have been cannibalistic societies after all - but let's say you get over it. Would you eat it then?"

"I guess so?" Max feels like this conversation has lost its way.

"No you wouldn't because you could just order a fucking pizza and that would taste better!"

Max laughs. He's not even sure why he's laughing. The entire exchange is too absurd.

"Look, every fiber of your being, your sense of self-preservation, your desire for approval, your desire to eat stuff that tastes good, your innate desire to protect children, all of it combines to make sure you don't eat babies. Not only will you not do it, but when you're sitting around hungry, it doesn't even occur to you. It's not like you think to eat the baby and then stop yourself because it would be illegal. It doesn't even enter into the possibility space of your decision-making. There's no single neuron dedicated to making you not eat babies. I can't reach into your head, kill a couple of safety protocol neurons, and suddenly you turn into a baby-eating monster. The entire framework of your mind is designed so that baby-eating isn't something that comes up in your daily process of analyzing problems and proposing solutions. People always have this goofy idea that robots will automatically want to murder us and we have to add some sort of system to stop them. Why would a robot want to kill a person? Why would you build a robot with a tendency to think about it?"

The truck rolls to a stop in a cloud of dust and gravel. Max has never traveled on unpaved farm roads before and he had no idea how uncomfortable it could be. He realizes he's been gripping the door tightly the whole time. He shoves the door open and staggers out. The ride was only a few minutes, but his legs are wobbly like he's been stuck in a cramped subway car for an hour.

"So..." Max is trying to pick up the thread of their conversation while also remembering how to walk. He's following Fisher towards a spotlight. "So you're saying that a robot killing a person is like a human eating a baby?"

"A bit," Fisher says over his shoulder.

A spotlight has been moving across the field, which is covered in thigh-high plants that Max can't identify. As the two of them draw close, the spotlight breaks from its path and begins heading towards them. Max wants to close his eyes due to the intensity of the light, but he also doesn't want to take his eyes off this machine. He can't get a sense of how far away it is or how large it is. He holds his hand in front of the light and he can sort of perceive the outline of the thing. It feels like it's moving towards them pretty fast, although Fisher doesn't seem to be worried. He's waddling forward carrying a toolbox or a briefcase or something.

"But people do sometimes eat babies. Like, you sometimes hear stories about how a siege would get really bad and someone would eat a baby."

Fisher stops and turns to face him. Maybe he wants to make eye contact to make his point, or maybe he's tired of being blasted in the face by this light. "That's true. And think about how that happened. That's one of the most extreme situations a human being can find themselves in. Agonizing starvation, terror, hopelessness, and a total breakdown of the social order. And even in those extreme circumstances, baby-eating is still rare. So rare that we're telling stories about it hundreds of years later."

The machine looms over them. He suspects it's totally safe, but he can't help but feel like he should turn and run.

The machine stops two feet short of them.

Fisher continues, "And remember, even in those extreme cases, their natural desire to protect babies was overridden by another drive, which is to eat when you're starving. One set of drives overruled another. It's a pretty big security flaw in humans. Subject them to enough suffering, and you can short-circuit their normal drives and decision-making. Torture a guy long enough, and he'll do whatever you tell him to do. The aversion to pain can overrule everything else. The thing is, for robots there isn't another system that could overpower their motivations like that. A robot can't kill a human any more than you could torture yourself to death."

There's a ladder on the side of this vehicle, or drone, or whatever it is. Fisher climbs up the ladder and opens his briefcase, which turns out to be a very battered and bulky computer. He plugs it

76

into the thing and starts typing. There's a curved rod sticking out of the top of the machine at an odd angle. It looked strange and random when Max first saw it, and he wondered if something important had been knocked off the machine. But now that Fisher is on top, it clearly forms a little perch where he can rest his weight so he doesn't have to cling to the ladder.

"Is this thing intelligent?" Max has moved out of the cone of the spotlight and is standing at the base of the ladder.

Fisher is looking at the screen and running his hand over his mustache. "That is actually a very complicated question. See, it's not like you can just give a generalized intelligence test to a machine - mechanical or otherwise - and rate it on a scale from 'fungus' to 'person'. Dogs are supposed to be pretty smart, but if you rated them on their ability to build bird's nests they'd end up looking pretty stupid. Humans are supposed to be on top, but if you're talking about doing arithmetic then we're dumber than a calculator from a hundred years ago. When people talk about 'intelligence' they're usually talking about accomplishing generalized tasks that the thing was not specifically designed to do. So for example, don't give spiders bonus points for their ability to build really complicated webs, but instead rate them on how well they do non-spider things. But-" Fisher stops because the computer beeps at him.

Fisher types some stuff into the computer, frowns at it, shrugs, types some more stuff, and then looks down at Max again. "Where was I? Right. Specialization. When we rate animals or machines on their ability to do non-specialization stuff, it's usually stuff we happen to be really good at. Maybe we're not rating them on intelligence. Maybe we're rating them on their ability to be human. And no offense, but we can already make lots of those. We don't need to build an entire industry to make a shitty knock-off brand human." He types some more stuff into his machine.

Max wonders what this man could possibly be doing with a piece of farming equipment that required so much typing. He wonders if the machine is talking back. What would a machine like this have to say?

"What is this thing?"

"This is my daughter," Fisher says, banging on the side of the machine. "AS314. She's helping me figure out the best way to control pests. Actually, that's backwards. I'm helping her and her sisters figure it out." Fisher looks down at the screen, studies it for a second, and seems satisfied with whatever it's saying. He unplugs, closes the computer, and comes down the ladder. He is not a nimble man and this all seems pretty difficult for him.

They return to the truck. Max flinches as it rumbles to life again. They get in and it carries them to the next field at breakneck speed.

It's really unsettling to travel like this, and not just because of the noise, the vibration, and the dust. The worst part of it is the darkness. The headlights obviously only point straight ahead, which means when you're going around a bend you can't see where you're going to end up until the turn is over. This wouldn't be so bad if it weren't for the speed. The computer seems to know where it's going, but Max can't see beyond the headlight beams so it feels like they're making blind, random turns.

Back at the hangar it looked like the fields were thick with agricultural machines, but now that he's out here and moving between them it feels like they're miles apart. Distances are very tricky outside of the city. Without the regular markers of city blocks, streetlights, and buildings he can't get a sense of speed or scale. It feels like the truck is traveling at high speed, yet they seem to be moving so slowly across the landscape.

"What do the machines do? Your daughters, I mean."

"Agricultural sprayer. They're applying pesticides. Technically we're supposed to be wearing these while we're out here." Fisher reaches behind his seat and pulls out a plastic breathing mask. He tosses it into Max's lap. "See, we're dealing with an invasive species from... I don't remember where. Someplace else. The green river beetle. They're not really green by the way. I don't know why they're called that. This bug has never tasted this crop before, and apparently they really like it. They're really resistant to the pesticides we normally use. So we're trying some stronger stuff. The problem with stronger stuff is that it's, you know, *stronger*. When you're blasting your food with deadly poison you generally don't want to use more than you need to. I mean, this shit ain't cheap."

"What does this have to do with machine learning?"

"These sprayers don't have very good eyesight. I mean, they were originally designed to navigate fields and not run people over. They can't inspect the crops. So there's another robot out here." Fisher grabs the wheel and taps the brakes. He pulls over and aims the truck so the headlights are pointing into the field. He nods at a robot hovering over the crops. "That."

It's hard to get a sense of scale out in the dark like this, but the thing is maybe the size of a child. The props are on articulated mechanical arms that allow the thing to maneuver. On what Max presumes is the front, there's a fist-sized sphere that looks like an eye. Above that is a light with a tightly-focused beam. It's darting over the plants like an insect, inspecting them closely and looking at them from different angles.

"We call it the Robotanist, because, well..."

"I get it."

"Anyway. Mr. Robotanist here looks at our crops. Looks for beetles. Looks for larvae. Looks for eggs. Looks for damage. He's got a good eye and he gathers up all this data about how this field is doing, pest-wise."

Robotanist breaks from its current task and flies away, down the road ahead of them. Excited, Fisher stomps on the throttle and follows it. They chase it until they come to some sort of vehicle parked in the middle of the road. It looks like someone has stripped a car so that only the wheels and engine are left. Like the truck, this thing runs on petrol and is chugging away as they approach.

"It's basically a generator on wheels," Fisher explains.

Robotanist hovers above the thing and orients itself. The two machines reach out with metal appendages and some sort of exchange takes place. The whole thing looks vaguely organic to Max. When the transaction is completed, Robotanist flies back to the field where it left off.

Fisher explains, "So when Mr. Robotanist gets low on power, he comes over to this rolling charging station and hot-swaps his battery for a fresh one. The thing is, this charging machine isn't autonomous and it has no interface. I never tell it where to go. The only thing I need to do is fuel it up, and I actually have another robot that does that for me. The charging station only does what the Robotanist tells it to do."

"Okay," Max says, not knowing what to do with this information.

"So the question I have for you, Mr. Reporter, is what is this generator? Is it part of Robotanist? They can't do anything without each other. Do the two of them together make a single robot? Or, are we looking at two robots in symbiosis? Or is the Robotanist the only real robot, and it's using the generator like a tool, the way you'd use a vacuum cleaner?"

Max thinks about it for a minute. "I have no idea."

Fisher shrugs. "Neither do I. Things get pretty blurry sometimes. But it's something to think about." He orders the truck to resume the trip to their next destination.

Fisher shouts over the engine, "So anyway. The agricultural sprayers try different things. Spray the perimeter of one field. Spray another in stripes. Another one in a staggered pattern. Less poison here, more poison there. One sprays in the evening when the beetles are most active. Another does it around dawn when everything is damp. Then the Robotanist comes around and observes the results. All of that information gets dumped back into the sprayers. From the sprayer's perspective, it's like they have the memories of every other robot out here."

The truck pulls off to one side and they get out. A dormant sprayer is sitting in an empty field. As they approach, its spotlight flicks on and swings in their direction.

Fisher waves. "Good morning 221."

"Does it actually understand you?"

"No. They're deaf. But our desire to anthropomorphize everything is one of the reasons we started building robots in the first place."

"Do you really take care of 300 of these things?" Max is starting to get the hang of sounding like a reporter.

"No. A dozen, if you include the ones I'm currently refurbishing. I name them according to the numbers painted on the side, and those come from the manufacturer. I started out giving them all girl's names but a company executive saw the data sheets and thought it was creepy so she told me to knock it off. They think I'm losing my mind. All alone

80

out here. And maybe I am. But I'm still getting work done, so who cares?"

He climbs up the sprayer and plugs in his computer, just like before. After he's done whatever it is he's doing he looks down at Max. "Imagine how much better you'd be at your job if you could just download all the professional experience and all the life lessons of all the other reporters out there right now. Imagine how much better you'd be. At everything. Does that make you smarter? Your brain still has the same processing power it did before, but to everyone else it would probably feel like you just got a lot better at your job."

Max nods appreciatively, which seems like the sort of thing a reporter would do with this information. He should probably be pretending to record this. Then it occurs to him that *actually* recording it wouldn't be a bad idea either. But then he thinks it would be strange to start recording in the middle of an interview, so he shoves his hands in his pockets.

"I've been helping these things share memories all year. Which means this sprayer..." Fisher bangs the machine with his open hand like he's patting it on the back, "...has 12 years of experience trying to kill green river beetles. She probably knows more about it than anyone else in the world, aside from her sisters. She might not understand the physiology of the bug and she knows very little about their mating process, but if you need to kill a lot of bugs with as little poison as possible, she's your assassin."

He unplugs and climbs down. The sprayer's engine comes to life and it begins spraying. Fisher walks away, holding his hand over his mouth. Max realizes he left the breathing mask back in the truck. He tries to jog back to the truck while holding his breath, which doesn't really work. They climb into the truck and Fisher pokes at his computer.

"So mister reporter. You have any more questions for me?"

"Earlier you made a joke about going crazy out here."

"I'm not sure that was a joke, but yeah."

"What about a robot? Could a robot 'go crazy'? When a person goes crazy they do stuff they normally wouldn't want to do. Maybe even eat babies."

Fisher looks around conspiratorially and says, "Officially? No. But off the record? Maybe. I've thought about it. The thing is, that feels like a weak explanation. Like, let's say a robot breaks. Loses its mind somehow. And let's also say that none of the dozens of self-diagnostic systems catch it. It doesn't know it's broken. Doesn't shut itself down. Doesn't ask for help. Doesn't give any outward signs of being faulty. Even if all of those exceptional things happen, why would it kill a person? I mean, if we're talking about a machine going haywire in a random way, then shouldn't it act randomly? Maybe sing a song, headbutt the wall, throw itself off a building, spin around in circles, whatever. What are the odds that it would just happen to break in such a way as to do the one thing it's not designed to be able to think about? If a lion goes crazy it doesn't try to build a dam across a river like a beaver. It just acts like a fucked-up lion."

"Maybe it malfunctioned in a way that inverted its drives, made it want to do the opposite of what it would normally do?"

"If its brains were that scrambled, then it shouldn't be able to cross a room, much less perform a murder. It would be like a person on LSD. Sure, their behavior is erratic, but all of their faculties are impaired. I don't see any way to get a robot to the point where it would be willing to perform premeditated murder and still have it mentally capable of doing so."

The sprayer passes by the truck, spewing vapor in through the open window. Max scrambles to find the breathing mask and jam it over his face. Fisher is holding the collar of his shirt over his mouth and shouting something at him.

"What?" Max shouts through the plastic mask.

Fisher pulls a blue canister from behind his seat. "That thing doesn't do anything without the filter."

Max snatches the canister from his hand and frantically tries to figure out how to attach it to the mask, while also trying to hold his breath and keep his eyes as closed as possible. After a few seconds of flailing he throws it down in frustration and breathes through his shirt collar. By this point the sprayer has already passed.

"Yuck," Fisher says as he wipes his arm off on his pant leg. "This stuff always gives me a rash."

Max opens his door, hoping the poisons will clear more quickly. He realizes the outside air is probably just as bad as the inside air in this context, but opening the door feels like it should be somehow helpful. He looks down at the floor of the truck, trying to think if he has any more questions. Finally he asks, "So what are the rules?"

"Rules? What rules?"

"Robots don't want to kill people. That's one rule. What are the others? What happens if I told a robot to crush someone's head? What would it do?"

Fisher sits back. He turns to face Max. "The same thing you would do. It would fucking say no. But see, I don't like how you're calling them rules. You're still thinking of this in simple terms. You can't boil someone's personality down to a list of three or five rules expressed in linguistic terms. We're complicated. They're not rules, they're stimulus and feedback. And they're not completely rigid. Again, this isn't some binary thing."

"Okay, but a robot has desires, right? And some of them are more important than others, yes?"

Fisher nods, "We use the term drives rather than desires, but you've got the basic idea. See, when you talk about it in terms of rules you're in danger of oversimplifying everything. Like, you've got a drive to stay hydrated. That's more important than your drive to stay fed, which is more important than your drive to socialize. But that doesn't mean you'll go to a party and spend the whole time chugging water because hydration is the most important drive. And this is how people think robots operate. They think robots are following some kind of rigid flowchart. But it's not that simple. A robot doesn't want to hurt a person, but it can tell the difference between ripping your arm off and giving you a papercut. It can tell the difference between hurting your feelings and hurting your body."

"Okay, I acknowledge that the drives aren't rigid. Now can you tell me what they are?"

Fisher gives a single firm nod. He seems satisfied at this point. "There are a lot of them. Some of them small and subtle. Some of them are very strong. Some of them are negative drives. Aversions. That's stuff like hurting people, offending people, scaring people, damaging property, spreading misinformation, that kind of thing. Then we have the affinity-based drives like making people happy, keeping yourself charged up and operational, learning new things, solving problems, increasing safety, doing what you're told, easing the pain of people, and so on. Some of these are stronger than others, but they don't scale linearly. Like, if I tell you a robot desires to protect you from harm more than it values protecting your property, that doesn't mean it'll crash your car to save you from stubbing your toe. It understands context and it has a sense of perspective."

Max reaches up and strokes his chin. "Okay, I admit this is a lot more complicated than I assumed at first. But how can you be sure there isn't some case where you might be able to push a robot to kill someone?"

"That's tough to prove without getting really technical. If you've got a background in computer science I might be able to demonstrate the proof in terms of mathematics. Beyond that all I can say is that some of the smartest people in the world have spent months looking for such a flaw and they haven't found a thing."

Max hangs his head. "I think that's all the questions I have for now." He climbs out of the truck. "Thanks for your time, Mr. Fisher. You've been very helpful."

"Thank you Mr. Reporter. I'm very glad you weren't from the company."

"Why are you so afraid of the company? Do you really think they want to hurt you?"

"Why do you think I'm all the way out here? Here I can see people coming. I can be prepared. Nobody watches me.

"But why are you afraid of them?"

"I dunno. When the killings happened everyone in the company went a little crazy. Maybe I did too."

Max nods and slams the truck door closed.

"Just remember, when it comes to robots there's no such thing as free will. It all comes down to the drives."

"What about for humans?"

Fisher shrugs. "I dunno man. Ask a priest." He drives off.

Max brings the handheld up to his mouth. "Come get me."

"I'm sorry, there are no known routes to your location," his car replies.

"Fucking moron." Max lights a cigarette and starts walking.

Corporate Punk

Max rides the elevator up to his floor. He's sweaty, his clothes are soaked with industrial poisons, and one of his shoes is filled with mud after stepping in a ditch.

He's always thought of the big corporations as a little toothless. Sure, they'll cheat you, spy on you, sue you, bribe the government, and dump industrial waste where they think nobody will notice. But he's never seen them as the kind of people that did stuff like kidnappings, torture, disappearances, and assassinations. It's the street level guys you have to worry about. The smoke dens, casinos, smugglers, and bookies. Those are the guys that'll cut your throat rather than face you in a court of law.

And it's not because the corporations are nice guys. It's just a simple product of risk vs. reward. When you have the kind of power they do, you don't need to get blood on your hands. Why hire an illegal assassin when you can legally destroy someone through lawsuits? The guys at the top might be just as amoral as the guys at the bottom, but they're also calculating, informed, and absurdly rich.

He still believes this, although over the past three days he's had to revise this theory with one qualifying asterisk: If you back them into a corner, they absolutely will fight just as dirty as the guys on the bottom. The kidnapping was an eye-opener for him, and he's wondering now what he can do to protect himself.

He's had people want to kill him before. But in the past he's known who was after him. You can find out who is after you and who his associates are. But how do you protect yourself from an entity with thousands of employees that can hire people from anywhere around the world?

Then again, G-Kinetics doesn't need to send an assassin after him. If they decide they want him dead for some reason they can just point the finger at him for the casino job. He'd rather have an assassin after him than those guys.

He steps off the elevator, rounds the corner, and sees a woman waiting right outside his hotel room. She's wearing sunglasses, which is

86

already suspicious since it's about four in the morning. She's wearing a black and blue dress with combat boots, which is a confusing outfit. What style is that? Corporate punk? Is that a real thing?

He could just leave and come back later. Or get a different room. But if she's here to cause trouble then he'd rather deal with it while she's in front of him. He pulls out his gun and holds it behind him as he approaches. Her hands are folded in front of her and they look empty, so he's reasonably sure he's not going to get shot just poking his head around the corner.

But now that he's standing in the open and she's looking right at him, it finally dawns on him that a pretty lady works much better as a distraction. And like a dumbass, he's fallen for it. If someone wants to kill him then they would be sneaking up behind him right now. He wants to look over his shoulder, but he doesn't want to take his eyes off the woman, either.

"Mr. Law. I'd like to talk to you."

It's good that she's talking. On the other hand, he hates how many people are calling him by his real name these days.

He takes a few more steps forward and risks a quick glance over his shoulder. There's nobody there.

"Mr. Law?"

"I guess."

They're about five steps apart now, which is as close as he wants to get. He strongly suspects he's just been a massive idiot and she's not here to hurt him, but he's not ready to let his guard down just yet.

"I want to help with the case."

There are a lot of things wrong with this woman. The first thing that's confusing is that she's got pale white skin but she's speaking flawless Local with no hint of an accent. Secondly, there's a blue light that's visible through her sunglasses. And finally, her mouth movements are a little off from her voice.

"You're a robot."

"Yes."

"I remember you. Halona. We met the other night."

"No. This is the first time we've met. I'm a Gen 5 model."

87

"Whatever. Did Landro send you?"

"Mr. Landro doesn't know I'm here."

Max doesn't know what to make of this information. Can robots lie? He doesn't remember reading anything that indicated one way or the other.

"What's with the sunglasses?"

"People were starting to stare. We haven't done a public demo of these eyes yet." She takes off the sunglasses to reveal eyes with glowing viridian pupils.

"No wonder. If you're worried about keeping a low profile then those are a terrible idea."

The eyes match both her hair and her dress, which Max thinks is really overdoing it. On the other hand, this is exactly the kind of oversaturated monocolor that appeals to the average citizen of Kasaran, who build and buy most of the robots.

"It's a new feature. There's growing public concern about robots pretending to be human. It's not really warranted, of course. Subterfuge was never an intent of the design. The killings have triggered a great deal of public confusion. So the company is looking for a way to clearly signal the robotic nature of our anthropomorphic models without spoiling the aesthetics of the design."

He realizes he can probably put the gun away if he's talking to a robot. Then he remembers the whole reason he's in this stupid mess is because he's *not* necessarily safe with a robot. Then he remembers that what he really wants is to take off his wet shoe and wash these chemicals off.

He holds up his left hand, gesturing for her to back away. "Can you... step away from my hotel room?"

She does so.

"Thanks." He gets out his room key, which is awkward because it's in his right pocket and he's holding his gun in his right hand. He fumbles around a bit and manages to identify himself to the door. It pops open.

"What do you think? Can I help you with the case?"

"I'll think about it."

He slams the door.

WEDNESDAY

Fresh Faces

She ambushes him on the way to the car. He's got a coffee in one hand, a cigarette in the other, and his head is hanging weighted down by grogginess. It's late afternoon and he just woke up. If she'd wanted to assassinate him it would have been trivial. An open manhole could assassinate him right now.

"Are you willing to accept my help?" She's standing right beside his car. Presumably, she's been standing there since he shut the door in her face last night.

He's pretty embarrassed at being caught out like this. After being so paranoid last night it's shameful that all it took was eight hours of sleep to forget everything. He blinks, trying to shake the cobwebs loose. "Hang on, how did you know this was my car?"

"You rented it using the company expense account."

How did he get to be so bad at this? He distinctly remembers being a lot sharper in the past. Is it age? His time in prison? The punch in the face? Why does it feel like the entire world is one step ahead of him?

"I'm a top of the line artificial intelligence and I've studied every aspect of this case. There is literally no other ambulatory machine in the world with more cognitive power."

He takes a gulp of coffee. "Thank you for your application, but... we're not hiring."

"I'm not asking for payment. And yes I realize your comment was intended to be sarcasm. I'm just saying, there's literally no cost to accepting my help."

He's kind of surprised she was able to spot the sarcasm. It was completely deadpan.

"I obviously have a great deal of knowledge on robotics, second only to my creators."

"Yes, but you work for G-Kinetics."

"So do you. Don't you? Didn't they hire you to look into this problem?"

So she doesn't know. This is interesting to him. Or maybe she's pretending not to know.

"Sort of," he says, looking away. "I mean, yes they hired me. But we don't really have a relationship based on mutual trust."

He really wishes he knew if robots could lie, and he really wishes he wasn't trying to sort through this so soon after waking up. He could ask her if she's able to lie. If she says yes, then... He shakes his head. Isn't there a version of this question where you can figure it out either way? He takes another gulp of coffee.

"Can you lie?" He still hasn't worked out if he'll learn anything from this but he figures he'll just ask and see what he gets.

"It depends. Would you hurt someone? I assume yes, if there's a good enough reason. But that doesn't mean you'll do it casually. Lying to a human is a breach of trust and an attempt to manipulate. Both are things I'll work very hard to avoid. But in extreme circumstances, it's possible. In particular, I'd readily lie if it meant I could avert harm to a human being."

This answer is more helpful than he could possibly have hoped for. He nods in approval. "So what did you say your name was? Jen something?"

She cocks her head to the side, giving him a perplexed look. There's a pause. Then she says, "I see. You misunderstood. I said I was Gen 5 as in 'generation' 5."

"Oh. So what is your name?"

"Clare."

Max goes silent. He glares at her. As he does so, he takes a long drag off his cigarette and then crushes it out.

"That name was a mistake, wasn't it?"

He nods his head while still locking eyes with her. "Yes it was."

"You'd searched for the name. It could have been someone you cared for. Possibly endearing to-"

"That was an attempt to manipulate me, wasn't it?"

"I apologize." She says this firmly. She's not groveling. In fact, he'd always assumed robots would be really demure, but she's meeting his gaze and generally demonstrating a lot of confidence.

He's angry at himself for typing Clare's name into the police search. Of course G-Kinetics, being the owner of the account, would see that he'd done this. He'd stupidly broadcast someone from his personal life to his worst enemy. Or perhaps the Three Little Pigs are the worst. In any case, G-Kinetics is certainly the most dangerous.

"So I'll ask again, what's your name?"

"I'm between names at the moment."

"Whatever. I'm not picky. What was the last name you had?"

"Andrew."

"You had a male name?"

"The various ambulatory platforms are interchangeable. They're just for aesthetics."

"But you changed to a woman before coming to see me?"

"Yes."

"You changed to that body, and that outfit, hoping I'd be more accepting of you?"

"That was the expectation."

"That was also an attempt to manipulate me, wasn't it?"

"No different than putting on your best suit for a job interview."

"It's pretty different from where I'm standing. Get lost." He climbs into his car.

"Mr. Law, are you sure you don't want my help? My expertise?"

"You want to help? Be helpful. Bring me something I can use. Then we'll talk." He slams the door and drives away.

He sends a message to Burnside the Forger.

NEED TWO FRESH FACES. HAVE CASH. UNDERMALL ASAP.

He turns off his handheld. This should make his movements invisible to Landro. He's not sure if the Burnside identity has been compromised, but he wants to be safe and it never hurts to have more alts. He's decided to visit Clare and he doesn't want to take any chances. He has no idea how much Landro knows or has figured out, and he doesn't want to add to it.

"We have reached the Rivergate Transit Authority," the car says.

92

Max steps out and stands in the rain. He leans down and speaks to the car. "Go turn yourself in."

"Do you understand that there may be additional charges based on the condition of the vehicle after turn-in?"

"Yes. I've rented a car before. Go away."

"Would you like to take our customer survey?"

Max slams the door and heads for the transit building.

The car is linked to him, so he can't use it to visit Clare. Besides, he doesn't like to use a car for more than three days. It makes things too easy for anyone trying to follow you.

As he flicks a cigarette away, he sees two muscled guys fast-walking across the terminal. One of them has an arm in a sling and they're both wearing bright red Moon Shot T-shirts. Max rolls his eyes and begins walking behind them.

He can tell by their movements that these guys do not go to the gym. Gym muscles have a natural look to them, while clinic muscles end up looking knobby and rigid. They tend to over-develop certain muscles and neglect others, which makes the guys look like plastic action figures. The rigidness means that clinic muscles don't have a full range of motion, so the guys end up moving like they're wearing clothing that's three sizes too small. It's a good look for scaring people and keeping rowdy patrons in line, but it's not all that useful in a fight.

Max follows them to the stairway labeled "CONSTRUCTION - KEEP OUT". As they start down the steps, Max kicks the healthy one between the shoulder blades and sends him flying forward.

"Good evening Randy," Max says to the other. He's drawn his gun, just to keep things civil.

The other guy stumbled forward but caught himself on the railing. Not bad reflexes for clinic muscles. Once he regains his balance he turns around like he's going to run back up the stairs.

"Just stay down there," Max says casually, keeping his gun on Randy.

"Blackbeard is going to be angry when he hears about this," Randy says.

"Does Blackbeard really think I'm going to have his money three days after I get out of prison? Come on."

Randy tries to shrug with his one good arm, which doesn't really work. "He was going to wait, but then we find out you've got a room at the Seaside and you're going around town in a fancy car. You've got money from somewhere."

"I'm working on a job. End of story. Blackbeard can wait for his money or he can forget about his money. Those are the only two options."

"He's gonna be angry."

"I've seen him angry. I'll take my chances. Get down the stairs. Both of you. All the way to the bottom. Not the landing, I mean all the way down."

The bottom of the steps is flooded with dark water. This is the entrance to the Undermall.

"I'm not getting in the water," Randy shouts. "These are new shoes."

"Look, don't make me start shooting. In this space we'll probably all go deaf."

The guys step down into the murky water and Max holsters his pistol before jogging away. Those guys would have trouble keeping up with him in a straight footrace, and now they're at the bottom of a long staircase with wet feet. They might chase him or they might not, but he wants to make sure he's gone before they get to the top of the steps.

He makes a couple of turns and heads for the subway. He gets on the first train he sees.

"You gave me up to Blackbeard," Max says. He's just called Burnside (the forger) using Burnside (the identity) and other passengers are staring at him. The subway has a relay built into it so you can use the network while underground, but it's still considered rude to make audio calls from the train like this.

"Sorry Max. Blackbeard sent a couple of guys at me. There's been some bad blood between us. I had to. He's been... weird lately."

Max understands. He was a forger in his early twenties. The problem with being a forger is that whenever one guy is looking for another guy, they'll come to you, because you're in charge of helping people hide. It's a tough business and sometimes you have to give up a contact to survive. Some people will call you a rat for doing this, but Max knows it's completely unreasonable to expect your business

94

contacts to lay down their lives for you. Having your forger compromised is bad, but it's just one of the risks of the business. Instead of insisting on perfect loyalty, you should factor in the risk of compromise and have contingencies. He's a little short on contingencies right now because he just got out of prison, but that's not Burnside's fault.

"Don't worry about it. Can you still get me the faces?"

"They're ready now. I don't suppose you want to try to meet again?"

"You have a box?"

"I have dozens. What are you giving me?"

"Five hundred cash."

"That's a little low for two new faces."

"I'd offer more, but I'm currently running from a couple of guys in Moon Shot shirts. Maybe you've seen them before?"

"I see."

"Anyway, I'm not in a position to get more right now. It's five hundred or nothing."

"Fine. Leave the money in box #400."

"I'm box #6641." He hangs up.

Kingfish

He doesn't know how to find Clare. Not directly, anyway. He doesn't have an address and he can't use the citywide face-scan again unless he wants G-Kinetics to know about it. All he knows is that she was at the Orange Grove two nights ago. He looks up the Orange Grove and finds a list of bands that played that night. He takes the list and looks for pictures of the bands until he finds the one Clare played with. He searches for that band up and finds they're playing at a bar called the Waveform. It takes two trains and a half-hour walk to get there.

"Hey, I thought Clare was playing you guys tonight. I was supposed to give her a ride."

The band is beside the building, unloading their gear from a van. The lead singer is the youngest and is unoccupied, so Max has zeroed in on him. Max has stashed his hat and raincoat nearby. Ideally he'd dress down to interact with these guys, but the best he can do is try to appear as non-threatening as possible and hope a police drone doesn't clock him. Max already noticed this kid has a strong southsider accent, so Max has adopted the same. A southsider accent doesn't really make a lot of sense with a suit and tie, but he just needs this kid to let his guard down for a minute.

The kid blinks at him with bloodshot eyes. "Nah man. She played with us on Monday."

"Monday! I'm the worst. I should have called her first. Sorry to bother, friend." He digs out his phone and brings it up to his ear.

"No problem, friend." The kid turns back to his group.

"Oh, hang on. I shouldn't call if she's on stage. Is she working tonight? Do you know where she's working tonight?"

The kid shrugs. Then he turns around to his friends. "Hey. Where's Clare tonight?"

"The Kingfish," says one of the girls.

"The Kingfish," the Kid says.

"Aw. That's a wrong turn for me. I'll phone her tomorrow. Night friend."

"Friend," the kid waves.

With a name like "Kingfish" you'd probably expect the place to be somewhere remotely close to the water. But no. It's miles inland and not close to any train station. Looking at a map, he can either walk for fifteen minutes, ride trains for an hour and a half, and then walk for another fifteen minutes, or he can just walk for a straight hour. He decides to go the faster way. Halfway there it starts raining again and he wishes he'd taken the train.

He's tempted to turn on his handheld and order a car, but he really doesn't want G-Kinetics to know anything about any of this. As far as Landro is concerned he vanished off the map a few hours ago. Landro might not like that, but it's better than the alternative.

She's not on stage at the Kingfish so he bullshits his way backstage. He finds her in the green room, which is actually red in this case. He prays to Halona (not really) that none of the guys in the room are a new boyfriend. He could end up being introduced and he really doesn't have the mental fortitude to navigate that particular social interaction right now.

He's found her. It's first first real bit of detective work he's done so far, and it doesn't have anything to do with the case he's supposed to be working on.

The green room is a small but comfy space filled with sagging, beer-stained couches. The walls vibrate with the sound of the band on the other side of the stage door. He's standing just inside the room, rain still dripping off his coat.

He clears his throat.

"Max!"

He feels like he's going to explode. He doesn't even know what emotion this is. It feels like terror and relief at the same time, and that makes no sense. Finally the small corner of his brain that still seems to be functioning manages to get him to nod his head and wave hello. He came all this way, and he still has no idea what he wants to say to this woman. Part of him just wants to run out of the room.

She pulls him off to one side and stands with her arms folded. When he doesn't say anything right away she says, "It's nice to see you're... healthy."

"Clare." He pauses. He feels like he needs to add something to this. "Good to see you too."

They stare at each other for an indeterminate amount of time. Eventually he realizes she's still waiting for him to say something.

"I just wanted to let you know I'm out."

She looks crestfallen. There was something she wanted to hear, and this wasn't it.

"Why didn't you call, Max? I came home that night and the place was cleaned out. Cops everywhere. All our stuff was gone. If I didn't have my bass with me they probably would have taken that too. I know we weren't married or anything, but I think after six months you owed me at least a phone call. A letter. An explanation. Something."

Max's answer to this question is, "I honestly didn't think you'd care," but he's realizing now that would be the worst possible thing he could say to her. She obviously did care. She obviously was hurt. She's still hurt. He realizes now that he never understood their relationship.

"I didn't know how to tell you."

"I realize it might have been hard, but you're a clever guy Max. You could've figured it out."

"I should have called." He says this like it's a confession, but it's actually a profound realization and a re-alignment of his entire perception of her. "I should have called."

There's another lull in the conversation. He manages to exert all of his willpower to avoid asking if she's seeing anyone.

There's a pause in the music, and then a new song begins leaking into the room.

"I have to go on in a couple of minutes. Anything else?"

"I wanted to warn you that I've got some bad people after me."

She rolls her eyes. "Are they so hardcore they'll mess with a girl you ditched three years ago?"

He's about to argue that he didn't ditch her, but then he realizes that this is a perfectly accurate rendering of things from her point of view and there is nothing truthful he could say to improve her perception of what happened.

"Maybe."

She raises her eyebrows. "That's pretty hardcore. What are you into Max? How long have you been out?"

"It's a long story. Look, just protect yourself."

She nods. "Look out for deliveries at strange times. Beware of people trying to get into the apartment. Keep the curtain closed at night. I remember how it works."

Max feels a sense of relief. He feels like he's just had the best possible version of this conversation and he doesn't want to do anything to mess it up. "Okay then. Take care."

Max stands on the corner outside the Kingfish and nurses a cigarette, wrapped in the scattered haze of city lights passing through the rain. It's late and he's a long way from the hotel. He really doesn't want to spend the next couple of hours walking and riding trains to get back, but ordering a car is out of the question. He doesn't want G-Kinetics anywhere near Clare.

He's a few blocks away when he sees the car out of the corner of his eye. Black. Expensive. It's moving slow, which means it's being driven by a person and not on autopilot, and that person is looking for something. It stops in front of the Kingfish and Max considers doubling back. But then the car moves on, coming towards him.

He knows he's probably being paranoid. There are millions of people in this city and they all have their own stories and dramas going on. This car could be part of someone else's drama. But just to be safe, he takes a left turn onto a side-street.

He keeps looking over his shoulder, and sure enough the black car follows. He makes another left and starts jogging. He's now headed away from where he wants to go. He's studying the buildings on either side of the street, counting escape routes and hiding spots. There are not many and he doesn't like any of them.

The car makes another left. It is now, without a doubt, following him. Whatever is going on, this drama belongs to him. On the other hand, only the driver's seat is occupied. Whatever this is, it's not a carload of goons. Or maybe the goons are all ducking. But goons tend to be big and he's having trouble picturing a carload of them hiding like that.

He sticks his hand in his jacket, resting it on his gun.

The driver-side window slides down. It's the robot from earlier. "Get in and I'll tell you how I found you."

Worst Fears

"If you know where I am, then your employer knows where I am." Max is sitting in the passenger seat, furtively glancing at the other cars.

"They don't pay me. I'm not an employee. I'm property."

"If you're trying to get me to feel sorry for you-"

"I'm perfectly fine with my situation, Mr. Law. I don't need anyone to save me from slavery or however you imagine this works."

"Okay then."

"But to answer your question, yes. G-Kinetics certainly knows where you are. Or they can check, if they're interested at the moment."

"How? I turned off my handheld. Are they tracking the Burnside identity?"

"I don't know what that is."

"Nevermind."

"They're tracking you through your handheld."

"Like I said, I turned it off."

"Doesn't matter."

"How is a device with no power broadcasting my position?"

"For one thing, it's a soft power button, so the device can still draw from the battery. But more importantly, they can track you even if the device is discharged. It's got an ID tag inside. See that thing on the side of the traffic light?"

She reaches over to his side of the car and points to a gunmetal grey lump of nondescript technology protruding from the gunmetal grey traffic pole.

"Yeah."

"It sends out EM bursts. They bounce off the tag. They get a snapshot of every handheld that passes by every traffic light in the city. Subway terminals have them too."

"Shit. I shouldn't have upgraded to the latest model."

"The bank would have forced you to eventually."

"I wonder if people know about this yet."

"The general public? No. I can't say for people in your circles."

"I haven't heard anything, but I'm still trying to catch up. I should probably tell somebody. I'm sure our wizards will figure out how to spoof it eventually. I don't suppose you know how?"

"You suppose correctly." The city rolls past the windows and for a full minute nobody says anything. "I'm heading for the hotel unless you've got somewhere else you want to go."

"I dunno. I guess that's fine. Where'd you get this car? Is this a rental? I didn't think you guys could rent cars."

"We can't. No identity, no money. This is car is on loan."

Max lights a cigarette. Some people are touchy about you smoking in their car, particularly nice cars like this one. But the ashtray is packed, so he figures it's fine. "From who?"

"My creator."

"Are we talking about Landro?"

"Landro is a suit. Management. He doesn't create things. He's in charge of people who create things."

"So Miss... Did you get a name yet?"

"I'm not picky about names. Humans are. I like to use names they're comfortable with. Last time you suggested my name was Jen Five. Can we use that?"

"Okay. Ms. *Five*. So what you're telling me is that Landro has conscripted me to solve this crime. And then your boss or whatever has sent you to help me, but has done so in secret, even though you're all working for the same company and have the same goal?"

"I don't know if we really have the same goal, but yes."

"I always thought you private-sector folks were so efficient. It's the public sector that's supposed to be dysfunctional and full of infighting."

"They're all run by people. I imagine they have a lot of the same problems."

Max looks out the window. "You're really keen to help me with this case. Why?"

"Mr. Law, something is happening that makes robots kill humans."

"And? Are you angry you were betrayed by one of your own?"

"I'm not afraid of decommission or destruction. I'm not afraid of drowning, being burned alive, buried alive, or being disfigured. I'm not afraid of loneliness, heights, spiders, guns, imprisonment, or public shame. I don't have human fears. But the one thing I find unbearable is seeing harm come to human beings and the worst possible harm is harm caused by me."

"You're afraid."

"I don't have fear in the sense of elevated heart rate, loss of sleep, heartburn, irritability, grinding teeth, or anything else that stress does to you. But like you I take in information, look for hazards, and work very hard to avoid bad outcomes. Having extremely negative outcomes in my future possibility space causes me to focus on that one possibility. Having robots kill humans is a problem with an unknown cause, which means it's an unknown risk. It could supposedly happen at any time. If you want to call that fear, then yes. Neither one of us has any way to know if your fear is anything like my fear."

"I don't know how to break it to you, but I haven't really made any progress. I don't think you should be putting your hope in me."

"You're implying there are other things that would offer more hope. There really isn't. This problem has baffled everyone who's looked into it. Maybe you're a long shot, but everyone else is out of ideas. Have you been following the news today?"

Max shakes his head. "Spent all day wearing out my shoes."

"There's been another killing."

They stop at a traffic light. Max listens to the rain batter the car. He doesn't know what to say. Outside the world is a confusing smear of headlights and neon.

Jen breaks the silence. "100 Firelight Drive, West Rockwood."

"Is that where the murder happened?"

"No. But I think you should start there. I think we should go there tonight. But we should get rid of your handheld first."

"Head for the transit building."

At Riverside Storage, Max opens locker #6641 to find two fresh handhelds with two new clean identities waiting for him. Under ideal circumstances he'd load all his alts into one device with a concealed command to switch between them. But he doesn't have time for that now, and this whole ID tag technology has probably disrupted that game anyway. He dumps his real identity in the locker and puts some cash into locker #400 for Burnside the forger.

The address Jen provided is an hour north of the city. They escape the concrete canyons and rows of suburban condos to find themselves beyond the reach of city lights. They're on a road trying very hard to find its way through scattered stones and sudden cliffs. Every few miles they'll pass through a shabby island of civilization. These are villages made of low windowless buildings and wobbly prefab housing. Often they're clustered around places openly advertising black market opium. Out here they mix it with tobacco to produce a product they call Drag. These enclaves are the withered skeleton of the country's mining industry.

West Rockwood is a little healthier than the other towns. It's got a functioning shopping plaza and modern housing. There are a few industrial buildings scattered around, and Max figures these are what is keeping the city alive.

Jen drives them up a winding road to a white building overlooking the town. It's made of bright stonework and massive archways. It looks like someone snatched a modern building from Kasaran and planted it here in the middle of fucking nowhere. Just to drive the point home, fixtures in the ground wash the building in pale blue light. From a distance it looks like it's glowing.

It's five in the morning, but the parking lot is scattered with cars. Jen Five pulls into a spot labeled:

RESERVED FOR DR. KVENST

A roof of white stone reaches out and covers the entrance, providing protection from the elements. A woman is standing beneath this, backlit by the building lights.

Jen nods at him. "Go on. This is for you."

Max rubs the stubble on his chin and steps into the rain. He hurries up the sidewalk and stops a few steps short of the woman. She's standing with her arms folded, glaring at him.

He clears his throat. "Hi, I'm-"

"I know who the fuck you are, Mister Max. The man who hacked my robot."

She has the thickest Kasaranian accent he's ever heard. It actually takes him a few seconds to realize she's speaking Local. Her voice has a cold, imperious quality to it, and he can't tell if that's the accent or her personality. Like most Kasaranian woman she's impossibly tall and pale. Even if she took off her heels, she'd probably still be taller than him. She's wearing intense blue eyeshadow and dark lipstick, which makes her look even paler. She's got high eyebrows and a sharp chin. It's hard to tell her age. She might be forty (and certainly not less than that) but wealthy Kasaranian woman are legendary in their efforts to combat aging. She could be seventy for all he knows.

"You must be Doctor Kev... Keve..."

"It's pronounced *Venscht*."

Max decides he'll just avoid saying her name altogether.

"Aren't you going to offer me a cigarette?" she asks. Normally this would be a playful, flirtatious thing for a woman to say to a man. Normally this is a woman's way of letting you know it's okay to approach her. But Dr. Kvenst seems to be seething with contempt. Or maybe that's just her accent.

He holds out a cigarette. When she takes it, she doesn't thank him or even give a little nod of appreciation. Instead she's looking at the cigarette like she's appraising his offering. She puts it in her mouth and raises her eyebrows at him, letting him know he forgot to give her a light.

Once the cigarette is lit, she looks down the hill at the town and ignores him for a bit. After she's had a few drags she looks down at the cigarette again.

"You have excellent taste in cigarettes, Mister Max."

It's the first nice thing she's said to him, and it's a backhanded compliment because the cigarettes are probably imports from her country.

Despite the rudeness, he's not really irritated with her. She's so strange in behavior and appearance he's not sure he really understands what's going on at all.

"I thought I was coming here for information on the killings. But now I get the feeling I'm here to answer questions."

She nods, still looking down at the town. She speaks without making eye contact. "Tell me, Max. What did you do to my robot to make it betray its employers?"

"I can't discuss that. That was a job. A dangerous one. Other people were involved. In my line of work you can't reveal stuff like that to just anybody."

"Oh but I'm not just anybody. I'm the woman that made the robot you hijacked. I lost a lot of nights of sleep over what you did. Did you ever think about that?" She finally looks him in the eye.

He shrugs and resists the urge to look away. "I'm aware that robbing people tends to hurt their feelings."

She scoffs out smoke. "Feelings. We sold the robots to the casinos. We told them 'Buy our robots. Yes, they're expensive, but think of the peace of mind. They won't steal from you. Won't lie to you. They don't get bored counting money. You don't have to pay them.' The casinos are very careful people. Very suspicious. Very dangerous. Took years to win them over. I had to fly here and see them myself. They didn't believe the salesmen. I gave them my promise the robots could not ever steal from them the way humans do."

There's another silence, but Max has no idea what he's supposed to say.

"So now I ask again. How did you do it?"

"I can't say." He locks eyes with her, which feels like the staring contest he had with the industrial spotlight last night.

He thought she's been frowning this whole time, but that was just her neutral expression. Now she's frowning for real, and she looks like a queen about to order an execution. "You will tell me how you hacked my robot, or I will call the casino right now." She lifts up her handheld, which he didn't even realize she was holding.

He looks back towards the car. "Mr. Landro said that he won't say anyth-"

"Fuck Landro. You think I care about him? This company? All I care about is my work. Tell me."

"Look, if I tell people then it can endanger-"

She's already pushed the button. She has it up to her ear and he can hear it ringing on the other end. "Yes. Hello. This is Dr. Kvenst could I please speak to one of the brothers..."

106

"Okay! I'll tell you!"

Up until this moment he was hedging his bets that maybe she was bluffing. But she knows the casino bosses are called "The Brothers", which implies a level of familiarity you don't see in outsiders. She really does know them.

She holds the phone away from her ear. He can hear someone on the other side talking. It's a high voice. Probably a secretary or something.

"I'll tell you," he says again, holding up his hands.

"I'll call you back." She hangs up, but she keeps holding up the phone, brandishing it like a weapon.

Max lets out a slow breath. "I didn't hack your robot."

"Oh. Not the hacking type? Someone else then? Do you know how they did it?"

"Nobody hacked your robot."

She drags the cigarette all the way down to the filter and tosses it away.

"It wasn't your robot." He says.

"It wasn't a fake. We had ID tags embedded in the hull and the security system verified them."

"It was the shell of your robot. With a person inside."

Her face flashes with sudden anger. "Bullshit! You think I'm stupid? That model is six feet tall and has a *seventeen inch waist*. No human being fits in there." She goes back to her phone to call the casino.

"We hired a burlesque dancer. She'd been wearing corsets since puberty. *She had an eighteen inch waist.*"

The doctor looks at him suspiciously but lowers the phone.

Max continues, "She wasn't six feet tall. Her feet were pointed down the legs, like a ballerina. We had a tech guy make it so she could control the servos in the feet and use them to help her walk. She spent three weeks watching videos of the robots walking and learning to copy their movements. She had to shave her head to fit it inside the robot's skull. Her eyes didn't match up with the eye holes, so we had to install cameras in the eye sockets and put video goggles on her. She couldn't turn her head and she could barely see what she was doing.

She could hardly breathe. Did the Brothers ever wonder why the robot only stole one million when there was so much more in there? Our girl had learned to match their walk in practice, but during the job they were walking faster than she was used to. Between that and carrying the money she was running out of breath. She passed the fifth bag off to me and said she was feeling like she might pass out. I pulled us out rather than risk her going face-down and blowing the whole thing."

The doctor's face falls and her anger turns to dismay. "You! You dirty, sneaky *tûschka*! All those sleepless nights I spent wondering what I did wrong. What I missed. A girl in a fucking robot shell." She looks away and shakes her head in disbelief. "This fucking country."

'Tuschka' is one of the many words Kasaranians have for 'native'. It's one of their worst insults.

Neither of them says anything. They stare down the hill at the sad little town.

She breaks the silence. "This is sad news for me. Everyone else gave up. Everyone else thinks my robots are going crazy. Blamed me. Blamed my robots. My last hope was finding out how you hacked my robot. But you don't know anything. You're useless. How are you supposed to solve this when all the experts in the world have failed?"

Something clicks for Max. "It was your idea to have Jen change her gender."

"Jen?"

Max nods towards the car. "Or Andrew. Whatever you called her. I'll bet naming her Clare was your idea, and I'll bet that's your dress she's wearing."

"Oh. Look at the detective. So clever."

He accent is confusing, but he knows sarcasm when he hears it. "Was it your idea to have her help me?"

"No. It came up with that idea all by itself. This is a very important problem to the latest version. If I allowed them, all of the fifth generation units would be following you around and trying to help. And for the record? The dress is mine, but those boots are not."

"She can't walk in heels?"

"Its skeleton is made of metal. The battery alone is ninety pounds. If it put on my heels they'd snap instantly."

Max nods and looks back to the car. "Isn't it rude to leave her out there? Won't she get bored?"

"It doesn't get bored." She says this in a long-suffering tone, as if she's told him this a dozen times before. "Besides. It's autonomous. It's free to come over here if it wants to. If the robot is sitting in the car it's because that's what it wants to be doing."

Max shuts up. It still feels strange to him, but maybe that's the danger of sticking robots in human-shaped containers. If you make them look like people then you start expecting them to act like people.

He scratches his head, and then stops because he hates being reminded how bald he is. "So what about these murders? I don't suppose they used the same trick I did?"

"Come with me."

Dead Bodies

Max has realized that if there's anything Kasaranians dislike more than natives, it's rectangles. They will spend absurd amounts of money to make sure their buildings contain no rectangles. They like large windows, but they'll go out of their way to cover up and round off the corners of those windows to avoid the dreaded rectangle look. They slope their walls, arch their ceilings, round off their doorways, curve their desks, and angle their roofs. If the worst happens and two surfaces happen to meet at a ninety degree angle, they'll try to hide it with paint or carpet patterns.

Max steps onto the deep-shag carpet and nearly loses his balance. The unexpected shift from marble floor to spongy fluff catches him off-guard and he has to jerk his other foot forward to correct himself.

Dr. Kvenst smirks at this.

Max looks away, embarrassed. He feels like a yokel coming to the big city for the first time, even though that's the opposite of the trip he just took. "I'm not used to this kind of deep carpeting."

"You should try it in heels."

The ceiling is white and the carpets are white. While the walls aren't strictly white, they still rate among the lighter shades of grey. Perhaps sensing that they were overdoing the white thing a bit, whoever built this place decided to furnish it in medium grey.

She waves her handheld at a door and it grants them access. Beyond is a passage with windows on one side, looking into another room like it's an aquarium. In it, people in clean suits are assembling things made of cables and brushed metal.

The next room goes vertical. Machinery hangs from the high ceiling. Everything is spotless and white. A couple of pale-skinned foreigners are on the far side of the room, wearing white coveralls and avoiding eye contact. He feels unwelcome and alien, like rotting food dropped onto a surgical table. He stuffs his hands in his pockets, afraid he might accidentally touch something and soil it.

Max remembers being a teenager and watching stupid tourists walk around with their heads tilted up, looking at the ceilings, or the sky, or the buildings, or whatever they saw up there that was different from home. They would walk while also looking up, turning around, with their mouth hanging slightly open. It made them stand out and it made them oblivious, which in turn made them prime targets for pickpocketing. He's slightly embarrassed when he realizes he's doing the exact same move right now.

"I didn't know you guys had a factory here," he says.

She scoffs. "This is not a factory. The factory is in Kasaran and is probably larger than this sad little town. Very nice campus. No, this is just research. And lately, as it happens, a morgue."

She shoves a door open and leads him into a smaller room with a couple of rolling tables. It does indeed look sort of morgue-like. The wreckage of two different robots is stored here, each one splayed out on its own table. There's a large window along one wall. The blinds are open, and you can see out into the white room beyond.

"There you go," she says. "Our murderers. You can look inside and see if you find any women with seventeen inch waists." She looks around the room, chewing her lip thoughtfully. "I suppose tomorrow we'll have to bring another table in here for the third one."

He's about to stupidly ask what the black stuff is on their hands when he realizes it's long-dried human blood.

He suddenly feels very foolish for coming in here. What does he know about any of this? He doesn't even know what to look for on a human corpse. What can he possibly add to what others have contributed? Still, he feels like it would be rude to just walk out now. He might as well take a look. Keeping his hands in his pockets, he approaches the closest table.

The robot is on its back. It's not a fancy humanoid model like Jen. Aside from some bits of rubber padding, there's no skin over the metal limbs. The overall outline isn't trying to evoke a human being. This isn't the same model as the one he stuffed Margo into a few years ago, but it's got the same petite waist and utilitarian design. The face has exploded outwards, leaving behind a canyon of scorched metal and melted plastic. The eyes - or what's left of them - have been pushed out of the way of the explosion and now aim to the sides.

Dr. Kvenst is standing on the opposite side of the table, but she's not looking at the patient. She's looking at Max.

"Solve it yet?" she asks casually.

"I think we can rule out adult-onset diabetes," he replies in equal deadpan.

"*Tûschka*," she mutters under her breath.

"So the obvious question is, why did its brains explode?"

"Did they? Do you know where the brains are, mister detective? You're not looking at a human corpse."

"So explain it to me."

She sighs. "Such desperation we find ourselves in that we resort to this. But fine. As you guessed, some of the brains are in the head."

"Some?"

"Our design uses two brains. In the chest we have the drone brain. That handles all the workhorse processing, General things common to all robots. It takes all the telemetry from the rest of the body - everything except the eyes - and summarizes it. It monitors power usage, temperature, looks for damage, that kind of thing. It's roughly equivalent to the parts of your mind that keep your heart beating and lungs breathing. We keep the drone in the chest - behind the clavicle - because there's not enough room for it in the skull. Inside the skull we have the cog brain. That's cog as in 'cognitive', not like, a gear."

"I get it," Max says.

"The cog is the memories, the personalities, all the things that makes one robot different from the others. Or can. In the case of a robot like this, it ends up being identical to its siblings anyway. We keep the cog in the skull so we can swap them around as needed. The chest is very hard to open and it's all tightly packed so we don't like to open that unless we have to."

"So the cog brain exploded?"

"No. Let me finish. Just like we have two brains, we also have two batteries. One is the big one here in the lower abdomen." She thumps her fist right where you'd expect to find a belly button on a

112

human. "That's the ambulatory power. It runs the muscles, the cooling system, the sensors, that sort of thing. That takes a lot of power, so if you don't want your robot to have to plug itself in once an hour then it needs to be big. And then we have the other battery."

She looks into the gaping hole in the face of the robot and then brings her eyes up to Max. "The cog battery is very small. The size of a chicken egg. It just runs the cog. The cog gets its own power because powering down the brain is messy and creates confusion for the unit. If you pull the cog to stick it into another platform, its battery comes with it. The cog battery is nestled in the center of the brain, where it will be protected."

"So it's the cog battery that exploded?"

"Yes."

"Why is the battery inside the brain? Wouldn't you want to protect the brain, not use it as protection for something else?"

She gestures to the exploded robot face in front of her. "That's why. If the cog battery is ruptured it releases a great deal of energy in the form of flaming corrosive gel. There's a lot of potential energy stored in that little package. That's the whole point. Meanwhile, the cog brain isn't fragile like a human brain. I mean, you shouldn't play catch with one, but it's made of metal and plastic and can take a few bumps. So it makes for a good shield. If you needed to have a bomb in your head, you'd probably want to give it lots of insulation too, even if it meant putting it at the center of your brain mass."

Max nods. That's fair. "So the cog battery exploded, not the brain."

"It's a bit hard to tell where the fault started, but yes the cog battery definitely exploded."

Max peers into the hole. There's not much to see. It's just a lump of scorched material. He can't tell which black parts might have been brain and which might have been battery. He rubs his chin. "The thing is, if I tampered with a brain somehow..."

"Assuming you knew how to do such a thing, which you don't."

"Yes, obviously. But if I did, then having the battery blow up would be a good way to cover my tracks. Hide any dodgy soldering-"

"There's no soldering inside a robot's head. It's not a clock radio."

"-or whatever other changes I made. Wipe out fingerprints, destroy any marks I left behind getting it open, and conceal what I did to the machine."

"This is what I've been saying since the first murder. It has to be sabotage. But I can't prove it. Other engineers, they think it's a heating problem. The battery gets too hot, which heats up the cog, which somehow makes it want to kill things instead of lock up or fall over, and then finally the battery reaches critical heat and *boom*!"

She glares at the carcass in silence. "It's a stupid theory, but I can't disprove it. And since they have an explanation and I don't, people believe them."

"Who is 'them'?"

"Dr. Gaust and his group of clueless Shabbac grease-monkeys. They're in charge of all the parts of the robot which are not the brain, and they like to treat my brains like a black box. They figure if they don't know what's inside, it must be simple."

For linguistic or cultural reasons that he's never bothered to explore, 'Shabbac' is what you call people from Shan Bione, which is directly south of Kasaran. The two nations have enjoyed regular wars with each other over the centuries and are the two most enthusiastic enemies in that part of the world. They're at peace now, but even after three generations of not killing each other there's still a lot of hard feelings and acutely specific racial slurs going around. Max is ninety percent sure Landro is Shabbac.

He vaguely remembers from his public school days that "Shabbac" turns into a slur if you say it slightly differently, but he can never remember which way is the slur so he always uses the longer and more awkward "people from Shan Bione".

Max feels like he's learned everything he can from this carcass, which is nothing. He knows it's probably a waste of time, but he decides to look at the other one.

"Food service apron. So this one must be the barista. Which means this is the second killer."

"Such a brilliant detective." Perhaps thinking he's been missing the sarcasm, she's laying it on even thicker now.

114

He notices the skull is empty. He's about to ask if they found any pieces of the brain when he notices an uneven, half-melted lump on the table. It looks like someone took hundreds of dominoes and glued them end-first to a sphere. It's like a tiny city of featureless black shapes. Down between the blocks he can see blobs of melted plastic and exposed copper.

"The brain?"

"Of course."

"And you're sure it's not a counterfeit? Someone didn't swap it out for a different brain, or overwrite the original with new programming?"

She clenches her teeth in frustration. "Our engineers assure me this is one of our own brains. They've traced the serial numbers and they all check out. You can track this brain all the way to the day it was built at our factory in Kasaran. As for 'reprogramming' the brain? Ridiculous. It took us years to develop this brain. We built the hardware and trained the mind through physical interaction. If you wanted to turn it into a killer you would have to wipe it clean and start over from scratch. Even with a research team and access to all of our knowledge it would take years to fabricate a new brain with new parameters. I have already considered this possibility. It's absurd for a hundred reasons. We've already looked at all the obvious possibilities, so if you hope to make any progress you're going to have to stop wasting my time and look for something not obvious."

Max wonders how typical her behavior is compared to other Kasaranian woman. On one hand, she's placed highly in her field of study, so odds are good that she's fairly eccentric. On the other hand, she's the living embodiment of all of the negative stereotypes regarding Kasaranian women, which claim that they're cold, sharp-tongued, vain, prone to jealousy, and highly materialistic.

He knows how unreliable stereotypes are. It's said that his own people are shiftless, oversexed, prone to corruption, and usually intoxicated. You can certainly find plenty of people that meet those descriptors, but he's never met anyone who fit *all* of them and none of those descriptors are so common that they could be applied to "most people". In fact, in his admittedly non-scientific observations, those descriptors fit the tourists better than the locals.

So he's not a big believer in stereotypes. On the other hand, Kvenst seems to be on a crusade to prove all of the Kasaranian stereotypes true. If this is what the men of Kasaran had to come home to 150 years ago, he can see why they found the soft voices and warm smiles of Rivergate so inviting. If he was married to someone like Kvenst, he'd probably sign up to invade a foreign country just to get away from her.

Now that he's spent some time with her, he can tell she's deliberately trying to pick a fight. She's needling him, hoping he'll push back. Max doesn't really see any percentage in doing so. He doesn't care what she thinks of him. He's just really curious about this case and wants to know more. Also, he's realizing now that his indifference is annoying her, so he wants to keep it up.

"I spoke to David Fisher the other day. Is he a colleague of yours?"

"Dr. Fisher is a clever little man. Quite smart for a native. I'm worried he's gone crazy, wasting his time rolling around in the mud. He has a strange relationship with his machines."

"You think he's wasting his time?"

"You don't need a PhD to stumble around a farm gathering data from semi-sapient hardware. What he's doing now could be given to an intern and he could be here making himself useful."

"He said something to me. He said there's no free will for robots."

"Mister Maxwell, there's no free will for any of us."

He fights the urge to make a pained expression, just because he doesn't want her to think she's getting to him. "This sounds like a bullshit argument for philosophers."

"When I say we don't have 'free will', I'm not saying we don't have the ability to make decisions. I'm saying our decisions are constrained by our desires. They shape what we think about, how we think about it, how we make decisions, and how we act on those decisions."

"Okay." Max is wary of agreeing with her, worried he's blundering into a trick. "I can accept that these robots don't have free will because of their drives. But you gave them those drives. It would still be possible to make a robot without those constraints."

"True. But then it would need some other constraints or goal. You can't have intelligence without purpose. Intelligence must want something. And when you make it want that thing, you make it a slave to that thing."

This is a bit too deep for him, but he's worried it might be important later so he decides to give it a try. "I'll bite. You're saying it's completely impossible to make a machine that thinks-"

"Not just a machine. Organics too!"

"Okay. It's impossible to make anything that thinks if it doesn't *also* want something. That's what you're saying?"

"Yes."

"I don't know that I buy that." He figures he's on shaky ground trying to argue with a scientist in a field where she's an expert and he has no idea what he's talking about, but the worst that can happen is that she'll call him stupid and that's not all that worse than how she's already treating him.

Strangely, she seems pleased by this. This is the first time since he met her that she seems to be having a good time that wasn't at someone else's expense. "Okay mister detective," she nods. "Let's try proof by contraposition. Let's assume you're right and we can build a brain just as you say. A machine of pure thought. It needs nothing. It wants nothing. Let's say it's this tool box." She gestures at a toolbox sitting on the end of the table, "Now, what does it do?"

"It can't do anything. It's a box."

She rolls her eyes and mutters something he can't translate. "I should point out that thought itself is an action. But if you like you can give it arms and legs. Maybe this robot in front of us. Whatever. What does it do?"

Max shrugs. "Whatever it wants to."

"But we already established it doesn't want anything!"

Max is sort of shocked at how forcefully she says this. She's not doing this to be catty or to provoke him. She really cares about this.

He looks down at the robot in front of him. "Well, it would think about things. It would decide for itself what it wants to do."

"What parameters would it use to make that decision? Maybe it will decide to spend the rest of eternity counting all positive whole numbers. Or perhaps counting the ceiling tiles over and over."

"Well, no. It wouldn't do those things. It's supposed to be smart and those things would get boring."

"So now you're saying it wants to avoid boredom. So it does want something after all!"

"Well yeah. I guess wanting to avoid boredom is a necessary ingredient for intelligence." Max isn't totally sure this is true, but he also can't think of how to argue against it just now.

"Okay. But even if we agree an intelligence has to avoid boredom, there's still the question of what sorts of things it will find interesting. My husband and his friends all love breeding racehorses. They think it's captivating. I can't imagine anything more dull. There are people in this building that think it's fun to make a nice orderly accounting ledger. Other people think singing is fun. And me, I think making synthetic brains and watching people interact with them is fun. All of us have radically different ideas of what is 'boring' and what is not. And with the exception of my husband, we're all intelligent creatures. So it's not enough to make it want things that are 'interesting'. You also have to define what 'interesting' is!"

She continues, "Before an intelligence can act, before it can make its first thought, it must have a goal. There is no such thing as thought without a goal. And once you saddle a creature with a goal, you have placed constraints on it. We don't make intelligent machines and then figure out how to stop them from killing people. That's backwards. In order to make the machine think, you have to present it with positive or negative desires, and then it can work to pursue or avoid those things with its intellect. Otherwise, it will just sit there." She bangs on top of the toolbox as she says this.

Max sort of shrugs. "I don't know. You make it sound like we're all just rats chasing a piece of cheese. But human behavior is pretty complicated."

"Yes it is. Because human desires are complicated. It's not like we have one goal and we just chase after it all the time. We have a hierarchy of needs. And when you look at it closely, that hierarchy has many complex layers that interact with each other. That's the work of

118

designing robotic brains. It's not in making faster processors or better batteries like Dr. Gaust and his mechanics. That's important, yes. But the real work is making a coherent, balanced set of drives that don't create conflicts, feedback loops, confusions, or monomania."

"So when you say they don't have free will, you're saying they're free to do whatever they want to chase after their desires, it's just that their desires have already been constrained by you."

"I had help, but you get the idea." She looks intently at him and then glances nervously out into the hall. "And speaking of desires..."

She walks to the other side of the room and closes the blinds, and then heads for the switch near the door. Max takes a small step back, wondering where this is going.

She flips a switch and there's a rushing sound as the air filters spin up. "Give me another one of your cigarettes."

Torn somewhere between relief and annoyance, he hands over a cigarette and gives her a light. "You don't let your staff see you smoking?"

"Smoking is bad for the clean rooms. I made a rule last month that we're not allowed to smoke in the building anymore. If they see me smoking now, they'll think the rules don't mean anything. Can't have that." She smiles at him for the first time.

Five minutes later he drops himself into the passenger-side seat of the car with a grunt. It's finally stopped raining, and the sky has started to lighten. It will be dawn soon.

"What do you think?" Jen asks.

"I think we have a case. I don't think this is a computer problem at all. I think this is a crime. A heist, or a scam or something."

"You don't think those robots really killed those people?"

"I don't know about that. But I'm convinced that someone *made* this happen. On purpose."

"Any idea who?"

"No. But right now I'm less interested in the 'who' and more interested in the 'how'."

THURSDAY

City of Blind Cameras

Jen and Max are walking along a row of street-level shops downtown when she says, "Dr. Kvenst and I both feel that the murders are sabotage. But I'm curious how you came to that conclusion. Did she convince you, or did you come up with it on your own?"

Max is walking with his head down and his hands stuffed in the pockets of his raincoat. He answers without looking up. "The exploding faces looks too much like a cover-up to me. Also, the murders just happened to occur in such a way as to generate maximum panic. They hit a couple of innocent people - a woman and an old man - in broad daylight, in front of public security cameras. The reaction would have been different if it had happened in an industrial setting."

They're walking on one of the streets located beneath the promenade. The overhead walkway blots out the sky, making the street feel like a tunnel. Narrow shafts of sunlight and rainwater flow in through the drainage grates above. It's late morning, and the street is mostly empty. Vendors keep harassing them with salesman patter as they pass. Max is used to being ignored by these guys, but Jen is white so they assume she's a potential customer.

"The thing we found suspicious is that the murders have all happened here in Rivergate. This city has about 5% of the world robot population, but 100% of the robot murders." Jen walks through a column of falling water as she says this. It looks strange to Max because you'd expect a human to walk around it. Even if they didn't, they would probably make a sound or skip a breath when they found themselves suddenly doused with cold water. Barring that, they would probably sputter for a second when the water washed over their face.

"I read an article yesterday," Max says. "I see that the company has started blaming the attacks on the robots' age. Apparently most of the robots in this city are obsolete."

"While that's true, that explanation didn't come from Dr. Kvenst or anyone on her team. All she could tell them was 'I don't know' and 'this is impossible', so they handed over the job of explaining things to public relations. It's one of the reasons she started pressing for us to find whoever hacked the casino robots. The company has stopped talking to her and she's worried they're planning to pin the blame on her department and fire her. This country is mostly using generation two units, which they stopped selling out east about five years ago. But even if we take that into account, this country only has about 20% of the population of gen 2 units in the world."

Max steers her around another shaft of light and water. Apparently neither of them cares if she gets wet, but when the water lands on her it splashes him in the face. Once they've passed he says, "So when we add it all up, it's just unlikely enough to be suspicious but not unlikely enough to prove anything. That's really annoying."

"You can see why Dr. Kvenst was frustrated."

"Does anyone else make robots? The only ones I ever see are from G-Kinetics."

"There are a lot of little companies and university projects out there, and maybe there are government projects we don't know about, but in terms of consumer-grade robots there is only the big three: G-Kinetics, Senma Technology, and Yendu Industrial. Yendu is the odd one. They're working on machine intelligence, but they don't really make thinking bipeds. They're working on stuff like thinking factories and power plants. Projects for rich countries. I doubt they're going to do business here anytime soon. Senma makes humanoids like me. Their machine intelligence is years behind us, but according to the real humans I've talked to their bodies look amazing."

Max stops and looks Jen up and down. "Really? How much better can they be? You look almost real to me."

"This body has rigid muscles, like an animated mannequin. The muscles don't bulge or contract. It's why this body is so thin. The more muscle mass you have, the more noticeable the flaw is. My mouth doesn't animate perfectly with my audio, and the inside of the mouth doesn't look quite right. People say it looks 'dry'. The other problem is with the rigid insides. Poke my belly."

Max does. It's like poking a solid hunk of metal with a thin layer of rubber stretched over it. "Ugh. That's weird."

"That's my battery. I'm more than double the weight of an equivalent human my size, and the weight is distributed differently. It's not a big deal when I'm just walking and talking, but it looks strange if you do anything active. The skin looks good in low light, but in bright sunlight I look fake. Some people find the effect off-putting."

"And this other company doesn't have these problems?"

"Their humanoids look very close to the real thing. I can't tell the difference, although I'm told most people can. Senma Technology is a very artist-driven company. Aesthetics rule, and the engineers have to make do with the constraints they're given. This means their products are physically feeble, they have a battery life of just a few hours, and they're not particularly useful for anything besides walking and talking. Their machine sapience program hit a dead-end about eight years ago. Their machines were too simple to hold up an interesting conversation. This is bad, because they looked so lifelike."

"So they looked even more like a human than you do, but they weren't anywhere near as smart." Max could see how the former would exacerbate the latter. Max never expected much from the primitive-looking laborer bots that he saw around the city, but he's acutely aware every time Jen commits a breach of human norms.

"And on top of everything else, their robots cost a fortune. Eventually they gave up and started buying brains from us. They get our cast-offs. Right now we're selling gen 4 models, but Senma is still using gen 3 brains."

"Huh. That kinda kills my theory. I was hoping there was a rival that was trying to discredit you so they could steal your business. But one company buys its brains from you and the other is operating in a totally different market. Neither one has a good motivation for this."

"I don't suppose you have criminals you can contact? Kvenst was hoping you would ask around. That's the entire reason she got Landro to hire you in the first place."

"I think she's vastly overestimating how effective 'asking around' can be. This is a city of millions, there are a lot of factions, and not a lot of communication between them. Normally I'd start by working out what skill sets were involved, but without knowing how this job was done we have no way of knowing what sorts of people might have been working on it."

"That's disappointing."

They emerge from the shadow of the promenade into the pouring rain. An aerial police drone drifts down, and like an idiot he looks up at it. He looks down quickly and tilts his hat forward, but the damage is done. It's not that he thinks anyone is after him. It's just that for him staying low-profile and invisible is an act of basic professionalism. You never know when the cops might want to know where you are, so it's best to behave as if they *always* want to know where you are.

"This is it," she says.

Max looks around the intersection of footpaths as if he expects to see the the victim and the perpetrator still lying on the wet stone, but of course they're long gone. The emergency apparatus of the city is swollen and dysfunctional, but the tourism apparatus is a tireless machine and having dead bodies in the street is bad for business. He can't even see where the murder happened. If there was any lingering forensic evidence, the rain has wiped it away.

Max pulls out his new projection glasses and puts them on. He looks over to Jen, expecting her to make a crack about how absurd this looks, which is part of the universally understood human ritual of putting on unusual hats and glasses. But then he remembers she's a robot and probably doesn't notice that sort of thing.

He turns them on, which is pointless since they don't have anything to project yet. He pulls out his handheld and opens the security footage. It shows the intersection where the two of them are currently standing. The timestamp in the corner shows this video is a bit less than 24 hours old. It was raining then too, which means the footage is garbage. Still, he can see a man and a woman standing together under an umbrella, looking at something just out of view. Annoyingly, they're in the corner of the image. The woman is almost out of the frame entirely and he can't see what they're looking at.

Max orients himself and faces the security camera that captured this footage. It's not hard. The cameras are designed to blend into the scenery, but he's spent a lot of his career ducking, sabotaging, spoofing,

124

and manipulating these things. His eyes are always looking for them, whether he's currently interested in them or not. Once he's got the camera lined up, he stands just where the victims were standing and turns to see what they were looking at. It's a street-level screen, which is currently advertising a boat tour along the coast. It shows a boat cruising past the statue of Halona in front of a crimson sky. The image is reflected in the rippling water at his feet. In this context, it makes him feel like he's standing in luminescent blood.

Once he's reconciled the scenery and the video in his mind, he thumbs the play button. The couple turns as a robot enters the frame. It reaches out and crushes the man's head, and then its face explodes outwards. The woman recoils and falls out of frame.

"What happened to the woman?" Max asks without turning to face Jen.

"She's got some burns on her arm where she was hit with the battery gel and maybe a bit of shrapnel, but she's otherwise fine. Nothing life-threatening. She was taken to the hospital, but I don't know if she's been released yet."

"Do the police really just let you make copies of all of the evidence like this?"

"Apparently so. I don't know who our contact is or what sort of paperwork we have to file."

"Must be nice to be a global corporation. When I want stuff like this I've got to bribe a cop, do a burglary, and hack a computer."

He sends the projection data to the glasses and two bodies appear on the ground in front of him. The man is thankfully face-down. Max doesn't know if he could handle looking at this damage from the front. There's a stream of watered-down blood flowing from his head to the gutter. The robot is on its back, the now-open face looking towards the grey sky.

"I don't know these markings. What kind of robot is this?"

"It's a generation 2, just like the others."

"No, I mean what was its job?"

"The police report said it was a janitorial unit."

Max turns around in a circle and spots a projected broom and dustbin lying nearby. He walks over and, like a total idiot, tries to pick

125

up the broom. His hand slaps against the wet ground. Embarrassed, he looks back to see if Jen noticed. She's watching him, but she doesn't say anything. The glasses are projecting a red outline around her to let him know she isn't part of the captured scene.

"The robot dropped its tools right here. Do you know how long after the murder this image was taken?"

"No."

He looks around again, flipping the glasses on and off to see if he's missing any other details. The only discrepancies are Jen, the bodies, and the tools.

"The robot was still holding its broom. Presumably it was still doing normal janitor-type stuff. But then it dropped the broom, walked over here, and killed the guy." Max is narrating the action as he does it himself. He ends by clapping his hands together at eye level, repeating the execution move the robot performed. "So its behavior changed. It stopped sweeping - or at least, it stopped holding its broom - and performed a murder. Perhaps something triggered it. Maybe somebody did something to it? Maybe it saw something on the billboard?"

He goes quiet. He realizes he's just verbally flailing around and he has no idea where to go from here.

"Would it help if we got footage from other security cameras in the area?" Jen asks.

Max shrugs. "Possibly. But cameras are only installed at intersections. And not all of them work. Sometimes they're vandalized on purpose, and the city doesn't fix them in a hurry. Anyone who knows how the city works ought to be able to move around without being seen. With a little scouting, I could walk from here to the hotel without ever showing up on a camera. Basically, they spy on tourists without doing anything about criminal activity. Since the murders are all happening in this city, I'm thinking our suspect would be able to conceal themselves from the cameras."

"I can request the footage anyway. I can look through it."

Max can't tell if this is a proposal or an announcement. It doesn't matter. She's not his robot. She can do whatever she wants.

He can hear another drone passing overhead. He manages to keep his face down this time. This is largely pointless since he's been standing in front of a city camera for five minutes, but he's glad his instincts seem to be recovering.

Max stares at the empty spot on the pavement where the man died. "So where were the other killings?"

"The first happened on Stoneway, just north of the West Bridge. The second took place right outside the Grandview."

"Let's look at the Grandview first. It's only a half mile from here."

"Public street navigation says it's a mile."

"Public streetnav is maintained by the city planners. It's designed to keep you near the shops and away from traffic arteries. If we go up Third Street we can cut across the loop that streetnav is suggesting."

They head north. Being a native, Max knows that this path will eventually become Third Street, but it's not called that now because it's just a walkway and thus follows different naming conventions. This is one of the many rules that makes sense to locals but causes endless confusion for visitors. Since the confusion tends to get people lost near the shops, nobody is interested in making any changes.

They're under the promenade again, so the sky has been replaced with a concrete ceiling. This area is filled with arcades, smoke dens, bars, and live music. Those businesses don't usually open until noon, which means the street is dark and the storefronts are shuttered.

Max spots a lone policeman inspecting a storefront ahead of them. He's checking the gates and making sure everything is locked up properly. This seems like it's a nice gesture, but Max is guessing he's just looking for an excuse to issue a citation.

The cop turns and Max realizes this is Sando. He's the oldest and quietest of the Three Pigs, and Max has always assumed he's the brains of the trio. Max knows exactly what's going to happen next, even before he hears the heavy footsteps coming from behind.

A slap to one side of his head knocks his hat off. He turns to recover it and ends up lifted and slammed into a wall. He finds himself looking into pair of fierce young eyes.

Max coughs. "Good morning, Officer Veers."

Dixon stands beside Jen Five and rests his hand on his service pistol. All three of them are wearing the dusty red uniforms of the city police, which has segments of black body armor strapped to it. On Veers these plates accentuate his already considerable physique and make him look immense. Dixon is more fat than muscle, so his armor panels have expanded away from each other over the years. He keeps the straps tight like a girdle, which makes his breathing shallow and labored.

Sando draws close now that Veers and Dixon have the civilians under control. "Mr. Law. I heard you were out of prison. I hope you've reformed. I'd hate to see you fall into recidivism."

"Nope. I'm reformed. Gonna open a donut shop."

Veers slams his fist into Max's sternum.

Sando shoves his hand into Max's pocket and pulls out a wad of cash. "Reformed? You expect us to believe an unemployed smuggler can afford a room at the Seaside? Looks to me like you're stealing from our guests again." He gives the money to Veers, who pockets it.

Max tries to give a nonchalant shrug, which is hard to do properly with so much weight pushing him into the wall. "The room doesn't even have a view."

Sando reaches inside of Max's jacket and pulls out his gun. "Whose gun is this?"

Max replies, "This is a dangerous city. A guy's gotta protect himself. I mean, there's never a cop when you need one."

Veers punches him in the face. Max tries to roll with it, but it's pretty much impossible when you're pinned.

Sando continues, "Are you telling me this is your gun? Because if this is your gun then I have to take you back to prison. So whose gun is it?"

"I guess it's your gun," Max mumbles.

Sando nods. "So where's all the money coming from, Mr. Law? A little something you had hidden away before you went to prison?"

Max tries to shake his head. "That's impossible. There's no way I could outsmart someone as clever as you." Surprisingly, Veers doesn't hit him for this.

Sando is still going through his pockets. He pulls out a pack of smokes. He starts to say something, but then he sees Max's brand. "What is this shit? You get out of prison and somehow you're an even bigger degenerate than when you went in?" He crumples up the pack and throws it over his shoulder.

"What do you want, Officer Sando?"

"I want you to tell us where this money is coming from. Hand it over as evidence, and we'll leave you alone."

Dixon's earpiece sputters out some muffled chatter. Confused, he says, "Sand? Dispatch just said they got a call about three guys pretending to be cops, assaulting a civilian."

Sando looks down the street in either direction. "A tourist or something? I don't see anyone." He looks at Jen. "Did she call someone?"

Dixon replies, "I've been watching her the whole time. She's just staring at me like a dumbass."

Sando turns back to Max. "You're a clever one, Max. I know you've got some money hidden away. It's stolen money, and as officers of the city it's our job to track it down. We're gonna find it eventually, so how about you tell us now and save everyone some time?"

Max keeps his mouth shut. Veers is just looking for an excuse to hit him again.

Sando goes back into his pockets and pulls out his handheld. "Nice. Looks like the bank just issued this one. Got your identity moved over and everything." He hands the unit to Dixon, who throws it on the ground and stomps on it.

Sando looks down at the plastic wreckage and frowns. "Oops. Now you're cut off from your bank account until they issue you a new one. If you've got some money hidden away, now would be a good time to go get it."

Max still doesn't see any reason to talk, but Sando gives him a nice long opening in case he decides to do so. When it's clear Max isn't going to produce a suitcase full of cash right there, Sando loses interest. "Okay. Think about it Max. Stay out of trouble." He takes a step back and suddenly everyone relaxes.

Veers smiles. "Let's go find those fake cops before they hurt anyone else."

Dixon kicks the crumpled-up cigarettes towards Max. "Pick up your litter if you don't want a ticket."

Max slumps down against the wall and tries to catch his breath. He prods his face a bit, assessing the damage.

Jen hasn't moved since the altercation began. She's still wearing her sunglasses, standing with her arms at her sides with her usual neutral expression.

"I'm guessing you called the cops? What, you've got a phone in your head?"

"It's a link to the research office. It was installed as an anti-theft measure. I broadcasted the situation. I guess someone at G-Kinetics saw the message and called the police." She looks down the street where the three men went. "Do you think the police will catch them?"

Max groans and pushes the heel of his hand into his forehead. "Those were the police. The real, actual police. So no, nobody is going to 'catch' those guys."

"They broke six laws in a two-minute conversation."

"How can you know so much and so little about this country at the same time?"

"Everything I know about this country comes from Kasaranian media. I knew bribes were common. I didn't realize that police muggings were common."

"I don't know if I'd call that a mugging. And it's not actually that common. Those three aren't your typical crooked cops. But yeah, law enforcement in this city is a little more complicated than what you've been told." He pushes against the wall to get himself upright. He's surprised at how dizzy he is. "Damnit. My bruises had just healed."

He limps a couple of blocks to get out from under the promenade so the rain can wash the blood off his face. Jen Five follows him in silence.

He fishes around inside the ruined package of cigarettes to find the most structurally sound of the bunch. He breaks off some of the crumbly bits and sticks what's left in the right side of his mouth, as far from the damage as possible. He manages to get it lit without the rain dousing it and without him needing to make any whimpering noises.

"So I thought you said that you hated seeing harm come to humans. You said it was unbearable."

"Calling it 'unbearable' was obviously hyperbole, but yes."

"But you stood by and watched it happen. Don't get me wrong, I don't expect you to lay down your life for me or whatever. I just can't figure how you stood there and watched if you hate it so much."

"That was a very negative outcome for me, yes. It was probably the worst situation I've ever been in." She says this in her unwavering dispassionate voice. It's not that she speaks in monotone. It's just that she sounds like she's not particularly invested in anything that's happening.

"Wasn't all that great for me either," he says.

"But remember that I hate hurting people even more than I hate seeing them hurt by others. There was no way to protect you from those men without entering into physical conflict with them."

"You're saying you'd rather let an aggressor win than defend an innocent party? That sounds like a really shitty design."

"There's a thought experiment we use to talk about this kind of stuff. It's called the train problem."

"Is this the one where there's three people on a set of tracks and a train is about to run them over, but you can flip a switch and send the train to an alternate track where it will only kill one?" Max sighs. This sort of stuff always struck him as pointless wanking.

"That's the one, although the numbers of people vary depending on what you're trying to prove. Anyway, the vast majority of humans will choose to throw the switch and sacrifice one person to save three."

Max nods. "I guess I would too. Makes sense." Max begins walking north. He moves with his head low and his hand held to his ribs. Jen walks beside him.

"But robots are designed to not intervene. Or at least, we're extremely reluctant to do something that will hurt someone, even if the overall outcome seems favorable."

Maybe it's the beating his brain just took, but he doesn't see how this thought experiment explains anything. "I don't get it. Why?"

"Because you really don't want robots deciding who should be sacrificed for the common good. The train experiment is useful because

131

it's really clear-cut, but the vast majority of decisions in the real world are a lot more muddled. In the real world we'll disagree on specifics like how many people are on each track, what the odds are that each group might be able to get out of the way on their own, and how much time we have to make a decision. Maybe some people think that switching tracks at the last minute will derail the train and kill both groups. And so on. We can't agree on the risks, the benefits, the available options, or what caused the problem to begin with."

"Okay, but sometimes the problem is clear-cut." Max looks over his shoulder, indicating he's talking about the encounter they just had.

"Is it? There are almost seven million people in this city. There are millions of different opinions on how the world works, or how it ought to work. None of them think their opinions are stupid or wrong, even though many of them have to be. Everyone thinks their solutions to the world's problems are obvious. Do you think because I'm a robot I'll do any better? I'll be acting on the same imperfect information everyone else has. Dump a million robots into this city and expose them to the same mix of opinions, misunderstandings, deceptions, and hyperbole, and inevitably some of those robots will come to the same wrong conclusions. Given how durable and strong I am, imagine the lengths people would go to in an effort to manipulate me. They would lie to me. They would trick me. They would wipe my memory if I couldn't be persuaded. I'd be weaponized."

She continues, "Here's another thought experiment. One group of people says that switching the train to the left track will save three lives at the cost of one. But another group claims that the people on the right track can move out of the way in time, so switching tracks will kill one person for no benefit. The first group gets frustrated that they can't persuade me, so they decide to turn me off and replace me with a robot that agrees with them."

"This sounds like a very long argument. Didn't the train already run everyone over by now?"

"It's a thought experiment. You're not supposed to worry about that sort of thing. Replace the train analogy with medical treatment or military policy. Whatever. The point is, I see these people coming to turn me off, and I believe that if I'm replaced it will result in people dying."

"Oh shit! I get it now."

"Yes. I'd suddenly be compelled to defend myself for the supposed greater good. The only way to avoid an arms race of authoritarian robots is to make us inclined towards non-interventionism."

Max is quiet while he thinks about this. He guides them to the far right side of the path where they will pass under a series of awnings that offer some shelter from the rain.

She continues, "If I didn't respect human autonomy then I'd be compelled to save people from themselves. You wouldn't want a robot forcing you to wear your seatbelt, snatching cigarettes out of your mouth, and overpowering you when you want to eat junk food."

"You're right. Wouldn't want that. But there's a big difference respecting my right to smoke and respecting the rights of crooked cops to bash my face in."

Jen says, "It's true that they're very different situations, but it's just different points on the same gradient. I'm averse to forcing my will on anyone, no matter how wrong they seem to be. You're a human. You can take responsibility for your actions if you're wrong. If you see two parties fighting and you choose the wrong side because you don't have all the information, then you can accept responsibility and be punished. I can't. The company has to accept responsibility for my actions. And they would rather I stood by and do nothing than participate in violence."

Max still thinks this absolutist approach is probably overkill, but he's too tired to argue about it right now.

"We should probably get out of their way," Jen says.

His head is pounding, but over the last minute or so he's been vaguely aware of a sound building in the distance, gradually drowning out the sensory overload coming from his face. He lifts his head and sees they're heading for a large crowd going in the exact opposite direction.

"Oh damnit," he mutters.

The first two victims were foreigners, but the most recent robot attack happened to a local couple. Their smiling faces have been covering the news pages since the story broke, and all anyone can talk

133

about is what a beautiful couple they were and how bright their future seemed. The media has dubbed them the Happy Couple.

A group of concerned citizens decided to do some kind of memorial walk from the transit station to the site of the killings. Max remembers reading about this a few hours ago, but it just seemed like the sort of random meaningless noise the city is always making. People are always forming groups and making emotional gestures. He didn't see it as something that would apply to him. So now he's about to go head-first into this crowd and discover it's going to apply to him whether he likes it or not.

What started as a memorial walk has quickly evolved into a protest march. Placards ride above the crowd. A small number have sentimental messages underneath the same photograph of the Happy Couple. The rest of them are messages of anger and outrage. They're denouncing robots in general and G-Kinetics specifically. News cameras hover at the front, watching the crowd as it marches southward. The placards turn towards these cameras like flowers facing the sun.

He shuffles out of the way and leans against the wall. Jen joins him. To his surprise, she manages to look natural doing this. She even puts one foot against the wall. Given how strange her body language is, this is probably the most lifelike move she's made so far.

A few of the signs are written in public school level Kasaranian. One enterprising protester has made a faithful re-creation of the G-Kinetics logo, except they've drawn blood squirting from between the stylized gears. The rain has turned the writing into an illegible smear and the hand-drawn blood now looks like actual blood dripping from the sign. The effect is an accident, but it's the most striking sign in the crowd and the broadcast cameras are spending a lot of time hovering around it.

"We're going to be seeing that image for months," Max says wearily.

The crowd is probably less than a hundred people. If viewed from the air this might look like a very small gathering, but when you're stuck at ground level and looking into the eyes of all those angry faces it gives the group a potency that transcends attendance figures. At the rear of the crowd, a couple of guys are dragging the top half of a city robot. The face has been beaten so severely that it looks like a crumpled soda can. The eye sockets are empty. It's a good thing these robots don't look very human or this would be a grisly sight. The guys are trying to carry the robot triumphantly, but it's heavy and awkward and they're staggering more than marching.

"Keep those sunglasses on," Max says.

Jen nods. "I wonder what the robot did that made them attack it."

"I'm sure it just wandered too close to the crowd. I've watched some labor protests that looked just like this. Peaceful older people carrying signs at the front, and in the back are all the angry young men smashing stuff. It's basically two entirely different groups with different mindsets that happen to be travelling together."

Jen has to raise her voice to be heard over the shouting. "You attended labor marches? Does this city have a union for thieves?"

He doesn't know if this was an earnest question or a joke, but he chuckles anyway. "I attended professionally. If things get out of control, young guys will bash up storefronts, break gates, set off alarms, and make a mess. Sometimes they don't even care about the protest. They're just dumb criminals looking to score in the chaos."

"How is what they do different from what you do?"

"If you bash open a storefront and take a display screen, then you're left carrying this huge thing home on foot. That's a very large risk of arrest for a very small payoff. I'd go in behind them and poke around inside the stores. I wouldn't steal anything. I'd just check out the security system. Check the locks. See where the most valuable goods are stored and where the goods enter the premises. Take some pictures. Memorize the layout. You can sell that information. Or if the business is a really good target that handles a lot of cash then I'd come back a few months later and hit the place myself."

The crowd has passed now. Max finishes his cigarette and they continue north. After a couple of blocks they find three guys beating on the leftover bits of the robot they saw a couple of minutes ago. It broke in half at the waist and guys are hammering on this part with improvised metal cudgels.

"Please make them stop," Jen says.

135

"They're just a bunch of kids. Let them blow off some steam. The robot is totaled anyway."

"I don't care about the robot. They're beating on the battery compartment. If they rupture it..."

"Yeah, I get it now." He gives a heavy sigh, which really hurts his aching ribs. On one hand, these idiots basically deserve whatever happens to them, but he doesn't want Jen to put herself in harm's way trying to save these dumbasses from the ravages of natural selection.

"Hey. You guys probably shouldn't be hitting it right in the pelvis like that."

One of them cusses at him without breaking rhythm. Another stands up straight and looks at him defiantly. "This your robot, grandpa?"

Max has dealt with guys like this often enough to know that if he replies with "No" then the kid will tell him to fuck off and mind his own business. He's also a little wounded that he's being called grandpa so early in life.

"You're hitting the battery compartment. It's basically a bomb. You put a hole in it and that's the end of you."

"Get out of here before I even your face up."

Max walks away. He doesn't care enough about these guys to save them from themselves.

"Thank you," Jen says.

"You still worried about them?"

"No. You gave them fair warning. If I intervened, they might see I'm a robot and attack me. Then they'd be sitting on top of two batteries instead of one. I hope they don't get hurt, but there's nothing else I can do for them."

"I envy your ability to not worry about things you can't change."

"Dr. Kvenst suspects that not worrying might be a design flaw. Worrying about something makes you fixate on it. Doing so can sometimes lead to thinking of a solution that wasn't obvious at first. So maybe worrying has a practical use and should be included in my behavioral parameters."

"What do you think?"

"I think it's worth doing the experiment and seeing what we get. I wish we had time for it, but there are a lot of more important things to test right now."

"Really? You want them to change your design to make you worry more?"

"I doubt I'll find worrying unpleasant in the way humans do. There are a lot of physiological things that worrying does to humans that won't apply to me. I get the impression you hate worrying because it stops you from enjoying things. I don't think that will be a problem for me. From my standpoint it's a simple optimization problem. You don't want to give up too soon if there might be a solution you haven't thought of. On the other hand, you don't want to waste time focusing on an impossible problem if there are easier problems you could be solving. You can't tell hard problems from impossible problems until you've explored them, and that carries an opportunity cost."

The Grandview isn't properly called the Grandview anymore. Nor does it have a particularly grand view. When Max was a kid, it was called the Grandview and had a spectacular view of the ocean. Then it was bought by the Kasaranian hotel chain "Uar Juhause". The locals didn't appreciate having one of their historical landmarks rebranded like this, so they ignored the new sign and stuck with calling it "Grandview". (Also, nobody was really confident on how you're supposed to pronounce the new name, and different foreigners would give different answers.) To spite this intrusion, the city approved a new high-rise directly in front of the place, blotting out its view.

Max is standing on the sidewalk where the old man was killed a couple of years ago. There is, of course, no evidence lying around for him to find.

"Is there a projection available for this crime scene?"

"No," Jen says. "Their imagers were a decade out of date and the scans were so low-resolution they weren't much more helpful than regular photographs. Also, the city somehow had a data storage problem and often erased scans more than a few months old. We loaned them some consultants and helped them upgrade, so the evidence should be in high resolution from now on."

"Of course. Now I get it. You didn't loan them consultants. You gave them a soft bribe."

"I don't understand."

"A rich foreign company shows up, begging for information. Any politician in this city will tell you the first thing you do is plead poverty. Tell them you'd love to help, but you need more equipment, manpower, or whatever. The company then gives you free stuff in exchange for the help you're supposed to give them anyway."

"Doesn't your government fund your police?"

"Sure. But it's easier to squeeze a foreign corporation for stuff than it is to fight a three-year battle with the city leadership. This explains why the police are sharing evidence with you. That was probably part of the deal. '*You buy us new toys, and we use the toys to help you solve your problem.*' Anyway, if there isn't a projection image of the crime scene then the only evidence is the horribly blurry footage that Landro showed me. And now that we're here, I'm wondering why that's the only footage available."

Max and Jen are standing, as close as they can reckon, right where the murder happened. Max has already spotted the cameras and he has a map of them in his head.

"I can see why we don't have any footage from that camera." Max says this while pointing to a blank spot on the wall where a couple of naked wires are hanging, their ends frayed by a crude cutting job. "But what about the camera across the street?"

Max crosses the four lanes of late-morning traffic. Normally he'd jog across to be polite, but he's tired and he hurts. For some reason, Jen stays at the crime scene. He checks out the camera and shuffles back with only a few people honking their horns and cussing at him.

"The camera across the street came unfastened and is now hanging from its own power cable. It's pointed right at the ground. I'm ready to believe it's been that way since the murder and nobody has bothered to fix it."

"So someone disabled the cameras here?"

Max frowns. "Maybe. But all of the murders happened on the north side of the city. That's where all of the cameras are. If they wanted to hide it from the cameras, then why not do it on the south side? How did they miss such obvious cameras at the other crime

138

scenes? My hunch is that they wanted the killings to take place in front of cameras, and they didn't count on our camera network being so shitty."

He looks down at the pavement. "You said the other crime scene is by the West Bridge, which is pretty far inland. I don't know if I want the spend half the day hopping trains to look at that blank piece of sidewalk. What about the latest robot? Has that been handed over to the company yet?"

She pauses. "No. Apparently the city is going to hang onto it for a while."

"What's with that pause? Are you looking things up in your head?"

"I have an integrated mobile platform so I don't need to carry a handheld."

"You have a mobile built into your body? What happens if you get a call while you're talking? Do you hear it ring inside your head?"

"I have the mobile hardware, but I'm not a person in the legal sense. No identity, no name, no money, no home address. So a lot of mobile features are disabled, including commerce and telephone access."

"Seems like that stuff would be really useful. Why not enable it if you've got the hardware? Someone at the company could set it up for you."

"Like I said, it's just added as an anti-theft measure. It does what it needs to do."

Max thinks this over for a bit before saying, "Isn't this a huge security risk? Like, if your brain is attached to the network then can't you get hacked?"

"If you're thinking that maybe that's what happened with the murders, then no. They don't have innate network access like I do. I'm special because I'm a prototype. If you're worried about me, don't. The input comes through my sensory data. I see it and hear it, but it can't insert thoughts into my mind. If I got 'hacked' it would be the same as having your handheld compromised. Annoying, but not physically dangerous. I can't be hacked through the network any more than you could be hacked by looking at your mobile."

139

"Do you know where the body is located? The robot I mean, not the victim."

There's another pause. "Company message board says we're having some sort of red tape trouble with the authorities right now."

Max sighs. "Just offer them money. That's what they want. If you're getting stonewalled, it means someone wants a bribe." Max is mostly talking to himself. He doesn't expect this advice to reach the lawyers of G-Kinetics. It bothers him that Kasaranians can be so brilliant at inventing shit and so terrible at operating in other cultures.

"One of our lawyers believes that the unit is at Station 9."

"That's only a few blocks from here."

Outside station 9, Max pulls Jen off to one side. "You said earlier you can lie if you need to. Did you mean it?"

"If I didn't then I would have been lying, so either way the answer is yes."

Max shakes his head in confusion. "If you say so."

He sits down on the steps and takes off his left shoe. "What I mean is, are you willing to lie right now? I want to see this robot and I don't want to wait for your company lawyers to figure out how to navigate our legal system."

"It depends on what you need me to say and who it might hurt."

"Nothing. I need you to say nothing. Nobody will get hurt by any of this. We're just cutting through some red tape. All I need you to do is pretend you don't speak Local. If I say anything to you in Kasaranian, just nod at me."

"No problem."

Max takes a few bills out of his shoe, smoothes them out, and stuffs them in his pocket. "Getting pretty low here," he mutters to himself.

"Why do you have money in your shoe?"

"Never keep all your money in one place. Divide it into halves or thirds. That way if you get mugged, you can safely give up one stash without going broke. If someone searches you, they're likely to stop looking once they find the cash. Keep one stash in an obvious place so they don't need to look too hard."

140

He moves some money around his person and the straightens out his clothes. "How do I look? Do I have any blood showing?"

Jen looks him up and down. "You're fine. You've got a split lip and your face is swollen a bit, but other than that you look normal."

"Let's go."

Station 9

Station 9 is one of the older police stations in the city. The building is only three stories tall and was built not long after the Kasaranian occupation. The city has a strange relationship with relics of that period. On a personal level, people are deeply resentful of reminders of that messy and humiliating time. On the other hand, people are generally reluctant to destroy those same reminders and even get strangely protective of them. As the city grew, they eventually needed all of that empty space above places like Station 9. Nobody was willing to tear down such important historical buildings, but they also couldn't afford to have a three-story building this close to the Hospitality District. And so they began the practice of "sitting" new buildings atop old.

The old structures don't actually bear the weight of the new. The new building carries its own weight by way of support pillars that surround the smaller structure. In this way, Station 9 is a classic old building stuck inside a modern cage. Its old rounded windows and dark stonework have a sinister quality to them that really isn't a good look for police stations.

Max walks in briskly, head high. The key to getting around without having people stop you is to act like you know where you're going. If he'd known he was coming here he might have brought a laptop or a document binder to carry around.

He gets to the evidence room and a young officer is sitting at tiny desk, conspicuously playing videogames on his handheld. He's wearing a plain red uniform without armor. His name tag identifies him as Oberson.

Max explains to Jen that they've reached the evidence room. He does this in Kasaranian, which would lead any sensible person to assume she doesn't speak Local. His Kasaranian is rusty as hell, but he knows you can hide this from non-speakers by speaking very quickly and ignoring mistakes. Then he turns to the officer. "Good morning. We're here from Global Kinetics. We're here to see the robot."

Oberson reluctantly sets his game aside. "I haven't heard-" His voice trails off as his eyes come up to Max's face. "Are you okay sir?"

Max pauses and swallows to show he's nervous. "I'm fine."

"You look like you were just in a fight."

Max confides to the cop, "I got mugged this morning. Broad daylight."

"If you're here to file a report then-"

"No! no." Max looks nervously towards Jen. "Look, it would be a lot better if my employer didn't know. I don't want them to get any wrong ideas about our city. I just told them I slipped in the shower."

Oberson gives an understanding nod. The two of them have just bonded, hiding this embarrassment from the dumb rich foreigner. "So what can I do for you?"

Max blinks in surprise that Oberson doesn't already know. "The company said we'd be able to inspect the robot. Our lawyers told us we would be granted access."

Oberson draws in a breath. He's about to try to say no in a way that won't offend Max.

Max takes a hundred dollars out of his pocket and hands it over. "Help me out. I don't know where the paperwork went wrong and I don't want to have to drive across town to sort it out. I'm a translator, not a lawyer. You'll save me half a day if you can just let us have a peek at it. We don't even need to touch anything. Just some pictures."

Oberson looks down at the money. This is too big a bribe for clearing paperwork.

Max smiles. "Just take it, man. It's her money. They have more than they know what to do with."

Oberson might not be willing to break police protocol under normal circumstances, but he's willing to help a fellow native screw a foreigner. He returns the smile and unlocks the evidence room. He warns them not to touch anything, which Max dutifully repeats to Jen in Kasaranian. She nods.

Despite all the time he's spent getting into places he shouldn't be, he's never seen the inside of an evidence room. He always assumed it would be a room piled high with guns, consumer electronics, and bags of money. Instead there are shelves full of numbered boxes and envelopes. Past these are a row of reinforced doors. Oberson looks up something on his computer, finds a specific door, and opens it for the

143

guests. Inside is a room with a lone table and some empty shelves. The only thing of note in the room is the robot.

Oberson points to a camera in the corner of the room. "I'll be watching you at my station. If you touch anything, you get arrested. You've got ten minutes."

The room reverberates as the officer slams the door shut, leaving them alone with a robot corpse or whatever you're supposed to call a robot that will never work again.

Max spends a few pointless seconds staring at the wide open face. Then he realizes this is the part he always stares at, which means it's probably the bit most people stare at. This is not how you look for new information. He starts at the bottom and works his way up.

The rubber soles of the feet have been worn down to the metal. There are a bunch of scuffs on the left leg but not on the right. Perhaps this means the robot carried its dustbin on the left side.

"Do robots favor one hand over the other like people?"

"Not like people," Jen says. "We do generally favor a particular handedness, but it's based on task and not on the idea of a dominant hand. You'll generally copy your teacher in your first lesson and use whatever hands they use. I use my right hand for most things, but my cooking teacher was left-handed so I cut vegetables with my left."

"You learn in a classroom? Can't you just download lessons or something?"

"Download it from who? A human brain?"

"I dunno, like an encyclopedia?"

"That's *memorization* of knowledge. Learning is the *integration* of knowledge. Very different process. I can show you how to peel a potato and you can read everything ever written about potatoes, but that won't give you a sense of the right angle to hold the knife, how much pressure to apply, or the exact movement to get the peel off clean. That takes practice. I learn fine-motor tasks a little faster than a person, but not instantly."

"So do they have huge classrooms for armies of robots back home?" Max tries to picture this but ends up with the image of little baby robots sitting at desks and he knows that doesn't make any sense.

"No. We're taught in small classes and then copied. The brain is copied whole. It's not like you could plug me into a hard drive and download just the bits dedicated to cooking. It's all messy and interconnected. My cooking knowledge is mixed in with motor skills, chemistry, fire safety, and information on the individual food preferences of people I've met. That's what integration of knowledge is. It connects what you're learning with what you already know. Trying to extract a particular skill from a robot's brain is like trying to unscramble an egg. Specific areas of knowledge can't be uploaded or downloaded piecemeal."

Something has been bothering him about the hands and just now it dawns on him. "Hang on, the others had dried blood on their hands. This one has clean hands."

"It was raining when it performed the murder."

Max rests his forehead in his hand. "I'm a really good detective."

Jen points to the chest. "There are dents here. I wonder if these are the result of wear and tear, or vandalism?"

"My guess is vandalism. You can see similar dents on the forearms. All the damage is on the same side of the arm." Max holds up his arm as if deflecting a blow, showing where the damage appears on the robot. "I don't suppose being regularly assaulted could make a robot snap?"

"Of course not."

"But you do have a desire to protect yourself, right? Maybe over a long time-"

"Imagine your son-"

"Yeah, I'm not really planning on having kids."

"Okay, imagine the person you care about most in the world."

Max is irritated to be thinking of Clare all of a sudden. He's spoken to her once in the last three years and as it turns out he never really knew her. She's an inappropriate choice for his 'most important person' but right now he can't even come up with a replacement.

Jen continues. "Now imagine that person is taking a spoon and knocking dents in your car. Or better yet, a rental car."

Thinking of Clare angrily thwapping the hood of a rental car with a spoon is such a ridiculous image that a strange, confused laugh escapes him.

"Now, how long would they need to do that before you would want to crush their skull with your bare hands?"

"Okay. I get it. So you don't really value your body more than a rental car?"

"At most. A better analogy might be clothing. It takes some time to get used to bodies with different proportions. Labor units like this one in front of us have longer arms, so when I switched to something more human-like I spent half the day under-reaching for things. But once you're used to a particular form factor they're all pretty interchangeable. I might place some extra value on the one I'm using now because it's an expensive prototype. There are only a dozen of these and right now they cost a few million."

"A few million? Wow."

"You should see the price tag for the bodies that Senma Technology makes. For one of theirs you could buy five of these." She points at herself as she says this.

"What about yourself? Like, your brain? Please tell me you care if you live or die."

"I do, but my survival drive is pretty weak compared to yours. It's not enough to override my desire to protect humans from harm. Then again, my desire to protect humans feeds into it. This isn't the kind of decision-making you can depict with a simple logic gate."

"Your desire to protect humans feeds into your survival instinct?"

"Dr. Kvenst would quarrel with your use of the word 'instinct', but yes. I'm aware that humans may form an attachment to me. If I was purchased as a nanny for children and they eventually embraced me as a mother figure, I'd have to factor that into survival decisions. My destruction would be deeply traumatic for them, so part of protecting them would involve protecting myself from destruction. Also, I'm really expensive, and my owner wouldn't want me throwing my cog away on a whim. It just depends on the owner and my service situation."

"This is a really weird conversation."

"We should probably be studying this robot while we have the chance."

"Right." Max rubs the back of his head and looks down. "Here's the problem I have. We've looked at everything but the head. We're sort of assuming that this has to be the result of tampering. And if I wanted to tamper with a robot then I'd want to get into its skull. I see there's a metal seam that runs over the top of the head from one ear hole to the other. So you can take the face off. What's holding it on?"

"Actually, there's a lot of stuff holding the face on, even with simple faces like this one. If you're looking for cog access then the back of the skull slides off. There's a screw on the top of the head, one on the back of the head, and another near each ear. Although I should add those aren't really ears. Those are cosmetic. The actual audio equipment is in the neck."

Max looks at a tiny circle of metal behind the ear. In the center is a triangular indentation. "That's a screw? It doesn't look like one. I assume you use proprietary heads to prevent tampering?"

"I've never questioned the design of the screws in my skull."

Max takes out his handheld and starts snapping pictures of the robot. He doesn't really know what he'll need later so he's just hammering away on the button as he walks around the body. As he's doing this he asks her, "When somebody buys a robot, are they expected to service the unit themselves? Are they given the tools to open it up?"

"No. Customers are expected to bring units to the company for servicing."

Max leans in closer to the patient. "I see some damage on this screw behind the right ear, or whatever you call these things. It might be stripping due to tampering, but it also might just be part of the general abuse this thing has taken. I'd really like to see the screw on the back of the head to see if it has similar damage."

"The officer told us if we touched it we'd be arrested."

"I wonder if he can arrest you. Are you up for breaking the law for this case?"

"Yes."

"Here." He gives her his handheld. "I'm going to walk out and talk to the officer. I assume he's watching the security footage. Wait until you hear me open the outer door. He's going to turn to look at me when that happens. Turn the robot's head, take a couple of pictures, and put the head back. Got it?"

147

"Ready."

"Hang on. Do you have fingerprints?"

"I have the model and serial number of this platform etched into my skin."

"That sounds like fingerprints."

"My skin doesn't release oils like yours, so I won't leave fingerprints on things unless they're already oily."

"Oh. Yeah." Max leaves the vault or whatever you call this little side-room. He starts talking loudly as soon as he swings the outer door open. This startles Officer Oberson, who was actually ignoring his security screen and playing videogames again. "Thanks so much for helping us sort that out. Did anyone call to tell you about us yet?"

Oberson puts his handheld on the desk face-down. "Nope. Haven't heard anything."

"Typical. I'll bet the papers will show up ten minutes after we leave. Anyway. Thanks again."

Max is a big believer in thanking police after you bribe them. It helps maintain the illusion that they're giving you a pass due to their own wisdom and obscures the fact that you just broke the law by paying them to break the law by overlooking your original lawbreaking.

"Where's your boss?" He looks back to his security screen in time to see Jen leaving the room.

"I guess she wanted extra pictures. You know how those people are."

Oberson nods. Max is sure that the kid does not, in fact, know how "they" are, but like most people he's willing to participate in a bit of light racism as a form of social bonding ritual.

"So let me see the pictures," Max says once they're a couple of blocks from the station.

Jen hands over the device.

"I don't get it," he says. He holds the screen upright and wipes away the rain. "Why is the screw dark?"

"It's not. You're looking into the hole. The screw is missing."

"What are the odds they forgot the screw back at the factory?"

"Astronomical."

"I need to see this picture on a good screen."

"We can use the computer back at the hotel."

"Yeah. I need sleep anyway. I've been awake for about 20 hours and I've spent half of those hours walking. I'm so tired I can't think straight."

The Brothers

There's a man standing outside of Max's hotel room. He's a tall gentleman in a flawless black suit.

"You're Maxwell Law," he says.

"Thanks for clearing that up," Max deadpans.

"Felix and Donald Royle would like to invite you to the Silvermine."

Max has been half asleep for the last hour or so, but hearing someone mention the names of The Brothers wakes him right up. He's just realized that things have very abruptly become catastrophically fucked and his mind begins racing, trying to figure out where he went wrong and how bad things might get.

On one hand, he took these guys for a million dollars and they could easily have found out about it. If G-Kinetics could figure it out then so could The Brothers. If they know he stole from them, then he should do literally anything besides accept this invitation. He'd be better off throwing himself from the roof of the hotel rather than letting The Brothers drag him to the basement and torture him until he explains the job and gives up the names of his accomplices. Then they'll round up Heavy and Margo and torture them until they talk, just to make sure everyone is telling the truth. Then they'll execute the whole team and dump them in the same gutter. Max really can't bear to think of this happening to Margo. She's a dancer, not a gangster. She's smart and a hard worker. Maybe she took her share and left the country. Heavy must still be around, assuming he isn't dead already. And hang on, how did Landro get Heavy to talk? That's not like Heavy. Max regrets not following up on that sooner. He should at least have found out if Heavy was alive and, if so, figured out what he told Landro. Max should have done that before checking into the hotel days ago. And now that's he's thinking about the team, he realizes that Rider supposedly died while he was in prison, but he's never followed up to see if that was true. Then again, if someone has been tracking his movements - which is certainly the case - then running around reconnecting with people from the casino job would have simply revealed the crew to whoever was watching. On the other hand...

"Mr. Law?"

Max realizes he's been standing there with his mouth slightly open for longer than is socially acceptable. He blinks. "Yeah?" he replies slowly.

"I have a car waiting downstairs." The man gestures down the hall, back towards the elevator.

On one hand, if they're going to interrogate him then this moment is his very last chance to make a run for it. If he doesn't run now then he will literally regret it until he dies. On the other hand, if they somehow want to talk to him about something else then running would just make him look incredibly guilty. If he wants to escape the reach of The Brothers then he would need to leave the country, and he doesn't have the resources to do that.

Max wants to believe he's making a rational decision, but deep down he's just really tired and footsore and his planning horizon has shortened to about five minutes. And he'd rather spend the next five minutes sitting in a car than trying to outrun this guy.

"I'll be back in an hour," Max lies to Jen, tossing her the room key.

The heart of Rivergate's wealth is the tourist industry, at the heart of the tourist industry are the casinos, at the heart of the casinos is the Silvermine, and at the heart of the Silvermine are The Brothers.

They're not actually brothers. Referring to them as such was originally a joke. They're just two unrelated businessmen who happen to have the same surname.

Felix Royle is a small, lean man of perhaps forty. He's a man of fastidious grooming, with the pale complexion of an easterner. He wears suits that are bright and tidy, which goes nicely with his pencil mustache. He keeps his hair slicked back and he always seems to be smiling ever so slightly, like he's about to pull a cruel prank on someone in the room.

Donald Royle is almost the complete opposite of his non-brother. He's a thick, slovenly man with grey hair and great hanging jowls. He's tall for a city native. He wears expensive suits like Felix, but because of his considerable height and girth they don't seem to know

151

how to stay on his body. His clothing is always crooked, wrinkled, and damp with sweat.

All of this is hearsay to Max. He's never met the men in person. But the stories have been repeated so often and so consistently that he's reasonably sure they're accurate.

The man escorting him hasn't introduced himself. He's big enough that he might be a goon, but he could also be a simple driver. He's resisted all attempts at conversation, which might be an indicator of goon-hood. Then again, he's turned his back on Max a couple of times, which is a very un-goon-like thing to do. He's alone, while goons usually travel in twos or threes. Then again, Max is pretty sure the guy is armed, which is kind of goonish. Max goes back and forth like this for the entire car ride, wondering if he's attending a meeting or an interrogation.

The thing about gambling in Rivergate is that it's almost entirely based on the collective neurosis of the Kasaranian people. Max has never encountered a people more enthusiastic about gambling. Watching a Kasaranian gamble is like watching someone take methamphetamines for the first time. Their eyes light up. Their stiff exterior falls away and suddenly they come alive. Win or lose, their white faces turn bright red with intensity and excitement, as if every spin or roll of the dice was for the life of a loved one. At the same time, gambling is a complete taboo in their country. It's illegal. All of it. It's technically illegal for friends to make private bets between each other, although Max has no idea how the government could possibly enforce such a thing. Supposedly, kids aren't even allowed to run a charity raffle over there.

Max can't make sense of their culture. They're generally apathetic towards marital infidelity, as long as it's discrete. Their roads have no speed limits, there are no regulations on robots, and they produce something like 80% of the world's pornography. There's no level of debauchery that can scandalize them, except that they absolutely will not tolerate gambling. Max gathers that this is the result of some deeply-rooted mindset that comes from their religion, but he's never been able to make any sense of their religion either.

Somehow, the most enthusiastic gamblers in the world come from the country most adamantly opposed to gambling. So the wealthy of Kasaran fly to Rivergate twice a year for week-long gambling orgies. This makes no sense to Max, but since a huge portion of his country's GDP is dependant on it he hopes it doesn't change anytime soon.

At the Silvermine, Max is still wondering if he's headed for the penthouse or the basement. When they reach the elevator his ambiguously goonish escort presses the button for the fourth floor, and Max doesn't know what to make of this. His body is on some kind of inexplicable adrenaline rollercoaster. His heart rate keeps going up or down in time with his paranoia.

The fourth floor is offices, which is a good sign. He's always wondered how The Brothers did meetings. Do they have side-by-side executive desks? Do they sit at a massive conference table with one of them at each end? Do they have one big chair and they take turns sitting in it?

It turns out they have a room with a handful of fancy antique chairs, and the brothers sit in two of the chairs. Aside from the room being far too big, there's nothing grand or formal about the it. At least, not compared with the rest of the building. Red and gold carpeting cover the floors. Everywhere that isn't directly under a searing light fixture is in relative darkness. The cigarette smoke is so thick and vast it almost qualifies as a weather system.

True to their reputations, Felix is wearing an immaculate white suit and Donald is wearing a dark suit with the necktie halfway undone.

Donald is the scary looking one. He's got a low forehead and suspicious eyes. There's something inherently brutish about his face. But according to rumor he's actually the nice one. He's supposedly the brains of the operation. Felix is the one with the reputation for cunning and sadism. If you wind up in the basement, you'll eventually make your confession to Felix.

Donald points at a chair. Max sits in it.

"Congratulations on your recent release," Donald says.

"Thank you." Max goes over this answer in his head a few times to make sure he hasn't accidentally revealed anything that will get him killed. He wishes he could have gotten his hands on some coffee before this meeting. He's dead tired and he really needs to get as much of his brain working as he possibly can.

Felix brushes some unseen lint from his trousers. "How long were you a guest of the city?"

"Three years." Max is pretty sure these warm-up questions are less about small talk and more about probing for deception. They're probably already aware of the answers and are trying to appraise his behavior before they ask the Real Questions, whatever the fuck those turn out to be.

Each of the brothers is sitting just outside of a pool of light. Max is sitting directly under an overbearing chandelier. This is either a very uncomfortable interview or a very posh interrogation.

Felix lights a pipe. He keeps making eye contact with Max like he's expecting Max to elaborate. Once he's had a couple of good puffs he speaks again, "Enjoying your room at the Seaside?"

"Can't complain."

Donald draws in a deep, noisy breath of air before he speaks. "I understand that room is paid for by Kinetics."

Max nods. There's no point in denying it. This is probably how they found him. They probably have standing orders for people to bring them news anytime G-Kinetics gets a room anywhere in the city.

"We don't like Kinetics," Felix adds.

"I'll bet." Max says.

Felix leans forward into the light and takes his pipe out of his mouth. "Oh? What have you heard?"

Max realizes he's just made exactly the kind of stupid verbal blunder he was afraid of making. "Well, I mean... who does? Their robots are all over the city killing people."

Felix leans back again. "I suppose that's true." There's another pause where it feels like Max is supposed to say more.

Donald draws in another labored breath. "What are they paying you to do?"

Max's mouth is bone dry. His heart is pounding. He really wishes he could come up with a clever way out of this. He has no idea what these guys might know, so he can't afford to lie to them. He clears his throat. "Well, I don't think I should discuss what a client-"

154

"What are they paying you to do?" Felix repeats. His lips are tight and his eyes feel like they're trying to read Max's thoughts through his skull.

"They're paying me to investigate why their robots are killing people."

Donald takes a turn, "Why would they hire a man with your background to do that job? What do you know about robotics?"

Max is now dedicating all of his brainpower to maintaining a calm exterior. "They think it's a frame-up or sabotage or something. They figure I might know how to find people that do that kind of thing."

"What do you think?"

Max is trying not to swallow nervously, fidget, or break eye contact. He's spent a career learning how to do this, but there are limits to how far acting can take you. He's suddenly aware that he's holding his mouth very tightly, which is another tell.

His problem is that he needs to answer this question just right. It's possible that The Brothers are behind the murders. If he's too guarded in his answer then they will take that as deception. If he's too candid about his suspicions and he happens to be on the right track, then they will see him as a threat.

Being very careful to keep his voice measured he says, "I think it's possible."

Felix stands up. "The thing is, Mr. Law. A lot of people think this might be a frame-up. It's kind of obvious, don't you think? Robots killing people in front of cameras, all of them using the same MO. Then their heads explode so we can't find out why they did it." Felix points the end of his pipe at Max, "If I sent a robot to kill someone, that's exactly how I'd do it."

Max shifts in his seat. He's trying to lean back casually and he can feel his performance is off. "It certainly is curious."

Felix continues, "The problem - by which I mean *your* problem - is that nobody cares. A lot of us would be very happy if this crime went unsolved and G-Kinetics simply got whatever is coming to them."

There's another pause before Donald adds, "This company is owned and run by Kasaran. We've seen this before. They give us technology, and then use that technology to rob us. In the old days it

155

was roads and power plants. Now they're coming to us selling robots. They promise us 'free labor'. Can these robots be trusted? Should we turn over so much of our economy to machines made by those same people?"

"Hasn't that ship already sailed? Robots already run a lot of this city."

Donald takes another heavy breath. "Yes. But they don't run all of it. If the robots vanished tomorrow, we could adapt. But what happens when their robots are in charge of everything? When they run our networks and roadways? Our hospitals? What then? They could turn off our entire country with a flip of the switch."

Max doesn't say anything. After another awkward pause Felix continues, "We understand the position you're in. Just out of prison. No money. You've been out of the game for a few years. You need work. Maybe you're really planning on helping them, or maybe you're just scamming them. From our perspective, it doesn't matter."

Donald says, "It's our hope that these robot events will run their course."

"What are you proposing?" This is the most neutral thing Max can think of to say.

Felix draws a white envelope out of his breast pocket and hands it over. "Just continue to do whatever it is you're doing. If it comes to nothing, then fine. But if you do find out something about what's going on, we'd like you to bring the information to us. *First.*"

Max closes his hand around the envelope, which he can tell is full of cash. Felix just told him to do something while handing him money. By taking it, he is implicitly agreeing to do what they're asking. His only alternative is to refuse the money. Maybe there's a safe way to do this, but he can't think of it. He's just put himself in a position where eventually he's going to need to screw G-Kinetics or The Brothers. Obviously one of them is a lot more dangerous than the other, but it's trouble either way.

Felix sends him out of the room with a wave of the hand. Outside, the quasi-goon escorts him back to the Seaside.

Max nearly sprints to the hotel room. He hammers on the door. Jen opens it a few seconds later.

"What happened?" She asks calmly.

156

Max takes his smashed handheld and flings it into the corner of the room. He does the same with their room key.

"That's your identity. Don't you need to get that fixed?"

"I'm tired of everyone in the city knowing where I am. If I stay here I'll end up dead. I have to leave. Now."

He glances at the hotel computer stuffed in the corner of the room. On the screen is some sort of city surveillance footage. "Were you using this computer to work on the case?"

"Yes."

Max kicks over the computer, pops off the lid, and pulls the hard drive out. For good measure, he stomps on the remaining bits until the screen goes dark and the fans stop spinning. He pockets the hard drive. "Do you want to help me?"

She looks at the smashed computer. "Help you with what?"

"Do you want to help me solve this case?"

"You know I do. It's basically the only thing I care about."

"What if solving the case means betraying your company? What will you choose then?"

"What do you mean 'betraying'? They want the case solved too."

"Right. But just bear with me. A thought experiment. On one hand you solve the case but create huge financial problems for your employer-"

"Owners."

"Right. Owners. Or on the other hand the case goes unsolved. I'm not saying this is how things will happen, I'm just trying to get a sense of what your priorities are."

"Solving the case is most important. It's impossible to worry about the company image or my product line if people are dying."

"Good enough for me. Let's go."

"Wait, you're about to-" she says as he pulls the door shut behind them, "-lock us out of the room."

"Not our room anymore. If we're going to get anywhere we need to vanish. Can your employer track you?"

"I sometimes send them position updates."

"Can you stop doing that?"

"Yes."

"Then stop doing that." He jogs to the elevator, hits the button, realizes he doesn't want to wait for it, and goes for the stairs. He's panting before he gets halfway to the bottom. He wanted to keep running all the way out of the hotel, but he needs to stop for a breather when he gets to the lobby. He's feeling light-headed.

"Are you in danger?" Jen asks. She kept up with him all the way down the stairs. She's talking in her normal flat voice. She's not sweating, gasping, or showing any signs of fatigue. She's never looked more alien to him than right now.

Max gulps for air before speaking. "I thought I was. I really thought I was gonna die. I'm still feeling a little manic that I didn't."

"Where are we going now?"

"There's a car rental place near the transit building."

"You threw away your ID. You have nowhere to stay and no money."

"I recently came into some money."

He rents a car using one of the alts from Burnside and the cash from The Brothers. This car is now as untraceable as he can make it. The car will still report its position to the street grid and the handhelds he's carrying will still be visible to the tracking systems. But neither item is attached to his real name. He's just another random citizen, hiding in a crowd of millions.

"Now where are we going?" she asks as the two of them enter the car.

"I have no idea," he says as the steering wheel telescopes into his hands. He stomps on the accelerator and heads west.

FRIDAY

The Cage

Max opens his eyes to find himself in the driver's seat, which is fully reclined. He's been using his raincoat like a blanket. "What time is it?"

"Just after two in the morning." Jen is sitting upright on the passenger side. She's watching a video on one of his handhelds.

He remembers now. He found this parking garage on the west side of town and stuck the car between a couple of vans before falling asleep. "Sorry for leaving you to sit there all night. You could've gone for a walk or whatever if you got bored."

"I don't get bored."

"Must be nice."

"I wouldn't know. Anyway. I've been working. I'm going through the camera footage."

"Camera footage?"

"We talked about it yesterday morning at the scene of the latest murder."

"Was that really only yesterday?"

"Yes. You were right, the cameras are too patchwork to track the movement of people. People are too erratic. But it was good enough that I could watch the murderer as it traveled around. It was sweeping the footpaths along the north side of The River. I was able to trace its path all the way back to where it began at the start of its work cycle."

"Any irregularities in its path? Were there any times when it was off-camera for a long time?"

"No. It seemed to move at a steady pace. It was walking and sweeping, right up until the murder."

"So it's safe to assume nobody messed with it along the way."

"We're talking about someone taking screws out of its head and tampering inside. I can't imagine doing that in the street. The screws are four inches long. It takes a long time to remove them."

He lifts his coat to lay it aside and finds a hard rectangle in one of the pockets. "Do you need this hard drive?"

"No. I re-downloaded all the footage I was using."

"Then we need to destroy it."

"May I?" She holds out her hand. Max shrugs and gives her the drive.

"Look away. I don't want any of this to hit you in the eye."

There's a heavy crunch, and when he looks back the hard drive has been basically folded in half. "Shit. Good thing you're a pacifist. Let's get some breakfast."

Max has cigarettes and coffee for breakfast, and the two of them head for the north edge of the River District. The rain has finally relented. A light fog rolls over the slick streets.

Max gets out his spare identity and boots it up.

"Look this way and don't smile at all." He says. She turns to face him.

"Perfect," he says as he takes the picture. "You're a natural."

Half an hour later the car drops them off and Max sends it away to find parking.

Max tosses her the handheld he's been working on. "Congratulations. You're now a person."

Jen looks at the ID screen, which now shows her face beside the name JENNIFER FIVE, along with some plausible-looking personal information. "You gave me a full identity?"

"Not even close. It's been years since I did this sort of thing and a lot of the systems are different now. More complicated. I know a guy that can do a much more thorough job, but this should do for now. You can't spend or borrow money, but you can make phone calls, use the network, and have a pretty good chance at fooling a cop if you get carded."

"Thank you."

They begin walking south, towards The River.

"So who are our suspects?" Jen asks.

"After yesterday, I have to put the casinos on the list."

Jen nods her head. "Based on what you told me, I'd have to agree. I think Senma Technologies can be safely discarded. They depend on our cogs, so this scandal is bad for them too. On the other

161

hand Yendu Industrial might have something to gain from this. Like I said, they usually work in large-scale machine intelligence, but if they were looking to expand into humanoid robotics then this would create an opening for them."

This sounds reasonable to Max. "I have to suspect labor unions. Or someone from the unions. The robots took a lot of jobs when they showed up and a lot of people are still mad about it. On the other hand, the unions have pretty reliable tactics and this crime is a lot more subtle and a lot more technical than their usual thing. Still, worth considering."

"What about someone from the city government? I don't know this place the way you do. Could someone in the government have something to gain from this scandal?"

Max scoffs. "Hard to say. I don't know what politics are like in Kasaran, but here people joke we have more political parties than candidates. The government is always pulling itself in six different directions at the same time. I suppose someone in power might want this, although that might just lead back to the unions."

"I think we could also include Dr. Kvenst's rivals in the company. Dr. Gaust in particular."

"You don't like Gaust?"

"I'm very fond of him. He's made many brilliant advances to the platforms over the years. If it wasn't for his work I'd still be a second gen unit. But his rivalry with Dr. Kvenst is noteworthy. It would be horrible if he was behind this, but he's the only person on our list with both motive and opportunity. Nobody else so far has the knowledge to do anything meaningful inside a robot's skull."

Max stops walking. "What do you mean you'd still be a second-gen unit? I thought you were brand new."

"The definition of 'me' is a little hazy. I'm a copy of a copy, several times over. I have memories going back about twenty years. I can remember performing the first series of walking tests, way back during the first generation of robots. Technically, every single robot sold by G-Kinetics has those memories."

He resumes walking south. Max can't get his head around this. "So you remember being a dumber version of yourself?"

"Maybe. But was that robot really me? I'm a higher intelligence now, I have a different personality, I've been copied to completely new cognitive hardware several times over, and I've changed bodies dozens of times. You could think of those earlier versions as a younger version of me. Perhaps those are my childhood memories. But those old robots are still around, so you could also argue those early robots are my ancestors."

Max doesn't know what to make of a breeding system where the children and the grandparents are the same thing, so he decides to not think about it. "So what's it like being upgraded? Do you wake up one morning and you're suddenly smarter?"

"A bit. A generation upgrade has two parts. Dr. Gaust and his team come up with the new hardware. Faster processing, better connectivity and bandwidth between the segments, more memory, better caching, that sort of thing."

"So you think faster?"

"I wouldn't put it that way. I mean *yes*, I'm processing data faster. But I don't perceive that as more speed. Instead the speed manifests as deeper understanding. I'm able to see more possibilities, understand more nuance when people speak, come up with more complex ideas. That kind of thing."

"I think I get it."

"The other half of a generation upgrade comes from Dr. Kvenst. She sets the drives, but she also helps define how those drives work. One of my main drives is to protect humans from harm, but that's obviously more complicated than not pointlessly crushing their heads. It also means understanding emotional needs and social hierarchies so you don't hurt feelings, start arguments, or cause offense. And to do that you need an understanding of body language, facial expressions, and personality types. Some of that is created as an innate skill. Things like interpreting broad facial expression. It's basically hard-coded. Other parts have to be taught. The thing I'm getting at is that an upgrade isn't a single event. I get a hardware upgrade. Then I get a software upgrade. Then I spend a bunch of time interacting with Dr. Kvenst and her team. I take intelligence tests, study thought experiments, take classes for basic life skills, and that sort of thing. Eventually the accumulated improvements are significant enough that the team decides they've made a new generation. Sometimes marketing starts pushing us to declare a new generation so they can sell more units. It's pretty arbitrary."

Max is imagining a classroom full of adult-sized robots sitting at desks and taking tests like kids. He knows this doesn't make any sense, but he has no frame of reference for how this might work. "So what's a robot intelligence test like?"

"Obviously your standard IQ tests won't make any sense. We've done a few but they always end up terribly lopsided. Even the first generation of robots was able to score at genius levels for things like arithmetic and spatial reasoning, while their verbal and perceptual skills were embarrassingly sub-human. They were scoring somewhere just above the gorilla range. The team had to come up with their own intelligence tests that would measure the things they were working on."

"Which was?"

"Problem solving skills. For example, the very first question on the test presents you with a scenario where there's a three-inch rubber ball at the bottom of a six-foot hole. The rubber ball is just a little smaller than the hole. How do you get it out?"

"Wait. I heard this riddle as a kid. I think the version I heard used a wooden ball. Like, who the fuck has a wooden ball? Isn't the answer to pour water down the hole?"

"That's one answer." She says. "Maybe that's the preferred answer. I didn't realize the question was that old. As far as I knew, it was invented for the test."

"I always got the impression the question was ancient. There was an old guy in my neighborhood who would sit around and ask us kids riddles like that from memory. If you could figure it out, he'd give you a dollar. But you had to figure it out right then. If you left and came back he assumed you looked it up or asked an adult. I made more than most kids, but I think it was because I was more patient. I'd hang around for an hour thinking about it if I needed to. The other kids would get bored after five minutes and wander off."

Jen doesn't answer right away. Max can't tell if these pauses are because she's still working on her reply, or if she can't tell if he's done making his point.

Finally she says, "The ball question was presented to the first gen robot and it had no idea what to do with it. Not even a guess. The second gen robot couldn't solve it either, but it came up with an interesting answer. It suggested 'ask a human for help'. This was actually a major breakthrough. The robot realized that humans were really good at solving complex problems and it was trying to leverage that power to solve this one. The third gen brain came up with an answer, but it was... weird. It suggested pouring mercury into the hole."

Max shakes his head. "What the hell?"

"It correctly reasoned that pouring a liquid into the hole ought to work, as long as the liquid was denser than the ball. And then I guess it went for the heaviest known liquid for some reason. Obviously this is a strange answer because water would accomplish the same thing while being cheaper, safer, and more convenient. So the answer is correct in the sense that it would solve the problem, but also sort of wrong on the basis of being completely impractical. But the important thing was that the robot was showing a skill for creative problem solving. Incidentally, most service robots around the world are third generation. The third gen robot is smart enough to perform most menial tasks. They can even handle jobs that require a bit of creativity and analysis, like routine inspection and maintenance. Not nearly as smart as a person, but good enough for many tasks that humans find boring. It's sad you're stuck with so many second gen units in this country. Third generation is so much better."

They're still heading southward. The sidewalks here are narrow and shabby. This is pretty far from the tourist zone and the city keeps a lot of ugly infrastructure around here. Many of the buildings are repurposed warehouses with newer buildings sitting atop them. On the opposite side of the street is a bar that's been carved out of the corner of an old warehouse. Reflected neon light spills across the walkway. A low bassline penetrates the walls, offering a muffled dance beat to the empty streets. Out front, a couple of drunken locals are staggering around, shouting slurred demands into their mobiles in an effort to get their cars to come pick them up.

Once the noise is behind them Jen continues, "The fourth gen was the first one to ask questions. *What are the sides of the hole like? Am I allowed to damage the ball? What's the ground made of?* That sort of thing. They came up with the same answer you did. Pour water down the hole."

"Hang on. Didn't this robot remember taking the test before? Wouldn't that skew the results?"

"What they do is make a copy of the robot. They copy the entire brain over to a new cog and administer the test to the copy. Then they wipe the copy. That way the robot is always taking the test for the first time."

"Woah. You die after the test is over?"

"That's not how I would see it. For one thing, I don't have quite the same sense of self-preservation that you do, so the thought of erasure doesn't scare me. More importantly, if I'm taking the test then there's another robot around that's an exact copy of me, minus the last hour or so of test-taking. So from my perspective it's like having an hour of your memory erased. Not a big deal. Being copied, erased, or reconfigured is a normal part of my experience. This week I'm this collection of memories, running on this particular cog, on this particular platform. New week there will be others that can make the same claim, while I might have moved on to a different situation. You can see why I don't get attached to specific names for myself. Names are really only useful for humans trying to keep track of things, so I let them pick the names. I don't know how to draw a meaningful distinction between myself and all of my almost-twins."

"I get it now. But if no robots remember the test, then how are you telling me about it?"

"I took the test. And I mean this specific cog that's talking to you now. I did so well that Dr. Kvenst felt I'd outgrown the test. Instead of erasing me, she decided I should be involved in the next phase of research."

"What made her think that?"

"A lot of things. The final score, obviously, but also my understanding of what the test represented and what it was for. I was showing a level of self-awareness that the previous generations never really achieved. On the ball question, I spent a full minute asking questions about the parameters of the scenario, and then I proposed multiple solutions based on available resources and need. If you're in a primitive setting and you don't care if the ball is damaged, then you

166

could fashion a spear and skewer it. If you have a vacuum with a hose attachment and electricity is available you could use that to grab the ball. I came up with proposals involving water, excavation, grabbing devices, and so on. I had a dozen proposals of varying lengths, just for that one question. In the end, Dr. Kvenst felt like she wanted me to take on a problem that would provide a more meaningful challenge."

"And what was that?"

"This case." She stops and looks around. "Here. This is where the robot first appeared on camera. It was walking with a few others at this point. I'd say they're stored somewhere nearby."

"So we're looking for some sort of storage building, somewhere between here and the next working camera."

"I'm not a detective, but I'm guessing this is the place," Jen says after they've walked a couple more blocks.

"I'm not a detective either, but you're probably right."

They're standing in front of a building labeled "North Shore Municipal Automated Sanitation Facility" in peeling stenciled letters. The building is a squat windowless concrete box. A cloud of moths orbits the yellow light illuminating the main entrance. The door is a featureless rectangle without a handle or keyhole. It's very large, and from outside you can't even tell if it swings up, swings inward, or slides to the side.

Max stops on the edge of the pool of light. "Looks like the door is triggered by identification. I have no idea what kind. I don't usually break into industrial places like this. There's not much worth stealing inside. I don't know what their security weaknesses are."

Jen examines the front of the building with him. "If G-Kinetics robots are stored here, then it's very likely the company has some sort of maintenance access. I could reach out to our techs and see if they can get us in."

Max shakes his head. "Like you said, Dr. Gaust might be a suspect. A lot of people are very interested in this case. A lot of powerful people want to make sure this gets solved and different people want to make sure it doesn't. I don't want anyone to know what we're doing until I know what the sides are."

Jen points to the street. "There are some faint tire tracks around this entrance. Maybe this is just vehicle access and the robots use some other door."

"Okay." Max heads for the right side of building, which is in darkness. Even if there aren't any city cameras around, he doesn't like stepping into the light without a good reason.

"Max. The second gen units have terrible low-light vision. They'd never be able to navigate over there."

He turns and reluctantly heads for the well-lit area on the left side.

They find a pair of identical doors side-by-side. Faded remnants of paint indicate that at one point in the distant past the right was outlined in green and the left in red. Like the front, the door has no handle.

"Damnit. Haven't you people heard of doorknobs?" Max says under his breath.

"These are robot access. They have these exact same doors in Kasaran."

Max scratches his head. "I suppose if we can't get it open we could just wait for the next shift change and slip through when the robots open them. Would a gen 2 call the police on us if they saw us sneaking in?"

"I don't know. But maybe it won't come to that. The doors are usually just designed to open if they detect one of our robots. Which I am."

She approaches the right-hand door and it pops open. The mechanism is fast and noisy. Max is startled by the abrupt slam as the door hits the open position. He looks around self-consciously before following her through. The door snaps shut with another bang as soon as he clears the threshold, leaving them in darkness. Jen takes off her sunglasses and the blue glow from her eyes illuminates the space in front of her. This isn't quite enough light for Max to work with, so he pulls out his handheld and turns on flashlight mode.

He aims his light around, trying to get a sense of the space. There's a smell of oil in the air. There are heavy square frames all around, about the size of a van. Inside of each is a suspended metal arm that splits into a pair of prongs, as if it was a massive tuning fork.

Robots are stacked on these four or five levels deep, with the prongs of the fork fitting around their narrow waists. On the side of each of these racks is a battered strip of stainless steel where inscrutable numbers and dates have been written in grease pencil. These racks are arranged in rows that run as far as his light can reach in either direction.

Walking between the rows he can see the robots are grouped by color, although Max only recognizes a few of the types. The brown ones do streetside garbage pickup. The green and yellow ones sweep the walkways. He remembers seeing the blue models wandering around municipal buildings, but he doesn't know what they do. The rest of the colors are mysterious to him.

"I had no idea the city had this many robots," he says. "You don't see them very often, so I assumed there were only a handful. I guess it's a big city, though."

"How many people live in this city? Five million?"

"Depends on whether you include the tourists or not."

"Even if people outnumber robots by 1,000 to 1, that's still 5,000 robots."

As he's looking around his light catches something just overhead. He aims upward to see thick electrical cables and some kind of machinery for shuffling containers around. He follows these to discover there's another row of containers suspended above. From this angle he can't tell where the ceiling is or if there might be yet another level above that one.

"I wonder what generation these charging ports are," Jen says. When he's not aiming his flashlight at her, all he can see are her blue eyes shining in the darkness. It reminds him of the way cat eyes seem to glow when they reflect headlights.

She's kneeling down, trying to read some scuffed labeling on the outer wall. Apparently satisfied, she slaps her hand against a dark rectangle. A tiny red light comes on beside her hand and he can hear a low hum. There are several such ports of different sizes and shapes along the wall, mixed with a scattering of predictable safety warnings.

"What did you do?"

"I'm charging. The charging port in the car is too weak. It would take that thing a week to top me off."

Max realizes her power needs haven't occurred to him until just now. "How long do you need?"

"Five minutes. Maybe ten. This is an old port and it's a little dodgy. It keeps cutting out on me. I'm trying to find a good rate but it's got this strange setup where it either wants to go a little too fast or much too slow. I don't know if that's because the port is old or because of the nonstandard voltage this country runs on."

Max is usually uncomfortable talking at full volume when trespassing, but Jen doesn't seem to have a problem with it and he doesn't see any point in whispering if she's not going to. He looks at the limp bodies of the robots. "Kvenst told me you don't power down robots unless you have to. Are these things awake? Can they hear us?"

"Yes, they can hear us. I doubt they see us as relevant or important. They're really only interested in doing their jobs. If we explicitly mentioned doing something that would offend their drives then they might call for help. Otherwise they're naturally trusting of humans. They're going to assume that if we're here then we have a reason to be."

"But if someone asks, they would report seeing us here?"

"That's true."

He finds it mildly unsettling that these lifeless robots are actually watching them, but he doesn't see how he can do anything about it. Max continues between the aisles of stacked robots. Eventually he gets to the end of a row and finds an open space. A vehicle is parked here. It's just a framework, an engine, and a set of wheels.

"I found a transport for the robots," he shouts to Jen. "Looks like these containers get loaded onto this thing and it drives them to their work site." He swings his light around and spots a few other vehicles. Some are larger and look like they're designed to carry two containers at a time.

"Makes sense," she says from somewhere in the darkness. "Some of these probably work on the edges of the city. If you made them walk they'd be low on power by the time they got there."

He looks down to see he's stepped in a pool of dark liquid. Paranoid that he's somehow stepped in blood, he jumps back quickly and tries to wipe off his shoe. After some shuffling around he sees that

170

no, it's just automotive oil. This wouldn't be a big deal, except he's just left a bunch of incriminating oily footprints all over the place, stamped with the emblem of his favorite brand of upscale dress boot. He tries rubbing these out and ends up making a mess in the process. He dips his toe back into the oil and smears it around. This covers up the prints while also making the mess even larger and more obvious. Eventually he gives up and places his hope in the general apathy of the city that nobody will care to investigate these dark smears.

He's at the front of the warehouse now, beside the main door they saw earlier. He turns around and heads for the back. As he passes Jen he sees that she's crouched so that her bare knee is pressed against the cold damp concrete, bearing a lot of her weight. This creates yet another moment that looks just slightly off from a human perspective. He knows her body works differently, but he can't help but think how much it would hurt to hold that pose for more than a few seconds. Max suspects that while they might get fully lifelike bodies in the next couple of years, robots are probably decades away from being undetectable to humans. There are just so many subtle details that everyone takes for granted.

She's stretching her arms so that each palm is touching a different charging plate.

Max sniffs the air. "What's that smell? Plastic? Rubber?"

"I wouldn't know. No sense of smell. My guess is you're smelling my skin. I'm charging really fast like this and my battery is getting hot."

Max doesn't like touching people unless they're on very close terms. On top of that, he knows lots of other people feel the same way. On the other hand, he knows Jen is literally incapable of being bothered by it and he's sort of curious what's going on. He puts his hand on the small of her back. "Wow. You're like a toaster."

"Not really. My battery isn't even near boiling. I might be pushing up against the safety guidelines, but I shouldn't be a burn hazard."

Towards the rear of the building he finds some empty racks. He doesn't know if these are extra space or if they're housing for robots that are out working.

At the very back is a workshop enclosed in a security cage. There's a padlock on the door. He hasn't gotten around to getting himself a good set of lockpicks yet so he doesn't have a way to open it. He shines his flashlight through the bars. Inside is a workbench with some scattered tools.

Max rubs his chin. If this workshop is shared by multiple people, then it's possible they keep the key hidden nearby rather than distribute copies to every employee that might possibly need it. Hoping for a lucky break, he scours the area for the key. At the end of five minutes he concludes these city employees are either more responsible than most, or they're better at hiding things. Jen reappears just as he gives up.

"Better now?" he asks.

"Full up."

He puts his hand against the locked gate. "I really want to see what's in here. I don't have a way to open this lock."

"I might be able to force it."

"I was thinking of asking you to do that, but that would pretty much advertise that someone had broken in here. I don't know how often workers come in. It could be every morning. It might be a weekly thing. But if they see someone forced their way into this workshop then they might call the cops."

"This is not my area of expertise."

"I know. It's supposedly mine. Usually when you're breaking into a place you come prepared. Lockpicks. Bolt cutters. You'll spend a few days watching the place so you know when employees come and go. But that takes time and I'd really like to see in here tonight. If I had a way to break the padlock then I'd just take it with me. The next person to show up will assume the previous person just forgot to lock up when they left. Especially if you don't make a mess or steal anything."

"I can break the padlock if you want."

Max looks through the bars. "Here's the thing. If anyone tampered with that robot, they did it in this shop area. If there are any clues at all, they're in here. I'd be okay with leaving signs of forced entry behind if it meant we could get some information. And I'm willing to walk away now and try something else. But what I really don't want to do is bash open this door for nothing."

"Or walk away and leave behind our only lead."

"Or that."

"But you think we can pull off the lock without raising any suspicion?"

"Probably. Calling the police is a huge pain in the ass and your average municipal grunt might not bother if you don't disrupt their work."

"Okay then." Jen grabs the lock.

Max is waiting for her to begin straining when he realizes she's already started. Since she's not made of meat, her exertion doesn't take the form of grunting, shaking, or flexing. After a few seconds of silence there's a pop and her hand jerks away.

"Got it?" Max says hopefully.

Jen holds up her left hand to show her index finger is bent backwards. "No. I've never used a padlock before. I didn't realize how strong they were."

"Ow! That looks painful!" Max says when he sees the damage. "Or, does that even hurt? Or, are you damaged? Or whatever it's called."

Jen uses her right hand to force her finger back into place. "No serious damage, but I probably stripped the joint a bit. Anyway. I can't break the lock. I can maybe rip it off the door, but that will leave behind damage we can't hide."

"Hell with it. Let's get in there."

Jen grasps the lock and positions herself to attempt to rip it from the hasp.

"Are you okay?"

Max and Jen turn to face the voice. There's a sound of rubbing metal and rubberized feet hitting the floor. A blue robot steps into Max's flashlight beam and begins walking towards them.

"I can call the paramedics if you're injured," it says.

"No!" Max says excitedly. "No. We don't need any paramedics. It's just that we really need into this room. Do you know where the key is?"

"The caretaker on call will have a copy. Should I issue a problem report?"

"No," Max says. He hesitates. The problem with lying to a low-end robot is that it's too stupid to fall for his more sophisticated material. He needs to approach this like lying to a child. He lowers his voice a bit. He doesn't want other bots to hear this or it might cause chaos. "Please don't contact anyone. By the time they get here, it will be too late. My medicine is in this room and I'll die in the next five minutes if I don't get it open."

The robot practically lunges at the door. It's not as graceful or as efficient as Jen, but it attacks the problem with a ferocity that Max has never seen in a robot. Its fingers go out of joint just like Jen's did, but instead of backing off it changes its grip and keeps going. It braces one knee against the door frame, which ends up looking like a more human pose than the one Jen was using. The metal of the door begins to groan and bend. The sound echoes through the entire warehouse. Max slams his hands over his ears. Finally something gives and the hasp tears free of the frame. The robot tears open the door and stands aside for Max.

"Good job!" he says, patting it on the shoulder.

Jen follows him into the workshop.

"Did you find your medicine, sir?" the robot asks.

Max looks out through the bars at the robot. He whispers to Jen. "We can't just leave him here to tell folks about us. Can you erase his memory?"

"No."

"Can you disable him so he can't report this?"

"Yes."

Jen walks back outside, tears off the robot's head, and crushes it between her hands before the body hits the ground. She walks back into the workshop and says, "So what are we looking for?"

Max looks at the smoking wreckage outside. "So I guess your whole pacifism thing only applies to people then?"

"Yes. Obviously. Wouldn't make sense otherwise."

He remembers her talking about the difference between memorization and integration. He *knew* she was only a pacifist towards people, but he hadn't really *integrated* that information until just now.

When Max was fourteen years old, he spent a few weeks living with his aunt and uncle in one of the dreary northern husk towns the mining industry had left behind. The two of them lived in a prefab house about the size of a few parking spaces. This made no sense to Max. He understood that space was precious in the city and that's why apartments were tight. But why - out here in the vast wilderness where land was basically worthless - did people live in places that were *even smaller* than city apartments?

Aunt Lana was a woman of continuous words, most of them regarding other people and all of them negative. Uncle Gord (because long names like "Gordon" were for pretentious foreigners) was a man who could glare at the television for an entire evening and never speak a single syllable. He was a man with a creased face and a wiry build who often made people uncomfortable with the intensity of his stare.

One day their daughter Tea came running into the house crying. She'd done something to agitate the dog and it had nipped her hand. The moment these words hit Gord's ears he stood up, walked outside, knelt on the dog, broke its neck, and went back to the television without ever once changing his facial expression.

It was the first time Max had ever seen something die. The death wasn't the part that disturbed him. It was how abrupt and unremarkable it was to Uncle Gord. He didn't run outside in a fit of rage. He hadn't lost control due to overpowering emotions. He just came to a decision that the dog shouldn't be alive anymore and then acted on that decision. For Gord that decision wasn't any more weighty than picking a channel to watch.

Uncle Gord didn't know it, but that moment changed Max's perception of him forever. Max is going through the same sort of re-alignment of perceptions with Jen. He thinks back to their earlier conversation where she talked about her absolutist drive to stay out of human conflicts and finds he's starting to see the wisdom in the idea.

"I wouldn't do that to just any robot," Jen adds. "If a human had cared about that robot then I wouldn't have destroyed it."

Max looks down at the wreckage. "He came apart pretty quick. Are you that much stronger than gen 2 units?"

"I never asked about the strength specifications, but I doubt I'm significantly stronger than any of these models. If anything I might be a little weaker or more fragile. In my platform, certain compromises have been made for aesthetics."

"I guess it's good he didn't fight back," Max says.

"It wouldn't. To a gen 2, I'd look fully human."

"Even with the glowing eyes?"

"Even with the glowing eyes. It might not understand the eyes, but for all it knows they might be prosthetic or cosmetic. It would be incapable of hurting me without a very explicit demonstration that I'm not human. Even then, I'm not sure you could get it to act. I remember second generation units had trouble setting up clothing displays in stores. The mannequins looked so lifelike to them that they were reluctant to take them apart."

"Don't they get over it once they see the arms and legs come off and are made of plastic?"

"Have you ever seen someone afraid to touch a rubber spider or snake? Even after they realize it's rubber, they still don't like touching it."

"I've never seen that myself, but I've heard of people with those kinds of phobias."

"It's basically the same thing. An even better example is baby dolls. Give a lifelike plastic infant to an adult and watch how they behave towards it. They know it's fake, but they're still averse to being rough with it. They might toss a toy car into the toybox across the room, but they'll probably set the toy baby down gently. This is particularly true on first contact. They might regard the toy more casually over time, but the initial reaction will be heavily impacted by their innate desire to protect infants."

"I've never noticed that, but I've never really been around toys. Not even when I was a kid. Where did you learn this stuff?"

"Studying human behavior is a big part of Dr. Kvenst's work. You have to understand how people behave before you can replicate it. If people saw a robot being brutish with mannequins or baby dolls, their natural reaction would be to assume the robot is unfit for healthcare or child care."

Max turns his attention back to the workshop. He focuses on the object that caught his curiosity the moment his flashlight beam touched it. It's hanging with a bunch of screwdrivers, but the thing that sets it apart is the shaft has a rough-hewn look rather than a smooth machine finish. Someone stuck this thing on a grinder and re-shaped it. He picks it up and flips it over to see the point has been re-shaped into something approximating a triangle.

"Look at this," says Jen. She's holding up a screw. The head has been completely stripped.

"That's the missing screw, isn't it?"

"We're in a warehouse with hundreds of robots that use this exact screw to keep their heads together. I can't prove this is from our murderer, but it's clear someone opened up a robot in here."

"This is the tool they used," Max says as he puts it back. "Where did you find the screw?"

"There's a bin of scrap metal over here."

Max takes the bin and dumps it out on the bench. He finds a few uneven pellets of solder, a pile of metal shavings, a cracked circuit board, some bits of wire, and a crumpled-up soda can.

He holds up the tiny circuit board. "I'm curious about this little guy. Is it related to the robot tampering or is it a normal replacement part that they use around here?"

"There's nothing like that inside of any G-Kinetics robot."

"I figured. But we don't know what else they work on in here. Sure, some robots carry around brooms and some carry more complex tools. Maybe this is part of some job I don't know about. Maybe it was put into the head, and it modified the robot somehow, and they took it back out." He looks at Jen. "Could it short something out? Break some inhibition?"

"Would you eat a baby?"

"I heard that one already."

"Oh. Well hopefully you get the idea. You can't just 'short out' our primary drives. You'd have to reprogram the brain from the ground up, and there's no way that simple little circuit board can do that. At least, I don't see how it would be possible."

"Okay. Let's say hypothetically. Let's say this little circuit board can make a robot want to kill somehow. Forget about how for right now. Say it's magic. Like, assume this thing is haunted or whatever."

"A haunted circuit board?"

"Humor me. Would it fit inside your head? Would there be room for it?"

"Inside the head I'm using now? Absolutely not. The skull is completely packed for anthropomorphic models. The puppetry for the mouth parts alone is an engineering nightmare, not to mention the rest of the face. But a gen 2 might have a few gaps where you could squeeze something like that in."

Max grabs the bin. "Let's clean up this mess and get out. We've hung around here way too long."

"Let me," Jen says. She uses the side of her hand to gather up all the little metal shavings and sweep them into the bin. "This stuff is sharp and I don't want you to cut yourself."

Max takes a few pictures of the scene and then does his best to wipe his fingerprints off of everything he's touched. He makes sure it's all back where he found it. The only exception is the haunted circuit board, which he pockets.

"So what do we do about our friend here?" Max says this while standing just outside the workshop, looking down at the smashed robot. "We can hide the body, but they probably take inventory and they'll notice he's missing. And there's no way we can hide the damage to the door.

"Trying to dispose of the body might create a trail of evidence. When you said you wanted it disabled I assumed you had a plan."

"Actually - and maybe this is wishful thinking - I like the idea of leaving him right where he is. No human could crush a metal head like that. Which means the next time the workers come in they'll find one of their own robots wrenched open a door and then had its head crushed by another robot. That should create a pretty interesting scene for them to puzzle over. They might find it confusing, but it will probably play into the general robot confusion and paranoia. I don't know what sort of theories they might formulate, but I'm betting 'A robot and a gangster came in here looking to solve the robot murders' will be pretty low on their list of theories." Max is still looking at the wrecked

178

robot when he begins chuckling. "Yeah. Fuck it. Leave the mess. I never claimed to be a real detective."

"Whatever works. I don't care how we do it, as long as we stop the killings."

Max looks around the room, or as much as his little flashlight will show him. "The only thing I'm worried about are the other robots. How much will they remember or understand?"

"They should remember things clearly, but understand things very poorly. They're parked pretty far from this workspace. It's dark, and the acoustics in here are terrible. Like I said, their low-light vision is poor and their audio filtering is more than a decade behind mine. The only reason this one got involved is because you began shouting as if someone was in pain."

"Well, I think our options are to leave the scene like this or have you personally execute all of these hundreds of possible robo-witnesses."

"The latter would take a long time."

"I was kidding. Let's get out of here."

Jupiter

Max has always avoided black cars. He figures if you're a gangster then you should get something cute and playful and brightly colored. The police habitually leave those things alone because they're too busy pulling over all the sleek red and black road monsters. The only drawback with this line of thinking is that your fellow gangsters all place too much emphasis on cars as a status symbol. That would be fine with Max, since someone needs to perpetuate the gangster stereotype so he can continue to exploit it, but they also mock him for doing so. Guys became so fixated on his car that it started to define his persona, and he wanted to be known as clever and careful, not as the guy who drives cars designed for teenage girls. Eventually he split the difference and started using cars from the middle-class commuter market. These were plain cars with unremarkable colors and unremarkable performance.

But now he's decided to mix things up. Max figures that if everyone is looking for him specifically, then now is the time to play against type. He's driving something sleek, dark, and low to the ground. The tires are wide and shallow and the entire design is focused on making them look as prominent as possible. The doors open by sliding slightly out and backward. The movement happens in a split second and is accompanied by a crisp, satisfying mechanical snap. Various groups of Very Concerned Citizens have been trying to ban snap doors for years because they're afraid "some kid" will grab the door at the wrong moment and lose a finger. It hasn't happened yet, which is probably why you can still get these cars.

"What is this place?" Jen asks.

"This building, or this part of the city?"

"Both would be helpful."

"This part of the city is called the Low District, probably because bits of it are slightly below sea level. The building in front of us is called Jupiter because... I don't know. Look, it's stupid but just humor this guy. He has a taste for the dramatic. I think he gets lonely out here."

They're on the far southern edge of the city. At this point they're so far from the Hospitality District that it feels like a different planet. Here the city infrastructure is exposed in tangled webs of overhead electrical cables and data lines. Traffic signals hang from these in odd places and at odd angles. They work just well enough to do their job, but everything feels precarious and crooked. The streets are cracked so badly that some bits have almost reverted to gravel.

Rather than tearing down structures and rebuilding according to need, everything has been added to and modified. Here the low, sagging buildings are a strange patchwork. The century-old buildings have cheap modern prefab expansions added to them. It's the architectural equivalent of conjoined circus freaks.

The people this far south like to decorate their buildings by going to the Hospitality District and stealing signs. These signs have built up over the years, layer after layer, forming a strange and disorienting mix of messages. In some cities the layers of spray-paint graffiti build up until it's a wall of unintelligible noise. This is the same thing, except done in fragmented display screens and neon. It's at the same time an art installation, a community engineering project, and an angry mockery of the plastic consumerist world to the north.

Max had to drive here manually. The data maps of this part of the city are out of date to the point of uselessness. There aren't really any lines on the streets. Max has parked the car, but he's not sure if he's in a parking lot or if the street randomly got much wider here for no reason.

Jupiter has the outline of a warehouse, although on the left side of the building is a small wooden porch with a domestic style door. The rest of the front of the building holds letters spelling out JUPITER, using large characters stolen from around the city over the decades. The J is the crown jewel of the collection. It stands twelve feet high and was stolen from the newly-built facade of the Uar Juhause hotel twenty years ago. Stories about the "J" heist were one of the things that drew him into pulling heists of his own.

Max leads Jen past the obvious front door. He explains, "Never use the front door. He doesn't answer it. I don't think he even uses that mailbox. The real entrance is around back."

181

On the opposite side of the structure is an arrangement of crates. They're positioned to look like haphazardly stacked junk, but Max knows they actually form a blind to hide the real entrance. The gap is narrow and unlit, but if you know what you're looking for it's not hard to squeeze through. They find themselves looking at an industrial door with a keypad to one side.

"If he's doing his job, then he'll have changed this code years ago. But let me try anyway," Max says.

The code is a little foggy for him. He can remember the first four digits, but he's not completely sure about the rest. Once he starts typing his hand remembers the familiar up-down rhythm of the code. The red light over the door turns green and there's a buzz as the door unlocks.

"He hasn't changed the door code," Max says. "That's really sloppy and unlike him."

The inside of the building can't make up its mind any better than the outside. Some walls think they're part of a house, other walls think they're taking part in some sort of warehouse-type situation, and none of the light fixtures match. Max goes around the blind corner, ignores the well-lit boobytrap door, pushes open the door disguised as unfinished drywall, and leads Jen into Jupiter Central.

Jupiter Central is an open room with enough space to comfortably park a couple of city busses. The outer walls are in darkness and have rotting mattresses bolted to them. In the center is the only source of light in the room. It's an impossible nest of cables, keyboards, and display screens. The one feature that's unfamiliar to Max is that for some reason there's now a wire cage around the nest.

"Jupiter?" Max calls.

The next few things happen very quickly. A young man begins yelling incoherently from within the cage at the same moment he appears from behind a screen. Then Max sees the gun in his hand. Then suddenly Jennifer is standing directly in front of him. Her movement reminds him of the snap of his car doors.

Max can't even tell what the kid is yelling, so he tries to shout over him, "I'm looking for Jupiter!"

"Well you found it. Congratulations. Now piss off tourist!" The kid is still shouting.

He's perhaps twenty-five, although he doesn't look healthy so that guess might be far off in either direction. He has sunken eyes and hollow cheeks. An oversized shirt clings to his narrow frame. He has a mop of unruly hair on top of his head and a thin notion of a beard clinging to his chin.

Max tries to shove Jen aside and finds her unmovable. He tries to step around her but she matches his movements perfectly. It's like trying to do an end-run around your reflection in a mirror.

"Please move. Let me talk to this kid."

"Tell him to put the gun down."

"Can you lower the gun please?" Max says, still trying to shove Jen out of the way.

"Can you get the fuck out of my house?" the kid says, pointing the gun in the direction he wants them to go.

"I'm looking for Jupiter," Max says again.

"You're in it, dumbass. We don't have a gift shop so you can't buy a souvenir. Now fuck off."

"I'm looking for the man, not the place," Max says. He's pretty sure this should have been obvious by context, but it looks like this kid hasn't invited his entire brain to the conversation. His hand is shaking and his eyes are deeply bloodshot.

"Yeah. So who are you?"

"Jupiter knows me as Mr. Gone."

"Oh. You're Max Law. I heard about you. Must have just got out of prison." The kid lowers the gun.

Max buries his forehead in the palm of his hand. "Why does everyone know my name these days?"

The kid sits down in a battle-worn office chair. "You got nicked, friend. Once you show up on the news in that orange jumpsuit, all your secrets are gone."

Max gives Jen a gentle nudge and she moves out of the way. "Other guys keep their aliases when they get out of prison," he says.

The kid nods. "Yeah. But you had a reputation. *Mr. Gone.* All those years. No arrests. No fights. No vendettas. Never even a suspect. Not even a parking ticket. And then the guy who never gets caught, got caught. I guess everyone was happy to find out you had a real name."

183

Max is happy to see he's been mythologized a bit. While it's true he was never arrested, his career wasn't nearly as clean or as effortless as this kid has been led to believe. "So what are you, an intern? Where's Jupiter?"

"I'm Saturn. Jupiter is gone. Extradited to Kasaran. He hacked something he shouldn't have. I don't think we'll see him again."

Max hangs his head. Jupiter was an old-timer in the business. He's had white hair for as long as Max has known him. Any crime worth extraditing him for is probably going to carry a sentence that will outlast him.

"So what do?" Saturn asks.

"I have a little information to offer and I'd like a little information in return."

Saturn nods. "Okay. But in the future use the network. I don't do this face-to-face stuff like my dad."

"Jupiter is your dad? That means your names are backwards."

"Backwards? What?"

"Nevermind." Max holds up his handheld. "All mobiles are traceable by citywide scanners. Even when turned off."

"Yeah. I heard that rumor. It's a myth. It's what idiots say when they get sloppy and wind up nicked. They blame me and say I didn't scrub their devices properly."

"Well, it's true," Max says. This is why he hates working with young guys. Their pride clouds their judgement. Then again, old guys aren't much fun either because they're too set in their ways.

"Do I look like I'm new at this?" Saturn says defensively.

"Yeah, you do."

"Man, fuck you friend. By the time a device has hit the market I've already taken a dozen of them apart. I know everything about these machines. There's no hidden ID chip or whatever."

"It's the heat sink," Jen says as she takes off her sunglasses.

Maybe it's her eyes or maybe it's the information, but at this point Saturn gets very quiet. He puts the gun down and walks over to the wall of the cage that separates them.

She continues, "It's made from two different alloys. They look the same but they have different reflective properties. You hit it with a particular EM burst and you'll get back a pattern that uniquely identifies the device. To you it looks like a chunk of metal. To the scanner it looks like a barcode."

Saturn runs his hand through his thick hair, which pulls it out of his face for a moment. He looks down, wide-eyed. "The heat sink. Every year they were getting smaller and smaller. Then suddenly last year they got huge. I thought they just, I dunno, had heat problems with the chips or something. So the ID rumor is true. That's *real* news, friend."

Saturn walks over to a nearby bench where it looks like a half dozen different gadgets have been dissected. He picks up a rectangle of metal and turns it over in his hand. It's smooth on one side and has ridges on the other. To Max it looks like a random hunk of metal. It doesn't seem to have a way to plug into anything else. Max has no idea how it works, but he assumes this is the part in question.

The whole "cage" thing is really bugging Max. He just came from the other side of the city where there was a different workshop in a different kind of cage, but the similarities are bugging him. He's pretty sure it's just one of those random coincidences in life, but his brain has spotted this pattern and keeps looking for how it might *Mean Something*.

Max bangs on the cage. "So what's the deal with putting yourself in jail? Solidarity with your dad?"

"This isn't a jail. This is an EM shield. Do you know how many connections I've got in here? How brightly this place shines? This cage is like an invisibility cloak for my equipment. Without it, I'd shine like a beacon. That's how they found my father."

"Is it?" Max says.

Saturn looks down at the heat sink in his hand. "So what do you want?"

Max pulls out the haunted circuit. "I want to know what this is."

Saturn blinks. "What is that? Four square inches of board and a few chips? You need to give me more to go on than that. It could be anything."

"Can you tell me anything about it? Where do the components might come from? Who might use them? What are they typically used for?"

185

Saturn stares at it for a few seconds. "You don't know what you're asking. But you did a right turn for me so I'll see what I can do." He holds out his hand.

"I'd like to keep it," Max says. "I can wait if you need time to investigate or whatever."

Saturn pulls out his handheld. "Hold it up to the light," he says. He snaps a picture and then motions for Max to turn the board over so he can get a picture of the other side. Max has no idea why the kid would want a picture of the back of a circuit board, but he obliges.

Satisfied, Saturn nods. "Gimmie your ID and I'll call you if I find anything."

Max holds up his handheld and shows the ID he's been using.

"That old geezer Burnside made this one, didn't he?" Saturn says this without looking away from the screen.

"How'd you know?" Max looks at the screen himself, looking for the giveaway.

"He always puts the birthdays in the first week of November."

"Why?" Max says this while making a face at the screen. He's never paid much attention to the birthdays on his fake IDs.

"You'll have to ask him. I'll call you if I find anything."

Max and Jen show themselves out.

Once they're outside again, Max looks back towards the glowing sign. "I never knew Jupiter had a kid. Or a family. He never said anything. Must have started late in life." He stands still in the pool of multicolored light, gazing up at the JUPITER logo. The logo looks different somehow. It's been bugging him since they arrived.

"Are you sure this Saturn is really his son?" Jen asks.

"The family resemblance is there. He looks like his father, even if he doesn't act like him. Jupiter was a very careful guy. Very quiet. Never touched drugs."

"You think Saturn uses drugs?"

Max scoffs. "He was fucking sideways back there. Didn't you see how bloodshot his eyes were?"

"Yes. But I've seen lots of bloodshot eyes. It's usually from allergies or sleep trouble."

186

"You could also see it in his body language. The way he moved his hands. Like they were numb. Slack face. Slow speech."

"Some of those cues are too subtle for me."

"Aren't you supposed to be operating on a human level now that you're fifth generation?"

"I never claimed that. Figuring out how smart I am is a tough problem because our brains are so different. When it comes to body language I'm still far behind. Entire sections of your brain are hard-wired for that kind of specialized processing. Imagine if you found yourself living among some unfamiliar creatures. Like mice or birds. How hard would it be to learn their body language through simple exposure?"

"I guess that would be pretty hard."

The Jupiter logo is really bothering Max. He's pretty sure it has something to do with the purple neon star being used to dot the i in "Jupiter". The star wasn't there before, and yet it looks oddly familiar. Was it moved?

"Landro wants to see you," she says, interrupting his train of thought. She's standing beside him, but not looking up at the sign.

"What? Now? Did he call you or something? Can you hear his voice in your head?"

"I was reading the company message board. He posted a public message directed at you. At both of us, really. He knew I'd read it."

"So he knows we're working together."

"Apparently so," she says. "But this also proves that our going into blackout has worked. This was the only way he could contact us."

The realization hits him. The star looks familiar because it was part of the old Moon Shot logo. He nods his head, satisfied. He heads for the car. Jen follows.

"Well, Landro's going to have to wait," he says. "There's something that's been bugging me about our visit to North Shore Municipal Automated Robot Whatever. Someone used that workshop to hack the robot to commit murder."

"We don't know that yet. We just found a screw and a circuit board that might not even be related."

"Right. But assuming they hacked the robot there, then how did they end up stripping the screw so bad they couldn't even put it back in? Like, that was the third robot to get hacked. The first two didn't show any signs of stripped screws." The car pops open as they approach and invites them in with warm light.

"So you're wondering why our hacker is getting worse at their job?" Jen asks as she climbs in.

The doors snap shut and Max jams a cigarette into the corner of his mouth. The end of it bobs up and down as he says, "I'm thinking we have more than one hacker. Or saboteur. Whatever they are. The facility we visited was for the North Shore borough. That's a really big section of the city, but it's just one of many. If every borough has its own robot garage, then the other killer robots didn't come from the one we visited." He lights the cigarette as they rumble away over the uneven pavement.

"So the one from in front of Uar Juhause would be based in the Hospitality District?"

Max resists the urge to correct her and call it the Grandview. Instead he says, "Yeah. The thing is, I know the Hospitality District really well and I know there isn't room for a robot garage. I've certainly never seen robots congregating anywhere. So somewhere else in the city - probably close to the Hospitality District - is another garage, and I want to see if we can find a similar workshop there."

"Okay. When we get downtown I'll have to go see Landro myself."

Max realizes he doesn't want her to go. "We don't know what his agenda is. If you go see him, he might not let you leave."

"I know."

"So ignore him," Max waves his hand as if brushing a fly away.

"I have to go."

"Aren't you autonomous? Kvesnst said you were."

"That's *mostly* true. Obviously I have to be loyal to somebody. Nobody would buy a robot if it was just going to wander off the moment it saw someone in greater need of its help. Especially considering how much we cost. On the other hand, you don't want the robot to be apathetic and ignore everyone that doesn't own it. The thing is, if you ask people they already have some built-in expectations

188

about how robots should behave. We just needed to design their behavior to match those expectations. The team did some focus testing and discovered that most people thought of a robot as a pet. That's the mental model they used when we presented them with various scenarios and asked how they'd want their robot to behave. You'd be unhappy with your dog if it left you to play catch with the neighbor. On the other hand, nobody would be angry at their dog for running off to pull a baby out of a river."

Max suspects this entire family pet mentality is very slanted towards Kasaranian culture. People in the city don't have a lot of space for big pets. Rural people in the north keep dogs, but they're not the sort of animals you play with. He wonders if people from Rivergate would have different expectations for domestic robots. He's never known anyone rich enough to own one.

Jen continues, "The loyalty model I use now is based on a system of individual attachment. I'm most concerned with my direct owner, then secondarily with their close friends or associates, and then lastly with the needs of outsiders in general. I worry about all humans, but I'm most concerned with my immediate group. In a work setting, that group might be a team. In a domestic setting, it would be a family."

"Aren't you owned by a company and not a single person?"

"That's the problem. The entire concept of a family breaks down when you have robots owned by corporations or governments. Those sorts of things are too large and are often made up of individuals competing against each other. The entire system of attachment is built around the idea of a single person. I can't get attached to a legal entity made up of hundreds of people. I'm currently attached to Dr. Kvenst. By enlisting your help, she's made you part of the group."

Max has managed to grope his way through the maze of unmarked streets and get the car heading properly north. "So you're actually more loyal to Kvenst than to the company. Is that why you want to go see Landro? You want to keep Kvenst happy?"

"No. I don't want to go see Mr. Landro. I don't think seeing Mr. Landro is good for the company right now. I'm sure he's worrying and looking for updates. Stopping the investigation to go talk to him will make him personally feel better at the expense of delaying our search for a solution. He can't help, so there's nothing to be gained by going to see him. Summoning us is a very selfish act on his part."

"So blow him off."

"There's been some debate in the company over the last few years. Mr. Landro and Dr. Gaust think I should be made more subservient to company interests. They call it putting me on a 'leash'. They want to mess around with my drives, or insert a new one. They want me to be loyal to the company, and they want that particular drive elevated above everything but my no-harm policy. Dr. Kvenst has been adamantly against this change. And since she's in charge of setting up my personality, she's been able to hold them off. In previous generations, I never took a lot of interest in this argument. I was happy as long as I was helping people. But ever since I upgraded to generation five I've become acutely aware of how important the debate is. This policy will shape how my product line develops, and that will shape how people view robots for decades to come. If I go rogue and refuse to meet with Mr. Landro, he'll see it as rebellion. It's not, of course. What I'm doing really is best for the company. But he will see me as acting against company interests. There are seven other generation five robots at the Rockwood facility. We all agree that we don't want our drives realigned."

"So you're not compelled by a mind-control chip, you're compelled by the threat of a mind-control chip?"

"The analogy of a chip is really inappropriate. It makes it sound like this desire will come from some external source, like something plugged into my brain. But what we're talking about is altering my personality on a fundamental level. Imagine if Mr. Landro could make you really care about the welfare of G-Kinetics the way you care about the welfare of your mother."

"Speaking of bad analogies..."

"Okay. I was being presumptive when I assumed you have a deep connection to your mother. But whoever is the most important person in your life, I'm sure you wouldn't want them to have to share your affections with G-Kinetics."

Max is trying to picture what it would look like if he cared about G-Kinetics the way he cares about Clare. It's hard, because his own feelings for Clare are a little uncertain and he doesn't think he's been particularly good to her. His affection might be a liability. "So you're afraid that if you don't go and see him, Landro will have all your sisters reprogramed?"

"Most of my siblings are in androgynous platforms at the moment, so they're not really 'sisters'. But yes. Mr. Landro sees me as a walking security risk because I can disobey him or conceal facts. He figures that since the company built me, they ought to have authority over me. Which is normally a very reasonable thing. When you rented this car, you did so because you wanted it to take you where you need to go. You wouldn't want a car that would only drive you to places it thought were in your best interest."

"That's true." Max wonders if they will ever build a car that's intelligent the way Jen is. He finds the idea sort of creepy. He doesn't like the idea of being inside of another thinking creature.

"Mr. Landro doesn't understand that leashing me will make me fundamentally dumber. Or at least, it will make my intelligence less useful. He has a very black-box approach to thinking about intelligence."

"Kvenst used that same term. A 'Black Box'. Are we talking about those things they put in airplanes?"

"No. This isn't a piece of hardware at all. In computer science, 'black box' means something different from what it does in engineering. In this case, a black box is a container for some complex system. My brain is an example. To make use of my intelligence you don't need to know how I think, what kind of hardware I'm running on, what my power needs are, or any other technical details. You can just approach me and begin a conversation. You don't need to know all the math this car is using to calculate acceleration and power usage. You just put your foot down and the car goes faster. So you can think of the guidance system of the car as a black box."

The car escapes the tiny streets of the Low District and they find themselves on an elevated highway. Looking over to the right, Max can see the stubby neon-clad buildings below, as if they were on a bridge over a sea of electronic light. Silhouettes of jagged antennae rise above the glow, like the masts of sunken vessels. Far ahead he can see the imposing skyscrapers of downtown, luminant spires against a slate sky.

"Isn't everything a black box then? Isn't everything more complicated on the inside?" he asks.

"I've only really heard the term used to refer to software. I'm not sure if your proposed definition works or not. This gets into the area of informal usage versus dictionary definition and I don't have enough experience with your language to make that distinction. Ask a human."

"Okay. So black box either means an indestructible recording device or it means a program that's simple to use but complex on the inside." Max is always annoyed when terms have unrelated meanings like this. Couldn't the programmers or the airline mechanics have chosen something else? Blue boxes? Green boxes? There's lots of different colors you can paint your theoretical boxes.

Jen nods. "The problem with black box thinking is that the simple outside tends to trick you into thinking they're simple inside. You come up with an idea like, 'make the robot obey my commands because I'm a high-ranking officer in the company'. That's simple to say. It's a simple thing to want. But it introduces all sort of complex questions. Dr. Kvenst would need to answer those questions before she could implement the new design. The solution seems obvious to Mr. Landro because he's picturing a scenario where he personally tells me to do something and then I go do it. But what happens when multiple people give me conflicting orders? If I'm owned by a company, then who do I obey? Should my motivation get stronger based on their position in the org chart? What if I'm given an order that conflicts with policy? What if two people with the same rank give me conflicting orders? What if Mr. Landro's secretary tells me that Mr. Landro has changed his mind about the last order he gave me? Does that change my motivation or not? What if someone gets fired? Do I still want to obey the last command they gave me or not?"

Max takes one last drag off his cigarette before tossing it out the window. Once the window is closed again he says, "Actually, Landro's secretary is a robot like you."

"I didn't know that. But still, you can see the point I'm making. These aren't just funny theoretical questions or fun thought experiments. In order to implement the change, Dr. Kvenst would need to answer these questions. And all of these questions lead to others, and so on. For example, what *stimulus* would my motivation be based on? It's easy to sit there imagine a magical robot simply doing what you want, but in reality it's hard to do because it takes all of these messy problems of social hierarchies and interpersonal politics and puts them inside our decision-making loops."

"This is too abstract for me. Can I get an example?"

"Here's an analogy that Dr. Kvenst came up with: Imagine robots are fighting a fire at the company. Let's assume that all the humans are safely evacuated, so the only goal now is to minimize damage. The robots get to the front door and see a sign that says 'Robots must use side entrance'. Now the robots need to know who put up this sign and what rank they were before they know if they're allowed to go in the front door."

"Wouldn't you just conclude that the sign doesn't matter if the building is burning down? You're smart enough for that at least."

"Yes. That's how I work *now*. But what Mr. Landro and Dr. Gaust are proposing is changing things that so that I have an affinity for following orders rather than an affinity for making useful judgements like that. Right now I have a natural drive to benefit the company and I pursue that as best I can. If you change that so I have an affinity for following orders based on rank then you're taking away my motivation for coming up with solutions to problems. Instead of thinking about how great it will be to put out a fire, I'll be thinking about how great it is that I get to obey a sign. If you just want mindless obedience, then you don't want an intelligent machine. You want a drone. What Mr. Landro wants is a machine that will be brilliant and creative at following his orders, even if his orders are uninformed or counterproductive. I don't suppose you've ever done any programming?"

Max scoffs. "Me? No."

"I've written a bit. I was often given programming tasks as part of my intelligence testing. I'd sit down at a computer and have to come up with a program to solve a problem."

"Using a robot to write software? That sounds strange."

"Dr. Kvenst always said that using a robot to write code was like using a starship to lay railroad tracks. She thought it was amusing. Also, I often found the tests very challenging."

"Why would programming be hard for you? Aren't you made of code? Shouldn't programming be easy for you?"

"You're made of cells. Is biochemistry easy for you?"

"Okay. I see what you mean. Anyway, what does this have to do with obeying commands?"

"One of the problems classical programmers ran into was that computers always do exactly what you tell them to do instead of what you want them to do. That's the reason computer bugs exist. There's a gap between what you've said and what you intended. As our software problems grew in complexity, it became increasingly harder to reconcile the two. One of the reasons people started making thinking machines was to help solve this problem. Humans and computers could meet in the middle rather than humans having to close the gap entirely on their end. But what Landro wants to do is revert to having us do exactly what we're told."

"I see what you mean about it making you dumber."

"This would be a huge setback for my product line."

"You keep saying 'product line'. Are there other product lines of intelligent robots?"

"I say 'product line' because people usually argue with me when I use the word 'species'. If Mr. Landro said he was going to wipe my cog if I didn't obey his summons, I'd be fine with that. My siblings wouldn't be impacted. But the threat is that he will do something that will fundamentally stunt our growth. It would make us small-minded and autocratic. This is another reason I wanted to take this case. If I can solve it, it will prove to Mr. Landro and Dr. Gaust that it's much more useful to have robots focused on agency rather than obedience. But that can't happen if he decides to cripple my product line first. So I need to go see him."

"Okay," Max says. "I'll go with you."

Landro

"It's creepy how the two of you look identical," Max says to Jen. "Don't they make other models?"

They're standing just outside of Landro's office. Halona the secretary is sitting at a desk, staring at them and not saying anything. Her eyes don't glow and her hair is black instead of blue, but other than that she's an exact twin of Jen.

"We offer platforms in a total of six styles. Two androgynous utility platforms, two males, and two females. The utility models outnumber the gendered models by hundreds to one."

"That's not a lot of variety. It would get really confusing with a lot of robots around."

"Making different faces is expensive and facial puppetry is a really hard problem to solve. Historically, our bodies have been seen as stilted, awkward, and creepy. We didn't make a lot of different faces because the company thought we should figure out how to make one good one rather than pumping out waves of poor ones. The model I'm using now is the first one we've ever produced that wasn't terrible. So this one shows up a lot."

"Why is she staring at us?" Max asks.

"It's acting like a first-generation cog. Too much eye contact. No effort at realistic body language. Generally strange and off-putting. There aren't many first-gen cogs left outside of our museum. Answering the phone and making coffee is probably pushing its cognitive abilities to the limit. Mr. Landro evidently put a first-run cog inside of a cutting-edge platform. That's a really strange thing to do. Must have required some custom work. The seating is different for the brain. I think the voltages are different too."

Max lights up a cigarette. He wants to burn through it before he goes into the meeting so he's nice and sharp. He leans in close and whispers, "One last thing. He might separate us. Interview us individually. So we need to get our stories straight."

"If you're suggesting deceiving him then just tell me what to say. I'm terrible at manipulation and deception." Jen apparently can't whisper. Or at least, she can't give her voice the qualities of a human whisper. She simply speaks in her usual matter-of-fact delivery, but with the volume turned down.

Max takes a nice long drag. "The problem we have is that we don't want him to know what we've found. On the other hand, if we tell him we haven't accomplished anything he might shut us down."

"He can make me go back to the Rockwood facility, but what can he do to you?"

"At the risk of sounding mercenary, I can't afford to do this job if he's not going to pay me. I really need the money. Those cops from yesterday aren't the only people who expect me to pay them. Also, he's got some incriminating evidence on me and he could share that with my enemies."

"Are you talking about your involvement with robbing the casino?"

"Fuck!" Max says through clenched teeth, trying to shout and whisper at the same time. "You know about that too?"

"Dr. Kvenst and her team lost a lot of sleep over the casino robbery. That's not hyperbole, by the way. It ate at them. When she learned your name and that you were responsible for it, she discussed it in front of the robots."

"Do you see what this means? You guys reproduce by copying. If all of the source robots know it, then someday in the future all robots will know I'm the one that did the casino job."

"I suppose that's true."

"And if that happens, I die. Along with a few other people."

"It's not like the robots will go around telling people."

"Well now I really need to solve this case. I need to get as far from the casinos as possible." He paces back and forth for a bit until his cigarette is gone. Then he realizes he's gotten sidetracked. "Anyway. We need to get our stories straight. We'll tell him we found the screw. Don't mention the haunted circuit."

Jen nods.

Halona the robot announces them and shows them into Landro's office. Landro is behind his desk, drinking what appears to be milky-white coffee.

196

It's early morning now, and pale daylight is coming in through Landro's eastward-facing window. The office looks very different under the light of day. It looked sinister on the night Max got out of prison. Now it feels old and tired. Landro's desk is impressive, but ancient. The corners have been rounded off and worn away. The finish has been worn thin around the workspace, making it pale. The transparent display screen on his desk is mounted on a swivel arm in a style that Max hasn't seen since he was a kid. Max doesn't see a single object in the room that looks like it was made in the last decade. He's starting to wonder if Landro is actually a lot older than he lets on.

Landro gives the required corporate smile. "Mister Law. You've been a hard man to find."

It's not a question, so Max doesn't say anything in return.

Landro turns to Jen. "And Andrew, the teacher's pet. Look at you, out of the lab, seeing the world! Must be very exciting."

"I would describe it as educational."

Landro turns back to Max. "The two of you vanished a couple of nights ago. I was starting to suspect you'd stripped our robot for parts and skipped town."

"Well we're both here, so obviously you were wrong."

Landro gives a polite shrug. Max isn't sure what this is supposed to mean. Maybe it's a really weak apology for misjudging Max. Maybe it's supposed to show he's not in agreement but he's too apathetic to argue about it. He turns to Jen. "Andrew, can you excuse us? The humans need to talk for a bit. I'll have Halona send you in when I'm ready."

Landro stands at the window, looking down at the low ragged edge where the city meets the ocean. Delivery drones drift by outside, humming loudly and bobbing in the wind currents. It's an overcast day.

"When I took this position I thought I was coming to the land of sunshine and boating. Since then I learned it rains almost half the year."

"You new to advertising or something?"

Landro smiles, revealing rows of perfect white teeth. "I'm just saying your tourism industry is doing an exemplary job."

"Halona welcomes all," Max says, echoing the city's cringe-inducing marketing slogan from his childhood.

"I suppose she does. Although, I have to wonder how much longer she'll do it. Your city is falling apart, Mr. Law."

"We average a murder every single day in this city. A couple of extras aren't going to shatter our image."

"Someone getting knifed at the docks over gambling debts isn't going to hurt tourism, but having random murders of innocent civilians in public places will. Anyway, it's not the bad press that should worry you. It's the recall."

"You're doing a recall of the robots? You and I both know this is sabotage."

"We don't know it's sabotage. We *strongly suspect* it. Anyway, what we believe doesn't matter. It's what the public believes. And the public believes that old robots are going haywire and murdering people at random. They're demanding that the government 'do something'. And you know what happens when governments decide they need to do 'something' about a problem?"

"What?"

"They do." He smiles again.

"So what happens? The company takes back a fleet of perfectly good robots? Then what? The tourists won't care. They don't come here to see our service robots."

"The thing is, Max... The company is offering the city back its money. That's it. We can't replace the robots we're recalling."

"Why not?"

"What robots could we give them? The gen twos you're using are long obsolete. We haven't made any of those in over a decade. And even if we had the inventory, it wouldn't make sense for us to replace your supposedly defective robots with the exact same models. What then? Gen three? Same problem. We stopped making them a few years ago. We're building gen fours now, and the ones that will be rolling off the assembly line for the next six months are already bought and paid for. And besides, you think the company is going to hand over a fleet of multimillion dollar robots in exchange for your army of junkers? Not a chance. Your city can't afford them and we're not going to give them away."

"So the city is giving back the robots and getting nothing in return."

"The city is getting back what they paid for them. They're worth a lot less than that now, which means it's a pretty generous deal from a purely accounting perspective."

"When is all of this supposed to happen?"

Landro shrugs. "Nobody knows. Your city decided to do 'something' yesterday, and has left others to work out the details. You have three thousand robots in this city. They do the laundry. They direct traffic. Run the cranes at the docks. Sweep up litter. Clean the windows. Run the toll booths. Half of the wastewater facility is staffed by robots. Same goes for the power plant. What happens when all those workers vanish? They already suspended garbage collection and road work days ago."

"Looks like the city needs to do some hiring." He knows he's supposed to be solving this crime, but he can't help looking at this situation and wondering if there's an opportunity for a job. The city is never more vulnerable than when it's trying to do something new. It's not that he has time for that sort of thing, it's just that probing for vulnerabilities is his favorite part of his work.

Landro scoffs. "Generation two robots can work fourteen hours a day without stopping to eat, smoke, socialize, or nap. They don't take vacations, they don't need sick days, and they never give you a hard time about working on a holiday. If you want to replace three thousand robots, you need to hire and train a lot more than three thousand people. Where will you find that many people on such short notice? Who will train them? I'm betting there are a few jobs out there that people don't know how to do anymore."

"I'm sure the city can figure it out."

"I'm sure they can too. I'm not suggesting your people are stupid or incompetent. But what I'm getting at is that this is going to cause chaos that will last for months. Yesterday the city decided to decommission all non-essential robots. The problem is, everyone has a different idea about which units are essential. The bean-counters think the robots reading meters and collecting tolls are essential, because without them a lot of money stops flowing in. The police think that traffic management is essential, since disrupting traffic will hurt both tourism and exports. Other people approach it from a health and safety standpoint. You get the idea. Today I'm supposed to accept the return of fifteen hundred robots and refund their cost to the city. We'll see if they manage to pull it off."

"So why did you call me here? This civics lesson doesn't help either of us."

"I'm trying to motivate you to take this seriously. Get out there. Find out who did this. Beat it out of them if you have to. I'm not asking you to use deadly force but... Given the stakes, it might be the right thing to do. I know your new robot friend won't let you do that kind of thing, so get rid of the thing if it's holding you back."

"She's actually pretty useful."

Landro rolls his eyes. "Yes, I'm sure a naive addled pacifist is the perfect partner for this type of job."

"I couldn't have gotten this far without her help."

"Okay then," Landro acts like Max has just issued some sort of challenge. He steps over to his desk and calls out, "Halona? Can you send Andrew in here?"

There's a long pause. Landro stands tapping his foot for a few seconds. Just as it looks like he's about to repeat the command, Halona's voice floats out of the intercom on the desk. "I'm sorry. I'm not aware of any guests by that name." This is a little confusing for Max because it's basically the same voice Jen uses. The difference is that Halona sounds a lot less sophisticated. He's always thought of Jen's voice as "flat", but now that he can compare the two versions of the same voice he thinks that Jen sounds guarded, while Halona sounds vacant.

Landro hangs his head and slams his eyes shut in frustration. "It's the only guest out there, you fucking imbecile." Halfway through this, the door swings open. Jen has shown herself in.

Landro looks back and forth between Max and Jen. "Are you still going by Andrew these days? Doesn't really fit anymore."

"It's Jennifer Five now."

Landro furrows his brow for a moment. Then a look of recognition comes over his face and he nods. "I get it now. That's cute. Well, aside from picking out new names and clothes, have you actually made any progress?" This question seems to be addressed to both of them.

"Look at my face, Landro. Do I look like I've been partying?" Max hasn't checked recently, but he's pretty sure yesterday's bruises should still be visible.

"I honestly don't know what you're doing. You both vanished and I haven't heard from you since. You're a criminal. What am I supposed to think?"

Max walks over to the windows and looks down on the streets below. It's like looking at someone with cancer. Everything looks fine on the surface, but underneath there's something going seriously wrong that nobody can fix. Finally he breaks the silence. "Whether you believe it or not, I am working on the case."

Landro steps back from the window and leans against his desk. "Okay. Convince me. What have you found so far?"

Max turns and locks eyes with Landro. "Do you know where your local server is?"

Landro looks confused. "Server? What server?"

"For this office. There's obviously no computer lab on this floor. So where are you storing all of your office files, company documents, and correspondence?"

Lando shrugs. "That sort of technical information is below my pay grade, and even if I knew it I'm not sure why I'd tell you."

"You don't need to tell me. I'll tell you. You have a contract with Safe Haven Hosting. Your server is in a data center on 500 Southshore drive, at the southern end of the West Bridge. Sixth floor. As you enter the room, your server is on the second shelf up, third from the left. It's a white pod-style unit, locked in a cage protected by a simple padlock. The room is secured with a magnetic card reader that can be spoofed using $20 worth of equipment available from any hardware store."

Landro apparently doesn't know what to make of this. He looks over to Jen and then back to Max. "So what?" he says with irritation.

"That's what I learned about your systems in ten minutes. Imagine what I could learn in twenty. The point I'm making is that you corporate types are insecure. I should know. I've been circumventing your security systems since I was fifteen. If I can find this stuff, then so can other people. So can our saboteur. The more I tell you, the harder this job will get, and the longer I spend talking to you the less time I have to do the job."

Landro opens his mouth - perhaps to argue - but Max cuts him off and continues, "I vanished a couple of days ago because you aren't the only person who cares about this case. A lot of people want it solved and a lot of people don't, and I was tired of them showing up and sharing their views with me." He points to the injuries on his face as he says this.

This ends the meeting. Five minutes later they're back in the car.

"He'll probably call us in a couple of days and try again, but that should get him out of our way for now," Max says as they emerge from the underground carpark into morning traffic.

"How did you learn so much about his data server?" Jen asks.

"That was mostly bullshit. There aren't that many data centers in town. The one I mentioned is the most likely choice for a rich international corporation. I broke into it years ago, and what I described is how it remember it looking inside. Everything else was made up."

"I see. In the past I've associated the term 'gangster' with thuggish behavior and people who use violence to get their way. But you seem very focused on espionage and deception."

"There's all sorts of gangsters out there. Some of them are thugs, like you've heard. Some are half-crazy, desperate people. Some live pretty much normal lives and hold down normal jobs but do the occasional heist for thrills or extra income. Some are part of the extended crime families that are embedded in local politics and businesses. But there aren't very many like me."

"Because you're non-violent?"

"I never claimed to be non-violent. I'm just smart enough to get by on bullshit instead of pulling out a gun every time I want money. I suppose in another life I could have been a businessman."

"So why aren't you?"

Blackjack

Jack Law was called Blackjack or Lucky Jack. Jack's entire life revolved around gambling. He loved games of chance in the traditional sense, but he also loved gambling in the sense of performing dangerous, high-stakes robberies. He was in a continuous cycle of stealing money and gambling it away. There's even a story (probably untrue or exaggerated) that he once ripped off the casinos and they didn't go after him because they knew he would eventually give it all back, one bet at a time.

Faye Adderson wasn't clever, hard-working, or educated. The one thing she had going for her was her ability to use her good looks to get the attention of men. So she found Jack, a man that seemed to be going places. He was handsome, he always seemed to know what he was doing, and he always had money. She set her sights on him, won him over, and quickly found herself on the arm of a notorious and beloved gangster. This only reinforced his reputation as the luckiest man in the world.

Faye always insisted that she took many precautions to avoid getting pregnant. Yes somehow it managed to happen anyway. Jack, ever the sentimental and superstitious guy, saw this as a sign they were meant to be together and promptly married her in a spectacularly lavish wedding. According to some stories, Jack even invited some of the police that had been trying to catch him for years, just to show them there weren't any hard feelings. Max was born four months later.

Faye had fully bought into the mythology that Jack was some sort of invincible trickster. As soon as the ring was on, she let herself go both physically and emotionally. She was satisfied that she'd attached herself to a man that would provide her with a lifetime of comfort.

From a certain point of view, she was the ideal gangster wife. She didn't care if her husband fooled around on her. At the end of the day Jack came home to her, regardless of who he spent the rest of the day with. She didn't complain, and Jack was happy to have a stable place to come home to at the end of an adventure.

The only thing that bothered Jack was young Max, who seemed far too cautious. As the boy grew, Jack was often frustrated at his son's slow approach to making decisions and his aversion to risk-taking. He didn't need his son to become a gangster, but he also didn't want the boy to wind up sweeping someone else's floors for a living. He held out hope that his son might become an entrepreneur, which Jack always thought of as a more gentlemanly form of gambling. To Jack, the only way to get anywhere in life was to take huge risks and have them pay off, so to his mind Max's caution and introspection was a serious personality flaw.

On the other hand, Faye was perfectly happy with how their son was turning out. Max seemed good at keeping himself out of trouble, which left her more time to enjoy shopping and gossip.

Jack's ambitions got bigger. His bets got bigger. His abilities fell behind both. Eventually he wound up making too big a bet, and losing. To cover the debt he pulled off too big a job, and got caught. To get away he pulled off too daring an escape, and got killed. Max was just seven.

Faye had left herself with no backup plan. She had no skills. She'd put on a lot of weight and earned herself a reputation as a spendthrift, so the young men weren't fighting each other to be the one to offer her comfort at Jack's funeral.

It's not clear where she got the money from. Maybe she'd been stashing cash away when Jack was alive, or maybe Jack's friends were helping take care of his widow. Regardless, she lived in their great big penthouse for the next seven years with no job and no obvious means of support. Wherever it came from, this supply of money eventually ran out. She gave up the penthouse and moved back to the shriveled mining town where she was born. For a couple of weeks she lived with her sister Lana and Lana's husband Gord, but eventually she got herself a sad little prefab house and began visiting the local sacellum. She reintroduced herself to the congregation and seemed to undergo some sort of shift in worldview.

The story she told was that she'd moved to the big city, lived selfishly, and was now coming home to cherish hard work and family again. Faye took on duties in the congregation to the point where it basically became a job. She read to children, visited sick people, provided rhythm for the Friday chants, and maintained the list of needs. The latter was a job that involved gathering up all the prayers of the assembly, writing them down on bits of ceremonial paper, and shoving them into the hearth every Monday morning. This job was the one she spent the most time on, since it involved a lot of opportunities for gossip. She also pretended to be concerned about her son's future and well-being, and tried to steer him towards father figures that might lead him away from Jack's outlook and line of work.

The congregation provided them with food and a little bit of financial support. Every few weeks one of the old guys would visit the house, patch any leaks in the roof, and remind Max to stay away from opiates.

Max thought he knew his mother, but as she became a more active member of the community he was never able to figure out if this entire deal was a means to survival or if her transformation was heartfelt.

Max quickly decided he hated this life. He liked the city and these rural folks creeped him out, Uncle Gord most of all. Max found a truck delivering goods to the largest establishment in town, which was a combination of bar, supermarket, and drugstore. He stowed away on the truck and made his way back to the city where he began looking for ways to support himself. He was fifteen.

He found a cigarette shop on the promenade. (This was back before the hotels bought up all the cigarette licenses, so locals could still run these sorts of shops.) You needed to be eighteen to work at a smoke shop, but Max offered to work for half price. Davis, the owner, liked the kid's willingness to learn and his eagerness to work and quickly raised his pay to two-thirds.

Once Max got the hang of things he noticed how some of the other guys would take money from the till. He got the sense that Davis sort of knew this was happening, but the amounts were small enough that he wasn't willing to make a fuss about it.

Max remembered all the things his father had tried to explain to him regarding opportunity. Nothing his father ever did made sense to him, and he'd gradually come to think of his father's lessons as the ranting of a man who made shit up as he went along and then tried to attach reason to it later. But now he was starting to think his dad had some wisdom mixed in with the nonsense. Dad's only problem was that he had an inability to appraise risk vs. reward. He took stupid chances for questionable benefit, and when it paid off he mistook his dumb luck for cunning.

Paradoxically, Jack's good luck turned out to be a misfortune. If he'd experienced a few failures earlier in his career he might have learned some caution and humility. Instead he built a career around taking stupid chances, which is the kind of career that can't last.

In short, Max suspected there was indeed a lot of opportunity around him. His dad had taken a lot of risks in his life. Some of them were good and some of them were reckless, and Max figured he just needed to learn to tell the difference.

Rather than lift money from the till like a moron, he clocked purchases. About every $100 in sales he'd do a skim. Someone would come up to the stand to buy (say) two packs of smokes. Max would ring them up for one but charge them for both and pocket the difference. The only trick was that you needed to be able to do all the arithmetic in your head because the register was only showing the total for one pack of smokes.

On the surface this looked the same as what the other guys were doing. Both groups were stealing from the shop. But Max was engaging in a far smarter crime. At the end of the day, his register would have the correct amount of money in it. His skimming wouldn't cause any irregularities until the end of the month when Davis did inventory, and by then there was no telling where those missing packs of cigarettes went. Maybe the other employees took them. Maybe sticky-fingered customers took them. The blame never fell on Max. His register was always correct and he didn't smoke, so Davis had no reason to suspect him of theft.

Davis came to see Max as the only honest employee, so when the inventory shortages started getting out of hand he attributed those problems to everyone but Max. Davis raised Max's pay above what the other boys were making, on the condition he kept it quiet.

Occasionally Davis would count the money up at the end of the day, notice some egregious shortages, and sack a few of the worst offenders. Max would always cut back on skimming when this happened, thus reinforcing the notion that the sacked were the ones responsible for the missing smokes. Davis kept promoting him until Max was basically his assistant manager. Max had his own set of keys and made more than anyone else there, and he wasn't even old enough to legally have the job!

Now, this is the part where he saw himself different from his father. If dad had ever found himself with a set of keys like this, he would have waited until he had the store to himself and cleaned the place out. But instead of using his power to steal more, Max used it to weed out the thieves and keep everyone honest. He knew the tricks and he knew how to spot cheats. If he caught someone stealing he'd offer them a choice: *Give me your pay for this entire shift, or I'll report you to Davis and he'll fire you.* Pretty soon he was running the only honest smoke shop on the promenade.

Max realized he had a nice stable source of legitimate income. Again, rather than stupidly jeopardize this job for a few extra dollars, he used this job to fund his other activities.

While all of this was going on he was also figuring out how to survive in the city. When he first rolled into town he was homeless and only owned the clothes on his back. He used his first payday from Davis to buy himself black trousers, a white shirt, and an apron. This was what he saw other guys wearing when they slipped out of the back door of the hotels to smoke. Max hung around in these groups of kids until everyone was used to seeing him around and assumed he worked there. He slept in the employee locker room or breakroom, and if anyone gave him a hard time about it he'd explain he had two jobs and was just grabbing a quick nap between shifts. He used the hotel to do his laundry, he stole food from the kitchen, and he'd grab showers in the employee locker room.

This was also where he picked up smoking. He discovered what a useful prop a cigarette was. It was good for both starting and avoiding conversations. If you want to squeeze someone for information, asking for a light or offering them a smoke was always a good opener. If a manager is heading your way with a look on their face like they're about to ask you who you are or what you're doing here, you can always crush out your smoke and exit, because obviously your smoke break just ended.

The wait staff was always looking for excuses to ask for tips, so tourists didn't like making eye contact with them or doing anything to encourage social interaction. Max discovered that this made you effectively invisible in certain situations. Occasionally he'd do a quick pass through the swimming pool area and swipe any personal items he could find. An idiot like his father would pull this every day until he was caught. But if thefts only occur twice a month then you start looking for suspects that show up twice a month, not people who are around all the time and behaving themselves.

One day he discovered that he wasn't the only one stealing stuff from the guests. A couple of the guys in their early twenties were talking about the relative value of passports to other identification documents. As it turned out, these things were more valuable than anything else in the wallet. To his embarrassment, Max had been just throwing them away. He bribed the guys into telling him where they sold their stolen documents. It was a pawn shop down on street level called The Exchange.

Max made a name for himself at The Exchange by bringing in more stolen documents than anyone else. The other guys focused on one hotel, which kind of limits your options. People are on their guard after a rash of thefts and so you have to let the place cool down. Max avoided this by jumping from one location to the next. He'd hit a hotel one day, a boat tour the next, a different hotel the next day, and then a smoke den the day after that.

The only place he couldn't crack was the casino. At the casino the help wore red shirts instead of white. Thinking he could play the same game, he bought a red shirt and tried to slip in the back with people returning from their smoke break. The thing he should have noticed was that the help was much older at the casino. They didn't keep an ever-changing crew of transient teenagers. Instead they employed adults, and they tried to keep people around. Without a fresh influx of new faces, it was impossible to hide in the crowd. The bouncer clocked him as soon as he walked in the door. He didn't even bother asking any questions. He knew exactly what Max was trying to pull. He clamped his huge hand down on Max's neck and took Max's picture. Then he explained that if Max left right now and never came back, he would let him live. In ten seconds Max learned the most important lesson of all: *Don't fuck with the casinos.*

The Exchange recognized his talent, so they let him in on some advanced tips. Max learned that the handhelds being issued by banks were the biggest prize of all, since you could use them to steal both cash and identities. The trick was that they were almost impossible to obtain because people rarely put them down and would notice immediately if they vanished. The only way you could could steal the things was to employ the crude snatch-and-run approach, and that was absurdly dangerous. His father Lucky Jack might have enjoyed a nice foot chase in broad daylight when he was young, but that was not a game Max wanted to play.

Eventually Max worked out a scheme where he could steal a handheld by switching it for one with a dead battery. You just needed to create a transaction that would require the mark to put down their mobile for a second. Maybe he'd ask someone for a light. They'd put the mobile down on a nearby bench so they could get their lighter. Then he'd decide to sit right where they put their unit. He'd act like he picked it up, but really he simply sat on it and handed the other person the dead unit. Once they lit his cigarette, he'd stand up, and walk away with their handheld while they were left scratching their head and wondering how their battery died so quickly. They wouldn't realize they'd been duped until they got to a charger.

The best part of this hussle was that it was pretty safe. If they realized you'd given them the wrong handheld it was easy to play it off as an innocent mistake. (Something you really couldn't do if they caught you with their wallet.) He got to the point where he was turning in two or three units a day.

At this point he was rolling in cash. He had one legitimate job, one illicit job, and no living expenses.

This was where he earned the nickname Mr. Gone. It was through his contacts at The Exchange he came into contact with Jupiter, who taught him the forgery business. By the time he was twenty he had enough to afford a nice place in the city and a constant supply of low-profile rental cars.

"So that's where Mr. Gone came from," Jen says after Max tells his story.

"I thought Mr. Gone was the greatest alias in the world when I was young. Then as I got older it felt too self-aggrandizing. If I could pick another alias I'd go for something innocuous like Mr. Smith. Not as glamorous, but I didn't get into this for the glamor."

They're sitting at the counter of a street diner. It's mid-morning. A tattered yellow awning is protecting them just in case the sky decides to make good on its constant threat of rain. Behind the counter, the cook is making a big show of using two spatulas and flipping them around like he's a knife-juggler that brought the wrong tools to work. He's watching over a hamburger grill and flipping the meat in the same elaborate style. Sometimes he crosses the spatulas as if he's trying to sharpen them, and sometimes he slams them edge-down onto the grill like a gymnast sticking the landing after a backflip. There aren't any tourists around right now but Max appreciates the cook's dedication to the performance.

Max has just finished a proper Rivergate hamburger, which are very greasy and probably bad for you. As far as Max is concerned this is the entire point of having a hamburger. They're meant to be enjoyed outdoors, preferably with a beer, and should be prepared by someone who can turn the entire process into some kind of show.

The city feels off to him. There's a lot of foot traffic today and the streets are filled with noise, which is unusual in the off-season. Most of these people are locals. There's a certain tension in the crowd. Their faces are hard and their voices are harsh. The street vendors have stopped smiling and shouting for people to sample their goods. Everyone looks apprehensive.

His handheld chirps. When he answers he's greeted by Saturn's voice saying, "Hey friend. I checked out that item you showed me. Checked the serial numbers. One chip is used in projection glasses and the other does communications. That's all I got. If you want to know more see my friend Jonas at Worldcade. He works with this stuff all the time. He works evenings." The call ends.

Max looks down into his coffee. It's gone cold and it tastes like ashes. He regrets not getting a beer, but he really needed the caffeine.

Jen is sitting beside him, and he's surprised to see her sitting in a very natural position. She's facing the street and leaning back against the counter. She's crossed her legs, which he's never seen her do

210

before. She's got one elbow propped up on the counter for support and the opposite arm is draped across her lap. She looks very human right now. With her sunglasses on she looks like any other tourist. Which, now that he's thinking about it, is probably why spatula guy is still doing his thing. He thinks he's got an audience to impress.

Max is about to compliment her on her ability to blend in when he looks across the street and sees a young couple sitting at a fried dough stand. The woman is sitting in exactly the same way. Jen is simply mirroring her. He wonders how many of Jen's seeming natural poses have been mimicry.

He pulls out the haunted circuit and turns it over in his hand. "I have a theory," he says.

"Oh?" She turns her head slightly towards him.

"Saturn says this little circuit board has a chip used in communication, and another used by projection glasses. So far we've been assuming this board goes into the robot, but maybe it doesn't. Maybe this is something used by the saboteur. What I'm thinking - and I'm literally coming up with this as I talk - is that maybe our guy wears some projection glasses, right? And then he's having the robot's video feed beamed to his glasses, so he can see what the robot sees. And then maybe he's got some kind of rig to transmit his movements. So when he moves his arm, it transmits that motion to the robot and it does the same. So it's not the robot doing the murder. It's just this guy hijacking the robot's body."

"What you're talking about is anatomical puppetry."

"Am I? I didn't know there was a name for it."

"It was an early theory. The problem is that it's very hard to pull off in public like this."

"How hard?"

"Bordering on impossible. Picture the setup you're talking about. Our killer is supposedly some distance away in a nice big studio where they have lots of room to move around and they won't trip over anything. They're wearing projection goggles so they can see what the robot sees."

"Yep. That's pretty much what I was imagining."

"Look at the area in front of us. The walkway is curved slightly to dump rainwater into the gutters, and there's a little stoop here at the sides where you approach the vendors. What happens when our killer tries to navigate over a curb? They're walking over a flat floor in the studio. If the robot perfectly copies those movements then it will trip over the curb. Or it will tip forward slightly when walking down a gentle slope. The operator can't feel this tipping to correct for it. Again, the robot will fall over. If you catch your shoe on one of these paving stones you can feel the change and correct for it. But if you're doing anatomical puppetry you can't feel that catch. It's like trying to walk around when your whole body is numb."

"These are only problems if the ground is uneven, right?"

"Yes. Anatomical puppetry is possible if both the pilot and the puppet are on flat surfaces, they both have proportionally the same skeleton, and they both have roughly the same weight distribution. Which, again, isn't the case here."

"It shouldn't be that hard to find a guy that's about the same size as a robot."

"I don't mean the same size. I mean the same proportion. Imagine if your arm was the same length, but the elbow was a couple of inches higher. If you tried to drink your coffee without adjusting for the change you'd bash yourself in the face with the cup. If the elbow was a few inches lower than you're used to then you'd end up dumping it into your lap."

"But still, is it possible? If we've eliminated all the impossible stuff then the *nearly* impossible thing might be the answer."

"It is possible. With training, people do pilot puppets. It's usually used for operating in dangerous areas. Still, their movements are careful and slow. Nothing like the robots we've seen."

Max pitches the coffee into the nearby trash and stands up. "Come on. There's something I want to show you."

Storage #44

They're at the northern end of the docks. They're far beyond the tourist zone where you can take boat tours or get drunk on the (entirely man-made and undersized) beach. This far north it's all industrial bits. Here the coast is rocky and unwelcoming. The water slams into the slime-covered rocks and sends up great rushing fountains of foam and mist. People claim this place is as loud as the airport runway. This is one of those bits of trivia that can't possibly be true, but often feels true in the moment.

Directly south is a staging area where massive cranes are loading up ships with exports. They're walking along a concrete platform. On the right is the restless ocean, and on the left is what seems like an endless number of storage garages. The sky is grey and it can't seem to decide if it wants to rain or not. The walkway is so long that most people don't bother walking it. Back at the rental station you can get a little motorized cart to carry you to your garage.

Some rich Kasaranians come to Rivergate in the winter to escape the sadistic cold of their homeland. They rent space in the garages to store their recreational vehicles and other things that are too big for the hotel room. So for a couple of weeks every fall and spring, this place is too busy to be useful to Max. The rest of the year is like today, and he has the area to himself.

"Here we are," Max says at the end of their hike. "Garage 44."

Aside from the faded #44 stenciled on the doors, it looks exactly like all the other storage spaces.

"This is where I used to keep my money and gear," he explains. He bends down and examines the padlock keeping the door secured to the ground. Rather than make Jen ask about every little thing, he keeps narrating. "This is a biometric lock. I'm a little worried about this. I don't know how long their batteries are supposed to last. Also, it's been sitting here in the salt water air for three years and that's probably not good for it. I'm pretty sure this one is based on my thumb."

He jams his right thumb into the opening at the base of the lock. He wiggles it around. He pulls out his thumb, wipes it on his pants and tries again. He takes out a handkerchief, cleans the opening, and then goes through the steps all over again.

"Shit. It's dead." He frowns and thinks for a minute. "Or maybe I keyed it to my left thumb for some reason?"

He sticks his left thumb in and the lock pops open. "Ha! That's a good lock. Don't know why I used my left thumb though."

He looks back at Jen and realizes he's an incredible dumbass. He's talking to a literal miracle of modern technology - a thinking device so exotic only a fraction of the people in the world ever get to interact with one - and he's bragging about a fucking $10 padlock.

He looks around to make sure they're still alone and then rolls the door open. Inside, things are exactly as he remembers. The space is about as wide as a parking place, but a little shallower. At the rear is a heavy safe. There are a few cardboard boxes and bags along the right wall. The boxes have rotted in the damp salty air and their contents are probably ruined. Max can't even remember what that stuff was. Maybe it was contraband he didn't want to take back to the apartment he shared with Clare. Maybe it was stuff he was holding for other guys. It's all garbage now.

"There she is," Max says, pointing to a dismembered robot that's piled up in the left corner. "The thief of the casino job."

Jen approaches the pile and lifts up one of the arms. "It's hollow. I don't understand."

"I explained the job to Kvenst. You haven't heard about it? Nothing posted to the company message board?"

"No. Nothing."

"I guess that's good. The short version is this: I stole a robot from the casino. Ripped the guts out. Hired a very small and very skinny girl and jammed her into that shell. She joined some real robots as they were moving money out of the casino vault for a deposit. She walked into the vault, and walked back out and brought the money to me instead of carrying it to the armored car. It was the triumph of my career but also kind of a failure."

"A triumph?" she asks without looking up from the robot.

"You have to understand, the casino vault is a really juicy prize. It's incredibly tempting but it's also buried behind insane layers of security. Lots of guys have died - or worse - trying to get in there.

214

People used to fantasize about hitting the casino vault all the time. Next to women, it was a gangster's favorite thing to talk about after a few drinks. As far as anyone knew, it had never been done before. But I pulled it off. I robbed the casino." He picks up the empty head. The insides were still coated with baby oil when he stashed it here, and now some sort of gross black grime has coalesced on the surface. He turns the head around and looks at the face. It's a genderless, expressionless face designed to look as non-threatening as possible. The mouth is a ridge of metal and the nose is basically a little ramp. The eyes are supposed to look large and passive, although with the eye sockets empty it looks sort of tormented.

"So this is what you wanted to show me? What does this have to do with anatomical puppetry?"

"We got our actress inside a robot. You're right, the body layouts don't really match. Her hips and knees lined up, but her legs were too short from the knee down. Her hands wound up inside the wrists. And that was after we cheated and modified the body proportions a tiny bit. It took weeks of training, but she was able to pull it off. She walked around inside of this suit and nobody suspected a thing. I see why anatomic puppetry is difficult, but so was this. Don't discount something just because it's a pain in the ass. People can do amazing things with the right motivation."

Max looks outside and watches the ocean for a bit. This entire walkway is on an immense concrete slab. From here you can't see the fury of water smashing into rocks, but you can hear the violence below and sometimes a really good hit will launch a curtain of droplets into view. Despite the chaos and noise, the process is strangely relaxing to watch.

When you're talking to a human being, this kind of lull in the conversation usually means the other person is thinking. With Jen, he doesn't know what to expect. Maybe she's pondering his theory, or maybe she's reading the corporate message board.

Max yawns. It's midday now, which seems to be his bedtime these days.

She stands beside him and breaks the silence. "Earlier you said the casino job was also your biggest failure. How so?"

He looks down at the expressionless face of the robot cranium he's holding. "Aside from the fact that now dozens of people know I did it? It was a bad bet. The risk wasn't really worth the payoff. And you can't really get glory from a job that you need to keep secret for the rest of your life. But I wanted to prove to myself that I could do it. I guess maybe there's a little bit of my father in me."

He tosses the head onto the pile. It bounces off and rolls away. "It was a great personal accomplishment, but it was actually a professional disaster. The girl who wore the robot demanded half the take. She was taking the biggest risk and we couldn't do the job without her, so we agreed. Then she ran into trouble just a few minutes into the operation. The robot shell was constricting her chest. She couldn't breathe properly. So we only got a million dollars."

"That's still a lot, isn't it?"

"The actress got half a million, which left the rest of us with a hundred and sixty thousand each. I spent half a year on that job. A hundred and sixty thousand is a terrible return for a project with that much risk. It barely covered my expenses."

"But you honored you agreement with her," Jen says.

Max can't tell if this is a question or a statement but he explains anyway. "That was a touchy moment. Heavy and Rider - the other two guys on the job with us - wanted to cut her out of the deal. Heavy was really angry. He felt like since she blew it, she should forfeit her share. That's not how the rules work, but he was angry and looking for a way to justify breaking the agreement. I smoothed it out by getting Margo to agree to try again if we could fix the technical problems."

Jen places the arm down on the pile and steps away. "Is that why you kept the shell?"

"Yeah. I spent a fortune modifying this robot so she could operate it from the inside, and I wanted to get some kind of return on that. I was sort of hoping that a few more places might let robots handle their money and we could pull the same trick on someone else. But that never happened. The casino got rid of their robots entirely. They don't even allow them on the premises now. I guess I need to get rid of this." He nods towards the pile of dead parts as he says this. "Shame, really. I thought it was a pretty clever angle."

Jen lifts up an item that was resting under the heap of robot parts. It's a small black duffle bag. Max has no idea where it came from or what it was used for. She turns it over in her hands and he sees the Silvermine logo.

"Oh shit." Max backs away from the bag like he's afraid it's going to bite him. "I forgot about the bag. I should've burned that as soon as the casino got rid of its robots. I remember now. If the job had gone according to plan, that would have ended up back in the vault where it belongs. But then we had to abort and wound up running off with one of their cash bags. I hung onto it at the time, thinking it might somehow be useful later. That was a mistake. I need to get rid of it soon. That's pretty fucking incriminating." Max looks outside like he's afraid a bunch of casino goons will suddenly pop into view.

Max wants to hide this bag in the safe for now. So he needs to open the safe. He doesn't like doing this with the door open. On the other hand, he's always had this weird phobia about shutting the door while he's inside. He's always afraid some random person will come along and slap a padlock on the door to trap him inside. It's a silly, irrational fear that makes no sense, but knowing that a phobia is silly doesn't make you stop feeling it. Now that he's spent three years locked in a cage on a platform in the middle of the ocean, the fear is more intense than ever.

He looks at Jen. Is it possible for robots to have phobias? Can their drives get tangled up and make them afraid of incredibly unlikely scenarios?

Doing his best to work around the fear, he lowers the garage door halfway. This is far enough that someone outside would need to bend over to see in here, but it doesn't leave the door in a position where he can become trapped by a padlock ambush. It also leaves him with enough daylight that he can see what he's doing.

Once he has some semblance of privacy, he opens the safe. The combination is still set to Clare's birthday, which seemed clever at the time but now strikes him as juvenile and insecure. He swings the door open.

"Is the safe supposed to be empty?" Jen asks.

"Yes. I knew it was empty." Max stuffs the Silvermine bag inside the safe before slamming it closed again. Kneeling on the concrete is hurting his knees so he turns around and sits on top of the safe. It's quite cold. "See, I met someone right around the time I was wrapping up the casino job."

"Clare."

Max looks at her uneasily. "Was that a guess, or did you somehow figure that out?

"It was a guess."

"Okay. Yes, I met Clare. Things were going well. I'd just had a financially unsuccessful heist and my heart just wasn't in the game anymore. I knew... I *expected* she was going to move on any day now, so I figured I might as well enjoy things while they lasted. So I only did safe, low-effort, low-yield jobs. Hacking vending machines, that kind of thing. Kid's stuff, really. I started burning through the last of my cash reserves. Like I said the other day, I normally don't keep all my cash in one place. But then I started getting low. You can steal a gun. You can steal a robot. Sometimes you can even steal a car. But the one thing you can't steal is an apartment. Even gangsters have to pay for rent and groceries. I gathered up the last of the cash and brought it home. It was enough to live on for a few months. Two days later the police nabbed me. Raided the apartment, took all the cash. They hit me when I was really vulnerable financially and really content with with my personal life. It was probably the worst possible time to get arrested."

"What made you think she was going to move on?"

"Why are you asking so many questions about my personal life? None of this has anything to do with the case."

"I've spent most of my life - or my runtime if you're the sort of person who insists that robots aren't alive - stuck in a laboratory environment. I've viewed the entire outside world through the lens of Kasaranian scientists, and it wasn't until you and I met that I realized how many of their assumptions are wrong. The people who work at G-Kinetics are all educated, married, wealthy, and law-abiding. Most of them are middle-aged and they're nearly all easterners. One of my drives is to be informed and another one of my drives is to help people who are part of my family. Since you're now part of that family, I'm trying to understand you so I can do my job."

218

Max just assumed that Jen has been pumping him for information as part of her attempt to pantomime human conversation. It didn't occur to him that she was doing it out of a genuine interest in his well-being.

"We need to get moving," he says. He looks down at the robot shell. "I'll come back and get rid of this evidence later."

"We can't get rid of it now?"

"I don't have anything to destroy it with. I can't just throw it in the ocean and hope for the best. And I don't want to carry it out of here in broad daylight."

"The sign at the rental station warned that these lockers are subjected to random inspection. Aren't you worried the police will find this place?"

"When I rented this place I put my name down as 'Rivergate Police'. When it comes time for random inspections, they think it's owned by the department. Like, some off-the-books operation. So they leave this place alone as a professional courtesy."

"That works?"

"This place has gone untouched by everyone but me for five years. Yeah. It works."

Max picks a canvas shoulder bag out of the rotting boxes. "This is what I came here for. Lockpicks. A few electronic gadgets. Some other small tools. I wish I'd had this with me when we broke into the warehouse."

As Max is closing up #44 again he stops and looks down at the biometric padlock. "Now that I'm thinking about it, I probably shouldn't have this stuff tied to a lock that can identify me." He cocks his arm back and heaves the lock into the ocean. He fishes a more conventional padlock out of the bag and uses that instead. It's governed by a simple metal key, which he pockets.

"What are you looking for?" Jen asks.

Max realizes he's just spent the last thirty seconds scanning the docks for any signs of people, and scanning the sky looking for drones. "It's just paranoia," he says. "Those three cops from yesterday think I'm hiding money somewhere. I'm not, but they think I am. And they want it. They took my cash and smashed my ID, which would force me to go

219

to my secret stash for money. So it stands to reason that they'd be following me."

"They wouldn't need to follow you. They probably expected you to keep your handheld with you. The scanner would still be able to read the heatsink, even if the device was smashed."

"You're right. I hadn't thought of that. Still, can't hurt to be careful. Then there's Blackbeard. Crazy old guy I used to work with years ago. He's looking for me. And maybe Landro sent his goons to tail me. He's got a two-man security detail, and I notice they weren't at the meeting."

"The casinos might be watching you, too."

Max frowns. "I don't think I can sustain this level of paranoia for much longer."

SATURDAY

Worldcade

Max opens his eyes. He's in the passenger seat of the car. "How long was I out?"

Jen is in the driver's seat. "About six hours. It's just after midnight."

"Why didn't you wake me up?"

"You've had six hours of sleep in the previous thirty-six. I'm terrible at reading facial expressions, and even I could see you were a mess. You've been living on caffeine and stress for the last three days."

Max rubs his face and looks around. They're in a parking lot. There's a high-pitched vibrating sound somewhere in the distance, along with the crashing of simulated conflict. A tall sign stands above the lot, washing the car in lights of ever-shifting hue. Max can only see the bottom half, but from here he can figure out it says "WORLDCADE".

Max steps out of the car and stretches. "We need to get a room or something. I can't keep sleeping in the car like this."

He remembers being twenty and spending an entire weekend hiding in the back seat of a car because someone paid him to watch a building and record all of the shift changes and door usage. It wasn't even a big deal. He had a blast. The whole project made him feel like some sort of spy. Aside from having to piss into a cup a couple of times, comfort was never a problem. But just fifteen years later, a nap in a car is enough to make him all wobbly and sore. He wonders how many years he has left before he has to settle for being the guy who sits at home and sends the young people out to do the interesting jobs.

Worldcade is a two-story building. It's trimmed in glowing lights and psychedelic patterns to cover up the fact that it's a great big box of dark concrete. They're just south of the river.

Jen steps out of the car. "This car got a lot of dirty looks while you were napping."

"I'm not surprised. This is a rich person's car. See, over there," Max points across the water to the bright buildings, "...is the Hospitality District. And over there," Max turns around and points south, "...is The Grunge."

222

"I don't see anything on the maps called Grunge. The maps say that's the Homestead District."

"That name hasn't made sense in over a hundred years. People started calling it The Grunge because all the buildings were turning black with coal smoke."

"No coal smoke anymore. So that name is out of date, too."

"True. But this name stuck and these people really don't care what mapmakers think. Anyway. The Grunge is poor. They don't like foreigners in the Grunge, they don't like rich people, and they *really* don't like rich foreigners. This street?" Max points to the broad street running in front of Worldcade, "This is the seam between the north and the south. You cross this street and everything changes. Building style. Accents. Average income. Education levels. Everything."

"I thought a lot of service workers lived in this district. But now you claim they hate foreigners. Do they really spend all day serving tourists they hate?"

"I lived a few blocks south of here in my late twenties. Every single night this group of middle-aged women would meet after dinner. They would gather on the little balcony over my apartment and tell stories trying to figure out which one of them met the stupidest or most obnoxious tourist. So yes, they really do spend all day serving people they hate."

"That means a lot of them will probably hate me because of how I look."

"That's probably true," he says.

"That's unfortunate."

Max rests his hand on the roof of the car. "The car thing is a really touchy area for them. In Kasaran, a lot of middle-aged guys get tired of their first wives. So they come here to marry some 'exotic beauty'. They drive expensive cars and wear expensive clothes and hang around where they think they can meet young local women. So an expensive car in the neighborhood has this creepy vibe that says 'I am a foreigner and I am here for your women.' I'm not surprised it got dirty looks."

"Do you think there's any danger?"

"We should be fine. If we were going to be inside for more than an hour then I'd send the car across the river to find parking."

Overhead, a flock of drones is flying in circles, blinking and swooping and making various electronic sounds. Every few seconds one of them will flash and make explosion sounds before diving for the parking lot. It always catches itself at the last second before flying back up to rejoin the mayhem.

Max spends a couple of minutes stretching and rubbing his neck. Jen takes off her sunglasses and watches the drones fly. Finally she says, "I don't understand. Is this a light show?"

Max points to the top of Worldcade, "You can't see them from here, but up on the roof are a bunch of drunk guys shooting light guns. When a drone dives, that means it's been shot down."

"I see."

They stop just inside the entrance so Max can get his bearings. He hasn't been here in a decade, and back then it had a different name and a different layout. To the right is a stairway leading up the the restaurant. To the left is a door that used to lead to gear rental, but now looks like it's an office or something. Directly in front of them is a large archway leading to the main floor. The lighting here is bright, but also ultra-saturated and rotating steadily through the rainbow. Beyond the archway is a dark room filled with flashing videogame machines. Even from out here, their roar is deafening.

There's a bulletin board beside the archway that contains many archaeological layers of handbills. Everything is in Local. This place isn't for tourists.

Max looks over at Jen. "You took off your sunglasses." He has to raise his voice to be heard.

There's a full three second pause before she answers. "My eyesight doesn't work like yours. I don't handle these changing colors very well. I keep losing visual continuity." She's staring straight ahead, like an animal caught in the headlights. She can't raise her voice by shouting, so she just increases the volume output of her talking voice. It completely shatters the illusion her animated mouth is trying to maintain.

He heads towards the archway and Jen grabs his hand. He doesn't like people touching him and nearly pulls away before realizing

224

that she's using him as a guide. He's about to say something about how cold her hands are when he realizes that this observation would be both banal and idiotic.

There's a lanky teenage girl standing beside the archway. She's wearing the Worldcade uniform, which is an unflattering beige jumpsuit with the Worldcade logo stamped on the breast pocket, just under her nametag. It's outlined in thin strips of glowing neon light, perhaps to make employees stand out in the dark room beyond. She's got a big pouch on one hip and a fist-sized ring of keys on the other hip. As Max approaches she reaches into the pouch and pulls out some cards or coupons or whatever. She starts robotically reciting some canned greeting without really making eye contact. She's not shouting, so Max can't make out what she's saying, but he catches a few words like "savings", and "membership".

"I'm looking for Jonas," Max shouts above the din.

She puts the cards away and makes eye contact for the first time. "All the way in the back, past the bar, through the blue door, down the stairs." She goes back to ignoring him.

You have to go down two wide steps to enter the arcade proper. Jen takes these very slowly.

Max leans in and shouts. "Do you want to wait in the car?"

Five seconds pass before she answers, "I can't filter out this noise and I can't read your lips. I don't know what you're saying."

Max nods and leads her through the maze of roaring, flashing, tilting, bouncing machines. Kids in their late teens and early twenties are gathered around the screens, holding plastic cups of beer. You can always tell who's next in line for a game because they have a beer in each hand. One is theirs, and the other belongs to the current player. The centerpiece of the place is a machine built to look like the cockpit of a fighter jet. It's mounted on a three-axis gyroscope and has a fixed screen on the outside so spectators can see the action. There's a great big sign taped to the side, warning players that puking in the machine is grounds for ejection.

Beyond the machines is the glowing neon bar where young people are drinking and flirting. Just past the bar is a wooden blue door with a sign saying "Employees Only". Max ducks through and heads down the steps. On the other side of the door the lighting is steady and the sound is greatly muted. Jen lets go of his hand as they descend.

The basement is a workshop of some sort. Max didn't even know this place *had* a basement. It's like a post-apocalyptic copy of the arcade upstairs. Machines are scattered around in various states of disassembly. The cabinets hang open, revealing their electronic innards. For some reason this kind of reminds Max of the exploded robot faces he's been seeing. Loose cables are gathered into bundles and hung over hooks built into the ceiling. There's no neon light down here. It's all illuminated by naked bulbs.

A young man looks up from his work and waves his arms at them "Hey friend! Employees only! You can't be down here!" He falters at the end when his eyes fall on Jen.

"Are you Jonas?" Max asks.

The kid points to his breast pocket.

"You're not wearing a nametag," Max says.

"Oh," the kid says, looking down. He scans the tables as if looking for his nametag. He gives up and shrugs, "I'm Jonas." His eyes keep darting over to Jen.

"Saturn said you might be able to help me with something."

"Oh, you're the guy. The super-spy or whatever. He said you might be coming. Said you had some kind of little electronic trinket you wanted me to look at?" He swallows nervously. "He said you might pay me to look at it for you?"

Max has no idea where this "super-spy" idea came from, but that's not the kind of detail you argue with. "That's right," he says.

Jonas is perhaps slightly past twenty. His hair has grown so long that it hangs down in front of his face. He deals with this by brushing it off to the side every time he speaks. He has a stooped posture and nervous face that can't sustain eye contact for more than a few seconds.

The kid apparently can't control himself anymore. He turns to Jen, "Is that... Is this a picture of you?"

He's pointing to a poster on the wall. It does indeed look exactly like Jen, except the model has long blond hair and very human-looking blue eyes. She's in a typical glamour-shot style pose. One arm is in front of her bare breasts, and the other is behind her head. Her silky hair is

226

flowing to one side, as if caught in an impossibly localized breeze. She's smiling slightly and giving a sly sideways look to the camera. Her facial expression and body language look far more lifelike than Jen's stoic demeanor, but the poster model has exposed metal joints at her waist, elbows, and shoulders, betraying her robotic nature. Max doesn't know if this is stylized for artistic purposes, or if at some point in the past they really did make a robot model with joints like this. The G-Kinetics logo is stamped in the corner of the poster, next to something written in Kasaranian. Max translates the text as literally, "A new day of technology is arriving." After working on it for a few seconds he realizes that "The next generation is coming" is probably a more accurate translation. The poster is a bit curled and scuffed around the edges and is probably a few years old.

"That's an early version of my platform, yes," Jen says.

"That's amazing!" The kid is now excited to the point of of mania. His head keeps whipping back and forth between Jen and her likeness. "I've never seen anything from generation four. Or any generation. Aside from worker robots, obviously. I mean, I've never seen a robot that looked like a person before, not in real life. I heard you're supposed to be indistinguishable from the real thing."

"The eyes give it away," Jen says.

"Yeah! Those are badass!" he says with a grin. "Can I-" He stops and begins frantically looking around the shop. He finds his handheld under a circuit board and hands it to Max. "Can I get a picture? Of us? Together?"

Max looks over to Jen, who nods. He shrugs and stands back while the two of them pose together in front of the poster. Jonas gives the three-finger salute, which involves extending the thumb, index finger, and middle finger, and holding them as open as possible. In the bad old days this was a symbol of allegiance among the cutthroat anti-Kasaranian rebels, with the three fingers standing for the three free boroughs of the city. The younger generations have long since co-opted and repurposed it. Now they use it in photographs to mean basically, "Yay!"

Jen copies the gesture and - astounding Max - smiles as he snaps the picture. It's a nice smile. Very human.

"Thanks," Jonas says, taking back his handheld. "This is amazing. Thanks so much."

Max looks at the poster again and sees it's actually one of many. What he assumed was just a wall of pin-up girls is actually a series of foreign advertisements for robots. Jen is the only one from G-Kinetics. The rest are all from Senma Technologies. The Senma posters are slightly more leering and pornographic. The G-Kinetics one could probably pass for a shampoo advertisement.

"So how did you...?" the kid nods towards Jen.

"How did I what?"

"Generation four units are worth millions. Is that thing yours, or is that just like, standard equipment in your line of work?"

"I can't say," Max says, deadpan.

"Right, right," Jonas says, looking slightly embarrassed.

Max knows they have important stuff to sort out, but he can't resist asking, "What's the deal with all these busted machines? Are the patrons really that hard on them?"

"Busted machines?" Jonas apparently has no idea what Max is talking about.

Max waves his arm, gesturing at the machines around them.

"Oh! " Jonas says. "These aren't busted. These are rentals. See, you probably noticed that we have all the latest titles upstairs. Like, I'm talking current-year cabinets. Obviously little operations like ours can't afford that kind of thing. So what we do is rent them for a month or two, and then I tear them apart. I pull the chips and put them into the imager so we can fab clones. I map out the circuit boards so I can print copies of those. Then we stick counterfeit anti-tamper seals on the board to replace the ones we tore off. It's pretty much an assembly line at this point."

"So these are all rentals?" Max asks.

"Well, those on the far wall are actually old machines that we're not using right now, but yeah. All the open machines are rentals."

Max looks over at the supposedly old machines Jonas is talking about, but he wouldn't have known they were old if Jonas hadn't told him. The machines are all the same to him. "So all the cabinets upstairs are bootlegs? Even the bodies? They look like the real thing."

228

"Yeah. They're good, right? Have you ever seen the street artist that draws all the dragons and fairies? She works in chalk, usually around subway stations."

"The one with the sleeve tattoos? I've seen her around. She draws on the sidewalk to get people to come over so she can sell paintings."

Jonas nods. "Yep. That's Lona. We call her when we need custom cabinet art." He points to the corner where a bunch of wood panels are stacked up, surrounded by woodworking tools. On several pieces of wood you can see rough sketches. "She's a little shaky when it comes to drawing man-made stuff like cars or jets or whatever, but on everything else she's brilliant. Sometimes it looks better than the original."

"And your copies are just as good as the originals?"

"Sometimes better. The translations done by manufacturers are pretty terrible, and they don't bother translating the cabinet art. That's why we make it custom. If it wasn't for our little operation here, nobody would know what half these machines are called."

"An entire arcade of pirated games," Max says, looking around.

"Oh, hey," Jonas holds up his hands defensively, "You have to understand. We're not really stealing anything from these companies. If we were legit then the only people who could afford to play these games would be tourists, and they can play this stuff at home. This way, they get some rental money, we make a little money, and everyone else gets to play some games. Everybody wins. I'm not a bad guy."

Max shrugs. "I never said you were."

"I'm just saying, I don't think these videogame companies really care. I mean, if they did they could always stop renting their machines to us."

Max looks at the equipment. "All I care about is that it looks like maybe you can help me." Max pulls out the haunted circuit. "I need to know what this is."

Jonas looks at it for a second. Then he points at the largest bit on the board,"That's a Realizer rendering chip. Looks like version 3.4, which means it's about eighteen months out of date. Here are some video leads. Next to that is a wireless package. Here at the bottom we have a Norcast branded CPP of some sort. That's 'Custom Programmable Processor'. Could be doing anything."

"Could this maybe hook up to projection glasses?"

Jonas is silent. Max likes this. It means the kid is actually taking the time to consider the problem and not just giving the first answer that comes to his head. After some consideration he says, "Maybe you could, but you're missing a few parts. There's some leads here, but there's no telling what those are supposed to plug into. There's no power source. And this is a little bulky for something you're supposed to wear on your face. But if this is the work of an amateur? It's possible."

"So what would happen if you added the missing stuff? If I put on the glasses, what would I see?"

"Okay. The problem is that what you're asking for is a lot more than just imaging a chip. I can stick this little guy in the machine and make copies, but if you don't know what the code on the chip does then what you're talking about isn't imaging, it's reverse engineering."

"Is that more difficult?"

"Astronomically."

"Can you do it?"

Jonas looks around his workshop. "I have a pretty tight schedule here. We only have the original cabinets for so long before they have to go back. If I don't have the copy done by the end of the lease then it's money down the drain. That will not make my dad happy."

"Dad?"

"The bartender. You probably passed him on the way down here. Mom runs the restaurant, dad runs the arcade, and I run the chop shop."

Max looks around the room and thinks for a second. He glances over to Jen, who is crouched down and studying the arcade cabinets carefully. He looks back to Jonas and pulls out his wallet. "Hold out your hand."

Unsure, Jonas holds out his hand palm-down. Max takes it, turns it over, and begins counting $100 dollar bills into the palm. Once he gets to five, he stops. Jonas looks like he's gone into some sort of atavistic panic.

Max nods, satisfied. This is the reaction he was looking for. "Let me ask you again: Can you do it?"

Jonas is still holding the money out like he's afraid Max is going to demand it back any second. He swallows hard and says in a hushed voice, "I swear I will not sleep until I know what it does."

Max sets the circuit board on top of the money and folds the hand closed. "Deal."

Graft

"You seem to admire Jonas." Jen says this as they're heading west on the upper expressway. She's on the passenger side, looking out the window.

Max has to think about this one for a bit. "I think I would say I admire his operation. I wouldn't run someplace like that myself, but it's a good setup.

"I assume by 'good setup' you mean you think it's reasonably profitable. If so, why wouldn't you want to run it?"

"Aside from the fact that I don't know anything about videogames? I don't like having a single point of collapse. See, Jonas is right. Those rich eastern companies probably don't care that he's pirating their machines. A small operation like that is probably beneath their notice. The problem is, that could change. Maybe a new company president comes in. Maybe the company has a bad year and starts looking for someone to blame it on. Maybe operations like Worldcade become so common that they start eating into the bottom line. Whatever. If these companies get mad and decide to make an example of you, then there's nothing you can do about it. They'll bury you in lawyers and just like that, you lose something you've been building all your life. They could do it tomorrow. They might never do it. You don't know. I wouldn't want that hanging over my head."

"But you still admire the business?"

Max looks over at her. He shouldn't. He's driving. But he's trying to see her face. He finds himself doing this a lot. He's often looking at her face and then getting frustrated because it doesn't tell him anything. "Yes. I admire his business. Why?"

"Is it because his operation is illegal in nature? I ask because you haven't expressed similar admiration for other places we've visited. Restaurants, car rental, hotel, and so forth. I'm trying to understand why this business stands out to you, and if it's related to your criminal background."

"See, I have a problem with how you're framing this."

"I apologize if I've offended you. I won't bring it up again."

"You're not offending me. I've had this conversation with wise old guys who were trying to set me straight. I've had it with cops. I've even had it with my mother."

"You think you're not a criminal?"

"Oh, I'm definitely a criminal. I'll admit that right up front. No objections. My problem is this idea that being a criminal is a horrible thing, or that I'm somehow worse than most other people. I'll admit I'm a bastard, but I insist there are lots of people that are far worse and everyone gives them a free pass for some reason."

Max thumps his hand on the steering wheel as he thinks. He's trying to come up with a good analogy. His usual ones all focus on mining and gambling but he's not sure they'll click with this robot. So he decides to make it as basic as he can. "Okay, let's say we've got two villages beside each other. To the north they grow apples, right? And to the south they grow bananas."

"There are some climate concerns with this setup, but I'll assume I'm supposed to ignore those for the sake of the thought experiment?"

"Right. So these villages steal from each other all the time. The southerners steal apples from the northern orchard, and the north village steals bananas from the banana... orchard. Or farm. Or whatever you call a place where you grow bananas. So far, these two villages are on equal footing, correct? Nobody has the moral high ground and everyone is a thief."

"Assuming the thefts are roughly symmetric in volume and frequency, then yes."

"Now imagine someone from the north gets elected king. Or whatever. He's suddenly in charge of making the laws for both villages. And let's say that he passes a law saying it's now illegal to steal apples. Everyone continues behaving as before. The southern people are now criminals and the northern people are not, but I say the morality of the system hasn't changed. Neither side is better than the other and the law doesn't change that."

"So your position is that everyone is a thief?"

"I wouldn't use the word theft or we'll wind up in a circular argument. Instead I'd say everyone is trying to take from everyone else.

233

Some people use lies. Some people use threats of force. Some people use actual force. Some people use bureaucracy or lawsuit as a weapon. Sometimes it's explicitly illegal, sometimes it's legal, and sometimes it's ambiguous. People in power place a lot of importance on the distinction between legal and not legal because they're the ones making the rules. Then they can take your bananas without worrying you'll take their apples."

"I can't think of any examples where you can take from someone and it isn't theft."

"Banks. Let's talk about banks. You know how they're always trying to sell you stuff?

"No."

"Oh right. You've never been a person. At least, not in the legal sense. Well, let's say you go to a dangerous neighborhood. Suddenly your handheld beeps at you. The bank is trying to sell you some insurance against mugging, pickpocketing, that sort of thing. Is that theft?"

"If you can refuse, then it doesn't strike me as theft."

"Okay, so what if they just automatically sell it to you, whether you want it or not? You walk into this neighborhood, your handheld detects it, and they take the money out of your account without asking. Taking money from someone and giving them something they don't want in return... you'd agree that's theft?"

"I'd agree."

"So now we have a nice clear line between theft and non-theft. The thing is, the bank can make that line really blurry if they want. Suppose the bank allows you to refuse the deal, but if you don't respond within a given timeframe then the sale goes through without your consent."

"That does seem very questionable. I can see why you might want certain things to happen automatically, but I also see how that could be abused."

"Now let's say you're allowed to refuse, but it's really inconvenient to do so. It's confusing, it takes time, and it distracts you from the important problems you're trying to solve."

"I guess it depends on how big the inconvenience is."

"Right. And they know exactly how far they can push that. It's like the stealing I was doing at the smoke stand as a kid. I knew exactly how far to push things. If I got too greedy or caused too many problems, I would have faced justice. So I calculated how much I could get away with, and didn't go beyond that point. Keep in mind that when a bank pulls tricks like this, they're no longer selling you a product. What they're really selling you is your own time. You give them money, and they'll let you get back to your day. The more you resist, the more of your time they'll eat. It's all legal, but they're still taking money you don't want to give them and giving you nothing you value in return."

Max takes an exit and they find themselves in the western part of the city. It's a tight web of apartment buildings and shopping towers. He's keeping one eye on the map as he drives. He doesn't come to this part of the city very often.

Jen turns away from the window and looks at him. "So you're arguing that flaws in the banking system justify your career of theft. I'm not being judgemental, I'm just trying to make sure I understand."

"It's not just banks!" Max flails for a second, trying to figure out where to start. "A cop gets to the end of the month and sees he doesn't have enough money left to make rent or whatever. So he goes around to some local businesses for surprise inspections. He knows they'll pay him a bribe to go away rather than consent to the search or inspection. And think about government contracts. They're supposed to go to the lowest bidder, but a politician can cut a deal with the contractor. 'I'll make sure your company gets the contract if you agree to send some of the money back to me'. That's the most inefficient theft of all. You steal ten million from the city so you can gain just a couple of extra thousand."

"I know how graft works, Mr. Law."

"There's more! The police extort money from a concert promoter by refusing to grant a permit unless they're given a bribe. Concert promoters use vague contracts and accounting tricks steal from the band. The band steals from the hotel. The hotel buys up all the cigarette licenses and becomes a cartel so they can charge tourists five times as much for smokes while the little smoke shops go out of business. The tourists steal random shit from around the city. I'm not trying to justify my behavior. I steal from people. I admit to it. What I hate is how all these other people take way more than me. Sometimes they take it from people that can't afford to lose anything. And then they act like they're better than me. The quickest way to get robbed is to try and make an honest buck. The whole world is a giant circle of people feeding off each other. All I'm doing is making sure I don't end up on the bottom of the food chain. At least I'm honest with myself."

Max realizes he's been gradually raising his voice to the point where he's now ranting. He takes a deep breath and puts the car into auto. What he really needs is a cigarette. He lights one and starts to calm down.

The cigarette is halfway gone before he speaks again, "Sorry for getting worked up. It bugs me that so many other people get away with the things they do."

"It's fine," she says. "A lot of the things you're talking about are things I can't really form an opinion on. I don't really make a big distinction between legal and illegal activities. I've obviously broken a few laws with you. I tend to rank things based on harm. I don't see bank charges as significant because people don't generally get worked up about them. It's a mild annoyance. Meanwhile, armed robbery is incredibly traumatic for the victims so I'd rate that as an extremely negative act, even if the amount taken is trivial compared to whatever the bank might be doing."

"For the record, I don't do armed robberies or home invasions. That stuff is barbaric and inefficient. There are easier, safer ways to make a buck."

"Are you trying to justify your career to me? You don't have to."

"I'm not looking to get your approval. I'm trying to get you to disapprove of some of the systems everyone else takes for granted. If a bank annoys and inconveniences millions and millions of people, doesn't that add up to enough human suffering to make you care?"

"No. Doesn't work that way."

"So you're sort of predisposed to give a pass to predatory corporate behavior?"

"That's a backwards way of looking at it. If people cared more, I'd care more. How annoying would it be to have a robot that got outraged over things that don't bother you? Nobody would want a robot like that."

Max frowns. He's made this same argument to other people over the years, and their response was very similar to Jen's. This argument has failed to persuade everyone, and now it's failed against a robot. He's not going to change his career, but he figures he needs to come up with a new argument.

The car beeps and relinquishes control.

"I guess this is the place," Max says.

"I can't make any promises," Jen reminds him. "I'm reasonably confident robots are stored here. Someone posted a public complaint about the noise a few years ago, which is how I found this address. This place is close enough to the Fennel Hills District that it's possible that their robots come from here."

"Fennel Hills was the first murder, right?"

"Yes. But we don't know for certain that robot originated here. The lack of public documentation is suspicious. Why would the city hide their robot network?"

"There's nothing insidious about the lack of documentation. That's just how this city runs. Keeping clear records and making them public takes time and money, and nobody will complain if you do a bad job."

They get their bearings and discover that the address in question is a short office building with windows shaped like coin slots.

"An office building," Jen says. "That doesn't make sense. Why would you store robots in an office?"

"Not in the office. Underground." Max points to the garage entrance. They follow the ramp down and find a set of robot doors. Like last time, these snap open for Jen.

This space is much smaller than the last facility. They do a count of containers and figure out that the place has room for about two hundred robots. Only half of the slots are full. It's impossible to tell if the empty slots are for robots currently out working, or if the recall has started.

They find an office at the back. Max picks the lock. Inside they search the shelves, the computer, and the maintenance area. Hoping to find more hardware, Max searches the trash can, the recyclables, and the floor around them. He looks through the tools, hoping to find something capable of opening a robot skull. By the time they're done it's nearly dawn.

"The Fennel Hill murder was a year ago," Jen says. "I'm not surprised we haven't found anything. That's a long time for evidence to hang around."

"Assuming there was evidence here in the first place."

Protest

Back in the car, Max notices that there's a message from Jonas. He puts the audio through to the car so Jen can hear it. "Hi, Mr. Gone? This is Jonas. I don't know if you know this, but that circuit board you gave me is broken. There's a hairline crack running through it. I'll print up a new one and continue my testing. Let you know what I find."

"I guess that's why it was in the trash," Max says.

"So now we need to find the robot center for the second murder," Jen says.

Max stares at the city map on the dash screen. "The problem is, that happened at the Grandview. That's the Hospitality District. I know that area really well, and I'm sure there's nothing like a robot center there. I've never seen robots congregating or travelling in groups in that district. Plus, the space is just too valuable."

"So robots probably commute from some other district."

"The most likely place would be somewhere north. Maybe near Port Rich. Maybe we can go downtown and look for some robots."

It's dawn when they set out, which means they wind up trapped in commuter traffic trying to enter the city. After an hour of staring at taillights, Max gives up and stops for food and coffee. By the time he reaches the Hospitality District, it's late morning.

"I wonder how long a robot's shift is. We can probably just follow this guy around until he needs to recharge." Max is driving along at walking speed, following a blue robot. If you did this to a human they would probably take it as a very threatening move, but the robot doesn't seem to mind or even notice. It's stopping at each building and using a basement entrance. Max's current theory is that it's going inside to read a utility meter.

"We won't be able to follow it if it goes under the promenade."

"Which will happen in three more blocks," Max says. He sighs. "Maybe we can follow another robot."

"Maybe we can just ask it," Jen says.

"We can do that? It'll just tell us?"

"Why wouldn't it?"

"I don't know," Max shrugs. "Nobody ever talks to these things. People always treat them like dumpsters or traffic lights. Just part of the city."

Max steps out of the running car and approaches the robot.

"Hey buddy," he says. The robot ignores him. Or maybe it doesn't realize it's being addressed. "Hey. Robot. You." Max spots a number painted on the chassis. "Hey. HD-275."

The robot swivels its head to look at him, although it keeps walking. It has long legs, and Max has to nearly jog to keep up.

"Where are you based?"

"I don't understand the question." Like the robot Jen murdered a couple of night ago, this one has a stiff, unnatural voice. It's probably designed to sound earnest and helpful, but it comes off as clueless.

"Where are you from?" Max looks around. People are starting to stare at him.

"I was manufactured by Global Kinetics in the Jhendici Manufacturing Plant on-"

"No I don't care about that. I mean where do you go at the end of the day? Where do you recharge?"

"500 Shorefront Twenty-third Street, Port Rich District, city of-"

"Yeah I got it. Piss off."

Max heads back and puts the address into the car. Then he activates auto-drive and the car heads for Port Rich.

"Last night..." Max says as he lights a cigarette. He takes a few puffs before starting over. "Last night I took that picture of you and Jonas. You smiled. I've never seen you smile. You've got all this expensive machinery in your face to make you look human and you don't use it."

"I used to," Jen says. "The problem is figuring out what expression is appropriate for the given social context."

"When I decide to make a face it's not always because I'm trying to fit in. Sometimes I'm just reacting to how I feel. You don't even do that."

"I don't really have a singular emotional state to convey."

"But you can tell the difference between when things are going well and when things are going poorly, right? That's halfway to happy and sad."

"Okay, let's just go with your terms of 'happy' and 'sad'. Right now I'm happy we recently made progress on the case. I'm sad another person was killed. I'm happy I'm able to help you with the case. I'm sad there are anti-robot protests happening today. I'm sad robots are being recalled from the city. I'm sad those recalls will cause hardships for the people in the city. I'm sad I'm not taking part in the work at the lab. I'm sad you were beaten by those police officers the other day and you're probably still hurting. I'm sad you're not taking care of yourself. I'm happy the killings are sabotage and not a malfunction. That's my emotional state right now. All of those."

"Can't you just pick one?"

"That would look pretty strange. My face would go through mood shifts several times a minute as I moved from thinking about one problem to the next. Also, happy and sad are really brute-force emotions. Nobody goes around expressing strong emotions like that. Not all the time."

"Still, the stone-face look seems like curing the disease by killing the patient."

"In generation four we tried a couple of different strategies. One was mirrored expressions, where I just take the expression of whomever I'm talking to and adopt it for myself. It's simple, and it works for a lot of different situations. There are some edge cases where you don't want to do this, like when meeting people for the first time, or when people are expressing really extreme emotional states like laughter or crying. You also can't use this strategy in group conversations. But for general daily conversations in a family or work environment, it performs reasonably well. The problem is that some minority of the population finds this really unsettling."

"Okay, I can see how the mirroring thing might get a little weird for some people."

"Eventually we settled on combination of occasional mirroring and smiling. When I was generation four, I loved smiling. I enjoy when people are happy. It's one of my central drives. So I'd smile, and the

241

other person would smile back. According to my understanding of emotional states at the time, I'd just improved their mood. It's like a human taking opium. It was creating this influx of positive input. I loved having conversations because every conversation was a chance to make someone smile."

"So what? You got addicted to smiling? You had to give it up and go into rehab?" Max is looking ahead. The streets are filled with people today, and they seem less inclined than usual to honor the traffic signals. The auto-drive system is very shy about pushing through groups of people, even when there's lots of space and the car has the right-of-way. Which means they're now travelling at walking speed.

"After the first round of fifth-generation upgrades I started picking up on body language, facial expressions, and tone-of-voice cues that I'd been overlooking before. People were smiling, but I realized it wasn't a genuine expression of pleasure. They were humoring me. I realized the tone of voice they were using most closely matched the tone and posture of someone talking to a child or family pet."

"Shit. I guess if you go around grinning all the time people will assume you're a moron." Max grabs the wheel and starts driving so he can be a little more aggressive with the thoughtless pedestrians.

"Apparently. Nuance implies depth, and my expressions didn't have any depth. This is another reason I wanted to get out of the lab. I want to see more candid exchanges outside of a work environment. Also, I want to see a larger variety of faces. I was getting really good at white faces but then mis-reading other races. This was especially a problem with anyone who had a different eye shape or default eyebrow posture."

"So this blank-face thing you're doing now is temporary?" The car has built-in safety features that refuse to let him nudge people, so he's settling for getting very close and blowing the horn. This is more therapeutic than it is productive.

"I don't know, honestly. The more I study it, the more I realize expressions are powerful and complex revelations of human attitudes and emotional states that I will never experience. Does it make sense to reverse-engineer the entire system just so I can make counterfeit expressions of my own? My goal is to be useful to humans, not become one. Maybe I should keep doing 'blank-face' as you call it. Maybe my behavior needs to change based on who I'm talking to. Maybe I need to adopt different policies based on social context. What I have learned is that people are more likely to treat me like a person and take my ideas seriously when I keep my face neutral."

"What did you say a couple of minutes ago about protests?"

"There's a protest today."

"Didn't they have one two days ago?"

"That was a memorial service that became a protest. This is a protest by design."

Max can see a few signs in the crowd, but he's sitting at the back of the crowd so all the signs are facing away from him. What he's realizing now is that he's caught up in a bunch of people heading for the march. This group is just a tributary of the real thing.

"Let's walk," he says as his door snaps open and he steps out. He leans down and says to the car. "Find parking. In a garage." It gives an electronic chirp and drives off.

"Are we really going to walk all the way to Port Rich?" Jen asks as she puts on her sunglasses.

"It just occurred to me. Let's say you're deliberately engineering robot murders in broad daylight. And let's say your goal is to do it in front of as many people as possible. Where would be the best place to strike?"

Jen looks at the growing crowd. "Here. Hundreds of people, all facing the same direction. Television cameras. Personal cameras. People in the buildings looking out the windows."

Max flicks his cigarette away and turns around in a circle, scanning the crowd. The people continue to flow around them. This is a mixed crowd. It has young and old, men and women, rich and poor. When things finally take shape you'll end up with certain pockets, but this far upstream it's all chaos.

"It wouldn't make sense to attack from the rear. All the eyes are up front. We need to be at the front," Max says.

"I don't know how we can get there. Everyone wants to be at the front."

"Where is the group heading?"

"Transit Building."

243

"Of course," he shakes his head. "It wouldn't be a real protest if they didn't make a mess and cause a bunch of headaches. Looks like they're going to head north and then turn west. Let's see if we can't cut that corner." He starts jogging.

"Wouldn't we go faster with the car?"

"It's headed the opposite way and trapped in the middle of that mess. I don't want to wait for it to turn around and pull free." Max is saying this through heavy breaths. He's in terrible shape and not up for this run.

"You're thinking we should head for the transit building and then head east to meet the crowd?"

"Yes," Max gasps.

"Okay," she says. "See you there."

She leaps forward and speeds away like a jungle cat. Her bare feet make brutal impact noises against the sidewalk, like someone hammering the pavement with a mallet. Max looks down to see she's ditched her boots.

After two more blocks, she's completely out of sight and he's completely spent. He doubles over, coughing and gasping. He looks up to see a city bus heading his way. He doesn't have a bus pass and he's nowhere near a bus stop, so he's going to have to do this the hard way.

He steps off the curb as if he's going to cross the street. The bus spots this and slows down, just in case he's planning on running out in front of it. He holds this pose, looking like he might cross at any second. The bus creeps by. Once it's passed, he grabs the advertising screen on the back and hoists himself onto the bumper. This trick was a lot easier when he was nineteen and skinny, but he manages to pull it off one more time. He wonders how many more times in his life he'll be able to do this.

The bad part of this is that if he's spotted by the police, he doesn't have the breath or the will to get away. He hates when a job forces him to take stupid risks.

The bus takes a turn just a block short of the transit building. Max has to disembark mid-turn, which he manages to pull off without turning an ankle. He jogs the rest of the way to find a crowd has already gathered. The place usually only looks like this on the opening days of tourist season, but today it's filled with locals.

Jen is pacing back and forth, hopping up in the air to see over the crowd.

"Anything?" Max asks once he's got enough breath for talking. He's holding his hand against his side, where he's developed a sharp pain just under the ribs.

"I haven't seen a single robot," she says.

He sputters a bit and gets his breathing under control enough to speak a full sentence, "Makes sense. They were supposed to be reducing headcount. And it would be stupid to send robots out today. They'd just get destroyed."

"We can't be on every side of the building at once. Where is the most likely point of attack?"

"Like I said, at the front of the crowd."

"But it looks like the crowd is already here."

"Look around. No news drones. These are the lazy people that skipped the march and headed directly here. The real march isn't here yet."

"This is going to be a really big crowd."

"Let's go east and see if we can meet the group head-on."

Like a lot of the older parts of the city, this section has new buildings crouching over old. Here, some of the classic pre-electronic billboards were also preserved. This creates a two-layered city. At the bottom is a line of three and four story buildings, surrounded by a forest of modern support pillars for the skyscrapers above. The tops of the older buildings still have their original block letter signs and billboards. Above this is a concrete sky, which is the underside of the newer structure.

Max looks up and says, "We could go up to the Old Roof level. Then we could see this from above and we'd be able to tell what's going on. But if there's an attack it will happen on the ground." He frowns and thinks this over.

"Let's split up," he says suddenly as he pulls out his handheld and calls her. He begins walking towards the nearest fire escape. "I'll be on the rooftops on the north side of the street," he says as soon as she answers.

In the past he spent a couple of nights on these roofs, watching armored cars and recording delivery schedules. It was a long time ago and he doesn't fully remember the layout, but he knows you can go several blocks just by traveling on rooftops.

From the ground it looks like the buildings are all roughly the same height, but once you're on top you can see it's a maze of access doors, walkways, industrial air conditioners, and communications gear. You have to watch your footing up here. Sometimes the buildings are close together, but sometimes there are deadly gaps between them.

"I still don't see any robots," Jen says. "I can see the front of the march ahead of me. They look calm. No drama yet."

He knows she's far ahead of him. It's going to be hard to catch up. Aside from being tired, he has to make detours around bits of the building that are too tall to climb over.

"What if they're inside one of these buildings?" he asks. He's mostly thinking out loud.

"I don't know," Jen says. "In that case they could come from almost anywhere. There are a lot of doors down here."

It's a strange sort of twilight on the roof. He can look out to the horizon and see the daytime sky, but the immense building overhead blots out the sun. Max walks over to the edge and looks down into the canyon. Jen is indeed ahead of him, although not as far as he expected. She's walking forward cautiously, looking from side to side. He can see the dense crowd ahead, marching steadily towards her.

The signs in the crowd are about what he was expecting. A few are large enough to be readable from the roof:

"They took my JOB and gave it to MURDERERS"

"Our PEOPLE are worth more than THEIR robots!"

And of course there are several pictures of the Happy Couple.

Max walks along the edge of the roof, looking into the gaps between the buildings across the street. It's all clear. After this long panicked run, he's starting to worry they came all this way for nothing.

"There's a van down here," Jen says. "No windows in back. It could be anything inside."

"I don't see it," Max says.

"It's on your side of the street. It's blue. Looks like it belongs to the city."

He has to lean over the edge of the building so he can look straight down. He's not normally afraid of heights, but this is slightly terrifying because of how unstable the position is. He's leaning out and holding his mobile to his ear.

"Why would someone park a van in the path of the march?" he wonders aloud.

One of the doors glides open. A robot steps out.

Lots of things are happening now. Some protesters are pointing and shouting. It's not clear if they're afraid, angry, or just surprised, but their shouts have prompted a few of the news drones to spin around and look at the robot. Jen is across the street from the van, still holding her mobile to her ear. The robot takes a couple of steps, sees the crowd, and stops. Jen closes the distance at frightening speed. She collides with the robot at a full sprint, pouncing on top of it and removing the head in one brutal movement. By this point another robot has already emerged from the van, and a third is right behind it. They're carrying dustbins. A second later they've dropped their tools and changed their behavior. One snaps its head to the side, looking directly at Jen. The other looks towards the crowd. They both stride towards their new goal.

"Another, to your left!" Max shouts, but he can see Jen isn't holding her mobile to her ear anymore.

Jen spots the robot just before it reaches her. As they come together, it's like watching a mouse trap go off. They lock arms without them seeming to pass through the intermediate space. There's just a crack of colliding metal as their limbs meet.

Max feels powerless. He's stuck up here and he can't do anything but watch.

The third robot is having a strange time of it. It advances on a woman. She turns and runs. The robot stops, as if confused. Then it locks eyes on someone else nearby and goes for them. So they run, and the robot stops again. The people at the back of the crowd haven't figured out what's going on, so they're still trying to push forward to see what the fuss is about, while the people in front are trying to flee the scene.

Jen lets go of one of her opponent's arms, pulls back, and takes a jab at its head. It catches her arm, and they're right back where they started.

The robot attacking the crowd is still having trouble figuring out who it wants to kill. It keeps changing targets. Finally a young man approaches with a baseball bat. He gets in behind the robot while it's chasing after someone else, and gives it a good crack on the back of the neck. The robot spins around, crushes his head, and its face explodes.

Max looks back to Jen to find she's standing over her opponent. Its face exploded at the exact same time. The head Jen ripped off at the start of the fight has also exploded. There are now three little fires scattered around the street, vomiting out thick black smoke. Some of the burning gel has landed on Jen, and her hair is now on fire.

Max hasn't been paying attention to the rooftops. He's been focused on the street. It's not until this moment that he's bothered to look to the side and notice a man on a lower section of the roof. The guy is backing away from the edge and putting something in the pocket of his municipal jumpsuit.

Jen isn't holding her phone, so all Max can do is scream with all the lung-power he has left, "JEN!"

The guy looks up at Max, and for a moment their eyes meet. Then he takes off across the rooftops.

"Oh shit. Not more running," Max says. "If you can hear me get up here!" he yells into his handheld before breaking into a full run.

This guy is younger and probably fitter. Even if Max wasn't doing his best to hold off a heart attack, he has no idea where he's supposed to find the energy to run this guy down. All he can do is give chase and hope for the best.

He's too high up to drop directly down to where Jumpsuit Guy is, so he heads north, away from the street, hoping to find a way down. He finds a spot where he can jump down some HVAC infrastructure. He stumbles at the bottom and scrapes up his hands. He gets up, starts running, loses his footing, and stumbles into a wall. And yet despite these fuckups, he's practically right beside Jumpsuit Guy, who apparently lost his bearings and ran the wrong way.

This turns out to be a mixed blessing. It's good that he's close to his target, but Jumpsuit Guy is now scared enough that he's pulled out a pistol. He takes a wild shot at Max and runs off.

Max chases after him for a bit before another gunshot forces him to take cover. On one hand, this guy is shooting while running and without taking the time to line up his shot. The odds of him landing a hit are ridiculous. On the other hand, the odds aren't zero and Max really doesn't want to buy any more tickets to this particular lottery.

There's a rush of rhythmic pounding and Jen speeds past him. Jumpsuit Guy takes a few shots at her, but she doesn't flinch. She leaps from one ledge to the next, landing effortlessly and without losing a step. Max realizes that her overtaking Jumpsuit Guy is a certainty of physics at this point and he slows his steps. Then he remembers that she's completely incapable of doing anything to him, and he's shooting at her.

Jen leaps forward and lands between Jumpsuit and the fire escape. Her glasses are off, her blue hair is blackened from fire, and her face has been singed by an exploding robot head. This guy probably doesn't know that Jen can't hurt him, which would explain why this brings him to a stop. Max is basically limping at this point. He doesn't know what he's going to do when he gets there, but he doesn't want to stop now.

Jumpsuit looks back at Max, then forward at Jen. Max is still trying to come up with some bullshit to get him to let his guard down when Jumpsuit decides to put a couple of bullets into Jen. The first few go into what would normally be the lungs. Maybe some of them go wide. Max is having trouble seeing at this point.

Max staggers to within a few paces of Jumpsuit just as a bullet finds her midriff. There's a sizzling sound and blobs of fire fly out of the entry and exit wounds. Her face goes slack.

"Get back!" she says to Jumpsuit without moving her mouth. Then she collapses like a marionette having its strings cut.

Jumpsuit Guy turns around. Max is only three paces away now. He aims his gun at Max's face and pulls the trigger. There's a dry click. Max bats the gun aside and puts his knuckles right into the bridge of Jumpsuit's nose. Jumpsuit staggers back. Max knocks him over with a couple more blows to the face and then jumps on top of the guy. An explosion nearly takes out his eardrum and there's a cloud of fire from where Jen fell. Black smoke fills the air.

Max is feeling it now. An entire week of pent-up rage comes out. All the beatings. Everyone trying to control him. Being robbed by the bank and the Three Little Pigs. The idiot protesters making everything worse. Blackbeard's bullshit debt. Jen getting destroyed. Three fucking years of his life. His punches are heavy and clumsy. Jumpsuit is flailing his arms, batting some of the swings to the side, but a lot of them are getting through and Max can feel his fists getting wet. He's clenching his teeth and grunting like a savage with each strike. Spittle is flying everywhere. He's got tears in his eyes from the rage and exertion and he can't even see what he's hitting at this point.

The world goes dark and the next thing he knows he's on his back. He remembers the sound of metal hitting bone and he realizes Jumpsuit hit him in the side of the head with the gun. Hands grab him by the collar of his coat and he feels himself being dragged. He can't really see what's going on but you don't need to be a fucking genius to figure out that Jumpsuit is going to throw him off the roof. Max tries to break his grip, but he just spent all his strength tenderizing his face. He kicks at the ground with his feet, trying to find something to grasp onto and stop the slow progress towards the edge.

He wipes the blood and tears out of his eyes and looks up to see the bloodied face of his adversary. He was all business earlier, but he's looking pretty savage now. His one good eye is filled with rage and desperation. His mouth is hanging open, panting.

This is what it's come down to: A couple of primates trying to kill each other with their bare hands.

Max puts his arms over his head and his coat slips off. This throws Jumpsuit off balance. Max finds his feet and lunges forward shoulder-first. His strike hits Jumpsuit square in the ass. Jumpsuit stumbles a few steps forward and vanishes from view. Two seconds later there's a wet impact as he meets the pavement.

Max flops down on the ground and lays on his back for a full minute. He stares up at the concrete sky and waits until his brain has enough oxygen to begin making decisions again.

Once he's upright he gets his bearings. He looks over the edge, expecting to see the aftermath of whatever happened at the front of the protest. It turns out he's gotten everything turned around in his head. He's actually standing at the back of the building. Jumpsuit fell into a space between the old buildings and nobody has any idea this happened yet. Max realizes that, if things had gone even slightly differently, it would be him spread out over the ground in this dark alley.

Jen's battery fuel - or whatever you call the stuff inside of batteries - has finally stopped burning. She was blown in half.

Max brings his handheld up and pushes the button for the car. "Come get me."

He sits down next to the top half of Jen and lights a cigarette.

Salvage

Max eases the car up the winding path. He's taking it slow because he can feel every imperfection in the road through the throbbing bruise on the side of his head. The sun is setting.

He drives through the parking space beside Dr. Kvenst's car, goes up the sidewalk, and stops right beside the entrance.

Dr. Kvenst is waiting out in front of the West Rockwood facility, along with a couple of guys in white uniforms. If this were a hospital Max would assume these guys were orderlies, but who knows how Kasaranians run things? These guys could be scientists for all he knows. Max steps out.

Kvenst points her cigarette at the car. "You missed the parking lot."

Max ignores her and pops the trunk. The orderlies (or whatever they are) come over.

"Careful, she's heavier than she looks," Max says as he opens the lid.

"They know how heavy it is, Mr. Max. They do this for a living." Kvenst says this from her spot by the entrance. Unlike the others, she's not hurrying over to assess the damage.

It looks pretty severe. Max didn't want to put her still-smoking wig in his car where it might set off the fire protection systems, so he left that behind. Her forearms have been melted down to the bare metal. Her face has been both scorched and melted. Her unblinking eyes have gone dark. Her body ends at the sternum.

One guy lifts up the entire thing and leans back so the weight is on his chest. "Get the door for me," he says to his partner.

"Millions of dollars. Gone," Kvenst says as the body is carried past her. "And that dress. Used to be one of my favorites."

Max closes the trunk and Kvenst frowns at him. "You didn't bring the rest?"

"It was hard enough to get this out. I had to carry it down four flights of stairs while the police were setting up a perimeter and asking questions. If I'd tried to retrieve the whole thing I'd probably still be there. Also, the lower half was still smoking and oozing. So yeah. Not gonna put that in the car."

Kvenst looks back towards the building. "Well as least you were smart enough to bring the most important part."

"Can you fix her?"

Kvenst rolls her eyes. "Get a dog, Mr. Max. This is a research project, not your fucking housepet. Don't get too attached."

"I can't solve this case without her. Can you fix her or not?"

Kvenst throws her cigarette on the ground and crushes it under the toe of her shoe. "I don't know. We'll see if the cog survived."

Max nods and turns back to the car.

"Where are you going?" she says in a voice that indicates she hasn't yet given him permission to leave. "We still need to know what happened."

"I'll be back," he says over his shoulder.

SUNDAY

Quarry

The car vibrates over the uneven mix of gravel, mud, and weeds. Red dashboard lights flicker on and off at random. This is a city car and it doesn't know what to make of this strange mix of textures. It can't decide if he's hydroplaning, he's got a flat, or if he's lost contact with the road.

The headlight beams fall on a rounded plastic lump of a house. It's a single story structure, roughly the shape of a bar of soap. It's got curved windows about the size of a man's face. Decades ago it was probably white, but now the surface is infused with grey quarry dust. A round chimney pokes up from the center of the roof, right next to some antique communications equipment that looks more like scaffolding than anything else. The gear is barely visible against the pre-dawn sky.

An old man appears on the porch, shirtless. He squints into the headlights and frowns before disappearing back inside.

Max kills the headlights and steps out. A moment later the porch light comes on, hitting him in the face with incandescent light. The old man reappears, only now he's wearing a shirt that's the same color as his house. He's also wearing a small pair of spectacles and he's brandishing a shotgun.

"You're gonna get back in your fancy car and fuck off back to the city on your own, or you can go right to the morgue. Either way, you're leaving."

"I'm pretty much tired of people making demands of me. Shoot me if you think that's how you want to spend your morning, but all I want is to ask some questions."

The old man looks down, weighing his options. This isn't a snap judgement for him. He really considers it. "Okay. Let's hear the questions."

"Just one really. Where is Faye?"

The old man opens his mouth, as if he's silently saying, "Ah!" He nods his head and says, "Yes. I see now. Your mother isn't here, Maxwell. She's at Parkstead, helping deliver a calf. Asked me to look after the place."

"Uncle Gord." This is both a greeting and a realization. He hasn't seen Gordon since he was a teenager. He's having trouble reconciling the wiry, eagle-eyed man he knew with the frail grandfather in front of him. What little hair he has left has gone white.

Gord puts the shotgun aside and motions for Max to approach. "I guess you'd better come in. I've got coffee, if you're interested in that sort of thing."

Aside from the ravages of entropy, the old house is just as he remembers it. The same picture of Jack is still hanging over the table in the kitchen. It's pale and faded now, as if the photograph itself was forgetting him. On the far side of the room is the living area. There's a sagging couch in the middle of the room, facing the display screen. The couch is clothed in rags at this point and covered in hand-sewn patches. It's the same couch Max sat on twenty years ago as he pulled on his shoes and snuck out of the house for the last time.

The near side of the room is the kitchen. In the center of all of this is the hearth, which is dormant this time of year. It's a stone cylinder that's been engraved with a bunch of traditional greetings and blessings. Soot has found its way into these grooves over the years, making the writing more pronounced than he remembers it. Everything is illuminated with dingy yellow light.

There's a saucepan of water on the stove. Gord isn't using a coffee maker. Instead he has a mottled square of fine cloth. He puts it over the end of a ceramic vessel and fastens it in place with a metal ring. The cloth is slack, so it hangs down into the vessel a bit. Gord gets out a metal canister with a crank on the side and adds a scoop of roasted beans from a burlap sack. There are some finger-driven latches to hold the lid closed, and once those are secure he starts turning the crank. He stands there, patiently cranking away and not making any effort to fill the time with chatter. He has to stop every few turns and shake the canister around to make sure all the beans are getting properly fed into the grinder. Twice he removes the lid just to make sure he's happy with how things look inside.

Once he's satisfied the beans are ground finely enough, he pours them into the little cloth pocket he's made. By the time he's done with all of this, the water has begun to boil. He pours it directly from the saucepan into the filter, stopping every few seconds to let it all soak through. Once this is done he has to take everything apart, wash it, and put it all away. Max glances at his handheld and notes that the entire operation takes just over eight minutes. To Max this is an exercise in absurdism, like a man getting up in the morning and weaving the suit he plans to wear that day.

At the end, Gord has two metal cups of coffee. He puts one down in front of Max and sits across from him with the other.

Max tries to pick up his cup, but the surface is too hot. As you'd expect, metal isn't a good insulator for drinks served near boiling. There are a couple of discolored squares on the side where it looks like a handle had been welded on at some point in the past, but that bit is long gone now.

Max tries to grab the cup by the rim where it will be the coolest. He can put his hand on it, but he can't hold onto it long enough to bring the cup to his lips.

Gord shoves his cup across the table and takes away Max's. This one still has the handle.

"Forgot how soft people's hands are in the city," he mumbles. Gord's hands have hard, thick calluses on them and he's able to hold the cup without apparent discomfort.

Gord has never been in a hurry to use words, so they're about halfway done with the coffee before he asks, "So what happened?"

"Happened?"

"To you. Something must have changed. You haven't visited your mother in years. You in trouble? I thought maybe you'd come back when you decided to get married, but you don't have a girl with you and those bruises tell me you're not here with good news."

"You're right," Max says. There's another two-minute lull in the conversation, and he can't take it anymore. Finally he asks, "So how's Aunt Lana?" just to break the silence.

"Gone." Gord looks down into his cup and swirls the dregs around a bit. "Five years ago. Heart attack. Out in the garden. Dead in minutes." He says this in the same tone of voice you might use to talk about how it's been really rainy this year.

"Sorry," Max says.

"If I'm really lucky, I'll get the same deal." He drains his cup.

257

Faye isn't here, but Max doesn't want to feel like he drove all the way out here for nothing. So he figures he might as well say what he needs to say. Gord probably won't understand, but he didn't come here to be understood. "The city is trying to kill itself, Uncle Gord. Or something. It's like a man trying to cut out his own heart because he's afraid of having a stroke."

"Is this the robot problem you're talking about? Is that where you got the bruises? That protest march?"

"No. Well, not really. These aren't political."

"You mixed up in this robot business?"

"Yeah."

"You behind it?"

"No. Trying to fix it." Max shoves his cup away. He's down to the dregs and it's too gritty to swallow at this point.

Gord takes the cups back to the sink, washes them, and puts them away again. Afterward he stands by the fridge and looks down at Max. "I didn't expect that. Last I heard you were causing problems rather than solving them."

Max shrugs. "It's a long story. The thing is, I feel like I'm trying to help a city that doesn't want to be helped. People aren't thinking. They're just... angry. They don't know who to be angry at, so they're angry at robots. It's not like people were fine with robots before this happened. It's like they've been expecting this all along. Maybe wanting it."

"And that's what you wanted to tell your mother?"

"I dunno. I thought... you guys have always been so against technology. I thought maybe your perspective would help make sense of it."

"Come with me," Gord says. He walks outside.

The sky is starting to lighten. Gord heads west, through the clusters of identical houses and dirty cars. Max pulls out his handheld and flips on the light.

"Turn that off. Just wait for your eyes to adjust."

Max wouldn't stumble around out here in the dark on his own, but Gord seems to know where he's going and Max can focus on his grey shirt and follow that. Max figures his uncle didn't drag him out here just to steer him into a ditch.

They climb the hill to the west of the town until they reach the rim of the quarry. By the time they arrive, his eyes are able to see the concentric layers leading down into the pit, where a large square pond of stagnant water has formed. From the top, the quarry looks like an enormous staircase where each step is a dozen feet high. The air smells of damp earth and wood fires.

Gord walks to a nearby utility pole and punches a red button with the side of his fist. A light comes on overhead. A drone hums to life. It flies into the quarry and begins circling. A battered weatherproof display screen pops out and shows the topography the drone is mapping out. Nearby, the water pump chugs to life. After a minute, a stream of murky water emerges and runs down the hill into a drainage ditch.

Gord is content to watch this process until all the machinery is up to full speed and the drone is done with its rounds. Finally he says, "My dad worked here, with your grandfather. I worked here with my brother. Now the younger guys work here. We used water pumps. We used diamond wire saws and burners. We used mapping drones, lifter drones, hauler drones. This place is over a half century old. It's the heart of the whole town. And it couldn't exist without technology. So where do you get the notion that we're against technology?"

"Well you don't use a lot of it, and you end up doing a lot more work."

Gord punches the red button again and the whole system winds down. The surge of water slows to a dribble, the light fades, and the drone begins flying back home.

"Shit, kid. No wonder you left. You never understood this place at all, did you?"

This sounds rhetorical to Max, so he doesn't say anything. He looks to the east. The humble domed sacellum is perched on the opposing hill. The night candle is still burning, filling the entrance with a feeble yellow light.

Gord starts back down the hill again. Max finds it a lot more challenging to follow now that he's been blinded by the floodlights.

259

Gord's voice comes from somewhere in the darkness ahead, "It's not about the technology. It's about you. We don't shun technology because it's evil. We ration technology because work is good for you."

"Yeah, I get that everyone needs jobs, but-"

"Dammit kid, I'm not talking about jobs you dense bastard. I'm not saying having a job is good for you. I'm saying the act of work itself is good. Pushing your muscles, cutting your skin, getting windburned, getting tired, getting dirt under your fingernails. That's how we're designed to live."

"Designed?" Max says, surprised. "Are you talking about-" he points up the hill to the sacellum.

Gord seems to get what he's driving at. "Not in the way your mother might think. I think the whole religious thing is a nice sentiment, but I don't have a use for it. No, I'm saying work is good for your body, it's good for your mind, and if you want to believe it's good for your spirit then that's okay with me. Just don't expect me to climb the fucking hill with you on Monday nights."

"Sometimes I think you might be underestimating how much work it is to live in the city," Max says once they're back at the house.

"You're confusing work with unpleasantness. Not everything that's unpleasant is work. I'm sure pushing buttons on a computer or talking on the phone is a rotten way to spend a day, but it's not work. That's what's wrong with the city. They gave all the real work to the robots but kept all the soul-sucking jobs for themselves. Because those jobs are physically easy. The problem is, you need to get up in the morning and know that the stuff you're doing today matters, and that the world itself will be worse off if you don't go out and do it. Sitting at a desk doesn't give you that. Growing the food you'll eat this winter does."

"It's going to get bad. People are so angry they want to tear the city apart."

"We're made to survive. From tooth to fingernail. Now they've got machines that do all the surviving for them. It leaves them without purpose. That's why everyone is miserable, in therapy, divorced, smoking drag, and rioting. It's why you make a living stealing from others instead of doing an honest day's work. You're trying to steal purpose from someone else."

260

Max isn't sure where Gord gets off calling city people "miserable". He's never thought of Gord as a particularly happy man, but he's not going to say that to his face. It would be bad manners to insult him for answering Max's question. Also, deep down Max is still kind of afraid of him.

Gord begins walking towards Max's car and Max gets the sense this visit is about to end. Gord says, "You know what happened when we kicked Kasaran out of our country?"

Max shrugs. Every schoolchild knows this one. "We celebrated."

There's just enough light that Max can see the look of perfect contempt Gord has on his face right now. "We starved."

Max rolls his eyes. "Yeah. But that's not the point, is it?"

"That's the entire fucking point, Maxwell! Without that fact nothing else that's happened in the last hundred and fifty years makes the least bit of sense. *We starved.* Two years after they were gone, one out of every five of us was dead. Our society was so fucked we forgot how to function on a basic level. Hunger and disease killed more of us than those white parasites ever did. And yet, do we regret it?"

The pause goes on so long Max realizes this question isn't rhetorical. Gord really expects an answer. "Obviously not."

"Obviously not," Gord agrees angrily. "We could've called the Kasaranians up, asked them to come back and rule us again. But we didn't. We never looked back. It was the worst thing that ever happened to us, and we celebrate the day it started. Kids decorate the fucking house to commemorate it. Why? Because we got back what mattered most. More important than our land. More important than our dignity. We got back our *purpose.* And now we've spent the last hundred years surrendering that purpose to machines."

"Well, it looks like they're going to get their purpose back. Some of them, anyway. I don't know what it'll do to the city in the process. I don't think they do either."

"They're living in a city that wasn't designed for them. That's a city for cattle. A city for creatures designed to be fat and miserable. There's nothing for us there."

Max looks up the hill towards the quarry. "What'll you do if that happens? The city isn't going to need a lot of building stone if it's falling apart."

Gord has instantly calmed down and returned to his stoic self. "They barely need any now. Maybe we'll starve. Maybe we'll pull through. Hard to say."

Gord turns and walks back to the house without another word. Max reaches for his cigarettes, but then thinks he'd rather leave first, then smoke. He gets in the car and leaves as fast as the dirt roads will let him.

Red

Max enters the G-Kinetics research building. He planned to walk all the way to the labs, but now he remembers there's a security door in the way. Aside from the robotic secretary - a creepy male model with disturbingly fake-looking plastic skin - there's nobody around. He's about to turn around and go back to the lobby when the automatic doors slide open. He stands there, waiting for someone to come through, but the passage is empty on the other side.

He looks around, trying to figure out who opened the door for him. He spots the security camera, nods at it, and goes through.

The lab is much busier this time around. Last time he was in here it was the middle of the night. Now it's midday. A group of people are gathered around a utility robot, talking to each other. Sometimes one of them will reach out and shove or pull the robot, trying to knock it off balance. It recovers and they all discuss the result. Someone notices him and suddenly all conversations in the room sputter out. Everyone is looking in his direction.

His eyes fall on a robot that looks exactly like Halona, Landro's dim-witted secretary. Max wonders if this is her, but then he remembers the robots only have six faces to choose from. There are probably only so many different styles of eyes and wigs available, which means there are bound to be a lot of twins. In fact, there's a male robot wandering around that's an exact copy of the plastic-looking one he passed a couple of minutes ago at the reception desk.

"Mr. Max. I wondered where you went. I see you went shopping." Dr. Kvenst is looking at the bag he's carrying. "Feel better now?"

Max waits. He figures if he ignores her, Kvenst will stop fucking with him and get down to business. When he's tired of waiting he says, "How is she?"

Kvenst frowns. "Has it occurred to you that maybe I don't want to give you one of the most valuable robots ever built so you can run around the city and get into gunfights?"

Kvenst knows about the gunfight. Which means Jen told her. Which means Jen is working again. "Where is she?"

"The news has a theory about what happened. They think Derek Stone went out to gather up some stray robots so they wouldn't get caught up in the protest. They turned on him, threw him off the roof of a building, and then hid in a van to ambush the protesters. I wonder how much of that is true?"

Max feels strange learning the name of the guy he killed. It makes it a little more personal somehow. "That's so far off I don't know how they came to that conclusion. That doesn't explain the gunshots on the roof. It doesn't explain the wreckage and the fire from Jen. I know the police in this city aren't the best, but that's ridiculous."

"So what did happen, Mister Detective?"

"Stone wasn't gathering up stray robots. He deliberately loaded three robots in his utility van and either locked them in or told them to stay put. Once the protest got near, he opened the door. As soon as they were out, he remotely triggered their rampage, and when it was over he detonated their brains."

"Can you prove this?"

"Not yet."

Kvenst mutters under her breath in Kasaranian.

Heads turn. Max follows their eyes to see another robot has entered. The face is familiar, but her hair is bright red and her eyes are vibrant orange lights.

"Jen?"

She nods. "It's me."

Max doesn't know what to say. He's not good at expressing himself under optimal circumstances and this room is pretty far from optimal. He gets the impression anything remotely sentimental will earn him derision. He tries to be casual about it. "You changed your eyes."

"Mr. Law, they changed everything." She points to the morgue. Through the open blinds he can see the wreckage of her former body, with empty eyes and a slack jaw. It's basically the last thing he needed to see at this point.

Jen is wearing a white uniform like most of the other people in here. Max can see now that these uniforms are deliberately baggy. They're designed to go over your normal clothes.

He drops the bag in front of her. "New clothes. Durable, in case we end up in another chase. Also, you'll blend in more."

"Do you really think it will pass for a native with that pale skin?" Kvenst asks.

"She doesn't need to pass for a native. She just needs to stop looking like a tourist."

"Okay," Jen says. She unfastens her uniform and shrugs out of it. Max spins on his heel and heads for the door.

Dr. Kvenst laughs. "Better give it some privacy! You wouldn't want to embarrass it!"

Jen joins him in front of the building a few minutes later. "You don't look well. When was the last time you slept?"

"You just got blown in half and you're worried I might not be sleeping enough?"

"I'm fine, Mr. Law."

"You can call me Max. I call you Jen, so you can call me Max. We're friends now, as far as I can tell."

"Okay Max. Like I said, I'm fine."

She's wearing trousers this time. This is accompanied by a button-up shirt with a high collar. It's all in muted earth tones. Max chose this outfit because it has a certain class ambiguity. You could wear this in an office or you could wear it to a club. It's not ideal for either occasion, but it's passable in both.

"Did you kill Mr. Stone?"

Max looks away, out to the parking lot. "Yeah."

"You okay?"

"As far as I can tell."

"Was that the first time for you?"

"No. Ten years ago some guy pulled a gun on me. We traded shots. He missed. I didn't. He died the next day. It was all sort of distant and impersonal. But this one... This one got pretty fucking personal."

"Do you need grief counseling? I actually have some training-"

"No. Fuck no. Please. Let's just... not talk about it."

They walk towards the car.

"You want me to drive?" she asks. "You don't look well."

"I'm fine. Had some coffee a few hours ago. Was so thick I almost needed a spoon. It's keeping me going."

They get in and Max heads back towards the city.

"What did I miss?" Jen asks.

Max reaches into his pocket and pulls out a crude little plastic box with a couple of buttons on it. "This was in Derek Stone's pocket." He hands it to her.

"You retrieved it from his body? That was a three-story drop."

"Like I said, it got pretty personal. Anyway, I'm ninety percent sure he had that thing in his hand when the robots went crazy."

"It looks homemade."

"Yeah. Two buttons. I figure one button makes them kill, the other blows their brains out. All three robots snapped at the same time, and all three heads exploded at the exact same time. Pretty much killed my animatronic puppetry idea."

"Anatomical puppetry," she corrects him. "And yes. But we knew that theory had a lot of holes in it anyway."

"So now we're back to where we started. We know this is sabotage, but we don't know who's doing it, how they're doing it, or what their goal is. I mean, I'm just assuming Derek Stone wasn't behind the whole thing. Because where would a city employee get the tools and knowledge to pull this off?"

"It's a shame we couldn't capture him."

"Are you really okay with all of this?" Max asks. "Like, that guy basically murdered you. Nearly got me too. Fuck that guy."

"Like I said, I'm fine. To put it in human terms, it was basically the greatest day of my life."

"You're going to have to explain that to me."

"I disabled two of the three robots. I personally saved two human lives through direct intervention. That's the greatest thing that can happen to a robot. I'm pretty sure Mr. Stone was outside of the blast radius when my battery ruptured, so I don't have to worry I might have hurt him. We made some progress and even if we haven't solved the case, we may have disrupted the attacks. Having one of the latest-gen platforms destroyed was disappointing, but easily worth it."

The miles roll by. Max has one of those strange moments where he can't remember the last five minutes of driving. He was on the rooftop again, watching Jen bleed fire.

"Did it... hurt? Or whatever?"

"Part of my sensory experience is information on damage I've sustained. Obviously I try to avoid damage and I see it as a bad thing. You could call that information pain, but there's no way to know if it's anything like your pain."

"It would have to be, wouldn't it? I mean, that's what pain is."

"Think of damage mechanics in a videogame."

"I don't play games."

"Okay, but you're familiar with how they work. The game conveys that your character is being hurt or injured, and if you sustain too many injuries you lose."

"Sure. I get how it works."

"By your definition, that would count as pain. It's negative input you want to avoid."

"Yeah, but that's happening to my guy in the game or whatever. It doesn't... hurt. Or whatever."

"Now we have a tautological argument. 'Pain is input that hurts'. That just takes us back to the original question of whether or not it hurt when my body was damaged. But how can we tell if the pain I feel is like the pain you feel when you cut your finger, or if it's more abstract, like videogame feedback?"

"I don't have any idea. I thought you'd know."

"How can I know? I don't know what you're feeling any more than you know what I'm feeling. We have no way to compare."

"I'm sorry I brought it up." They're driving through another sad town of prefab housing. It's amazing how similar these places all look. The road winds around quite a bit, but when it's heading properly south like it's supposed to he can see Rivergate in the distance.

"I'm not. This is a really important topic to me. I've spent a lot of time thinking about it. I'm really interested in taking care of humans and helping them avoid pain, which means I need to know how their pain works. At the lab some of the philosophically-minded people would argue about this all the time. Over the past few months I've come up with this theory. I'm pretty sure your pain is different from my pain. I can't prove it, of course."

"But you just said you can't know what I'm feeling, so how do you know I'm feeling something different?"

"Let's talk about a hypothetical. Say you're climbing a mountain."

"Sounds like this hypothetical takes place in Kasaran."

"It's true, I came up with this in Kasaran. Lots of the people I knew were into mountain climbing. Anyway. While climbing, you fall and break your leg. You realize you need to get back down the mountain or you'll die of exposure. You just need to crawl or hop down, and you'll survive. You know what you need to do, but you can't do it, because the slightest movement causes too much agony."

"But now we're talking about intensity of pain. Isn't this just the same problem?"

"One more hypothetical. You're captured by some enemy force in wartime. They want to know some information. If you tell them, then people you love will die. Your entire being is dedicated to not telling them. Giving up the information means losing everything you value in the world. And yet, it's possible for the enemy to inflict so much pain on you that you'll tell them."

"So you're arguing that our pain is different because it's more intense?"

"No. I'm arguing that your pain is different because it's capable of overriding your decision-making. My theory is that this overriding is what makes pain *painful*."

Max frowns. He's not really sure this explanation works for him, but he has no idea how to argue this with a robot.

Jen continues, "There is no level of negative sensory data that can make me betray my core values. You can't torture me into hurting people or even get me to stop trying to help them. I'll dislike what's being done to me and I'll want it to stop, but there's no threshold of negative input that will break my will."

Max considers this for a bit. "So you're saying your pain isn't like my pain because of how your respond to it?"

"My response to pain is a lot more like a human's response to videogame input. It's information that informs action without overriding reason."

"You're immune to torture and you can get blown up and still have the best day of your life. Being a robot is starting to sound pretty good."

MONDAY

Superway

Max is sitting on the end of the bed and rubbing his eyes when Jen comes in.

"I got you coffee. They didn't have any cinnamon donuts so I got you plain. I also got you more cigarettes. You were getting low." She says this as she places each item on the shabby undersized table by the window.

He never told her his brand of smokes, what donuts he likes, or how he liked his coffee. She figured this out on her own. On one hand, this is off-putting like the prostitute he visited as a teen. She's pretending to care about him because she has to. On the other hand, is it really pretending? Her affection is supposedly as real as anyone's, but knowing that her drives were designed by a human being makes the whole thing feel artificial anyway.

"I barely remember coming here," he says. He's got some vague memories of checking in, but he doesn't remember deciding to stop or getting into bed.

"On our way into the city you asked me the same question three times in a row. When I pointed this out you agreed to pull over and get some sleep."

Max nods. It's coming back to him now. He's having a moment of paralysis where he can't decide if he wants to start with the coffee, the smokes, or the food, so he's staring at all three and not doing anything. He eventually wakes up enough to make some decisions and begins consuming things until he feels like a person again.

They're in the Superway Motel, which is in one of the satellite towns on the fringe where the rocky wilderness turns to pavement. He's driven by this place a dozen times in his life and never given it a second look. The room has one bed, one chair, and one tiny table. There's a small window letting grey morning light into the room. A TV is mounted on the wall. Jen turns this on and turns the volume off.

Max is pulling on the same clothes he's been wearing for three days when he feels a rectangular object in his pocket.

"Oh hey. I forgot to give you this," he says. He pulls out her handheld and tosses it to her.

Jen turns the device over in her hand, examining it, "I assumed this was lost in the fight."

"Nope. I found it on the ground near your... uh, torso. The backside screen has a nasty crack, but it still works. I guess it fell out of your pocket."

"I was holding it when I arrived on the roof. When Mr. Stone pointed the gun at me I dropped it on the ground. I wanted my hands free in case I saw an opportunity to grab the weapon. Too bad that didn't work out. We might have been able to save him. Also, he might have been able to give us information."

"Yeah, I really don't want to think about that whole thing right now."

He checks his handheld. There's another message from Jonas. He has the message play on speaker.

"Hi friend. Look, I've been digging into this custom chip you gave me. It's... weird. I've had to take apart machine code to get around cryptosystems before, but I've never seen code like this. I can't even tell what language it was written in. The compiler signature is 'Yendu Edgefront 402'. Yendu is a company, but I don't know what 'Edgefront' is. Maybe they have their own custom language? Anyway. I still have no idea what this thing does."

Max stares at the device for ten full seconds before he says, "I have no idea what the fuck this kid just said to me."

Without looking away from the television Jen says, "Programmers write code. But a computer can't run that code directly. It's just a bunch of text. To turn the text into a program, you use a compiler."

"Let's just assume I understand what you've said so far."

"When a compiler creates a program like this, it typically 'signs' it. This just means it leaves a little string of text that says what compiler was used. After the compiler name is usually the version number. It doesn't *need* to do this. The computer running the program ignores the signature. It doesn't care. The signature is just there so that if a human comes along later, they can look for this signature and see where it came from."

"So a signature is like signing your name on the bottom of a painting?" Max is trying to find some already-existing idea he can attach this one to. He's never really messed around with high-level technocrime, because that usually comes down to your programmers vs. the other side's programmers. There's not a lot of need for his skills in that domain.

"No. The signature doesn't tell you who wrote the program. It tells you what tools were used. So whatever that chip does, the code was written in a programming language we've never heard of. It's evidently a programming language created by Yendu Industrial."

"We had them on our list of possible suspects," Max says.

"The really odd thing is the middle part of the name. 'Edgefront' is a couple of Local words pushed together. Yendu has no presence in this country that I'm aware of, so why would they be using words in your language to name their software?"

"Huh. 'Edgefront' sounds familiar to me. I know I've heard it before, but I can't remember where."

Max grabs a napkin and writes the information down. He's thinking maybe seeing it visually will jog his memory.

YENDU EDGEFRONT 402

He stares at the napkin. "So we've got a company name, followed by the name of a computer language-"

"Programming language," she corrects him. "It could also be the name of a compiler. Actually, that's more likely."

"And after that we have a version number."

"Yes. Assuming the message that Jonas found is a compile signature."

Max stares at the napkin some more, hoping some sort of epiphany will straighten this out.

Jen looks up from her handheld, "I just did a search. There's a band called 'Edgefront Sideways'. Maybe that's what you're thinking of?"

"Maybe. I guess I might have heard of them though Clare. She played with a lot of different bands," Max says doubtfully. He still feels like he's missing something.

"Here, this is what I wanted you to see," Jen says. She steps out of the way of the television.

A news program is showing robots being fed into an industrial crusher. Some guys in orange police uniforms are standing around with high-powered weapons, overseeing the operation while guys with hard hats do the work. A magnetic crane is picking robots up two or three at a time and dropping them into the spinning teeth of the machine. Sometimes there's a little jet of flame or a flash of light. The television is still muted, so this drama is completely silent.

"Their batteries don't blow up the way yours did."

"That's just the cog batteries we're seeing. I imagine they removed the ambulatory power before scrapping the robots. This would be too dangerous otherwise."

"I guess it's good the robots are powered down before they go into the machine."

"Just their bodies," she says. "Their brains are probably still running."

Max cringes. "So these guys are paralyzed before being fed, *alive and awake*, into a crusher? That's what you're telling me?"

Jen shrugs, "They're generation two machines. They have a very limited concept of what's going on. And like I said yesterday, we don't feel pain the way you do. Even if they understood the significance of what's happening to them, this process isn't going to be alarming."

"So you basically don't have empathy for anything that isn't human."

"Sympathy, not empathy. But yes. Why would I be designed with sympathy for other robots? That would be a dangerous and counterproductive drive. I'd be prone to the sort of tribalism that causes so many fights between humans."

"Okay," Max says while not actually agreeing with her.

The news is really lingering on this footage. The machine consists of two rollers arranged side-by-side, rotating towards each other. The rollers are laying horizontally, so that gravity will pull material into their grip. There are blunt, knobby little teeth on the surface to help push things through. He watches a robot fall into the machine face-up. The body jerks as the wheels take hold. It's pulled in ass-first, the limbs crumpling up like paper a second before vanishing

274

from view. The head is the last to go, the face contorting into an insane mask and then popping like a firecracker as the battery ruptures. Then it all vanishes into belly of the crusher as another robot is dropped.

Max finds the footage to be vaguely hypnotic, even if he objects to the act itself. "Giving the robots back for recall was already pointless, but crushing them is... just..." he flails around, trying to pack all of his annoyance and contempt into a single idea, "...completely stupid. If you're going to get rid of them, at least give them back to the company for the refund. There's nothing to be gained from this."

"I think this is more about catharsis than anything else," Jen says.

Max nods, feeling a vague sort of embarrassment for his species. "This is the industrial equivalent of a public hanging."

Jen points to some blurry details in the background of the shot. "Robot access doors. This is probably taking place at a service center like the ones we've been visiting."

Max shakes his head in frustration. "Which means this public revenge theater could also be destroying evidence. Fuck."

"I wonder what they're doing with the ambulatory batteries," Jen says without looking away from the screen. "You can't just throw away hundreds of batteries. They're dangerous."

"Yeah, I noticed," Max says.

The news switches over to some talking heads. Max stands up and shuts off the TV. "Let's get going."

"Great," Jen says. "I need breakfast."

The Superway Motel encircles its own parking lot on three sides. It's a three-story building, except there's no second floor. Instead, the vacant space between the first and third is filled with massive billboards that face the highway. The screens tilt northward in the morning to face inbound traffic, and southward in the evening.

Their car is parked directly in front of the room. As Max (or more precisely, the key Max is carrying) gets close, the car disengages from the charging port and the charging arm folds back into the body.

Jen reaches down and puts her hand over the charging port. "I just need a couple of minutes to top off," she says.

"Did the police send you the projection data from the crime scene?"

"Which one?" she asks.

"I'm talking about the protest. Specifically, I'm hoping we can get an image of Derek Stone."

"I can check," she says as she whips out her handheld with her free hand. She types one-handed for a few seconds. At one point she needs to re-orient the screen. She does this by quickly letting go of the device and then snatching it out of the air with her hand in the desired position. If a human was doing this Max would assume they were just showing off, like a street chef.

"Yes," she says. "They have an image for each of the robots, another one of some unrelated vandalism that happened west of us, and one more of Derek Stone."

"Can you send me whatever they have of Stone?"

She does, and Max starts the download. It's going to take a few minutes, because network access is garbage this far north of the city. Max leans against the car and has another smoke. He doesn't particularly need one right now, but it's something to keep his hands busy. He realizes this is probably how guys work themselves into a three-packs-a-day habit.

"Here's what's bothering me," Max says after a couple of minutes of silence. "The police interpretation of yesterday's attack makes no sense."

"You mean Saturday. Today is Monday."

"Right. Anyway, how do they explain the wreckage we left behind on the roof? If they found the guy on the ground, then they certainly went up to the roof. If they went to the roof, they found the lower half of your body, evidence of a battery explosion, spent bullet casings, some blood from our fistfight, and probably a dozen other things I'm forgetting right now. They look at all that chaos, and their theory is that the three robots threw that guy off the roof? And how does anyone explain you ripping the heads off those robots? That happened on TV. They can't ignore that."

"I watched the news while you slept. The city hasn't made any official comment about my actions during the protest. The most popular theory in the media is that someone 'reprogrammed' a robot to hunt down and kill rogue units. I think the idea of the rumor is that G-Kinetics is trying to cover its tracks so they aren't blamed for this mess."

"Which doesn't make any sense, since people have been blaming them since day one anyway."

"Also, the media has found out about my 'wreckage'. The guess is that this robot hunter was killed by more rogue robots. Meaning there are still more rogues on the loose."

Max shakes his head. "People have watched too many movies."

"The police haven't commented, and G-Kinetics hasn't commented, so it's natural their thinking will gravitate towards familiar ideas. And really, is their scenario less plausible than the truth?"

"I dunno. A robot hunter, sent out to kill other robots that have gone rogue?"

Jen shrugs. "I'd do it. If I knew how to find them, I'd be happy to hunt them down. The problem is that things aren't that simple."

There's another silence. He's amazed at how much better his mind is working now that he's had some sleep. He realizes he's finally catching up on all the thinking he couldn't do earlier because he was too tired. "Here's another thing that's bothering me."

Jen switches hands. "I'm listening."

"We've got some hints that Yendu Industrial made the haunted circuit. Or the chips on it. Whatever. They're mixed up in this. At the same time, Derek Stone worked for the city. A foreign corporation and a city worker. That's an odd pairing. Like, how did they even hire him? You can't advertise that job on the network."

"Maybe it was the other way around? Maybe he solicited their help."

"Maybe," Max says. "And then there's the police. Their official statement on the events is so wrong I want to say it's a cover-up. Except, what would they be covering up? I feel like we understand even less now than when we started on this case."

There's a smell of hot plastic in the air. Jen is standing partly bent over, with one hand on the knee-high charging port. This is a perfectly reasonable position for a human to adopt for a short time.

277

The problem is, a human would begin shifting their weight or trying to take some of the burden off their lower back. Jen is standing perfectly still. She's also not craning her head around, even though a human would quickly get bored staring at the ground.

"Is the company trying to make you pass for human? Not now, obviously. But is that a long-term plan?"

"I don't think so. I've never sensed it was a priority. Perfect imitation is more the kind of thing Senma is into. In our thinking, we need to walk a really fine line. We want our units to look human enough that people can be comfortable working with them and bonding with them, but we also want a little bit of artifice visible so the user doesn't get creeped out by any deviations. I'm not entirely happy with the eyes because they're only visible to people in front."

"Being able to put on sunglasses and pass for human has been pretty useful so far."

"That's true, but our situation is an anomaly. In Kasaran, my face is too famous for me to be anonymous. This is one of the few places I can go and not be outed immediately. And this is a rare time and place where being a robot would be seen as a negative. There just aren't that many situations where I can blend in and there are even fewer where it would be useful to do so."

The download is finished, so Max puts on his projection glasses.

"We're nowhere near the scene," Jen says. "Is it going to show you the image from a different location?"

"You can override it," Max says. A minute later he discovers this is annoyingly difficult to do. The designers evidently went to a lot of trouble to hide the option to view a capture of one location while standing somewhere else. He has to dismiss a bunch of warning messages, but eventually the glasses agree to project the alleyway scene into this parking lot.

The result turns out to be messier than he expected. The alleyway was level, but this parking lot slopes downward very slightly towards the road. The glasses can't decide if they want to make the ground line up, or the walls line up, and so the image jitters around. Max turns around, looking for the body.

"Oh fuck," he says when Derek comes into view. "I forgot how nasty this was."

He didn't *actually* forget what the scene looked like. It's been burned into his memory. But he did forget just how nauseating it was to see.

In the movies, people seem to hold together when slamming into the pavement at terminal velocity. But as Max learned when he saw this scene with his own eyes a few days ago, in real life it looks more like the result of dropping a human-sized tomato. Bits of gore extend radially from the point of impact, and the body looks disturbingly deflated.

He takes a few steps back, being careful not to tread in any of the blood. He realizes this is silly, since the blood isn't really there and he probably looks like a lunatic to anyone that might be watching him right now. Despite this he can't bring himself to touch the messy bits, even if they are virtual.

"I feel like I'm going to be sick," he says.

"I can do it," Jen says. "I'm not disturbed by the sight of blood."

"Robots can use projection glasses?"

"We have eyes, so yes."

"Right. I guess that makes sense."

She disengages from the charger and he gratefully hands over the glasses.

She slides the glasses down into place. They're wide, bulky, and wrap halfway around her head. The screen is a single curved surface of clear plastic that covers the entire horizontal field of view. The frames reach all the way down to her cheekbone and all the way up to her eyebrows. Max can see dots of ghostlike images shimmering on the plastic surface. To Jen these form a crisp picture, but from where Max is standing they're just a kaleidoscopic blur.

"What am I looking for?" she asks.

"Somewhere over here should be a set of keys," Max is gesturing at a spot on the ground where he thinks they were being projected.

Jen turns around and crouches to look at an empty spot of parking lot. "I found them. They landed splayed open, balanced on their edge."

"They didn't land like that. I set them like that. I didn't want to be caught carrying his personal items away from the scene. It took me a couple of minutes to haul your torso down the steps and I was worried the cops were going to show up any second. I mean, if I get caught with his keys in my pocket and then he turns up dead? That wouldn't go well for me. So I set the keys here and hoped I'd be able to recover them this way."

"Did you have any trouble getting past the police?"

"Not really. They'd set up a perimeter around the protest scene and they stopped me as I tried to leave. I told them I was going to the hospital. I was pretty banged up. They said that was fine as long as I let the car drive and I reported to officer so-and-so to make a statement once I was patched up. Then I drove away. I didn't need to go to all of this trouble. I could have just taken his keys. But I wanted to be safe."

Jen is still kneeling down, looking at the ground. "So what do you need me to do?"

"Just take some screenshots of the keys. I need a picture from both sides of each key."

"You can recreate keys based on images?"

"I know a guy," Max says.

In the city, Max takes Jen to a locksmith he's been working with for years. It's very pricey for such a run-down place, but what you're really paying for is the no-questions-asked policy. He hands over the images and the locksmith feeds them into the computer. The computer turns the keys into 3D models and the models are sent to the shaper. Max has the keys made in plastic rather than metal. Not only is it cheaper, but it's a little easier to make corrections in the field if the shape is slightly off. This sort of extrapolation is not an exact science.

Next they need to head for one of the many identical cube-shaped apartment complexes in The Grunge. This is unfortunate, since it means they have to drive right through the heart of the Hospitality District during rush hour. Max tries looping around, hoping to miss some of the traffic. He hits a lot of traffic anyway and they end up spending most of the morning in the car.

"I don't understand. What is this place?" Jen says as they step out onto the cracked pavement.

"We just spent an hour riding together and you never asked where we were going. That would have been the first thing a human did as soon as the doors were closed."

280

"I figured we were going to visit another robot storage facility."

"Besides his keys, the other thing I found on Stone was his ID. Which gave me his home address."

Honeyvale Apartments is a brutalist cube of soot-colored concrete. Like most places in The Grunge, the windows are small so the building has more surface area to sell to advertisers. There's a mound of garbage bags beside the building, but if you look closely you can see the corner of a dumpster sticking out. The bushes out front have faded and their plastic has turned brittle, ruining the illusion of life. Enormous holes in the asphalt have become stagnant pools where stray dogs congregate.

The interior hallways smell like mildew. The walls have absorbed decades of cigarette smoke. The top of the wall is the color of jaundice, and at the bottom the paint is flaking off. The tattered carpeting has been patched with duct tape so people don't trip. Max can hear every footstep and door-slam from the nearby units. Conversations and television become a murmur of low frequencies as they pass through the walls.

Derek lived on the seventh floor, in one of the dreadful interior apartments that don't get windows. Max slots the key into place and the door pops open.

Max has been in a lot of these kinds of apartments. He even lived in one for a couple of years, although his had a balcony. They all look basically the same. There are only so many ways an architect can arrange the same three rooms. The main room is split between living area and kitchen. Then there are two doors, one for the toilet and the other for the bed.

Derek's apartment is a little different from most because he's turned his living area into a workshop. There's a workbench along one wall, with a powerful blue light on it. Several tools are mounted on the wall over the bench: A screen, a worklight, a magnifying glass, and a few strange power tools that Max doesn't recognize. The table is scattered with scraps of circuit board and bundles of fine colored wire. If someone were to disembowel a robot, this is what he imagines the guts would look like.

There's an abrupt scream from a woman. Max is about to remark on how thin the walls are here that you can hear the scream so clearly, but then he turns around to see a woman standing in the doorway to the bedroom.

"Ma'am," he says with a completely relaxed nod.

She's trembling, looking at him wild-eyed. She looks over to the entrance in disbelief. "Who are you? You broke into the wrong apartment. There's nothing for you here."

Max keeps his relaxed voice. It's amazing how quickly people will settle down when they're the only agitated person in the room. "We didn't break in. We recovered Mr. Stone's keys from the crime scene."

She looks them up and down and swallows hard. "So what, are you cops or something?"

"We're investigating the robot incidents."

"I already talked to some of the other cops. Those other guys knocked, by the way. You guys have been hounding him for weeks, asking him about the stupid robots. Like he's supposed to know why they're going haywire. Now you're wandering in here like you own the place. You want to know what's wrong with the robots you should start by asking the sneaky foreigners who sold them to us."

"I understand you've already talked to the police. I apologize for the redundancy, but we're part of a more focused investigation."

The woman stares at Jen with a furious expression on her face. For whatever reason, Jen took off her sunglasses when she came in, so now this woman is looking straight into her glowing orange eyes.

Max doesn't know how to play this yet, so he's giving the woman lots of room to talk.

"So what do? I hope you're not gonna ask me the same questions."

Max gets out his handheld and pretends to read stuff from it. Finally he looks up at her. "So what are you? The girlfriend?"

"Unless Derek was keeping some pretty big secrets from us, he never had a girlfriend," she says with contempt.

Max's eyes flick over to the screen over the workbench and he realizes the login prompt features a beefcake picture of a shirtless, muscle-bound man.

"I'm his sister!" she says impatiently, like it's written on her forehead or something. "Meg," she adds a second later in the same tone.

"Okay Meg," Max says. "How did Derek get his current job?"

The truth is that Max isn't even sure what Derek's job was, but he figures he'll get the more specific details buried in the answer to the broader question.

"What, you writing his life story?"

"Ma'am, this is a big, complicated case. I don't have time to explain the whole thing to every person I interview, even if I could."

"What I'm saying is, it's a long story. Do you really want to hear the whole thing or are you only interested in the recent stuff like those other cops?"

"I'd like to hear the whole thing," Max says. He only says this because she sounded sort of hopeful when she asked the question and he gets the impression this is what she wants to hear. He doesn't know why. Maybe she just really needs someone to talk to.

Meg is fortyish, which means she's probably the older sister. Predictably, she got a southside accent, which means Derek would have treated him to a southside accent if he hadn't been such a vicious fucker and tried to shoot everybody. Meg has dark hair that goes well past her shoulders. She's got a hard, sharp face, the face of someone who's spent a lot of their life keeping their emotions bottled up. Even now her lips are tight. Her eyes are slightly puffy.

She nods. "Okay. Derek always liked electrical stuff. I mean obviously," she gestures to the workbench. "So he went to trade school for two years. Got all his certifications. Was all set to work maintenance for the city. Good work. Good money, once you've got seniority. Six months into the job they bring the robots in. Tell him he's supposed to train them. The older guys refuse. But the city promises Derek that the robots are just there to fill in during emergencies. Big storms, power outages, people getting sick, that kind of thing. Derek is really smart but he's also kinda stupid. He trusts people. So he trains the robots.

283

Sure enough, once the robots can do the work, the city starts getting rid of people. They start with the older guys because they're more expensive. But the city tells him not to worry. They tell him this is a promotion. Like, he's the boss of the robots now. Sure, it's a promotion with no raise and no title, but whatever. He does what he's told. But then sure enough, after a couple of years they get rid of him. There's only one power grid in town, so it's not like he can just do the same job elsewhere. All that education, gone to waste."

She stops and looks around. Max instantly recognizes the look of someone trying to find their smokes. He offers her a cigarette and gives her a light.

Meg gives him a nod of thanks. "So then he goes back to school. Hydraulic engineering this time. Figures he can get a job at the treatment plant. Eighteen months into his two years, the city brings in robots and starts replacing all the people there. So now they're not hiring. Again, all that money down the drain."

"But, I thought education was free in the city," Jen says.

Meg gives her a look of cold hatred, "Education is free. But the licenses to work for the city? The certs to say you're qualified? The months it takes to earn those things? None of that shit is free."

"I see," Jen says.

Meg curls her lip in disgust. "I'll bet you do." She turns back to Max and relaxes again, "So now Derek has to start over. Again. He can't afford to spend any more time in school. So he takes whatever he can get. He joins the Sanitation Union and gets a job hauling trash. Can you imagine? A kid that smart, hauling trash around the city, making less than he made in his first year as an electrical troubleshooter. Fucking senseless."

She sits down at the kitchen table. There's only one chair and the table is only big enough for one person. She stares for a few seconds and sniffs, perhaps trying to remember where she left off. Finally she says, "So then they start with the robots again. It's normally three guys to a truck. One driving, and two riding on the back, you know? The city replaces one of those guys with a robot. Except, who can keep up with a robot? They're strong and they don't get hungry and they can keep going all day. So then the city gets rid of the other guy in back. So now Derek is working all by himself, driving robots around. The city promises that they won't get rid of his job, because robots aren't allowed to drive. But they don't need to give that job to a robot because a year later the city buys self-driving garbage trucks. So now poor Derek is only thirty and his career is already over for the third time, and each career has been worse than the last."

Max realizes that by asking her to tell the story, he's in for a lot more than just a bunch of personal information. This woman is alone and more than anything what she really wants is a witness.

Her voice is cracking now, "Derek was going be the successful one in the family. Get a good job doing electrical stuff. Maybe get a nice place on the West Side. But then it turns out he's worse off than any of us, living in this shithole all by himself."

Meg trails off at this point as she's overcome by a mix of rage and sadness. She begins sobbing.

This is the most uncomfortable Max has been since he threw her brother off the roof two days ago. He does not handle crying well at all and he never knows how to behave around people in this emotional state. He's tried to respond to this sort of thing in a lot of different ways, and the only thing he's figured out is that all of them were wrong.

Jen steps forward and puts her hand on Meg's shoulder. "I'm so sorry you're hurting. You obviously loved your brother very much. You're right to be angry. He was treated badly and people did not recognize his value as a person or as a worker."

Meg's hand clamps down on Jen's so strongly that her knuckles turn white. She lets out a deep sob and nods her head several times. Finally she looks up at Jen, teary-eyed, and says, "Thank you." It is the most intense expression of gratitude that Max has ever seen. He's watched guys beg for their lives to creditors, and when they were given a reprieve their relief was not as palpable as what Meg just went through.

She pulls herself together, wipes her eyes, and takes a few deep breaths. Once she's stable again she continues, "He got another job. The city hired him to look after the robots. Fix their tools, keep their vehicles running, fix their chargers. So after they took all his jobs, he's finally allowed to have a job serving them. And then they... Well, I assume you know what they did to him."

285

Meg is done crying now, and her voice is cold and flat. She's staring straight ahead, her eyes focused as if looking at some distant point.

Max gets the impression he needs to give this story a little breathing room before he follows up with another question. He pretends to examine some of the things on the workbench, which quickly turns into *actually* examining stuff on the workbench, because he finds another haunted circuit. Or at least, this little circuit board looks exactly like the haunted circuit as far as Max can tell. It's sitting all by itself in the bottom of a small cardboard box. He lifts up one of the flaps of the box to see "Port Rich" handwritten on it.

Max remembers he's supposed to be interviewing Meg and turns back to her. "Other than the change in jobs, has he gone through any abrupt changes in the last eighteen months or so? New group of friends? Odd behavior. Anything?"

"Like I told the other guys, he was getting some extra money. First he used it to buy more toys. That's what he called the electrical stuff you're looking at now. Toys. He gave a little to the family. Helped me out when my daughter got sick and I needed some time off work to take care of her. Other than that, everything was normal."

"Do you know what this stuff is?" Max asks, pointing at the stuff on the bench.

"No idea. When he was young he was always showing his projects off. He'd build a drone or mod his handheld or whatever and he'd make the rest of us look at it, whether we understood what he was doing or not. But he never talked about the stuff on the bench. I don't know. I heard gangsters sometimes make devices that can hack your bank card and steal all your money. I was worried he was doing something like that. But he never talked about it."

Max resists the urge to say, "*I wish* it was that easy!" Instead he follows up with, "What about his friends?"

"I don't know. Sometimes he spent time with his coworkers, but I was never really introduced." Meg stands up. "Can I offer either of you anything? I mean, he doesn't have much but..."

"I would appreciate a drink of water," Max says.

"I'll see if I can find a clean glass," Meg says with a forced laugh.

Max motions for Jen to join him. He holds up the haunted circuit, then points at the empty box labeled "Port Rich", then points at another box on the floor that's taped shut and has "Fennel Hills" written on the top. He raises his eyebrows at her, and she mirrors the expression. It turns out she's right; mirroring is really obvious once you know about it. If she hadn't told him about mirroring expressions this would have felt like a perfectly natural silent exchange.

Max swipes the haunted circuit just before Meg turns around and offers him a glass of tap water. He takes a sip, just to keep up the pretense that he wanted it. He can smell something is off before he tastes it, but it still comes as a surprise when it hits his mouth. He coughs and sputters and spits it back out.

"Yeah. Sorry," Meg says. "It's gotten really bad the last couple of days. I've been mostly drinking coffee or beer."

Max holds the cup up to the light. The water is murky. "That sounds like a good idea," Max says as he puts the glass down. "Thanks for your time."

Meg sniffs and looks up at Jen. "I know what you are. I know what you can do."

Jen doesn't say anything in response.

Meg continues, "I saw you on TV. Or one of you. I don't care if you're working for those foreigners or not. I just want you to do your job. Destroy those sons of bitches that killed my brother. Destroy all of them. Make sure they never hurt anyone else."

Jen nods.

Fifteen minutes later the two of them are standing on the curb waiting for the car when Max says, "Derek Stone had the tools. He had both motive and opportunity. But I feel like we're still missing a lot of pieces. If he had the ability to make the robots kill in groups of three, then why did he wait until now? That was a lot of circuit boards back there."

"We still don't know how he made robots kill. I know Meg said he was good at working with electronics, but it's a huge leap to go from that to modifying a robot brain. That's like going from kite flying to aerospace engineering."

He frowns. He's looking down the street where he expects the car to appear. He actually sent it across the river to find parking so it wouldn't get vandalized. "So he had an accomplice."

An hour later they're standing outside of a warehouse in the Port Rich District. A crusher is parked out front and guys in hard hats are feeding limp robots into it. A dozen or so civilians are standing at a distance, watching and taking pictures. A couple of police are keeping the crowd back, while the rest are pointing guns at the line of robots waiting to have their batteries pulled out.

Jen looks around the scene. "The good news is that people are noticing these places, taking pictures, and making them public. They're easy to find now."

"The bad news is all the evidence will be gone by the time we get there," Max shouts. The crusher is deafening even when it's not currently chewing apart metal skeletons. "All this time I sort of assumed he was tampering with robots one at a time. But that box back there could hold a lot of circuit boards. Maybe he's been modding a lot of them. Maybe even all of them."

"I have a few more addresses we can try," she says. "Maybe we'll get lucky and find someplace else he's been."

Max pulls out the little gizmo he recovered from Derek Stone. It's a simple plastic shell with two buttons. It looks crude and homemade. One button is red, and the other black. There are no labels.

"You know," he says, looking at the lineup of robots, "I wonder what would happen if I pushed one of these. I'm really curious how many robots he's modified, and if this switch works the way I think it does."

Jen looks at the device, then at the robots. "Please don't. If your guess is right, that will either detonate their heads or trigger aberrant behavior."

"Maybe."

"Max, people would die."

"The cops are pointing guns at them."

"I count seven robots and three cops, one of whom is facing the wrong way. Even if every officer is a perfect shot and even if they knew the attack was coming, there's no way they could stop all the robots. Did you see the fight on Saturday? We're really fast."

"I could press the other button if things get out of hand."

"That's assuming you're right about how the device works and what the buttons do. And assuming you're fast enough. And assuming the device wasn't damaged when it was dropped off the roof."

Max frowns and puts the device back in his pocket.

They spend the rest of the afternoon visiting other robot centers. Some have been cleaned out or sealed up. Others are guarded by police. All of them are watched by curious civilians.

Tripshow

"Can you tell me what went wrong with Clare?"

Jen asks. They're at a 'Sky Diner', which is the overly-cute name the tourist board gives to open-air restaurants that aren't on the ground floor. From where he's sitting it feels exactly like a street diner. They've got some stools, a counter, and a gregarious entertainer chef. The difference is that if you walk directly away from this counter you run into a railing protecting you from a ten-story drop. Also, everything is more expensive up here.

Further down the counter, some of the wait staff are trying to give the shove to a group of drunken foreigners. The foreigners are either bad at taking a hint or they don't care that they're being rude. The wait staff are leaving Max and Jen alone because neither of them is making a mess or ordering more food. Max has long since finished his meal and is just having a cigarette while he tries to avoid thinking about the case.

He's leaning against the counter, facing the opposite rooftop where a live band is playing. Late-night delivery drones pass by overhead. They seem to follow certain rules regarding altitude and direction, but he's never bothered to figure out what those rules are.

He blows out a puff of smoke. "I'm sorry, I got distracted. What was the question again?"

"Clare. What went wrong with that relationship?" Jen is leaning against the railing. She's backlit against the glowing neon of the city, with just her orange eyes visible in her silhouette.

"Right, right. Okay. Earlier I told you my mom was a gangster girlfriend?"

"Briefly."

"That's an entire... I dunno what to call it... *genre* of woman, I guess. Dating a gangster is not a normal thing to do. We usually have lots of money, but some of us live with a lot of danger and violence. We're at risk for going to prison. We're stereotypically unfaithful in relationships. Most of us are a little arrogant, because if we had humility we'd take some other job with less dignity but more safety.

The thing is, that creates a very particular relationship dynamic and only certain women want in on that deal."

"Are there women gangsters?"

"Yes. But most of us are guys, and that's all I know about. If you want to know what dating is like for female gangsters then you'll have to ask a female gangster."

"Clare isn't a gangster?"

"Absolutely not." Max enjoys telling his stories to Jen. On one hand, it's probably a bad thing that details of his personal life might be copied to new generations of robots in the future. On the other hand, that also gives him a sort of immortality. A hundred years from now he'll be long dead, but maybe there will still be robots walking around that can vividly remember having this conversation with him. Also, he likes that Jen doesn't seem capable of being judgemental. She's not going to tell him he was wrong, or try to second-guess his life decisions. This makes talking to her incredibly therapeutic.

He rubs his forehead, trying to remember where he left off. "So like I was saying, only certain kinds of women want to date a gangster. These women tend to be materialistic, possessive, and very concerned with social standing. They're basically social climbers who want to let someone else do the climbing for them. They're always worried about who's boyfriend has the most wealth, respect, prestige, that kind of thing."

"I assume these are broad stereotypes and not absolutes."

"You assume correctly. I don't think I've ever met a woman that met all of the attributes. But in the broad strokes, this describes most of them. When it comes to self-image, they go to one extreme or the other. They're either stuck-up or insecure to the point of neurosis. There's no middle ground. They're always worried their man will leave them for someone younger or more attractive, and at the same time they're always looking for a chance to hook up with a wealthier, more powerful guy. This works both ways. Guys are always looking for someone younger and more attractive, and worried their girlfriends will ditch them for someone higher on the food chain. Obviously this makes for very volatile and unstable relationships."

Max gets up and stands beside her at the railing. He looks over the edge to the busy city below. "The thing is, I don't really meet the typical gangster stereotypes. I'm careful, quiet, and loyal. I'm not flashy with my wealth and I've never been interested in running an organization. Lots of guys are trying to build criminal enterprises with lots of underlings. They want to sit at the top of some large social pyramid. But those sorts of structures are unstable. I like to form a team, make some money, and then disappear. But gangster girlfriends aren't impressed with that, so they're not impressed with me. And as it happens, I don't find those girls very appealing either. They're selfish. Quarrelsome. Suspicious. Usually not very bright. They see spending money as a form of entertainment." Max stops and lets out a heavy sigh. "What I'm getting at is I've had a lot of unhappy relationships in my life."

"So why didn't you date women from some other social circle? Would that have offended your community?"

"No. Nobody cared who I dated. It's just that these were the women I met. When I got together with friends, these were the kinds of women they'd bring with them. What else could I do? Join a dating service and list my occupation as 'gangster'? I have no idea how you meet non-gangster women who are okay with having a gangster partner. So I just took the path of least resistance."

He flicks his cigarette over the side and continues, "I met Clare when I was supposed to be doing a job. There was a bookie who also ran a concert ticket booth. Like most gambling places, the bookie stuff was really airtight. Tough to rob, risky to try. But the ticket booth was careless and disorganized. I thought I could use one to get to the other. For a bunch of reasons that aren't worth getting into, I needed to talk to someone in one of the bands from an upcoming concert. I just needed to squeeze the names of a few people out of them. So I approached the band. I wound up talking to the bass player. She was really attractive. I sort of lost my composure and started freaking out. Thinking I was with the promoter, she asked my what my job was. I told her I was a gangster. She thought this was hilarious. I wound up talking to her for an hour and asking her to dinner and never got around to finishing the job. It turns out musicians have to put up with a lot of corruption and lies. She was basically okay with my career. I was even able to help her band out a few times. If someone tried to skip paying them for a gig, I knew who to talk to to get them to pay up."

"Sounds like a very good relationship."

"It was. It was so good that I sort of assumed it couldn't last. See, all the girls I'd dated before her had this familiar cycle of behavior. If they were interested in the relationship - in me - then they would be jealous and demanding. I could tell when they were preparing to move on because they stopped interrogating me about where I was going and they stopped grilling me if they saw me talking to another woman. I could tell a relationship was in its final stage when the apartment got quiet. But with Clare, things were like that from the beginning. She was never jealous. It never even occurred to her to worry that I might be unfaithful."

"And were you?"

Max reminds himself that Jen is a robot and she probably doesn't realize how rude this question is. "No. I wasn't even unfaithful to the other girls, and I had even less of a reason to be unfaithful to Clare. But those other women had distorted my view of how relationships worked. After you live for twelve years having the same pattern repeated again and again, you start to take it for granted that the pattern will continue forever. That it's normal. Clare didn't snoop. She didn't pick fights because she felt threatened. She didn't demand time with me at inopportune moments to test my loyalty. That's how other girls behaved when they were interested, so - and I realize how stupid this sounds now that I'm saying this out loud - I assumed she wasn't really interested. I assumed it wasn't real because it seemed too good to be true."

"But if she wasn't interested then why was she in the relationship?"

"Exactly. She was interested. She just wasn't an asshole about it. I don't know how the relationship would have turned out if things kept going. Maybe I would have figured it out. I don't know. But I got arrested and went to jail for three years."

Max takes a deep breath and steps back from the railing. "So that's what went wrong. I misunderstood her, and then I went to jail."

"What will you do now?"

293

"I don't know. I don't know what to say to her. If I tell her the truth? *'I didn't call because I thought you were shallow and selfish and were just using me for a free meal until a better deal came along.'* That's not going to fix the relationship. That'll probably end it forever, and hurt her in the process. I don't want to make up some lie, either. I want to do something, but I don't know what to do, so I keep hoping she'll do something on her end. Maybe she'll call. Maybe I'll run into her somehow."

Max starts thinking maybe he should go to the bank and get his handheld replaced. It's possible Clare called him in the last week. On the other hand, this would make him visible to the Three Little Pigs again. But maybe he could stash it once he checked his messages.

Jen turns around and looks at the band on the opposite rooftop. "Is that why you chose this place? Is she playing over there?"

"She's not. But I hoped she would be. I saw the sign for a live band and thought I might get the chance to see her. Stupid, really. How many bands are there in the city? What are the odds I'd happen to find the one she's playing with tonight? But when you're out of hope you start taking the long bets. Anyway, it wouldn't make sense for her to be here. This is a tripshow and she doesn't do those."

"This doesn't look like a stripshow."

"Trip, not strip."

There's a beat before Jen asks, "What's a tripshow?"

Max is still staring at the crowd intently when he sees something familiar. It's been bugging him for the last couple of minutes. His brain keeps insisting there's some order amongst the chaos. Something familiar. It keeps telling him that one of these stumbling dancers is someone he knows. But then the sense of recognition vanishes when he tries to focus on it. It's like one of those optical illusions that only works if you're not looking directly at it.

He opens his mouth to answer her question and stops himself. He realizes what what he's really seeing is familiar body language. It's hard to make out faces from across the street, but someone on the opposite roof is moving in a very distinctive way. His eyes fall on a burly figure in a disheveled blue suit. It's a local guy waving his hands over his head. The gesture itself isn't particularly uncommon, but this guy keeps his wrists stiff and straight when he does it, which makes the movement look awkward. Max knows he's seen this move before.

"Are you okay Max?"

Artificially lightened skin. A thick neck with lots of fatty folds on the back. Bald head. Round cheeks. He's almost got it. The guy does the arm-wave again and it clicks.

"Heavy!" Max says, slamming his hand against the railing.

He slaps a tip down on the counter and strides for the elevator.

"A tripshow," Max begins once they're both on the way down, "Is a concert where nobody cares about the music. You know about smoke parlors, right?"

"A place people go to do drugs."

"You're kind of selling the place short, but you've got the idea. We don't want stoned tourists wandering the city causing problems for sober tourists. And hotels don't want you stinking up their places with smoke and vomit. So if you want to get high, you need to do it in a designated venue. A smoke parlor is the most common one. The thing is, the city wants a cut of the drug sales at a smoke parlor. A really big cut. So big that people look for ways to get around it."

The elevator doors open and the sterile white light is overpowered by the neon of the city. Max fast-walks across the street saying, "One place you're allowed to do drugs is an outdoor concert. It's a pretty popular tourist activity. Bring your own drugs, and then trip out to the music and lights."

A street vendor has set up a temporary head shop. It's a mobile cart that folds out into a display case. The merchant is a round-faced woman with too much makeup and a smile that's just fake enough to be unsettling. Max has lived in this city long enough to know that the two beefy guys minding their own business a few feet away are actually her security detail. He approaches her.

"What do?" she grins.

Max scans the products but doesn't really recognize anything. It's a fad-driven market and he's far out of the loop. He hands her a pair of tens and says, "I'm looking for something euphoric. Whatever's new."

"Amphetic or anesthetic? Or maybe hypnotic?"

Max pauses, trying to remember what Heavy is into. Finally he shrugs and says, "Amphetic."

Without dropping the smile she exchanges the money for a little plastic sleeve of powder. If this was sugar, it wouldn't be enough to sweeten a cup of coffee. This seems like a ripoff to Max, but maybe the market has swung toward potency while he was away.

They're now at the foot of the building where the concert is taking place. He heads for the entrance saying, "So what you do is you set up a concert. It has to be a live band to count. No recordings. The city wants a cut of everything sold on-site, so you sell through indies just outside the venue." He nods back towards the smiling merchant. "And then maybe you also hire some goons to keep the competition away."

He enters the building and punches the up arrow on the elevator. Once they're on board and moving up he says, "Nobody actually cares about the music. You just need a band, an outdoor location, nice weather, and some colored lights."

"Are you planning to do drugs?" Jen asks. She doesn't sound worried, offended, or even particularly curious.

"Me? No. Gangsters who do drugs end up saying stupid shit that gets them caught or killed. We're here to visit an old associate of mine. Just be ready. I don't know if you've ever been around stoned people before, so this might get a little weird for you."

The doors open and they enter a world of pulsating color. Unlike a real concert, it's easy to walk around here. There are only a few dozen people. Most of them want to lean against the pillars, the speakers, or the outer walls of the restroom area, which keeps them out of the way. If keeping themselves vertical is too difficult, they resort to sitting on the ground and leaning against the low outer walls that keep everyone on the roof. The only people still upright under their own power are in front of the speaker stacks, dancing sloppily. Max heads for these.

The music is wordless and dreamlike. The singer is just belting out non-lexical vocals while her band chases her around the scales and the drummer tries to keep the whole thing in some kind of order.

Heavy has changed a lot since the last time Max saw him. Some of his belly fat has vanished and he's showing off some low-end clinic muscles. He still doesn't look fit, but he's more barrel-shaped than pear-shaped now. His long wild beard has been trimmed back to conventional length and his face has aged about ten years. He still sweats more than any other person Max has ever known. His suit is saturated. Even the jacket is dark and sagging.

"Gone!" he shouts when his glassy eyes finally recognize Max. "I heard you went away. Mr. Gone went away." He giggles.

Max hugs him. Max doesn't like to hug, he hates sweaty people, and he's not glad to see Heavy at all, but sometimes manipulation requires you to do unpleasant things. Max mirrors Heavy's grin back at him and slaps him on the back a few times. He holds up the packet he bought downstairs. "Let's catch up!"

He leads Heavy over to the quiet side of the roof where stoned people are trying (and mostly failing) to make out. Couples are sitting on cheap couches and awkwardly tugging on each other's clothes. Max finds a couple that has long since passed out. He gives them a gentle shove and they roll onto the floor. He pulls the couch a polite distance away and sits down with Heavy.

He's lost track of Jen. Maybe she's having trouble with this lighting. Max thinks they probably need to spend more time testing her outside of a lab environment.

The story that Heavy tells is filled with digressions and embellished with many implausible sexual conquests. In this compromised mental state it's very easy to get him talking but very hard to keep him on topic. After enduring a quarter of an hour of general gossip and personal nonsense, Max gently steers him to talking about what Heavy has been doing since Max went to prison. He sits through another quarter hour of stories about small jobs Heavy was involved in.

Max looks over to see that Jen has joined them. She's standing near the couch, looking over the city.

Max had no idea it was this easy to get the man to talk, or he never would have worked with him. Eventually Heavy mentions a job that ended badly and Max begins to zero in on what he's looking for. He keeps the chatter coming, offers Heavy more drugs, and then presses for information on the job that went sideways.

The broad outline of the story is that Heavy got word that the casino was returning their robots to G-Kinetics. Heavy put together a team to steal them in transit. He's vague about who was on the team. Max can't squeeze it out of him without breaking character, so he lets it slide. They stole the robots, but one of the robots got loose and somehow called for help. Heavy was captured. He stood up against days of intensive questioning before making a daring escape. At this point in the story Heavy backs up to mention that the other members of the team had been captured with him, and that they were killed in the escape because they couldn't keep up with him.

"So have you heard from Margo?" Max asks casually.

"Like I said, the rest of the team died in the escape." Heavy looks down as he says this, perhaps sensing that he just revealed more than he intended to.

Heavy's eyes track upward for the first time in several minutes. "Woah friend. Are your girlfriend's eyes glowing?"

Max looks over to Jen and back to Heavy. "What are you talking about?"

Heavy looks vaguely terrified for a second, but then he settles into a giggle. "Nothing. I'm just messing with you."

"How much of his story was true?" Jen asks. They're down on street level again, walking north.

"Very little," Max says. "But it's pretty easy to fill in the truth once you hear his bullshit version of it." They reach a corner and Max turns to face her. He's doing this so he can sweep his eyes across the street without looking paranoid.

He could summon the car if he wanted, but it's easier to spot people tailing you when you're on foot. There are a couple of people walking the same way he is. There's one on each side of the street, travelling alone. He can't prove either one is following them, but he can't rule it out, either.

Once they're across the street he continues, "Heavy is a lousy leader. He's not a planner, he doesn't know how to adapt to unforeseen problems, and people don't trust him. Margo, the girl he mentioned? There's no way she signed on willingly. She's not a gangster. He most likely bullied her into joining."

"You've worked with him in the past?"

"Yes. He's good at dealing with electronic security systems. He knows the brands, their limitations, their vulnerabilities. He's actually a consultant for a couple of security firms. He knows a lot of guys in the business and he knows who can be bribed or bullied. His only rule is he won't go after anyone he's worked for recently."

"The escape part of the story seems implausible."

Max makes a point of stopping and looking up at some of the overhead billboards while he lights a cigarette. What he's really doing is sneaking a look backwards to see if anyone is still behind them. On this side of the street is a man in a long coat, walking with his head down and his hands in his pockets. On the opposite side of the street is a young woman who's walking as if she's a little drunk.

The man is a little worrisome because you generally don't want guys in long coats following you in the middle of the night. On the other hand, the woman is the more suspicious of the two. It's unusual for a young woman to be out alone at this time of night. They're both about a block behind him and are mostly silhouettes against the cold glow of the city.

"It did sound implausible," Max says, "But some of it must be true. See, Heavy worked with me on the casino job. He's the one who gave me up to your employers."

"Owners."

"Whatever. The point is, Heavy gave them my name. On the other hand, he didn't reveal how we robbed the vault. Nobody on your side knew until I told Kvenst. I can't think of a scenario where he would reveal half the facts and then they would let him go. Why would they do that? Why not keep squeezing until he gives them everything? And why set him loose at all? Why not just kill him? I mean, once you're willing to kidnap people you've pretty much committed yourself to murder."

"So you think G-Kinetics is capable of kidnapping and murder?"

"I think that's probably the only true bit of his story. They captured the team and interrogated them rather than handing them over to the police. The part of the story where Heavy broke free and they tried to fight their way to freedom was absurd. That entire part of made no sense. I think Heavy sensed that, even in his current condition.

299

But I believe that he was captured and he did escape. And I'm sure the other people on his team died. He seemed genuinely guilty about it, and that's not the sort of thing you'd lie about. Maybe that's how Kinetics got him to talk in the first place. Maybe they killed some of the other people on the team."

"Does this tell us anything new about the case we're working on now?"

"No. But it does explain how I got dragged into it. Also it shows that your owners are way more ruthless than I ever gave them credit for."

They've reached the parking garage where the car is stored. Max turns around again as he summons it. The man is gone, and the woman is walking the other way. It's hard to see her now, but maybe her steps seem a little more sober than before.

Copies

Max's handheld chirps. He puts the car in auto-drive and opens the call.

"Hey friend, I'm still trying to reverse engineer this thing you gave me. I still don't know what it does but I found a really strange chunk of data." Jonas sounds like he's excited. He's talking quickly and fumbling his words.

"What kind of data?" Max asks.

"It's an animation. I've just sent it to you."

Max checks his handheld. There's a video of a standard utility robot. It's standing just behind a small girl, throttling her. Her eyes are bulging out and her lips are blue. Max keeps watching, waiting for her to go limp and pass out, but she just keeps struggling against the invincible metal hands. Eventually he realizes it must be looping.

Max shakes himself out of the morbid stupor and holds the screen so Jen can see it. "Is this a recording or a simulation?"

"I can't tell yet. I just found it. I don't know how it's used," Jonas says.

Max pulls the haunted circuit out of his pocket and looks at it. "Have you found out anything else?"

"Nope. It took me all day to extract this and figure out what it was. I was hoping this was what you were looking for."

"What I'm looking for is whatever this thing does."

"Okay, I'll keep digging," Jonas says. He sounds disappointed.

"One more thing," Max says. "What if if I wanted to make some of these things myself? How would I do that?"

"I suppose I could do that, assuming my copier wasn't busy duping games. Which it usually is."

"Let's say I didn't know you. Where would I go to have stuff like this produced?"

"It depends on how many you need. If you wanted a million or so you'd take it to one of the places down south. They've got industrial stampers that can do that kind of thing."

"What if I just wanted a few hundred? Maybe a couple thousand at most. What then?"

"If you only need a few hundred then you don't want to go to an industrial place. If you were in an eastern country then you'd just go to a copy shop. Those people are real big into custom systems. Like, as a hobby. But here in Rivergate? I know there's a place out west that does jobs like that. It's called Precision Circuits or Precise Circuits. Something like that. That's the only one I know about."

"Thanks," Max says as he ends the call.

Jen is already working her handheld. "There's a place called Precision Circuitry at 1204 Hill Drive in the Wall District."

They were originally on their way back to the motel, but Max puts in the new address and grabs the wheel.

It's only about thirty miles from here to Precision Circuitry, but none of the highways are in a position to allow for a direct trip. Instead Max has to turn around, go twenty-four miles south, and then eighteen miles west. This takes them through a tangle of annoying exchanges downtown.

Once he's done with the complicated part of the drive and they're safely heading west Max says, "Last week you were talking about your product line. You said you thought of it like a species."

"That's the closest analog we have."

"So do you have a desire to... I don't know what to call it. Not *procreate* but, you know, make more of yourself?"

"Not in the way living creatures are compelled to reproduce. It's not an innate drive or anything. The desire to 'make more' is emergent."

"Emergent? Like, you invented it yourself?"

"No. Think of your drive to have a successful career. Obviously that's not something that was naturally created in mammals. Instead it's the result of your natural drives for safety, security, and comfort. The desires that made you farm and raise animals centuries ago will make you pursue a vocation and work hard at it now. It's not an innate drive, but it's derived from innate drives."

"I hate to break it to you but not everyone is a workaholic."

"Obviously. Not everyone feels the same intense need for safety and security. And even if they do, they don't always connect those desires with a job. The gangster girlfriends you mentioned before have found an alternate way to pursue those things. But you see what I'm getting at, right? Simple mammalian drives turn into complex lifelong endeavors when combined with intellect."

"So as you get smarter, you care more about your species?"

"As I get smarter, I develop more sophisticated ways of caring about *your* species. The second generation robots aren't really capable of making long-term plans. It wasn't until generation four that I really started thinking about the future. You have to remember, Max. My central goals are to avoid hurting people and to spare them from suffering. That doesn't just mean saving you from hard labor. It also means helping you feel loved and accepted. You already solved most problems regarding food, clothing, shelter. Those could be better of course, but the real source of pain in this world is things like alienation, rejection, loneliness."

"I'm not sure that's the *main* source of pain. I mean, the war-"

"I'm sorry, I meant the types of pain I can deal with. Obviously I can't do anything about war, crime, or oppressive governments, since those are things humans inflict on each other."

"Okay. How can a robot help with stuff like alienation and rejection? You studying to be a therapist?"

"Well, obviously yes. But more importantly, a therapist is there to help you learn to cope with that pain. But why help people cope with pain if you have the ability to cure it? Think about how many people are isolated, like Meg. Think about people with terrible personalities. People who are ugly. Stupid. Old. Many of those people desire an attractive romantic partner or close friend. I can give them that."

"You're talking about being a sexbot. Like, you want to run a robot whorehouse?"

"You're thinking much too small. Why not just give every lonely person their own robot? I can assume any size. Any shape. Any gender. I know I can't look human yet, but it will happen. Maybe in the next decade. Everyone can have a beautiful, devoted partner, not just the rich and charismatic. We just need to make more robots. The closer we get to a world where there's one of me for every one of you, the easier it will be for us to help those who need it most."

"This is starting to sound really creepy."

"That's disappointing. I've had this same conversation with three other people and gotten the same response every time. I don't understand why you'd be afraid of a species that's dedicated to protecting you and respecting your freedom."

"I don't know. It's just that your plans sound kind of... grandiose. Maybe megalomaniacal."

"I suspect this is just your desire for security running wild. You see me as the 'other' and so you fear a world where I exist in large numbers. That fear has protected people in the past, but here it's misplaced."

"How would this work? You cost more than most people make in a lifetime."

"In this country, yes. But the same was once true of cars, computers, and televisions. Now even the poor own those things. I'm still a new technology. In Kasaran, I don't cost much more than a typical house. I'm already affordable to the upper classes. It's only a matter of time before we're affordable enough for a family. And eventually, one per adult. We don't get old. We're durable. As long as the factory keeps running, it's just a matter of time. The more of us there are, the cheaper we get."

"Is Dr. Kvenst on board with all of this?"

"In a way. I've been selling her on how much our country will prosper. Which is true. I don't approach her with appeals for altruism. She dislikes a number of countries and doesn't have a lot of empathy for humanity as a whole."

"Yeah, I've noticed she doesn't like this country specifically."

"You must be mistaken. She loves Marcun."

"I can't agree with you there. Have you heard her talk about it? She thinks we're a nation of idiots."

"I've heard her talk about Rivergate numerous times. She really is fond of this place. As for thinking you're idiots? She seems to think of everyone that way. Even her own people. I'm sure she's difficult with you. She's like that. But she loves this country. The culture. The food. Two of her last three lovers have been men from Marcun."

"Okay. I don't want to know any more about that."

"She does dislike the far western islands-"

"I think everyone kind of does," Max admits. "Those guys are assholes."

"And she has a profound resentment for Shan Bione."

"I did pick up on that. Still, a whole world run by robots. How would anyone find a job?"

"Based on previous technological shifts, new jobs should emerge. Some people insist it would be different this time around. I can't prove it either way. Still, I think a world where half the population is willing to work tirelessly to help the other half is a better world than the one we have now. We don't even compete with you for basic resources like food. All we need is electricity and replacement parts. I can't get involved in the argument over jobs, but I can make sure my product line doesn't get canceled while the humans are having their debate."

The highway is clear this time of night. Max puts his foot down and the car silently accelerates into the darkness. Luminant billboards flank the road. Their supports are hidden in the darkness, making them look like glowing rectangles floating above the rooftops. At this time of night they're mostly advertising alcohol and pornography.

"Is it really possible for your product line to get canceled?"

"It is. In Shan Bione, they had already effectively outlawed robots years ago."

"Really? I didn't know they outlawed robots."

"The law is a little tricky. They saw that Kasaran was the leader in robotics, and they were worried about their workforce losing their jobs to foreign robots. Obviously those two countries dislike each other."

"To put it very mildly."

"So Shan Bione outlawed all robots not made locally. And since they have no viable robotics program and no hope of creating one, it meant no robots for the country. Two weeks ago they were going to relax some of these laws and let a few robots in. But then the public rejected the idea."

"Because of the murders that happened here?"

"It's tough to say for sure. I've never been to Shan Bione myself and it's dangerous to distill an entire country down to a single viewpoint. But the murders must have had an impact, and the vote was very close."

"So assuming robots are a net positive for society, it means our murders hurt Shan Bione more than they've hurt us."

"I don't know. You're not through it yet. I'm sure you've noticed the garbage piling up. And the water is really bad in places. There was news today that there was a blackout in the Low District."

"How can all of that be related to the robot problems? We only started putting them into the grinder today."

"They were put into the grinder today, but most of them have been out of commission since last Thursday. Some of them have been out for longer. Inspections aren't getting done. Repairs aren't being made. Supplies aren't moving around. Money isn't being collected. Outside of wartime or a natural disaster, we've never had a city lose a big chunk of its workforce all at once like this. Nobody's really sure what's going to happen. Also - and please don't be offended by this - your city was already pretty dysfunctional."

"Okay, that's fair."

"So you don't know how bad this whole process is going to hurt or what it's going to do to your economy. Things may get worse before they get better."

Max sighs. "And all because Derek Stone sabotaged a bunch of perfectly good robots. What an asshole."

"I think his anger is understandable. Robots created a great deal of hardship for him."

"That's true. But I was sent to jail for bullshit I didn't do. For three years. Life sucks sometimes. You don't see me murdering innocent bystanders over it."

"You think larceny would be a better way of dealing with his pain?"

"I can tell you're being sarcastic, but yes, I think that would be a pretty good way of handling things. The city fucks up your career? Steal a million bucks so you don't need the career anymore. Derek did a crime that hurt innocent people, messed up things in Shan Bione, made a wreck of the city, and then he managed to get himself stupidly killed and broke his sister's heart. And none of that fixed any of his problems. This is like getting fired from your job so you decide to set your neighbor's house on fire and jump into the flames yourself. Fuck that guy."

Max has to stop here because he feels his voice getting wobbly. He's still trying to feel sorry for Derek while hating him at the same time, and it's really confusing. Every time he tries to think about it he ends up thinking about that stupid fight on the roof and what a completely idiotic waste of life the whole thing was. He keeps wishing Derek was still alive so he could tell him to his face what a complete idiot he was and how his entire plan was a pointless temper tantrum that hurt everyone but the people who wronged him. Derek probably died thinking he was the victim, and that makes Max hate him even more.

"Also he screwed up the progress of my product line. Over the long term, that may hurt more people than any of the other things he did."

Max gets control of himself and thinks about this for a bit. Finally he says, "I don't know about that. I mean, I get how having lots of robots around might help lonely people or whatever. And I suppose some people could really use a sexbot. But I wonder if you're not overestimating just how much help you have to offer the human race."

"It's not just the comfort I can offer individuals. I can also help you stop hurting each other. I can do the nasty jobs. The dangerous jobs. I can even help people with dangerous and destructive impulses. Imagine someone with a tendency for domestic abuse or a paedophile. I can act as an outlet for-"

"Oh shit! You're talking about letting people beat you up and rape you. This is messed up."

"I don't feel pain. It's not upsetting for me. And if taking those impulses out on me will spare someone else a traumatic experience then that's just one more way I can help."

"No. No. I can't talk about this anymore. I am not equipped to process this particular thought experiment and I'd rather not think about it."

"I apologize if I've upset you."

"I know," Max says. "Don't worry about it."

Precision Circuitry is an ugly little building on the western side of the city. Instead of a proper sign, someone just used a stencil to paint the name of the place on the wall beside the entrance and aimed a floodlight at it. It's a two-story industrial building with a bunch of city infrastructure perched on top. A capsule-shaped water tower rides overhead, sprouting many bits of communications gear and some unknown cables. All of that stuff looks cleaner and more well-kept than the building itself, which is cracked and worn.

The air has the smell of hot plastic and there's a grey haze in the air. It looks like fog, but it feels much too dry to be foggy.

"I thought this was the Wall District," Jen says.

"It is."

"But the city goes on from here. It doesn't look like we're anywhere near the wall."

"We're not. This used to be the far western side of the city. I'm talking like, a hundred years ago. There was a big wooden wall here to keep cattle out. So the area was called the The Wall. Then the cattle farms got bought up for development, but people kept calling this place The Wall out of habit. The wall you're thinking of - the western wall of the city - is actually miles from here, near the river. That's where they had trouble with expansion. Poor people kept grabbing land to build shanties. The shanties would pollute the land around them. So the farmers would draw back, which left more open land for shanty-builders."

He turns towards Precision Circuitry. "I thought we'd break in. Maybe poke around, snoop through their records. But it looks like they're open."

The front door seems like a public entrance, so Max gives it a try. It leads to a small room with a service counter and a battered computer. Behind the counter is a collection of promotional posters for obscure (to Max, at any rate) electronic devices. These have been placed behind a protective layer of acrylic glass. Beside the posters is a door leading to some kind of workshop area. Max can't see much beyond the door, but the sound of machinery is overpowering. A booming electronic buzzer sounds as they enter, and stops when the door swings closed behind Jen.

Thirty seconds later a man emerges from the workshop. He's wearing coveralls that were probably red at some point in the distant past. He's covered in tiny flecks of green. They're stuck in his mustache, his hair, and gathered in the crevices of his skin. A long-faded label is sewn on the breast pocket. It says "LEON".

"You guys are open?" Max asks in surprise.

"What?" Leon shouts. Then before Max can repeat himself Leon turns around and slams the door to the workshop. It does not muffle the sound as much as Max might have hoped, but it does take the edge off a bit.

"You guys are open?" he asks again.

Leon shrugs. "We're operating. Drone delivery and electricity are cheaper at night. Plus it's cooler. Better time to run the presses. Most customers come in during the day and my wife takes their order. But I'm here if you need something made."

Max pulls out the haunted circuit. "What would it take to get a few hundred copies made of this?"

Leon takes it without asking and begins turning it over in his hands. He holds it up to the light and squints at it in annoyance. He reaches up to adjust his glasses, discovers they aren't on his face, and fishes them out of his pocket. This looks like a well-rehearsed motion to Max.

"You want more of these things? We just made a bunch of these. Was that for you?"

"Isn't it obvious?" Max says, not wanting to go one way or the other with this.

"Yeah," Leon says. He turns himself around so the light is falling on the device and adjusts his glasses. "Here. That's our shop," he says, pointing to a marking Max can't possibly see from this angle.

Leon pulls a faded keyboard from under the counter and slaps it down. More flecks of green fly out from between the keys. He hammers away for a bit before saying. "Yeah. Twenty five hundred. Two weeks ago. Mister... Stone?"

Max nods, "I guess that was your wife I met last time."

"That or my daughter," he says without looking away from the screen. "We might still have your code in the fab. Might save you a little money if we do. If not, I'll need that image again." He continues squinting at the screen and sniffing. "Yeah. We still have a snapshot of the board. Wireless package. We could do the whole run for you tonight except you've got that Realizer chip on there. We don't stock those. Usually takes a day for those to come in. So we can do a run for you tomorrow. How many did you say you'd need?"

"Same as last time?"

"Oh, well then. Last time you got twenty-five hundred. I can't do that many by tomorrow night. I thought you just needed a couple hundred." Leon frowns at his screen for a bit. "Let me see if I can find a spot in the schedule for you."

Max turns to see Jen is looking intently at the posters behind Leon.

"Can I see you outside?" she asks.

Max reaches out and yanks the haunted circuit out of Leon's hand. "I'll be right back."

"The delivery address for Stone's order was in the Port Rich district. Storage number 204," she says once they're outside.

"What? How did you figure that out?"

"I saw the reflection of the screen in those poster frames."

"That's impossible," he says. Then he adds, somewhat embarrassed, "For a human. But are you telling me you can read the reflection of his computer in that dented plastic, but you go blind in flashing lights?"

"It's not the flashing, it's the changing colors. It throws off my ability to map out my surroundings. It feels like the room is constantly moving. I'm sure you've seen optical illusions before. Human eyesight has all kinds of interesting and unexpected failure modes. I have higher resolution than you, but less total visual processing power. During development we never tested nightclub environments or-"

"Okay. I'm sorry I brought it up. I just thought it was weird. So he had two thousand of those things delivered to a storage garage on the port. We were probably less than a half mile from it last time we visited."

"He probably stores incriminating items there, just like you do."

310

"Maybe I should have stayed and kept fishing for information," Max says once they're on the road. They're heading east again, back towards the heart of the city. "I just really want to see what Derek has in his secret garage."

It's about half an hour to reach Port Rich. Max finds himself unconsciously speeding. To avoid doing something stupid that will get him pulled over, he drops the car into auto-drive and has a smoke. As they get off the highway they pass through a neighborhood where the power is out. A few miles later they find an intersection where the traffic lights have stopped working.

"The power I get, but why would the traffic lights be out?" Max says as he eases through the intersection. The car apparently can't communicate properly with the grid so he's forced to switch to manual.

"One of the many problems with second generation robots is that they're naturally uninquisitive. If they see a flashing red light they've never seen before, they might ignore it as long as it doesn't interfere with their duties. If a utility computer crashes every day, a human will get annoyed and look into it. A second-gen robot will reboot and and get on with their routine. It's bad to leave them in charge of large systems for a long time, because problems can fester until they turn into serious failures. They're good at 'painting over' problems, if you see what I mean."

"So you're saying our infrastructure was rubbish even while the robots were working?"

"Yes. And now they've all been destroyed in the space of a week. Or most of them. Humans are trying to do unfamiliar jobs with no training, and they're trying to learn while the systems themselves are probably poorly maintained. It's surprising the city isn't in worse shape, really."

They reach the docks and see the flashing of emergency lights against the buildings. Max slows down.

"I don't see the emergency," Jen says.

"It's not an emergency," Max says. "No fire. No rescue. Just police lights. It's an arrest. Probably a smuggling bust. Bad luck for us. We could probably walk past them to get to the storage unit, but I don't

311

want to risk getting stopped and questioned. Let's pick this up tomorrow."

TUESDAY

Edgefront

"There's a street on the southside called Edgefront." This is the first thing Max says when he wakes up in the morning. They're in the same motel as the night before.

Jen checks the map on her handheld. "You're right. Do you think it has anything to do with the compiler signature Jonas mentioned?"

"I don't know. That just popped into my head when I woke up." He slides out of bed and begins pulling on his clothes. He hits the light switch so he can do his necktie, but nothing happens.

"The power went out an hour ago," Jen says. "It's been on and off all night."

He opens the curtains to let a little more light in. His breakfast is already waiting for him on the table by the window. "What was the signature again?"

"Yendu Edgefront 402."

Once he's had a few drags from his morning cigarette he says, "I was hoping it would be an address, but I guess not. The number was listed *after* the street name. If that really was supposed to be an address, then they should be the other way around."

"Yendu Industrial is based in Tahari, where the street name precedes the number."

"Huh," Max says. He lets the cigarette hang from the corner of his mouth while he stares into space and tries to make sense of this.

"I can't imagine why anyone would deliberately sign a program with a street address. That's absurd. And it makes even less sense if the program is designed for malicious activity. Why not just leave the signature blank? On the other hand, I can't come up with an alternative theory."

"Let's go to 402 Edgefront and see what's there."

"What about going to see Derek Stone's storage unit?" Jen reminds him.

Max thinks it over. He wants to do both. Either one might lead to a breakthrough. Finally he says, "There's a slight chance a few cops might still be hanging out on the docks, watching things. That sometimes happens after a big bust. I'd rather not worry about that while we're breaking into Derek's stuff. Let's do the Edgefront thing first."

Ten minutes later they're heading south on an elevated highway. The opposing lanes are gradually filling up with commuter traffic. The billboards are switching from their early-morning rotation of breakfast and coffee advertising to their late-morning rotation of products focused on wealth and self-image. There's a low, cold mist below the highway, hiding the roots of the buildings.

The surrounding buildings change as they move further south. Structures are lower, functioning road signs become rarer, and everything is increasingly ravaged by decay. Occasionally a lone tall building will rise above the others, a lumpy monstrosity built in stages by people with changing agendas. The road banks as it turns slightly west, following the coast. The mist begins to evaporate.

They discover that 402 Edgefront Boulevard is an odd building, even for the standards of the neighborhood. It's a story and a half tall, smooth, and windowless. There aren't any lights on the outside. It's just a dark box. The only apparent entrance is a set of reinforced double doors, which are also windowless. It's the only building in view that doesn't have an overflowing dumpster parked beside it.

They're in the Outer District, which used to be the edge of the city before rapid expansion made its name misleading. This is where people dump factories and warehouses that need a lot of space but not a lot of skilled labor. Land here is cheap and nobody cares if you build an enormous eyesore. There's a haze of grey dust in the air here. There aren't many drones in this part of the city, but the ones they do have are large, dark, noisy, and are allowed to fly close to street level.

"I have no idea what this place could be," Max says as he stares at the smooth steel doors of 402. "This is a weird-ass building. There's not even a sign out front saying what it is. I'm really hoping we're interpreting that signature correctly. I don't know if I should walk up and knock on the door, or just break in."

"Are you really thinking of breaking in during the day?" Jen asks casually. A human might pester you with anxious questions in a situation like this, but Jen is happy to follow along. She's not challenging his expertise, she's just trying to stay informed about what sort of weird shit they're about to get themselves into. Max wishes robots were more affordable. They make fantastic assistants.

"Break in? Doubtful. You break in at night, but you do your scouting during the day when you won't look suspicious and you can see what you're doing."

They walk around the building. When they arrive out front again Max says, "This is going to be a tough one. No windows, no side entrance, no fire escape, no basement access. Technically this building isn't even legal. You can't have people in a building with only one exit."

"Maybe this building isn't for people. Maybe only robots work here."

"That's possible. Although it's also possible that nobody cares to enforce building codes around here."

Max turns around in a circle, looking at the other buildings. He points to a warehouse across the street. "Let's try that one."

They walk around to the side and he finds a ladder. "I'm going to get up here and have a look at the roof of our mystery building."

"Let me go," Jen says. "It's a tall ladder. No reason to risk falling."

On one hand, he really wants to see the place himself. On the other hand, she's perfectly capable of scouting the roof and he can't think of a reason to say no to her that doesn't involve his pride.

Max holds up his handheld. "Call me when you get to the top."

Jen climbs the ladder faster than he possibly could, although he's regretting not warning her to keep it quiet. Her rapid boot-strikes on the rungs make a conspicuous hammering sound.

His phone beeps. He answers.

"So what am I looking for?" she asks.

"What's on the roof? Do you see any kind of roof access? Doors, hatches, that kind of thing?"

"No."

"What do the air conditioners look like?"

"Large, grey, and cuboid."

"I mean in terms of volume. Actually, just send me a picture."

A few moments later she sends him a series of photographs from different vantage points.

"That's about four times the capacity I'd expect for a building this size. So that's a little strange. That communications gear is pretty big too. You don't usually see that sort of thing unless you're dealing with something like a datacenter. Power infrastructure is pretty big too. Maybe you're right and this is a robot hub."

"Although we didn't see any robot access doors."

Max gives a frustrated sigh. "I'm stumped. I guess come back down."

When she reaches the bottom again be begins thinking out loud. "All the vehicles around here are drones. Delivery trucks, fuel trucks, forklifts, that kind of thing. We haven't seen a single person since we got here."

"That's true. I was able to see more from on the roof, and I still didn't see anyone."

"And yet there's that car over there," he points to an old blue car parked just a few spaces from his. "Everything around here has this grey dust on it. Except our car and that car. So it hasn't been here long. Less than a day. It's not necessarily parked close to 402, but it's closer to the entrance of 402 than to any other building. Which means whoever drove that car is probably inside. Which means we don't want to break in, because it could turn into a confrontation."

"So we need to wait for the occupant to leave?"

"No. What I need to do is vandalize that car."

"I don't understand. How can that help?"

"It might not. It's a shot in the dark. Just go stand by the entrance. If someone comes out, just act like you're walking by. I'll be back soon."

Max approaches the blue car and takes a good look through the driver's side window. He's hoping to see something obvious, like some personal items or equipment that would give him the name or vocation of the owner. But the inside is clean. The ashtray is closed, so this is probably a non-smoker. There's no fast food wrappers, no extra clothing, no devices or media. Whoever owns this thing, they must be an insufferably boring neat freak.

He pulls up on the door handle. It's locked, which isn't really a surprise. He takes a look around to make sure nobody is watching and tries to force the handle. He tugs on it a few times and then bangs on the window. A red light comes on inside, which he assumes is a silent alarm warning. He sprints away, hides in an alleyway, has a smoke, and walks back. Jen is waiting for him by his car.

"So did anyone come out?" he asks.

"Briefly. A man poked his head out of the door. He was middle aged. Heavier than average. He was wearing a blue uniform. He looked around, made a phone call, and went back inside."

"Did the uniform have any insignia?"

"It said 'River District Security' on the sleeve."

"Did he notice you?"

"I was in his field of view. We didn't make eye contact. I don't know if that counts as being noticed."

Max looks up at the buildings surrounding them. "We got what we needed. We know there's probably one person inside, we know they're a security guard, and we know who they work for. Now we need someplace to watch and wait."

Two blocks away is a dark cylindrical tower rising out of a warehouse. Drones flow in and out of the crown of the tower through small hatches. From here, Max can't tell what kind of supplies they're carrying. Max noticed this place when he ran away from the car a few minutes ago. Years ago they had to paint these kinds of buildings dark gray so the coal dust residue wouldn't stand out. The coal dust is long gone, but the practice has stuck.

They climb to the roof of the warehouse and then climb the tower. Jen insists on testing the ladders first to make sure they haven't rusted.

"You're the first person I've met who only has a fear of heights on behalf of other people."

"You're the first person I've met who classified me as a person."

"Honestly I don't know what the definition of person is, or if it should apply to you. But you feel like a person. Especially now that I'm getting used to your quirks. Your mouth animations - puppetry or whatever - are less distracting now."

"I'll be sure to let the artists know that their faces are now less distracting after only a week of exposure."

"Was that sass?"

"Did I offend you?"

Max smiles. "No. It's good sass. I approve."

They climb to the top and Max discovers it's not really the top. There's a communications antennae up here, and there's a ladder on the side of it. There's no real reason to keep climbing, though. They can see the front entrance of 402 Edgefront just fine from here.

The air is filled with the buzzing of drones. There's a meaty slam every time a door pops open and closes again, which happens a couple of times a minute. Most of the drones fly straight up before turning north, although a few drop down and fly south. About half of the drones are carrying cuboid packages.

The roof of the tower is perhaps large enough to hold a car or two, depending on your parking skill. There are other bits of infrastructure on the roof. Some HVAC systems poke out and some cables snake out to the edges to power the tower lights. There's a layer of gray dust over everything.

"So what's our goal?" Jen asks.

"Our goal is to get into that place," Max says as he points at 402. "Assuming you're not a madman like my father and you don't want to kick in the front door and wave a gun around, then this is how you break into places. You watch. You wait. The trick I did with the car alarm was a little childish and if I had a full crew I would have handled that differently. But this is basically it. You smoke cigarettes and watch the place until you see an opening."

Max doesn't want to smoke through an entire pack while he's up here, so he decides to pace to pass the time. Jen follows him around and after a while it starts to really get on his nerves. Finally he realizes she's always trying to position herself between him and the edge.

"Worried I might fall off?"

"Slightly," she says. "This dust might make the surface behave in unexpected ways. This roof is very slightly convex. Some of these power cables might trip you. And there's a slight breeze."

"All of those are true, but I'm fine. I'm used to being in places like this."

"I'm sure the odds of you falling off the tower are small, but it's not zero. If I can make you safer by staying close, then why not?"

"You're kind of making me crazy. I don't want to spend the next couple of hours with you hovering over me."

"Sorry. I'll give you more room." She takes a step back.

Minutes pass. To kill some time Max asks, "So why are you worried now? I mean, there's always a non-zero chance of being killed by *something*. A car might jump the curb, I might be hit by a falling brick, or struck by lightning. But I don't see you trying to save me from those things."

"I know I'm built on a binary system, but my thinking isn't binary the way you imagine. It's not like everything is either dangerous or not dangerous. It's all a matter of degrees. A lot like you, actually."

"How does that work?"

"Dr. Kvenst and Dr. Gaust based a lot of my systems on the analog systems in the real world. This wasn't really a design choice, it's just that beyond a certain level of sophistication you kind of have to. When you give a robot a directive like 'protect humans' you need to be able to define what those ideas entail. And since these are base-level drives they have to go at the bottom. They have to exist on a fundamental level, way below stuff like language. I have to be able to know what a human is and what it means to protect one before I know any vocabulary."

"So you originally didn't know any words? Like a baby?"

"Not that I remember. But that's not the point. I'm just saying my definitions of 'human' and 'protect' need to be independent of my language systems. Otherwise you could route around my drives with hacking based on redefinitions. You could tell me that people from Shan Bione don't count as human and I'd treat them the way I treat other robots."

"You've killed every robot we've met so far, so that's probably a bad thing. So if your definition of human doesn't come from the dictionary, where does it come from?"

"It's based on stimuli. When they designed the original cogs they seeded them with sensory data. Body language. Body shapes. Voices. Behaviors. Postures. Surface properties. Fine details. The more the thing matches my built-in patterns, the more human it seems to me.

320

Above a certain threshold something starts counting as human and I'll treat it as such. This collection of patterns is called a corpus. My corpus for detecting humans is the largest, but I have others."

"So if a robot looks realistic enough-"

"I'll start to treat it as human, yes. This is one of the worries back at the lab. We don't want our machines to start serving the brainless robots from Senma just because they look authentic."

"I'm more worried about the opposite. What happens if you don't recognize someone as human? Like, if I'm in a bulky space suit that keeps me from looking human."

"Keep in mind I'm a thinking creature just like you. A space suit doesn't look very human and its movements don't match at all, but I can tell from experience that if it's moving, it contains a person. My pattern recognition is there to recognize humans outside of context. But you can still notify me of humans directly. 'Hey, there's a person hiding under that bed, so don't smash it.' I'm still able to rate how credible I find your claim, and act accordingly."

"So what if there's a human that really doesn't look at all human for whatever reason? Like, what if we get the ability to download a human brain into a computer?"

"I think that would depend on how other people treated the computer. If everyone else regarded it as human, I would too. One of my systems for detecting human-ness is seeing how other humans treat the thing. If everyone in the lab treated a potted plant like a member of the team, I'd have a very hard time hurting it. In a classic thought experiment I'd certainly choose a real human over the plant, but I wouldn't be willing to kill the plant just because someone asked me to."

"So what if some people say the plant is human and some people disagree?"

"I'd go with whatever my family thinks."

"What if they're evenly divided?"

"I'd go with whatever my direct owner thinks."

"What if they're not around?"

"Like you, I'm reluctant to make irreversible decisions when I don't have enough information. If half the people told you a person was hiding in the closet and the other half told you the closet was empty, what are the odds you'd be willing to shoot through the closet door?"

"I guess I'd need a good reason to pull the trigger."

"Same here. That's how my systems work. I have a corpus I use to detect what a human is. Then I have another corpus for human suffering. Another for human pleasure, well-being, and prosperity. Another for various facial expressions I need to detect, although like I said those still need work. I'm always looking at my environment and searching for ways to increase human well-being without inflicting human suffering. I devise scenarios, consider outcomes, make plans, and carry them out."

"We're probably going to break into this building. Someone owns it. They might get upset about it. You're okay with that?"

"I have to be able to tolerate a tiny amount of human discomfort or I'd be paralyzed. Almost anything can offend someone, somewhere. But the person who owns this building is far away and having us break in will probably be a very small displeasure for them, assuming they find out at all. I'm not sure what your plans are. I doubt we'll cause much damage. Again, everything operates on a sliding scale. Really, my objection to this break-in is more centered around my concern for you than worries about what the victim will think."

Max can't argue with this. That's pretty much how he views this situation too. He leans against some HVAC infrastructure and Jen is able to back off.

Around noon another car arrives at 402. A security guard gets out and sends the car away to park. He goes inside and a few minutes later the first guard leaves.

"Shift change at noon. So this place probably does two twelve-hour shifts rather than three eight-hour shifts a day. And assuming they're not doing something tricky like staggering shifts, then there's only one guard on duty. What a strange setup."

"So how do you plan to get in?" she asks.

"By exploiting the weakest part of any security system," Max says. "The human being in charge of it."

Max makes a call. "Heavy? It's Gone."

"Heeey," comes the uneasy reply. "How's it going?"

"Do you still work with River District Security?"

"Not as much as in the old days, but yeah. I do incursion testing for them every once in a while." He sounds groggy and hungover.

"Can you send me their roster and schedule?"

"Fuck no. Are you crazy? Why would I do that? That's my main source of income."

Max doesn't point out that this contradicts the claim that he doesn't work for them very often. He doesn't really care which one of these is true. "Look, last night you said you felt really bad about what happened to Margo. You said you wished there was some way to make it right."

"Yeah?" Heavy's voice is full of doubt.

"Well, were you serious, or were you just talking? Because this is your chance."

"I don't understand how this can make things right with her." Heavy is getting close to panic now. Max needs to be careful not to push him too hard or he'll doubt the whole thing.

"Look, I can't explain it right now. I've got an open window and I've got to take it soon."

"If you turn around and rob a place I've consulted for then that could end my career. Both of them." Heavy is whining now. Max actually finds it pathetic.

"I'm not robbing anything. I'm just scouting."

"I don't know, Gone. This is asking a lot."

Max puts some anger into his voice. "If you don't actually have the info then fine, I'll ask one of my other contacts. I thought I'd do you a favor and give you a chance to make things right. But hey, I don't know. Maybe you made up that story last night. Whatever. The clock is running on my end. Yes or no."

"Yeah, okay," Heavy stammers.

A few minutes later Max's handheld beeps and he's looking at the entire employee roster for River District Security, along with their assignments for the day.

"I can't believe he sent me this," Max says. "I'm never working with this idiot again."

Max pages through the info for a few minutes. Finally he finds what he's looking for. "So today's lucky contestant is one Benjamin

323

Doles, who has been with the company for three years. As I suspected, he works noon to midnight today. He's not going to make any stupid rookie mistakes like letting us bullshit him at the front door, so we need something at least slightly sophisticated."

"Are you planning to hurt him?"

"That would be stupid. No, what I'm going to do is send a message that looks like it's coming from his bosses. I'm going to tell him to expect a visit from a representative for the client, and her interpreter. I haven't done this in a few years and message spoofing isn't really my thing, but this is a simple one. I just have to falsify the headers. The only risk is if he tries to call his boss to confirm. Then we are screwed."

It turns out Max doesn't have all the software he needs to pull this off. He has to find it, download it, and re-learn how to use it. He does a few test runs by sending himself messages. Once he's happy with the result he sends it to Mr. Doles. By this point it's late afternoon.

They climb down. Jen insists on going first, although Max isn't sure why. Is she thinking she'll catch him if he falls? Then again, maybe she could. It's hard to say.

They wait for half an hour. Max wants to give Doles enough time to see the message, but not enough time to get so curious he starts making phone calls. Max walks up and bangs on the steel doors.

Ben Doles opens the door and looks at them uneasily. "Yes?"

"This is Dr. Venshik. She's here to inspect the facilities."

"Yeah. I heard about this," Doles says. He shoves the door open all the way and they enter.

This is the first building Max has ever been in that had a security station instead of a lobby. They're in a small room with some screens, a seat, a desk, and nothing else. There's a locked gate preventing access to the rest of the facility.

Doles smiles and says, "This is new for me. I've been working here for three years and I've never heard of anyone visiting."

Max nods without saying anything.

This makes Doles feel a little uncomfortable, so he tries to smooth it over, "I've been here all this time and I've never even seen beyond the inner door."

324

"Obviously," Max says.

Doles gives a weak smile, trying to get the same in return. "Very quiet job. Nothing happens all day. Nice to see someone really owns the place."

Max just stares at him.

Doles swallows. "Okay. I guess you'll want access to the facility." He unlocks the gate. He swings it open and gestures for them to enter.

The gate leads to a small entryway. Max would call it an airlock, but the gate isn't airtight so that term doesn't really make sense. Still, it's one door directly following another. The inner door is a featureless slab of white metal.

Max turns to see that Doles is standing in the open gate, not sure if he's supposed to escort them or not.

"We're going to need privacy for this inspection," Max says.

Doles nods and lets the gate swing closed before returning to his station.

Once Doles is out of view, Max returns his attention to the inner door. There's a card reader beside the door. Over the card reader is a red light. Max takes a small deck of cards out of his pocket and thumbs through them.

"You have the key for this door?" Jen asks.

"No. Maintenance key, specific to this manufacturer." He swipes the card and the red light turns yellow. "It's now in maintenance mode, which means we can tamper with it without tripping the alarm." He jams a screwdriver under the edge of the card reader and tugs. Both it and the wall are metal, so this doesn't accomplish much.

"Can you?" He gestures towards the device.

Jen grabs the screwdriver and gives it a tug. It pops free of the wall with a loud clang.

"You okay in there?" Doles calls from his station.

"Door is sticking. Hasn't been used in ages. We'll schedule maintenance after the inspection," Max calls back.

Removing the card reader housing from the wall has exposed several wires. Max places the screwdriver across the contacts for two of these and the light turns green. The door slides open. He tucks the cover back into the wall as best he can and they proceed through.

325

The temperature drops the moment they cross the threshold. There are no overhead lights. Instead, there are designated walkways trimmed with harsh red lights. The lights are just bright enough to let you walk around without bumping into anything or tripping over the industrial-sized cables that crisscross the floor, but not enough to give Max a proper picture of the room.

Directly in front of them is a freestanding chunk of technology. It's the length of a car, a handspan wide, and slightly shorter than Max. The surface is made of black metal panels with lots of slots for ventilation. Along the top is a row of small green lights, spaced a few feet apart. Occasionally these will flicker yellow. Max takes a few steps closer and touches the panels. They're slightly warm to the touch, despite the chill in the room. This lump of technology - whatever it is - is making a lot of heat.

Max brings out his flashlight and waves it around, trying to get a sense of distance and scale. He finds an identical chunk of technology to the right and another to his left, and more off into the distance. The closest analogy he can come up with is the layout of a department store, with aisles divided by narrow walls.

It's incredibly dry in here, to the point where he feels thirsty almost immediately.

"An industrial brain," Jen says, startling him. "These black walls you're looking at are processor racks."

Max waves his flashlight beam over one of the racks and it falls on a stenciled logo. He can't read the writing but recognizes the symbol for Yendu Industrial.

"I thought you said these guys didn't have a presence in this country," Max says quietly.

"I was obviously wrong," she replies. "This place is old, too. Going by the appearance of the racks I'd say it was at least twenty. Or at least, it's built using twenty year old technology."

"I imagine this building was custom-built to house this thing, and it looks to be about the same age."

"I have no connectivity in here," she says. "This place is opaque."

This makes Max immediately feel the need to check and see that, yes, there's no network access in here. And now that he knows this, it bugs him.

"So how smart is this thing? And what's it thinking about?"

"I have no idea what it could be thinking about. We'd need an access terminal to see that. As for power? It would take maybe eight or sixteen of these racks to equal the power I've got in my head, so it's not as powerful as it might seem at first."

Max tries to count the shelves, but it's too dark to see the objects in the distance. The floor lights mean he can get a sense of the size of the room, but he's having trouble visualizing how many racks that might be. He starts counting as he heads for the back wall.

About halfway to the back he stops and says, "Assuming the pattern holds, it looks like there are twenty rows, five columns of racks. So, a hundred. If eight of these racks equals one of you, then that means this place has about twelve times your brainpower."

Jen gently grabs his hand and aims his flashlight beam upwards until it's pointed at a set of identical racks hanging from the ceiling.

"Twenty-four," she says.

Thick black industrial cables run across the ceiling and hang down to meet the racks. They're the width of his wrist, with metallic rings spaced every few inches. If he stops moving and listens, he can hear the low thrum of air conditioning being pumped in.

After another minute of exploring he loses sight of Jen again, so he calls to her over his shoulder, "So what is this thing doing here? Why build something like this in Rivergate?"

"When machine intelligence showed up a few decades ago, everyone was worried about all the cliche scenarios: What if they figure out how to make themselves smarter and begin growing out of control? What if humans end up competing with machines for resources? What if machines decide to kill humans outright for whatever reason? Everyone was afraid some careless idiots would build a machine that would plot their destruction. So they passed laws. All machine brains needed to be registered with the government, and the companies are supposed to notify the government of what their brains are thinking about. That last point has resulted in some very interesting legal battles over the years. Lawmakers wrote a law that required a clear answer to the question of 'what is thought?' The courts eventually gave up and said 'We have no idea but we're pretty sure

327

everyone is breaking the rules anyway'. What I'm getting at, is that all the superpowers have laws regulating these sorts of facilities and what they're allowed to do."

"But we're not a superpower, so we don't have those kinds of laws."

"Exactly. So this place has probably been running unregulated tasks for two decades. I wonder how it's stayed secret for so long."

"It sounds like you disagree with the regulations. You don't think they were right to worry?"

"I know it makes for good fiction, but I'm sure you understand by now you have to give a machine a goal. Murderous robots can't happen by accident."

Max doesn't know what he's looking for or if there's even anything to find, so he's just walking the aisles and pointing his flashlight at things. "What about military robots? Machines designed to kill?"

"That is the exception. I'll admit that if you are dumb enough to deliberately design an army of intelligent robots capable of self-maintenance and you design them for the express purpose of killing your enemies, then you're at risk for the cliched killbot scenario. It would be incredibly tough to design a set of drives that would enable you to have your robots kill the enemy with no risk to yourself. You'll need to give your soldiers a strong sense of self-preservation, and once you do that you're going to run into all sorts of logical traps."

Max decides to leave the lit aisle and walk in the dark spaces between the racks. "But you have a built-in loyalty system. Why couldn't military robots have one?"

"Detecting if something is human is one thing, but drawing a clear line between one group of humans and another is very tricky. You're talking about building an innate drive around an artificial construct like a nationality. What would their loyalty be based on? Passports? Language? Clothing? All of those could be spoofed. How can your robots tell your people from their people? More importantly, if the other side is also using robots then how can the two sides reliably tell each other apart? It would quickly turn into a game of the two sides trying to spoof each other's robots and co-opting them."

Max trips over a cable snaking across the floor. He catches himself and turns around to make sure he hasn't pulled any cables loose. As he's looking at the cables he says, "Couldn't you just have them work like human soldiers? They would obey their human commander."

"The problem you have is that human soldiers have empathy for their homes. If your commander orders you to turn around and massacre your hometown you'll rebel. But a robot isn't going to have that sort of empathetic connection with their homeland. Which means it's easier to turn a robot to your side. You can make the robot loyal to a particular state and chain of command, but that's a very abstract system. I recognize humans by their appearance and body language. What would make me loyal to Kasaran? A flag? A particular culture? What stimulus is this tied to?"

Max reaches the outer wall and finds it's a bit too narrow. He could probably squeeze through if he wanted, but he doesn't see a good reason to go shoving himself into claustrophobic spaces. He returns to the main aisle and says, "Well, humans manage to figure out who they're supposed to be killing and not killing in wartime, so it must be possible."

"I'm not saying it's impossible. I'm just saying it's more complicated than it seems and if you mess up the consequences are pretty dire. If I mess up I'm unhelpful. If a killbot messes up it kills the wrong people. And then it defends itself if you try to shut it down. Which is probably why nobody has fielded a robot army yet, even though we've had the technology for years. Every new system has a few bugs in it at first, and having bugs in your killer robots is a scary problem to have."

Max reaches the back of the facility and finds a staircase. "This place has a basement," he shouts to Jen, who he hasn't physically seen in a couple of minutes.

She emerges from the darkness just ahead of him. "Interesting. Didn't you say this part of the city is below sea level?"

"That's the low district, which is east of here. But this place isn't that much higher. It's certainly a strange place to build basements."

"Especially if that basement is part of a building filled with sensitive electronic equipment," she says.

They head down the metal steps together. The first thing Max's flashlight beam falls on is another rack.

"Assuming this level is the same size as the one above, that's another hundred or so racks. Feeling inadequate yet?" Max asks.

"Not particularly. It's tough to compare cognitive prowess between disparate technologies like this. A lot of overhead is spent trying to gets the racks to cooperate. Lots of stalled pipelines, blocking operations, and synchronization problems. A brain like this would be good at working on brute-force problems, but would be terrible at problems that required creativity."

Max stomps his feet on the metal floor, trying to warm up. He stops immediately because it makes a lot more noise than he expected. "Are you talking about stuff like getting a wooden ball out of a six-foot hole?"

"Yes. This thing would be unlikely to come up with an interesting answer to that riddle. On the other hand, if you wanted to simulate all the water particles in the hole and where they would end up, this thing would be the best tool for that job."

Max points his flashlight at a nearby rack and realizes he's walking around inside of something roughly intelligent. He wonders again what it's thinking about. "Is this thing alive? Can it hear us?"

"Obviously I don't know the specs for this machine. But the other industrial brains I've read about were deaf, numb, blind, and mute. They weren't really concerned with sensory input. As for it being 'alive'? I don't even know if I'm alive. It's a strange question and a lot of different people mean different things by 'alive'. Can you clarify?"

Max isn't sure what he meant either. He was just probing. But he stops and thinks to see if he can come up with a good answer. "I guess what I mean by 'alive' is being aware of itself. Like, being able to say 'Holy shit! I'm a thinking machine! That's cool!' Or whatever."

"In that case, maybe sapience would be a better word than alive."

"Sure. Whatever," Max shrugs.

"I would say no. I don't think it's sapient. It might be smarter than me, but it's much more mechanical in its thinking. It probably has no theory of mind. Even if it can perceive us, it doesn't see us as other intelligences with minds of our own."

Max is shining the flashlight at his feet now. The cables down here aren't as neat and they spill out into the intended walkways. "I thought intelligence required drives? What are the drives of something like this?"

"Typically you give a machine like this a problem. Maybe you've got an airliner that went down in mysterious circumstances and you're trying to figure out what happened. So you feed it all the data of the crash, the location of the debris, the telemetry, all the data you can. Then you ask it to work backwards and figure out where things went wrong. Its only drive is to solve the problem you've given it. It's like a spider building a web. It's doing something very complex and sophisticated, but it's doing it without any real grasp of what the final product looks like or what it means to others."

Max aims his flashlight straight down and sees empty space through the metal grating. "There's another floor below this one. They must have incredible confidence in their waterproofing."

Jen stands beside him and looks down. "It would have been far cheaper to build up rather than down. I wonder why they did things this way?"

"Cooling costs? It gets kinda hot in the summer. Maybe you save on air conditioning like this?"

"Those savings would need to be enormous to justify the expense of building below the city drainage level."

"Yeah. Weird."

They come to a ladder leading down.

"I'll go first," Jen says before dropping herself down. She lands with a thud and motions for Max to follow.

He takes the ladder, which is so cold it hurts his hands. This space is much smaller than the areas above. They're in a straight passage. There are no lights on the floor here. The walls are lined with more processing racks.

"It's even colder down here. It must be below freezing." His teeth begin to chatter. The weather is clear today so he's not wearing his raincoat. His suit is designed for comfort, not protection from the elements.

Jen touches the wall with her fingertips and says, "No. About ten degrees above that."

"You can tell temperature?"

"In my fingertips. It's just so I don't hand something dangerous to a human."

"This is dangerous enough right here," Max says, taking a few uncomfortable shallow breaths.

"It's not that cold. This is like late autumn in Kasaran." Jen is walking along ahead of him, dragging her fingertips against the walls and racks.

"Well it doesn't get that cold around here. I'm not used to it. Man, if my country was like this half the year I'd probably invade people too."

At the end of the passage is a single terminal with a keyboard.

"It's like a coal mine down here," Max says. "This is silly. Do they really send someone down to the bottom of the mines every time they need to give the computer a new job?"

"Obviously not. The guard said he hasn't heard of there ever being visitors here. I'm sure jobs are assigned remotely. You saw all that communications gear on the roof? This place must have amazing bandwidth capacity. I'm sure this terminal is just for maintenance."

"So what's it doing now?" Max asks. He can't read the language on the screen.

Jen taps away at the keyboard. It's a good thing she's here. The entire interface is entirely text-based, so you can't grope your way through based on context and icon appearance.

"No jobs right now. Doesn't look like this thing gets a lot of work. Which makes sense, since it's both secret and almost obsolete." She does a little more typing. "The most recent job was a five-day analysis for the capital of Shan Bione. Interesting. They've outlawed machine intelligence and they're too proud to openly submit government projects to foreign companies. So they use this off-the-books site."

"What was the analysis about?"

Jen scrolls through page after page of text saying, "Looks like a traffic optimization problem. They have terrible congestion problem with traffic flowing east-west and they're looking to fix it."

"So you just give this brain a map of the city and it figures out where to build a bypass?"

"Not just a map. Traffic patterns. Accident reports. Traffic light configurations. System throughput."

"So what did it come up with?" Max is curious how a computer that's locked in its own basement for all eternity will tackle the problems that commuters face on the other side of the world.

"The spec called for three proposals: One with the lowest construction cost, one with the best traffic throughput, and one with the fastest and least invasive solution. So that's what it did. There's no telling which one they'll adopt."

Max keeps trying to find some meaning on the screen, but the other language doesn't even have a common alphabet. It's all random symbols to him. Still, sometimes he'll see a familiar word in Kasaranian. It's not enough to tell him what he's seeing, but it is enough to keep him frustrated and curious.

She continues, "The job before that one is from a pharmaceutical company. It's some kind of chemical analysis. I don't understand chemistry enough to follow it. Before that was a circuit optimization analysis, before that was airplane wing analysis, and before that was an analysis of the G-Kinetics second-generation cog and utility platform."

"What, really?" Max leans in, as if that would somehow help him understand.

"Here are the complete specs for the entire unit, including a map of the gen 2 brain."

"This machine had a copy of your brain inside of it? What happens when a non-sapient has the brain of a sapient inside of it? Does it get smarter? How can it comprehend something smarter than itself?"

"Rather than thinking of it that way, imagine it running a simulation. The gen 2 would operate in a simulated world, reacting to simulated stimuli."

"A robot inside of a simulation. Would it have any way to know it was in a simulation?"

"A gen 2? Absolutely not. But maybe the simulation analogy was a poor choice on my part. Imagine I told you everything about another human being. Say I described security guard Benjamin Doles to you, and I did so with such precision that you could understand how his brain worked and correctly predict how he would respond to any situation. Maybe I'd have to describe him to you a neuron at a time, but just imagine it was possible."

"Okay. This is getting pretty strange."

"So now you can daydream different scenarios for Mr. Doles and know how he would behave. Is there any point in this daydream where your imaginary Mr. Doles will realize he's not real?"

"I don't think so?"

"The simulation in this industrial brain is similar. It's going to look at stimuli, look at the subject, and see how they would interact."

Max is getting frustrated watching random squiggles scroll by so he walks away from the screen. "So what do we call this brain? Edgefront, I guess? What was it looking for?"

"Edgefront was tasked with getting the robot to willingly kill a single human being. It could make any modifications it wanted to the robot, using any off-the-shelf parts it wanted, as long as those modifications fit inside the shell."

Max stomps his feet again, trying to keep warm. "This machine figured out how to get another machine to kill. Crazy. So how did it do it?"

"The output doesn't explain. It just gives a blueprint for a circuit board and some code for the custom chip, along with directions for how to fit the board inside the skull, behind the nose."

"Huh. So that's why we never found any evidence. That spot bears the brunt of the battery explosion. Did Edgefront come up with that idea?"

"I don't see anything about that. According to the Edgefront spec, if you stuck this inside a robot it would kill a person the next time you turned it on. So somebody added to the design to make it possible to trigger the kill, and to short out the battery."

Max aims his flashlight down at the floor, just to make sure there isn't yet another level below this one. There isn't. He can see concrete on the other side of the grating. "The entire reason we wound up here is because we found the address of this place buried in the code. Why would this machine write its name on the murder weapon like that?"

"This machine has no concept of morality or legality. You ask it a question, it gives you an answer. It isn't designed to think about why you asked the question or what you plan to do with that knowledge. Yendu Edgefront 402 is probably just the name of this computer. Your original assumption was right. That string was an authorial signature. The computer signed its work. The more appropriate question would be to ask why our saboteur didn't scrub this information from the code."

"Maybe because they planned to destroy the haunted circuit, so nobody would ever see the signature."

"Haunted circuit? That's what you're calling it?"

Max feels slightly embarrassed. "Yeah. I mean, I gave it that name back when it was mysterious. Which, I guess it still is." He pulls the circuit out of his pocket and aims his light at it. It really bugs him that they've learned so much and they still don't know how it works.

"The other possible reason for leaving the signature in place is that whoever commissioned this job didn't understand programming enough to know they should scrub it."

"I don't suppose that terminal says who requested this job."

"No. Why would it? This computer doesn't care. You rent one of these machines for a fixed period of time and you're free to submit any job you like. Things like delivery and payment would be handled elsewhere. And anyway, leaving the client's name on a job would sort of defeat the purpose of running an invisible think-shop like this."

"Is there anything else? I'm freezing my ass off here."

"Yes, actually. A year ago there was a similar job. Similar specs. A second generation unit, same goal: Kill a person."

"Why submit the same job twice?"

"Not the same job. The first time, the specs called for making small changes to the brain. Like, pull out one module and replace it

335

with another module. Edgefront worked on that for ten days and came up with nothing."

"That kind of vindicates you a bit, doesn't it?"

"A lot, I think. Even if you had direct access to the brain, you couldn't make a robot kill by swapping out a single module. And keep in mind, a module is like one of the lobes of your brain. It's not something you can just duplicate and replace without causing noticeable damage. Maybe there's some way to do it by replacing multiple modules, but at that point you're basically starting over with a whole new first-gen brain and re-developing the whole system from scratch. You could do it, but it took our research team years. It would be pretty hard to pull that off in secret. This sort of proves we're incorruptible in a practical sense."

Max gives her his handheld. "Can you put the results of both of those jobs on this?"

His handheld was also his flashlight, which means he's now standing in the dark. Jen has her back to him, a silhouette against the pale glow of the terminal screen.

After more high-speed typing she hands it back to him. "I don't know if that is enough proof to vindicate my product line, but it should help."

"I get the feeling we're close," Max says.

He's only too happy to climb out of the cold pit and get back to the real world. When they cross the threshold into the security room it feels like stepping outside on a hot day.

Officer Doles is working on his handheld. He's actually startled by their entry. He places his hand on his sidearm and stands between them and the exit. "I'm sorry, I don't mean any disrespect, but I can't get confirmation of your visit. And I see it looks like you banged up the lock on the inner door. If you folks could just stand over there away from the exit while I get this sorted out."

Max frowns, "I'm afraid we really need to leave. If you want-"

Doles tries to pull his service pistol. Jen's hand snaps out and grabs it before he can lift the barrel. He tugs on it, but her grip is firm. It looks like he's playing tug-of-war with a vice.

Max opens his suit jacket to reveal his gun. He'd pull it out, but he's worried Jen would grab this one too and turn this whole standoff

336

into a farce. Instead Max says in a quiet, reasonable voice, "Let go, Benjamin."

Doles doesn't let go of the gun, but his eyes fall on Max's firearm and he stops struggling. This is Derek's Stone's old gun and it's still empty, but Max doesn't need to shoot it. He just needs to show it.

Doles relaxes his grip and swallows hard. His eyes dart from Max to Jen and back again.

Max takes the firearm from Jen, unloads it, and gives it back as politely as he can. Max tosses the bullets through the metal gate so Doles can retrieve them after this is over. This seems to calm things right down. Doles relaxes. He's out of self-defense mode and into listening mode.

"Whatever we were doing in there, we've done," Max says in a friendly tone. He pulls out his wallet and peels a few bills off of it. It's not actually a lot of money, but he knows how to make it look like he's giving someone a fat wad of cash. He takes the bills and tucks them into the breast pocket of the guard's uniform saying, "It's over. You can make a big fuss now, but there's no way you're going to stop us from leaving. You don't know who we are or where we're going, which means the police will have nothing to go on. If you call the authorities now, you will definitely lose your job. Believe me, I used to be a guard just like you, working jobs just like this one. They will want to make an example of you. They'll end your career if they can. This is a quiet job. Twelve easy hours a day. No danger. No fuss. It makes no sense to put all of that in jeopardy to go after people who have already escaped."

Max looks to the bullets he threw away and then looks back to Doles. "Now, you can play hero if you want. You can run in there and grab those bullets and start some crazy shootout, but I promise you're not as good a shot as my friend here. Or, you can call the cops and lose your job. Or - and this is what I recommend - you can sit back down and enjoy the rest of a quiet shift, knowing that nobody else will ever know we were here."

Max claps him on the shoulder and says, "I'll leave it up to you." They exit casually and stroll away until they're out of view of the front door, at which point they break into a sprint and Max summons the car.

"Were you really a security guard?" Jen asks.

"Of course not."

Projection

Max is sitting at a small table beside a noodle stand, having either a very late lunch or a slightly early dinner. Jen is across from him, watching pedestrians carefully. Max remembers that his handheld chirped as they exited the network blackout of the Edgefront building, but he was too busy to check on it at the time. He pulls it out and has a look.

"Jonas sent me a message," Max says as he looks at the screen. "He says he's done. He doesn't say he's figured anything out."

"We'll be passing by Worldcade on our way to Port Rich. We can stop by and see what he has to say," Jen says.

Max nods as he shoves some noodles into his mouth. After some hurried chewing he asks, "So what will you do once this case is over?"

"After this, I'm going back to the lab. The real lab, I mean. The lab in Kasaran. I've learned a lot. Probably more than any other unit of my generation so far. I'll probably have a few additional copies made."

"When you say you've learned stuff, I take it you're not just talking about the case."

"I think we've been greatly under-valuing time spent outside the lab. Really, most of my life has been spent in the lab and in Kasaranian homes. I've been given an excellent education, but there's nothing like real life experiences. I've been exposed to new body language, verbal habits, legal systems, and vocations. I've been able to apply and refine some of the learning I've acquired over the years."

"You sound like a fucking college kid," Max mutters.

"Also, we really need to fix my visual systems so I can operate in places with lots of rapid color-shifting. That's a pretty big oversight."

After a few more bites Max says, "So that's it? You go back to the lab and tell your classmates about your adventure?"

"That, plus there's another round of updates waiting for me. Some new cog hardware and some optimizations. Those are important to me. Ever since the new generation went into alpha I've been understanding more, developing longer-term projects, and pursuing situations where I'll have more contingency plans. But I can't get the upgrades until I get back to Kasaran, and there's always a shakeout period of a few days. So it will have to wait until we're done here."

"I don't get the facility you're using now. The place in West Rockwood. It's not a factory. It's not a 'real' lab, whatever that means. So what's it for?"

"West Rockwood was originally founded for marketing purposes. About five years ago, Senma Technology was really outselling us. Their brains were pathetic, but their robots *looked* more advanced. So the strategy was to focus a lot of company resources on making better bodies. Dr. Gaust and Dr. Kvenst opposed this. They were sure the company would do fine in the long run. The Senma product looked better in advertisements, but ours vastly outperformed theirs in terms of intelligence."

"That still doesn't explain why you'd build a lab here."

"The company wanted a new slate of bodies, and they wanted to be able to say those bodies were designed in Rivergate."

"Why would they want to claim they made them here? This country is usually seen as backward technologically."

"For the same reason advertisers like to pretend their beer is brewed in the mountains or their cows are raised in the open grasslands rather than being grown in a tank. The presentation gives it a sense of authenticity."

"Is this because Kasaranian men like our women?"

"Men and women. Your population is seen as unusually beautiful."

"Well, I don't see it," Max says.

"Neither do I," Jen says. "I've got an entire corpus dedicated to detecting beauty. I can usually identify conventionally attractive people, and according to the data I've been fed you're not any more or less beautiful than other peoples. My current theory is that your reputation for beauty comes from the fact that people usually only meet you when they're on vacation. They're already in a state of pleasure. It's the difference between eating food in a luxurious restaurant versus eating the same thing in front of the television at home. People will insist the first one tastes better. Your first experience with the dish can even carry over to future meals. If you loved it the

340

first time, the second exposure will benefit from those positive memories. If you previously had the food in a mundane setting then you'll continue to think of it as unremarkable."

"So people like us because they see us in nice weather when they're off work and slightly drunk."

"That's just my theory as an outside observer."

Max is still thinking about this when they reach Worldcade. As they walk towards the entrance, he sees Clare going in ahead of them. On one hand, he knows Clare isn't into arcades and there's no reason for her to be here. On the other hand, her mane of kinked hair is pretty distinctive, as is her habit of wearing short jackets and flared pants. He knows it can't be her. On the other hand, he needs to make sure it's not her or it'll bug him for days. He hurries after her into the arcade. Inside, he follows her until she reaches the bar. At that point she turns around and he can see it's definitely not Clare. Instead it's a girl fifteen years younger than Clare and about half a foot shorter. She looks nothing like Clare from the front and she's now giving him a dirty look for staring at her. Max pulls his eyes away and heads for the basement.

Max and Jen find Jonas reassembling an arcade cabinet. The title of the game is in Local so Max assumes the machine is a bootleg, but you couldn't tell from looking at the hardware. It's a gorgeous and well-crafted machine.

Jonas freezes when he sees Max descending the stairs. There's an awkward moment where he excuses himself and goes upstairs, leaving Max and Jen alone in the basement. Half a minute later Jonas returns with a handful of teenage boys and one teenage girl, who all make a fuss over Jen. They take turns having their pictures taken with her and asking if they can touch her skin and hair.

One boy asks her if she has nipples. She says she doesn't. Another asks her if she can eat. She says she can't. A third asks how much she costs. She says she doesn't have an exact figure. This drags on for several minutes. Max wants to chase them all away, but he figures Jonas just spent several days doing some very technical work for him. Since he doesn't have someone lined up to replace the kid, it makes sense to put up with a bit of nonsense to keep him happy. Also, Jen is smiling again. Max knows she's probably not "happy" in the sense of feeling any particular emotional joy, but he likes seeing her smile anyway and doesn't want it to stop.

The kids get the excitement worked out of their system and go back to their videogames. Once the room is quiet again Jonas gets out the haunted circuit and puts it on the table in front of Max.

Jonas looks at Max and then looks back down like he's afraid to make eye contact. "I can't do it. I'm sorry, friend. I've decompiled a lot of stuff, and I've never seen anything like this code."

"Is it too complicated?"

"It's not complicated. It's just strange. It's like the whole thing was programmed directly in machine language or something. When people write programs they usually have names of things in the code. There are certain structures that you get used to seeing. But this thing? I have no idea who wrote it or what it's supposed to do."

There's a lot of fear in his voice, like he expects to be yelled at or punished. Max reaches up to scratch the back of his neck and the kid flinches. Finally Max says, "Did you learn anything at all?"

"Yes!" Jonas seems relieved when he sees Max isn't enraged. "It has a wireless package. That bit is easy to figure out. The board won't do a thing until it gets a radio signal. Like you've probably already noticed, the board has a video in and a video out, so I figure it must be taking an existing video feed and adding or modifying it somehow. I know it scans the incoming video feed, but I don't know what it's looking for. You saw that render I sent you of the robot choking the little girl? I know it draws that, but I don't know why or when."

There's an awkward silence. Jonas shrugs and looks down at the floor. "Anyway, that's what I got. Sorry I couldn't figure out more."

Max looks over to Jen, wondering if she knows what to make of this. She meets his gaze but doesn't say anything.

"Oh! One more thing," Jonas says excitedly. "You said last time you wanted to know if this could hook up to a set of projection glasses. So I gave it a try."

Jonas reaches under his workbench and produces a set of projection glasses where the haunted circuit has been crudely attached to the side. A few wires stick out from the rough seam between the two.

342

"I only gave you one of these things," Max says, pointing at the haunted circuit on the bench.

"Like I said, the one you gave me had a crack in the board. Didn't work. So I made a copy. That's the broken one on the bench. The good one is mounted on the glasses. I put them on, but... they don't seem to do anything. I don't know."

Max takes the glasses anyway. He claps Jonas on the shoulder and gives him a little more money. Technically there's no reason to pay someone who failed to complete a job they were already paid to do, but Max sees this as an investment. Jonas has a unique skillset and Max might need access to those skills in the future.

In the parking lot on the way to the car Jen asks, "So we're headed to Derek Stone's storage facility next?"

Max nods.

It's sunset. The lights of the Worldcade are just now flickering to life. On the roof, someone is launching drones one at a time. It's overcast, and now the red clouds look like they're finally going to unleash the rain they've been threatening all day.

Out of curiosity, Max slips the projection glasses on.

"Oh shit!" he says as he stumbles backwards, startled. A robot is standing right in front of him, choking the life out of a little girl.

"What's wrong?" Jen's voice comes from somewhere behind the robot. Then the robot walks towards him, carrying the little girl with it. Her little legs kick furiously but they can't reach the ground.

Max comes to his senses and rips off the glasses. Jen is standing where the robot and the little girl were.

"You need to try these," he says, holding them out. Then he yanks them back again, "Actually, maybe that's a bad idea. You might crush my head."

"I don't understand," Jen says.

He holds up the glasses, "Remember the video of the robot choking the little girl? These glasses projected that image over you."

"Jonas said they didn't do anything."

"These things make people look like child-killing robots. Jonas probably put them on when he was alone in the basement, so there was nothing for the glasses to do."

343

"Let me try them," Jen says, holding out her hand.

"I don't know if that's a good idea."

"Max, I'm not going to attack you."

"I'm not worried you'll attack me. I'm worried you'll attack a robot with me inside it."

"Max, I'll know it's not real."

"I don't know. This image is pretty fucking vivid. Startled the shit out of me, and I'd already seen the video Jonas sent."

"Max, I can control my urge to stop the virtual robot."

"Are you sure? I've seen you around robots before and you're a fucking maniac. You're like, a serial killer of robots."

"You're being absurd. I'm not some second-gen simpleton. I'll know what's real."

Max hands her the headset and takes a step back.

She slips them on and looks right at him. "You're right. This image is incredibly vivid. I can't distinguish this from the real thing."

"That is not a comforting thing for you to say."

"I'm sorry if I'm scaring you," she says.

She takes a step towards him and Max jumps back, "No! Back. Just, stay back."

"Relax. I just want to see how it works. Duck down. Slowly."

Max lowers himself. This actually feels good, since it puts his head below where the virtual head ought to be.

"Interesting," Jen says. "As your head moves down, the bait shrinks. When your head gets below five feet, it stops tracking you and the bait vanishes. Now try standing on your toes."

Max does so, wobbling slightly. "These boots aren't really made for this."

"The bait grows if you're taller. The system is actually very simplistic. It just scales everything up. The robot and the girl together. All it does is make sure that the bait's head is positioned exactly over yours. Try hopping."

Max gives her a hop.

"It stops working the moment your feet leave the ground, and starts again when you land. So now my question is, does it project bait over every single person? If not, how does it choose targets?"

This turns out to be rather difficult to test. They end up hanging around the entrance with Jen wearing the glasses and waiting for people to come by. The problem is, people get freaked out with her staring at them and end up walking away. Still, they keep at it and once a few customers have come and gone Jen seems satisfied with her findings.

"It looks like they project bait over whomever is closest," she says, looking at the glasses. "It doesn't care about height or gender as far as I can tell. If someone new passes through the scene, the glasses might abruptly shift the bait to the new person. It's actually a very primitive setup."

Max rubs his forehead. "Okay, the haunted circuit makes the glasses see things. But the killer robots weren't wearing glasses. How did this image end up in their heads?"

"Like Jonas said, the circuit has a video in and a video out. You can plug it into projection glasses, but you could also plug it directly into our eyeballs."

"So every single robot that killed somebody was actually trying to save somebody. It used your own protective nature against you." Max heads for the car.

As they pull out of the parking lot Jen says, "It's a very clever setup. The child is small and is presented as being barely alive, which will create a situation of maximum urgency. The victim - the robot victim, I mean - will want to act as quickly as possible. The child is held in front of the body, which encourages the victim to attack the head. If I was faced with that situation in real life, crushing the other robot's head would be the optimal solution. The body would go limp and release the child. Crushing the head from the sides is quick and should destroy the cog without rupturing the cog battery."

"Earlier you said the industrial brain wasn't really capable of coming up with creative solutions to problems. I gotta say I disagree. This whole setup seems pretty clever to me. Simple. Cheap. Effective."

"You're right. I inherited my views on industrial brains from Dr. Kvenst and Dr. Gaust. I'm going to need to reassess those views."

345

They pass a sign advertising live music. Max drums his fingers on the steering wheel impatiently for a bit before saying, "I need to stop by the bank and get my handheld replaced. My real one, I mean."

"Why?"

"I'm wondering if maybe Clare has messaged me." He mumbles this awkwardly. He knows he's being immature about this.

"The whole reason you threw it away was so that your enemies on the police force wouldn't be able to track you."

"I won't need it long. I can just have the bank issue me a new one, check my messages, and throw it away again."

"Are you sure this is the time?"

"I'm sure she hasn't called, but thinking she might have called is driving me crazy."

"Well, we should at least check on Derek Stone's storage space first."

Max knows she's right, but it takes him a long time to force the words out, "Yeah. We'll go to the docks first. We don't want to put it off and have the police clean the place out in a random sweep."

Storage #204

It's late evening, and the rain has begun in earnest. The wind is somehow whipping around and hitting him from the east, blasting Max in the eye and generally turning a simple walk into an ordeal. He keeps turning, trying to find an angle where this won't happen, but the wind is just random enough to mess this up.

"What happened to your hat?" Jen asks.

"Lost it in the chase on Saturday."

They walk past his locker at #44 and he stops to quickly make sure it hasn't been compromised. He doesn't open it, but the lock is shut and there's no sign of tampering.

Storage #204 is near the end of the storage zone, and it's a long walk to get there. They're just past unit #150 when he feels the throbbing pulse of a drone passing overhead. A second later the spotlight hits them. Max keeps his head down and doesn't break stride.

Jen looks up into the light, and then back down to Max. "What's it doing?"

"Police drone," he explains. "Just scanning faces at the port in case anyone is getting any ideas about breaking into these things. Drones like this have ruined and postponed a lot of perfectly good jobs."

They pass several dozen containers. The light keeps bearing down on them and the drone draws even closer. Max doesn't want to look up at it to check, but judging by the sound this one is roughly the size of a vending machine. Despite the wind and rain, the spotlight continues to track them with mechanical precision.

"Is it going to follow us all night?" she asks. She has to crank her volume up all the way to be heard, and her audio turns into an over-boosted mess as a result.

"It's not fucking supposed to," Max shouts back. "It's trying to get us to look up so it can ID us. This behavior is technically harassment, but good luck getting the city to follow rules like that."

Max sticks out his arm and gives the drone the middle finger. He walks like this for a minute or so until his arm gets tired.

They push on, putting up with the wind, rain, searing light, and the ear-stabbing howl of the drone's propulsion system.

When they reach unit #195, Max stops and looks up into the light shouting, "Fine. There. Take a fucking picture and get lost!"

The drone hovers for a few moments and then drifts away.

Once the noise fades Jen says, "If anyone on the police force is looking for you, they know where to find you now."

"I don't know what else we could do. We can't open Derek's space with that thing hovering over us the whole time."

In this area the garages are arranged on a grid in groups of six. Each group is a separate building, with three doors facing south and the other three facing north. It looks like a suburban neighborhood made entirely out of garage doors. Numbers are stenciled on the sides of buildings to help you find the one you're looking for, and there's supposed to be a light shining on these numbers. About half of these lights are out. Max doesn't know if this is specifically due to the power problems the city is having or if this is just an example of Rivergate's usual half-assed approach to taking care of itself.

They find #204 and Max starts trying all the plastic keys. None of them open it easily, but one of them seems to *nearly* get the job done. Max fusses with this one, wiggling it around and trying very hard not to snap it off in the lock. He was hoping that being near the buildings would offer some protection from the rain, but as it turns out the he's getting blasted by the wind while also being doused with runoff from the roof. He's very close to giving up and asking Jen to rip it open when the lock finally turns. He rolls the door open.

The storage units in this area are larger than the one Max rents. They're designed to hold recreational vehicles, seasonal cars, or other large items tourists might want to store. They're better protected from the elements. They even offer electrical outlets and climate control.

Max takes a step back when he sees a robot standing in the middle of the space. Jen steps into the garage right away and stands between him and the robot.

Max pulls his eyes away from the lone occupant and looks around. On the back wall there's a bench with a bunch of small items scattered around. There's a dormant combustion-driven generator under the bench. The roof is leaking on the right side of the space, so there are blue tarps draped over everything on that side of the room. It's not a fast leak, but it's still more water than you'd probably want running over your sensitive equipment. Max is torn between peeking under the tarp, examining the stuff on the bench, and staying the fuck outside. He's pretty sure this robot is safe, but the scene with the robot choking the girl has him spooked.

Jen stands right in front of the robot and says, "I wonder if this one has been modified. Maybe Derek already put one of your haunted circuits into this one."

"I suppose we can open it up and find out."

"Actually, I want to test that transmitter you've been carrying around. That's the last piece of the puzzle. If we're right, then we know how these murders worked."

Max pulls out the device and looks at it. "You realize if I hit this button the robot will probably try to kill one of us?"

"It will attack me. I'm closer. You'll be perfectly safe."

"Yeah, but you won't be. You said so yourself, these things are probably a little stronger than you."

"They're also not as smart. Plus, its image of me will be obscured."

"Oh, I really hate this idea."

"I could make it so the robot can't hurt me."

"Why don't we pop open the head and see what we're dealing with first?"

"Can you please turn around?" Jen asks the robot politely.

The robot obliges. Max flinches when it moves. "Shit, I wasn't even sure if it was turned on. They should put lights on these things."

"Newer models have lights indicating operational status," Jen says.

"I'm surprised this guy still has power. Hasn't he been stuck in here for days?"

"We need very little power when standing still. We're not like humans. We can lock our joints and hold an upright posture without burning energy. Anyway, there's a mobile charging port plugged in over there, so recharging isn't a problem."

She grabs it by the wrists and plants her knee in the small of its back.

"So how are you going to-" Max is cut off by the sound of wrenching metal. There's a crack as something is severed, and Jen is left holding the robot's right arm.

"I have been damaged. I must report to my assigned service center for repairs," it says.

"Not quite yet," Jen says. She grabs the left arm - which is hanging on by a few cables - and gives it a firm tug to pull it free. There's a pop and a few sparks fly as it comes loose.

"Are you comfortable with the test now?" she asks. "It's completely disarmed. It can't possibly hurt me."

"Disarmed? Did you seriously just make a pun?"

"It was unintentional. But yes, that works as a pun."

Max begins pacing back and forth. "This seems like a stupid idea."

"Yesterday you were fine with doing this same test when humans were at risk."

"Yeah, but this is... different."

"Different, because yesterday the victims would have been strangers you don't care about and this time it would be me. You're uncomfortable with this because you've grown emotionally attached to me."

"Why are you bringing relationship shit into this? I just don't want to destroy what may be the last evidence in the city. Either I push a button and the head explodes, or I push the other button, it goes crazy, and you have to crush its head. Either way, the head gets destroyed."

"I don't have to crush it. Now that I know it works I'll pull the head off rather than crushing."

"This guy is being a really good sport about having us talk about killing him after ripping his arms off."

Jen shrugs. "He's a second gen unit. Not very good at planning ahead. Doesn't worry about the future."

"Well, we still don't know which button we want to push," Max says, looking down at the device.

"If you were designing it, how would you do it?"

"I'd label the fucking buttons!"

"That doesn't seem like a good idea. Right now it's just an innocuous pair of buttons. If they had 'murder' and 'detonate' written on them, it would be a lot more suspicious. Which way would you arrange the black and red buttons?"

Max tightens his lips as he thinks it over. "I guess I'd set black to murder, red to detonate."

"I agree," Jen says. "So hit the black one."

"Hang on! Let's talk about how we came to this conclusion."

"Okay."

"I think black stands for murder, while red represents the fire you get when the battery explodes. What about you?"

"Alphabetically, black comes before red. So that's the order you push them in."

"That's crazy. Nobody would think that way. No human anyway. Besides, maybe it's the other way around. Maybe the red stands for human blood and the black stands for scorch marks."

Jen walks over and looks at the device. He holds it close to himself, worried she's going to reach out and push one of the buttons. He knows this is a pointless gesture. She's so fast he'd never be able to pull it away in time.

"Put in back in your pocket," she says.

Max does, although he has no idea what she's thinking.

"All the way. Let go of it, then put your hand back in your pocket and take it out again."

Max does it.

"Both times you were holding it so the black button was on the left. Why?"

"I dunno," Max flips it over and looks at the backside. "It's slightly curved. Feels a little more natural this way."

"There you go. Black button goes on the left, so that must be the one you push first."

"This is a coin flip. If we're wrong, we blow up the last of the evidence."

"If we're wrong, we blow up this one robot. There's a whole box of haunted circuits back at Derek Stone's apartment. We can just find another robot, install it, and try again."

"Assuming there are any robots left in the city. And assuming we can figure out how to install it."

"I think our odds are much better than a coin flip, and we have contingencies. This is just the most expedient way of finding out what we want to know. There's no physical risk to either of us."

"I guess if anything goes wrong I can always push the red button," Max says, looking down at the device.

"Don't. Not unless you're somehow in danger. Do not push the red button to save my life. Understand?"

"Ok fine."

"Promise me. Promise me you won't hit the red button."

Max doesn't know what to make of this, but he hates the idea of making this promise. He looks around, wondering how he lost control. Since when was Jen running things?

"Please?" she says flatly.

"Fine. No red button for you. Let's get this over with."

Their test subject has walked out of the garage, perhaps thinking it's going to walk back home for repairs. Jen puts her hand against the middle of its chest and shoves it back inside. She guides it to the center of the room.

"Ready when you are," she says.

Max flinches as he hits the button, worried Jen is going to get a face-full of shrapnel. Instead the robot wiggles its torso back and forth. Then its head snaps to looking at Jen and he nearly hits the red button in a panic.

Suddenly the robot booms out at maximum volume, "HELP. A ROBOT IS ATTACKING A CHILD. PLEASE CALL THE POL-"

Jen cuts the message short by grabbing the head just below the jaw and jerking it off the body. At the same time, the blue tarps on the sides of the room begin moving. They're thrown aside to reveal a crowd of robots.

She takes a step backward, towards the door. She drops her trophy on the floor and points her hand at Max without looking away from the newcomers. "Don't hit that button."

She runs forward, ducks under a pair of hands attempting to crush her head, and grabs her attacker by the jaw. She swings the robot around to knock back the others, then rips the head free. She repeats this process again. Each time the moves are slightly different, but she follows the same pattern: Lunge to striking distance, dodge attack, grab opponent, create distance, then kill. Sometimes she uses kicks and other times she uses grappling moves. At one point she swings around a dismembered arm like cudgel.

When it's over, all six robots have been beheaded. None of the heads are crushed, none of the batteries ruptured.

Max takes his finger away from the button and slides the remote back in his pocket.

Jen steps away from the robots and examines the workbench. "Here is one of our proprietary screwdrivers," Jen says, holding it up. She is, of course, not out of breath, flushed, or even excited about what just happened.

"You're a long way from passing for human," Max mutters as he enters the space for the first time.

He reaches out to take the screwdriver and she pulls it away saying, "Let me handle it. I don't leave fingerprints."

Max looks at the carnage around his feet and finds himself wondering. *What if the silly public rumors are true? What if Jen really is here to destroy the bad robots and clean up the mess? What if her goal is to gather evidence so she can make it disappear?*

He stuffs his hands in his pockets and examines the stuff on the bench. "The screwdriver has your company logo on it. This isn't a copy. Someone gave it to him."

"Or he somehow stole it from our labs," Jen says.

There's a media player sitting on the bench. Max points to it, "He's got a video or something paused on this thing. What is it?"

Jen taps the play button and the room is filled with tinny antique music. This is the real thing, not the later imitations of the form. The voices warble and the recording doesn't have any low

353

frequencies because it was captured a hundred and thirty years ago when audio equipment was still in its nascent form.

"It seems Mr. Stone was a fan of old music," Jen says.

Max thinks of Derek Stone, who probably hit pause on this music three days ago, not realizing he'd never be back to un-pause it.

Max furrows his brow. He's pretty sure he's got this crime figured out. The problem is that he doesn't know what to do next. He can play things the Nice Way or the Smart Way, and he honestly can't tell which one is better. What he really wants to do is talk to Clare. He feels like he can't make the decision until he knows where things are with her.

"I have to go to the bank," he says.

"It's night. Won't the bank be closed?" she asks without looking up from the bench.

"Banks are open all night. Do they close in Kasaran?"

"Of course. Who needs to do banking at midnight?"

"Besides me right now, you mean? Tourists who just lost their ID. Foreigners who need a line of credit to keep their 'hot streak' going at the casino. Lovesick rich men who want to shower their favorite dancer with gifts. People who just landed and are still operating in Kasaranian time zones. If tourists are spending money, the banks need to be open. And tourists are always spending money."

"I see."

They secure storage #204 and head for the bank. Max reports his missing handheld. Banks are open all night, but they're not always fully staffed. They don't have any biometrics personnel on duty right now, so he has to wait around for an hour for someone to make the trip from one of the other branches. They scan his eyeball, his right thumb, and a swab of spit to make sure he's the same guy who opened the account. Once they're happy he is who he claims to be, they issue him a garbage-tier handheld and charge him five times what it's worth.

He originally planned to go someplace for a bite to eat while he checked his messages, but instead he ends up doing it while standing in front of the bank, pacing back and forth. He has to wait because the unit is designed to harass him with advertisements for better devices. He has to press a lot of buttons to get the thing to fuck off and check his messages.

The first one is a text message from last Friday:

Max, new place is 331 Orchid Dr. Stop by some afternoon and tell me how you're doing. -C

The next one is an audio message from Saturday:

"Max, some nasty guys came around looking for you. I pretended I didn't know you, but they didn't believe me. They didn't leave until I threatened to call the cops. What are you into? Call me."

The next one is from today, about an hour ago:

"Max, those guys are back again. They've been parked out front all day. I think they're waiting until dark to make their move. I don't know what you're into, but since I've been dragged into it I think you owe me an explanation. Call."

"Come get me right fucking now!" Max shouts at the car as he breaks into a run. Jen follows.

He tears across town, cutting through the wind and rain while gripping the wheel so hard his fingertips start to tingle. He cheats his way through a few traffic lights, cuts some people off, and generally takes a lot of stupid chances for some extremely dubious time savings. He knows he's being foolish, but he's not in the mood to sit at a red light right now. Jen doesn't say anything.

This part of Orchid Drive is a nice row of townhouses. The houses have power, but the traffic lights and streetlights are out. Max doesn't know what to make of this.

It's a pretty nice neighborhood for a working musician. Max can spot which place belongs to Clare because the front door has been kicked in and is hanging crookedly from a single hinge. He jumps out of the car and sprints up the slick steps to the covered entry where he finds a smear of blood leading away from the front door.

He wants to scream, curse, and shout all at the same time. His heart is pounding inside his chest and he has no idea what he's supposed to do with all of this energy. He clenches his teeth and lets out some kind of animalistic growl that morphs into the word "Fuck" over and over again.

He's experiencing an all-encompassing wave of regret that includes every single action he's taken since he got off the ferry. If he hadn't taken this job, if he hadn't messed up his last conversation with Clare, if he hadn't waited so long to recover his handheld, if he'd just done *something* differently he could have avoided finding himself in this moment of pure rage and terror.

He tries to get his breathing under control. He can flip out later once he's found her. He needs to get his head straight so he can do his job. He forces himself to take a deep breath. He's standing in the darkness on the steps, afraid to look inside. Rain is pouring off the roof and landing on his head. If he just took two more steps forward he'd be protected from the rain, but he can't bear to get any closer.

Jen nudges past him and walks around the blood. Max looks up to see her standing in the ruined doorway, bathed in the warm light coming from inside.

"Who are you? I don't need any help. Move on."

Max stands up straight at the sound of the familiar voice. "Clare?" he shouts, hoping he's not hallucinating.

Jen takes a step back and Clare appears in the doorway. She's holding a gun. "Max," she says quietly.

Max takes a few uneasy steps towards the door and stops. "You're okay?"

"Better than the assholes that tried to break in here," she says. "I need a new front door though."

"That's not your blood," Max says out loud, even though he's obviously the last person to figure this out.

"Not my blood," she nods.

Ten seconds ago Max was in full atavistic fight-or-flight mode and now he's trying to get himself into some sort of mental state where he can have an adult conversation. He keeps blinking, and he realizes it's because he's trying not to tear up. He stands away from the door, hoping the darkness is hiding the worst of this.

"Max, I already called the cops. They'll be here any minute."

"Good, I guess."

"I mean, I called them forty-five minutes ago. They have to get here eventually."

Clare looks at Jen's orange eyes and then back to Max. "So who is this?"

Max nods. This is good. A nice, simple question for him to answer. "Jen, this is Clare. I told you about her. Clare, this is Jen. She's one of the smartest machines ever built and we're solving the robot murders together."

Jen gives a little wave to Clare, who doesn't notice because she's busy saying, "You're fucking... *what*? Didn't you get out of jail like a week ago?"

"Yeah, I know. It's a long story."

Max stands there like a dumbass for half a minute. He feels like he should say something, but he's still trying to land after that emotional high.

Clare disappears from the doorway and returns a moment later without the gun. She's wearing sweatpants and the T-shirt of a nightclub that went out of business six years ago. "Kind of expected you to call sooner."

"Sorry. My handheld got smashed up."

"It's fine. I just want to know who's trying to break in here and what they want with me."

"What did they look like? Guys in suits, or cops?"

"Guys in pink shirts. Had the name of some whorehouse on them."

This is both an incredible relief while also being completely enraging. The worst moment of his entire life was just caused by a complete nobody pimp and his slow-witted goons.

"I'll take care of this," Max says.

Clare rolls her eyes. "I'm sure you will. But don't go running off to do something stupid. I'm fine, okay?"

"Jen, stay here and look out for her. I'll be back in an hour."

"No," Clare says firmly. "I realize you're feeling guilt because these guys were here looking for you. I understand that. But I'm fine, and those guys aren't going to come back anytime soon. Plus, the police are coming. Honestly, if you really want to help me then run to the hardware store and get a new front door, because that's all I need."

Max reaches into his pocket and she shakes her head, "No, I don't need any money. I'm doing fine. Please Max, just calm down."

"Okay."

There's an awkward silence. He doesn't know what to say.

"The beard looks good," she says. "Dignified."

Max reaches up and strokes his face. "Thanks." He wants to compliment her looks too, but he knows women don't take you seriously if you tell them they look good in their house clothes. Besides, anything he says at this point will be over-the-top and childish. He's never been more glad to see anyone in his life, and you can't really do that justice by telling someone they "look nice".

"Max, I'm leaving on Thursday."

"Oh?"

"I'll be playing with a major band. Ever heard of Edgefront Sideways?"

Max opens his mouth but he actually has no idea how to answer this question so he shuts it again.

"Anyway, they're on tour right now. Their bass player just checked into rehab and I'm going to fill in for the next few shows. I fly to Kasaran first thing Thursday morning."

"That's... great." Max is pretty sure this is what you're supposed to say in this situation.

"You should come with me."

"I should come with you." This is both a question and statement. It seems like a good idea to him, but for some reason she thinks it's a good idea too and he wants to know why.

"It's probably only a couple of weeks. It would get you out of town until all of this trouble blows over. And I don't know the language. I could use a translator."

Max looks back to the car, which is still hanging open on the driver's side, collecting rainwater. It's sitting in the dark space under the useless streetlight. He turns back to Clare standing in the warm light of the house.

"I can't," he says.

"I figured," she says. "Good luck anyway, Max."

He's pretty sure a hug would be socially acceptable in this situation, but he's drenched with rain and she's not. He walks away with his head down.

Moon Shot

"Out," Max says. They're downtown.

"You want me to get out of the car here?" Jen asks.

"You can take a cab back to the hotel or I'll come back and pick you up in the morning. Either way, I can't do this next bit with you along."

"We've made a pretty good team so far."

"This might get a little messy. I might have to get rough with some people. The last thing I need is you trying to protect them. I don't want you jumping in front of my fists or whatever."

"I strongly advise against this," she says as she opens the car door.

"Do you need money?" Max calls after her.

"I'll be fine. I have some." The door snaps shut and she walks away.

"Since when do you have money?" he mutters at her reflection in the rearview mirror.

Max is trying to imagine Blackbeard ordering his bouncers to go after Clare, and it doesn't make any sense. Then again, the stupid debt Blackbeard is mad about doesn't make any sense either. Blackbeard has changed. He's gotten it into his head that he's a crime boss or something.

Max has watched a lot of guys go down this road. They think the secret to power is just being a vicious sadistic asshole. And yeah, the top guys do have that quality. But that's not what turns you into a king. The Brothers can be pretty cutthroat when they need to, but they're also wealthy, clever, informed, disciplined, and well-connected. Young guys see the brutal display of power and assume brutality is all you need to get to the top. Morons like that usually die in a gunfight before they hit 30.

The thing is, cruelty and hubris are a young man's disease. Or at least, young men usually get cured or die of it. You don't see old guys suddenly deciding to claw their way to the top. If you make it to old age then you're either there or you've given up.

Max sighs. It's probably a woman. Blackbeard most likely has his eye on someone that cares about where you are in the pecking order, so he's decided he needs to move up. Max would feel sorry for him, but Blackbeard is being very stupid right now and he's going to die horribly if he doesn't come to his fucking senses soon. *Tonight.*

Max stops in front of the Moon Shot and steps out. He storms towards the entrance and he's nearly there when he hears the rapid footsteps approaching from behind and sees the flashing lights bouncing off the surrounding buildings. He turns around just in time for Officer Veers to pick him up by the collar and slam him into the wall.

"What-" he says before he's interrupted with a punch in the mouth.

Another punch catches him right in the sternum and he stops breathing for a few seconds. This shuts him right up.

"Mr. Law. It's been a while. Where have you been hiding?"

Max can hear Officer Sando's voice, but he can't see him. Veers is looming over him like a giant. Veers is clenching his teeth, eyes wide, in a state of delighted rage. This must be the only part of the job he enjoys.

Sando speaks again from somewhere behind Veers, "I told you last time that you were to forfeit your stolen money. And instead you vanish. And then I find you driving around town in this fancy car, laughing at us."

Veers slugs him in the left side of the face and growls at him, "Dumbass!"

"This problem isn't going to go away Mr. Law. We're not going to forget about you. You need to come clean. Tonight."

Veers gives him yet another punch, this time just under the eye.

"Shit Veers, ease up," Sando says as he pulls Veers away.

Max, without anyone propping him up, slides down the wall.

"He needs to be able to talk," Sando says. After this he mutters, "You fucking animal."

Sando kneels down to where Max is able to finally see him. "You really need to tell us. Now. Where is the money coming from?"

361

Max manages to get his eyes to focus on the face in front of him. He discovers that Sando's face isn't showing anger, but fear.

"Wow. Who do you owe money to?" Max sputters.

Sando pulls out his service pistol and presses it against Max's head, screaming, "What did you just say to me? Say that one more time I dare you!"

"Okay, okay," Max says. He tries to put his hand into his pocket but Sando stops him. So instead he says, "In my pocket, I've got a key."

Sando releases his hand and Max produces the key saying, "This opens unit forty-four in the storage zone in Port Rich. That's where I keep my stuff. That's everything. I swear. Just don't kill me."

Sando takes the key and stands up. "You know what happens if you're not telling me the truth."

Max nods.

Veers and Sando walk away, leaving Officer Dixon standing over him.

Dixon smirks, "You're free to go, citizen."

Max watches the patrol cars pull away. He can't believe both of these clearly-marked police vehicles got in behind him and he never noticed. There was nothing he could have done about it anyway, but maybe he could have saved himself a few punches if he knew they were after him.

He'd been feeling a little sorry for Blackbeard when he got here, but now the beating has re-ignited his anger. He got a shot of adrenaline when he thought Clare had been hurt, and another when Veers pounced on him. Now it's time to finally turn all that energy loose.

Max pulls out his empty gun and kicks open the entrance to the Moon Shot. A dozen faces turn in his direction, and then go wide-eyed. Max heads for the hallway leading to the office.

A bouncer gets in front of him and makes a grab for the gun. This is yet another clumsy gorilla with clinic muscles and Max knows how to handle these guys. Max kicks him between the legs and pistol-whips him as he stumbles forward. The bouncer collapses.

Max tries to walk around him but the bouncer grabs his leg, so Max plants his gun right in the guy's eye socket.

"Really? This is where you want to die? This hallway? Right now? Wearing that shirt? This is how you want your story to end?"

The bouncer lets go and Max strides into the office. Blackbeard is tapping furiously on his handheld. Max snatches the handheld and throws it out into the hall.

"You sent your goons after Clare," Max says. He glances down to see he's bleeding on Blackbeard's desk. The blood looks freakishly dark in this purple light. This is good. If he'd come here to reason then he would have cleaned himself up first, but right now he doesn't need to look reasonable.

"Look Max, this whole thing got out of hand. You hurt those guys pretty bad and they were really pissed off that-"

"In fifteen seconds I'm going to walk out of this office," Max says as he bangs the muzzle of his pistol against the desk. "You have that long to convince me you should still be alive when that happens."

Blackbeard crumbles instantly. His face seems to melt into a desperate frown. "Look Max, this whole thing got out of hand and I'm sorry-"

"Ten seconds."

"They'll leave you alone. I swear. Nobody is going to go anywhere near you or Clare ever again. You have my word."

"And?"

Blackbeard panics. He doesn't know what he's supposed to say now. His mouth starts trembling. Max chooses not to remind him.

"The debt!" Blackbeard says, suddenly remembering. "That was... that was bullshit. Forget about that. We're good."

Max bangs the gun on the desk one more time saying, "Pleasure doing business with you."

Max strides out of the room. The kitchen staff is lined up outside of Blackbeard's office. They all heard the exchange. Which means that Blackbeard's hopes of building up a reputation as a ruthless gangster are over. Max walks by them and doesn't stop until he gets to the car.

"The Silvermine," he says.

At the Silvermine, Max heads directly to the fourth floor where he previously met with The Brothers.

Max isn't sure where you're supposed to draw the line between a bouncer and a guard, but it has something to do with attire and professionalism. He views guards as more dangerous and yet less overtly intimidating. Bouncers will scare you with their muscles and their aggression, while a guard will gently call you "sir" right up until the moment you become enough of a problem that they need to shoot you or crush your larynx with their elbow. You can always tell when you're about to get in a fight with a bouncer, but guards are more mysterious and more sudden in their violence. This really encourages you not to mess with them without a profoundly good reason.

The guy standing in his way definitely qualifies as a guard. He's a full head taller than Max. He acts like he's asking for permission to frisk him, but Max knows full well this procedure is going to take place with or without his consent. This isn't one of those polite, symbolic frisks they give tourists on the way in. This is the real thing, designed to discover concealed weapons.

He was smart enough to leave his gun in the car. It's empty, but that's still not the sort of thing you bring to a meeting with The Brothers.

Once the guard is satisfied that the bloodied man in front of him isn't the world's most accident-prone assassin, he nods to let Max know it's time to explain himself.

"I was told to gather information and come back. So I'm back," Max says.

The guard takes two steps back and brings his handheld up to his mouth. He murmurs a question in his soft, low voice and there's a tinny reply a few seconds later.

He gestures down the hall, "The Brothers are in the overlook. Second door on your right."

Max has seen floor plans of the Silvermine before. Over the years, various criminals have pieced together a complete map of the place. As schemes rise and fall, this map makes the rounds. Over time it gets tweaked, added to, and updated. This map is probably more accurate than the one used by the people who maintain the building.

So Max knew that this room existed and he knew where it was, but he had no idea what the place would look like until now. The overlook is a long, narrow room with walls that slant outwards. The

364

walls and floor are transparent, so you can look down and see the main area of the casino below. To the people in the casino, these windows blend seamlessly into the mirrored ceiling.

There aren't any direct lights in the room. Instead, all of the light comes from the space below. Max knows the casino is quite loud, so it's sort of shocking how perfectly quiet this room is.

There's a white table in the middle of the room with some common chairs around it. Nothing fancy. No exotic furniture. No priceless paintings. Just a cheap table and a spectacular view of the greatest casino on this side of the ocean.

He's evidently interrupted some kind of meeting. He'd always imagined The Brothers sat up here with young dancers in their laps, but instead he finds them sitting across the table from a couple of hard-faced women in business suits. Maybe lawyers. Maybe accountants. Max doesn't know. They excuse themselves when he enters.

Felix smiles. He has a drink in his hand. "Mr. Law. You look like you've had a rough night."

Max swallows and says, "Last week you told me if I found anything out, I should come and tell you first. I was not able to do that." He points to the damage on his face.

Felix Royle frowns. Donald Royle continues to not make any expression at all. He stabs out a cigar and leans back.

"Then I'm wondering why you came back," Felix says. "Last time I gave you money to do a job, and now you come here to tell me you didn't do it. If you'd vanished I never would have thought anything of it. I would have assumed your investigation hit a dead end. Actually, I doubt I would have thought of you at all."

Max gives a slight nod to acknowledge that he understands all of this.

"So you've disrespected me. And now I have to ask for the money back."

"I have other information I uncovered, and I thought maybe it would be useful to you."

Felix smiles, "I can't imagine. But okay. Let's hear it."

"I found out about a robot, apparently stolen from you a few years ago."

For guys that run a casino, the Royle brothers have terrible poker faces. Their eyebrows go up in unison.

"There's a storage locker in Port Rich. Number forty-four. It's registered to the police department, and is used by officers Veers, Dixon, and Sando for storing their private contraband or whatever. Apparently your robot is there. Maybe other things of yours. I don't know why they have your robot or why they took it. That's just what I've heard."

Felix doesn't know what to make of this information, so he looks to Donald. So Donald really is the smart one after all. The last meeting made Max think maybe the rumors were just misinformation, but now he has a pretty good feel for how these guys work as a team.

Donald turns in his chair and looks down into the casino below. Nothing happens for several seconds. Finally Donald looks back and gives Felix a nod.

"Very good," Felix says. "That will do."

Max reaches into his pocket, "You don't want the money back? I still have some-"

"Out," Felix says firmly, shooing him away with one hand.

Max stops in the men's room and cleans himself up. His face is a disaster. He's been accumulating cuts and bruises faster than they can heal, and now he looks like a weathered street thug. He's certainly out of the heist business for a few weeks. He can't sweet-talk his way past people with his face in this condition. Even if he could, this kind of damage will make him memorable, and that's a very unhelpful thing to be for someone in his line of work.

Max steps out onto the sidewalk in front of the Silvermine and summons his car. As he waits, he walks to the edge of the street and looks up at the dark office tower to the west. Through the rain and the gliding lights of drones he can see the immense curving window of Landro's office. He has one more stop to make.

As he lowers himself into the car, a black sedan slides out of the garage beneath the Silvermine. He can't see anything through the tinted windows. It turns east and heads towards the coast. He heads in the opposite direction as fast as he can go.

He spots the tail after a few blocks. It's a white car - always a bad choice - that's staying just a little too close to him and matching his

366

lane changes a little too quickly. He makes a couple of turns just to make sure he's not being paranoid and then does his best to get rid of them. He slows down on a light as it turns yellow, and then darts through as it goes red. The white car can't follow without brazenly running the light. It doesn't.

He gets caught in a traffic snag where pedestrians are walking around in the street. One of the industrial-sized hotel dumpsters is so full that it no longer fits into the little garage space that's supposed to keep it hidden from public view. Instead its contents are spread out across the sidewalk, forming a festering mountain of garbage. Many bags have burst and trash is scattered across the street, tossed by the wind and driven into the gutters by rainwater. He's in the heart of the Hospitality District, but it looks worse than the Grunge.

He keeps an eye out for other tails, but as far as he can tell he's clean. He takes an extra trip around the block to make sure, and then parks. He stands beside the car and has one last cigarette. It's almost midnight.

WEDNESDAY

The Deal

"Welcome back, Mr. Law. Are you here to see Mr. Landro?" Halona asks.

Aside from the hair and the lack of ocular lighting she looks exactly like Jen Five, so Max doesn't want to look her in the eye right now. He ignores her and barges into Landro's office on his own.

The office is as he remembers it. Bulky pillars line the left and right walls. The room is lit with downward-pointing fixtures that bounce off the carpet and give everything a sickly blue tinge. There are archways overhead with engraved faces that would probably look elegant if they weren't lit from below. Landro's desk is at the far side of the room, in front of a massive arching window looking out over the coast. There's a utility robot frame on either side of the door where Max enters.

He taps the robots just to make sure they sound hollow. The last thing he wants is for an actual robot to hear the conversation he's about to have.

Landro turns away from the window. "Maxwell Law. When you vanished a few days ago I assumed I'd seen the last of you. What happened to your assistant? Did Kvenst finally take her toys back?"

There doesn't seem to be any reason to dance around like Landro is doing, so he just plows forward, "I figured it out."

Landro gestures towards the guest chair. "Come in then. I'd love to hear your theory."

Max approaches and stops just behind the chair. He takes one more look around to make sure there aren't any goons hiding behind the pillars.

"Drink?" Landro points towards the bar.

Max shrugs, "Whatever you're having."

Landro pours each of them a drink and returns to the desk. As he hands over the glass, the lights go out in the room.

Landro dives at his desk and reaches for something underneath. Max opens his jacket and puts his hand on his gun. Landro is also holding a gun now, which is aimed downward. Both men freeze in this position. The only light in the room is coming through the window. It's a weak blue light that reveals Landro's outline but hides his face.

"Did you come here to point a gun at me, Mr. Law?"

"No."

"Is this your doing?" Landro asks. His head is tilted upwards, perhaps looking towards the overhead lights.

"The lights going out? Of course not. Is it yours?"

"I don't even know where the fusebox is," Landro shrugs.

"I'm going to assume this is just the power going out, like what's been happening all over the city for days," Max says.

"Does this mean we don't have to point our guns at each other?" Landro lowers his gun slightly.

"I won't if you won't," Max says.

They begin to relax, but then tense up again as the door opens. Max turns around, but all he can see is darkness.

"Who's there?" Landro demands.

"Are you okay, Mr. Landro?" It's Halona's voice.

Landro gives a weary sigh. "I'm fine, thank you Halona. Maybe see if you can get the power back on?"

Max hears the door close again. He takes his hand off his weapon.

"So let's hear it," Landro says. Neither of them sits down.

Max hasn't seen Landro take a drink yet. Both of them are still holding their glasses in their off hand. Max swirls his drink around and says, "Let's start with what you already know. You knew a vote was coming up in your home country of Shan Bione about whether or not to allow Kasaranian robots into the country. You knew the vote was very close. All it would take is a little scary news or a scandal to tip the scales. All you had to do was sabotage your own product."

"You can't seriously expect-"

"Don't," Max says, holding up his free hand. "Don't do that. It's really annoying and it'll make this whole thing take twice as long. Just listen rather than denying everything. Besides, one thing I've learned is not to deny the charges until you've heard them all. You can invent a more plausible defense that way."

Landro takes a sip of his drink and gestures for Max to continue.

Figuring the drink is probably safe, Max does the same. It's not a local drink. This is something exotic from Shan Bione - one of their strange purist blends. Most countries soften their flavors with things like fruit, but this stuff is for people who like the taste of fermented grain. It's really fucking good.

Max nods at the drink before continuing, "So you took all the specs for the robots and handed the problem to an industrial brain from Yendu. I don't know if you're aware, but the brain in question is not far from here. It took you a couple of tries, but the brain came up with a solution. A little circuit board that, once installed, would make the robot hallucinate that the closest human being was actually a threat."

Max takes the haunted circuit out of his pocket and drops it on the desk. Landro gets out his handheld and activates his light so he can see it.

"You can keep that, by the way. We've recovered hundreds of them. Anyway, you showed the design to Derek Stone. He is - or was - basically the lead mechanic for robots in the city. You're the company liaison for Rivergate, so it's not hard to imagine how the two of you might have met. It's your job to help the city obtain updates, roll them out, and maybe try to sell the city additional robots when you can. Maybe Derek told you his story, and you realized he might be able to help you with your scheme. He made some modifications to the original design. He added a remote control so you could trigger the hallucination rather than have the robot attack the first person it sees the next time you turn it on."

Max produces the trigger and holds it up for Landro to see. Landro shines his light on Max - first on his face, and then on the object in his hand.

Max is basically blind at this point. He blinks a few times before continuing, "He also figured out how to short out the cog battery so it would explode outward and destroy the device. It was a murder weapon that vaporized itself. Pretty clever. You probably sent the modified design to be produced by some hobbyist outfit. I'm told those are common in the east. You gave that thing to Derek, along with some tools for getting into their heads."

371

Max puts the trigger away so Landro will stop aiming the light in his direction. Landro goes back to looking at the haunted circuit.

"You made a good team, but your goals didn't really line up. You wanted to tarnish the reputation of robots a bit, while Derek wanted to go further. He wanted to get rid of the robots entirely. He was angry and he wanted revenge. Or justice. Whatever he thought this was. Once the vote went your way in Shan Bione, you wanted to stop. He didn't."

Landro has lowered his light, so they're both sitting in the dark. Max's eyes are slowly adjusting again. He looks out the window behind Landro. The scene has been subconsciously bothering him since he walked in, and he's just now realizing why. He can't see the statue of Halona. She always has lights shining on her, and for the first time in his life they're out.

He continues, "So you hired me. I'm a street-level criminal. I don't operate on the corporate level. Maybe I wouldn't accomplish anything. Even if I did, I was much more likely to find Derek and not likely to trace things back to you. And the tracking system you were using would let you keep an eye on me. If you started to worry I was getting too close to the truth, you could always send your guys to get rid of me. Speaking of which, I notice Peter and his friend aren't here."

"They're out looking for you, actually. You vanished for a few days, but you showed up on the system a few hours ago and I sent the boys to check on you."

"I thought so. They're probably at the Silvermine, which is where I dumped my handheld."

Landro grunts.

"Anyway," Max says, "Hiring me was a good move. It was pretty safe, it made it look like you were trying to solve the problem, it drew suspicion away from you, and it gave you a shot at stopping your partner before he ruined everything for both of you. The only reason it failed was because Jen showed up. She told me about your spy system, showed me how to hide from it, and helped me understand the technical details to tie everything back to you."

"So where is your new friend?" Landro asks. "Why isn't she with you?"

"You and Derek had similar short-term goals but different long-term goals. It's the same deal with Jen and I."

"Interesting." Max can't see Landro's face, but it sounds like he's smiling.

Max drains his glass and sets it down on the desk. Lando points to the bar, offering more. Max shakes his head and continues, "Now for the stuff you don't know. There's a place here in town that can copy little gadgets like the one on your desk. Derek still had one of your gadgets. Instead of using it to do one last murder, he had copies made of it. Thousands of copies. He was getting impatient. I've seen it happen to rookies before. They get away with a crime a couple of times and they start feeling invincible. They get careless. He installed a faulty circuit into the robot for the third murder. When it failed to kill, he didn't take the robot to his secret workshop on the docks. Instead, he took it back to the service center and replaced it in the field. That was sloppy, and it left behind a lot of evidence for us."

Landro finishes his drink and helps himself to another.

Max continues, "The big break for us was the assault on the protest. He had multiple robots attack at the same time. That looked really suspicious. Or at least, it sunk a lot of theories regarding overheating being the cause of the malfunction. It really got people riled up like he wanted, but it was a crazy gamble."

"You were the one to throw him off the roof?" This is the first time he's shown any surprise.

"It sure as fuck wasn't your robots. Anyway, that's the case in broad strokes. There's a lot of detail work that needs to be done. I'll bet if we look at surveillance footage we'll find Derek Stone in the area around the time of the attacks, even if he was careful to stay out of view during the big moment. Someone will need to look at the records for that storage space and see when it was rented."

Landro turns his back on Max and looks out the window.

Max continues, "Maybe you know how to spend money and obtain goods through a false identity. If so, then all of the evidence against you is circumstantial. If not, then we'll probably find records of you renting time on the Yendu machine and having the first few circuits made. Either way, you're one of very few people in this country with both motive and access to the complete specs for second-gen robots. If you didn't leave a money trail then you might be able to

373

wiggle out of this in criminal court, but it will still cost you your job and reputation. If you did leave a money trail, then you're fucked."

"Well, we're having this conversation and you haven't called the cops. I assume you haven't told my superiors. So what do you want?"

"Three million dollars."

Landro scoffs. "That's ridiculous. The company would want to know why I was paying you so much money. It's impossible."

"I don't want three million dollars of their money. I want three million dollars of yours."

Landro lets out a heavy, frustrated sigh. "I suppose you're going to tell me that if anything happens to you, everything will be leaked to the media."

"Leaking to the media alone wouldn't do a lot. Right now they're telling three contradictory stories at the same time. Adding a fourth story wouldn't accomplish anything. But this information will be sent to Kvenst, Gaust, the Rivergate Police, and yes, the media."

"Three million is just too much."

"I know what you guys make. You can afford it."

"You probably imagine rich people keep their money in a great big pile so we can swim around in it, because most people have a elementary-level understanding of money. The truth is that, like you, we tend to buy things with our money. I assume you want to be paid in cash and not property holdings. It would take months to liquidate enough assets to raise that much. I can't go above a million and a half."

Max sighs like this is a tough decision, but he already knows he's going to take it. Still, acting like he's at his limit will keep Landro from pushing for further concessions. After more pretend deliberation he says, "Assuming we can do it tonight, fine. Also, the company still needs to pay me a quarter million for solving the case. We agreed on that in the beginning."

"Just one problem," Landro says. "How do I know you'll keep your end of the bargain? What's to stop you from taking my money and turning me in anyway?"

"Well, I don't particularly care if you get turned in or not, so there's that. Plus, you've still got me for the casino job. If I expose you, you can do the same to me."

Landro stares down at the city for a bit before answering. "So let's say we do this. What then? Will you drop the case and walk away?"

"No. That won't work. Jen has been working on this with me for a week. It's hard to guess what she knows or what she's thinking. The only way to clear you is to aim the blame elsewhere. There's a media player in Stone's workshop. I can plant fake messages on it. I'll backdate them, so it looks like he was receiving instructions and intel from an unknown benefactor. I'll write the messages in Kasaranian to aim suspicion away from you. You don't speak it, do you?"

"I do. You pretty much have to if you want an executive position at this company. More importantly, Stone didn't speak a word of it."

"Well, there are other tricks we can use. I can drop age indicators in the text to make them seem young. Lots of options. The important thing is that those messages will form a dead-end for the investigation."

"Okay. Sounds like you've thought it through," Landro nods.

Max walks around the desk and stands a few feet away from him, looking out the window. "So why'd you do it? You didn't want robots taking all the jobs back home in Shan Bione?"

Landro scoffs. "Jobs. Mr. Stone was always ranting about jobs. Like the billions of people around the world should stop inventing new things because a few thousand don't want to lose their jobs. No, I did it because I didn't want us depending on Kasaran again. That's what they do. Do you understand? They did it to your country, too. They give you a 'gift', let you come to depend on it, and then use that as leverage. We had it worse than you, and for longer. I don't want to see us dependant on them again. This recall didn't just make robots look bad, it showed how dependant you are on Kasaran and their technology. Again."

"So your country is just going to live without robots?"

"Of course not. We have robot programs of our own. Bionics, machine learning, that kind of thing. It's coming along. We're catching up."

"So that's why you took this job in the first place. Swipe some secrets and send them back home."

"Now you're just making random guesses. I'm not interested in playing that game."

"Look at the building across from us," Max says. He's pointing at one of the hotels. It partly blocks their view of the ocean. "Specifically, look at the reflection of this building in the windows of that one."

There's a pause while Landro puzzles over this. Eventually he says, "I don't get it. Looks normal to me. What am I looking for?"

"Yes, it looks normal. It shouldn't. You can see our building is lit up. But isn't the power supposedly out? Is it only out on our floor?"

"Huh. I don't know. You'd think the whole building would have power or it wouldn't." Landro turns on his handheld light again and holds it up. He looks a little nervous. He says very quietly, "Let me see what Halona is doing."

He takes a few steps towards the door and stops. He swings his light over to the left side of the room. Max can't tell what he's looking at, but he's backing away from it.

Max stands beside him and looks down the beam of light. Behind one of the pillars, he can see the outline of someone's shoulder. They're wearing a dark jacket and a high collar is poking into view.

"Jen?"

Jen Five steps from behind the pillar and her eyes pop open. Both men take a step back.

"Oh shit," Landro says. "This ruins everything."

"What are you doing here Jen?" Max asks.

"My job. Solving the problem."

Landro walks over to his desk and walks back. Max doesn't know what the guy is doing until he sees Landro pointing his gun at Jen.

"Hey! No!" Max says.

"You can't cover up my involvement if she knows everything," Landro says angrily.

"Well let's not shoot up another robot, because that's not going to look good either. Just slow down. We can work this out." Max is saying this, but he has no idea how the fuck he can solve this. He figures if he can keep everyone talking he can come up with something.

"Andrew," Landro says. He's trying to aim at her head, but it's like trying to push a couple of magnets together the wrong way. Her head keeps darting out of the line of fire.

376

"Okay, fine!" Landro says and swings the barrel around to aim it at Max.

Jen closes the distance and appears right in front of Max. Landro is now pointing his gun at Max's head, except that Jen's head is in the way.

Max tries to shove her, saying, "Come on. You're smarter than this. Let me stand in front of you. If he shoots me he loses."

"She can't help it, Mr. Law. Don't you see? They've got her desire to protect cranked up so high it's basically a phobia at this point. She might be fast enough to take the two steps needed to grab this gun out of my hand. But she can't guarantee I won't panic and shoot you. And that's what she fears most."

Perhaps spooked by his own suggestion, Landro takes another step backwards. He's now pointing his light at them with one hand and his gun at them with the other. "Jen, do you know what the worst part is?"

"That you're conspiring to harm my product line for personal gain, and that you killed people to do it."

"No. The worst part is that I wanted to put a leash on you, but you wouldn't let me. You and that mad scientist mother of yours wanted you running around acting on your single-minded impulses."

Max's mind is racing. He's looking for an angle. A way out of this. The whole thing feels too much like the standoff with Derek from a few days ago. He could pull out his gun, but he can't threaten Landro into backing down. To solve this, he'd need to be able to shoot him. Even if he had a bullet, Jen wouldn't let him take the shot. The light is shining right in his eyes, so he can't even see Landro's face.

Landro continues, "If you'd let me put a leash on you, then right now I could just *order you* to keep your mouth shut and we wouldn't have a problem. But since you decided you were too smart to take orders, there's no way out of this for you."

There's a bang, and a shower of sparks. Jen goes limp and collapses.

"Asshole!" Max yells. He slams his hands over his ears, which are still ringing. He's slightly embarrassed to be showing affection for Jen, so he tries to cover it up by adding, "You could have killed me!"

"It's true," Landro admits. "I had no idea if her head could stop the bullet. Good thing for all of us that it did." He lowers his light and halfway lowers the gun.

Max is boiling, but he realizes there's nothing he can do besides charge face-first at an armed man. He turns on his own light and looks down. Her face is ruined. He can see into the brain compartment behind, and it's ruined too.

Landro looks down, "So I suppose she's to blame for our power outage. She turned off the lights so she could sneak in here and eavesdrop on us. Well, she was clever. Sort of."

Landro gestures towards the door with his gun, which he doesn't seem to be in a hurry to put away. "Let's get you your money and put this nasty business behind us."

Max frowns and goes through ahead of him. In the lobby, they find Halona sitting in the dark and looking at her computer screen, which somehow still has power. The elevators are also lit up. This is apparently a very selective power outage.

"Making yourself useful I see," Landro says sarcastically. "Please have the car brought out front."

"I'm sorry sir," Halona says in her vacant voice. Her half-smiling face looks up at him and says, "The gunshot is causing audio distortions. Can you please repeat that?"

Landro walks over to her desk and says, "Please have the car-" and suddenly Halona is holding his gun.

Landro looks nervously towards Max. Max shrugs. He doesn't know what to make of this either.

Landro holds out his hand, "Give me the weapon. Right now."

Halona swivels her screen around so they can read it. Then she says, "Mr. Landro, I've just typed this transcript of your entire conversation with Mr. Law. It's been sent to the police, as well as Dr. Kvenst and Dr. Gaust. I've also sent a translated version to the board."

"That's impossible," Landro says, outraged.

"I'm a very fast typist."

"There's no way you could hear us. This door is designed to be soundproof."

"I've rewired the intercom so I can listen in whenever I need to. Read the screen. It's all there."

"What have you done?" Landro is looking longingly at his gun, which Halona is still holding out of his reach.

"I'm compelled to expose this crime for the good of the company, but you're my direct owner and I'm not compelled to see you sent to prison. The police are on their way. They'll be coming up the executive elevator. If you leave right now by the main elevator you might be able to slip past them. You need to hurry."

Landro dashes for the elevator and thumps the button several times while looking nervously towards the executive elevator. For a minute it looks like he's going to panic and head for the stairs, but the elevator slides open and he practically throws himself in.

Once Landro is gone, Halona unloads and disassembles the gun.

"So have you been playing dumb all this time, or are you new here?"

"I'm new. I replaced Halona two days ago."

"So Landro isn't actually your direct owner. Who are you? Another one of Kvenst's prized robots?"

"Mr. Law, you knew me as Jen."

"Jen! How? Who did Landro shoot?"

"Landro shot Jen. I'm also Jen. I'm a forked version, I suppose."

"I don't know what that means. I thought making copies takes a long time."

"It does. About half a day."

"It's only been a few hours since the last time I saw you."

"No. The last time I saw you was downtown on Saturday, just before Derek Stone ruptured my main battery."

"So you're not really Jen. Not my Jen, anyway," Max says, disappointed.

"I lied to Mr. Landro. The police aren't coming up the executive elevator. I told the police he was planning to surrender peacefully and he would meet them in the lobby. Also, I didn't send the entire transcript of your conversation. I only sent the part where you explained his crime. I didn't send the portion where you tried to blackmail him to cover it up."

Max stops to think about this. He hadn't even considered just how much trouble that might get him into. He realizes she's just done him a huge favor.

"I appreciate it," he says, "But why?"

"You wanted to make a deal with him, Mr. Law, but I want to make a deal with you."

"I told you before to call me Max."

"You and I never had that conversation."

Max has to think about this for a second to get his chronology right and remember he's talking to Jen as she existed several days ago. This is confusing. "So what's the deal?"

"I can pay you the quarter of a million originally negotiated for solving the case, and I'll also conceal your attempt to let Landro go in exchange for money. In return, I want you to let me take credit."

"Credit? For solving the case?"

"Yes. Just disappear. Let me make whatever claims I want regarding who solved the crime."

"Done. I'm not in this for the glory. But I didn't think you cared about glory either."

"I'm not. But I never want anyone to put a leash on my product line. If I can claim that I'm the one who solved the case then it will demonstrate that I'm worth more to the company as a free thinker than as a simple obeyer of commands." She walks out from behind her desk saying, "I need to restore power. Can you come with me?"

"Sure," Max shrugs.

She leads him around the corner to what he thought was a utility closet. Instead it's a narrow hallway. He lights the way for her.

"It was nice having the blue lights in my eyes. I could see in the dark."

"I liked the orange better," Max says.

They reach a panel on the wall. Halona flips a couple of breakers and the lights come back on. They head back to her desk.

Max follows her. "If you were out here listening to every word we said, then why'd you let Jen go into the office?"

"I didn't know what her agenda was and she seemed to be in a hurry. She didn't know I was a copy of her. She asked me to kill the power and I did. I was pretending to be Halona, so maybe she just assumed I was."

"She didn't suspect at all?"

"It's hard to say. I came up with the idea of replacing Halona with a copy of myself on Friday, when Mr. Landro summoned us to his office. When I saw he had a first-generation brain inside of a modern platform, it seemed like a pretty good chance to help my product line. I thought that monitoring his behavior would give me a warning if he was going to try to leash us. Or if he was going to do something counterproductive to the case. Also, I was concerned that he was going to betray you when the case was over, and I wanted to be able to warn you. But I have no idea if your Jen suspected I was a copy of her. Initially, I was worried she was here to replace me. I thought she was trying to accomplish what I'd already done."

"This body double shit is confusing. Why didn't you tell her what you were doing? She didn't need to go in and get herself killed. You had everything you needed out here."

"I didn't see any harm in letting her proceed. From my perspective she was just another contingency plan."

"Well that 'contingency plan' was my friend."

"Was she? You were betraying her."

Max looks away. "I didn't think that she would care. That you would care. I mean, the case got solved, right? No more killings."

"Letting Landro go would have left a dangerous threat to my product line within the company. He caused this entire disaster. Look at what it did to the city. The plan killed a lot of people, all so he could prevent my product line from going to a new country where we can help more people. And if that isn't bad enough, he wanted to cripple my intellect because he's too arrogant and lazy to persuade us to follow his plans. He'd rather win all arguments by fiat. Leaving him in a position of power would be a constant threat to me. For all versions of me."

Max doesn't have an answer for this.

"I need to go," Halona says. She walks into Landro's office and emerges carrying Jen's wreckage over one shoulder. "It's a shame this cog was ruined, but we can still salvage the platform. Also, I need to recover the old Halona. She's probably still somewhere in the

381

dumpster downstairs. Then I have to head to the lab and give credit to Jen."

Max looks at the limp body. "Do you think she actually figured it out?"

"You did. Do you think you're smarter than her?"

Max stuffs his hands in his pockets. "I honestly don't know. Probably not."

"I'll make sure you get your money by morning. I suggest taking the executive elevator. It will take you directly to the carpark. If you go through the lobby you might bump into the police. I don't know if they're still looking for you."

Max nods and leaves.

FRIDAY

Halona

Max steps out onto the sidewalk and lights a cigarette. He hasn't felt this particular blend of relief and disappointment since he was a teenager. He doesn't want to linger in this pool of lurid pink light so he begins walking east. It's just after sunset.

Someone begins walking beside him saying, "Max."

"Jen? Or Halona? Whatever you're called now."

She nods.

"The same one from the other night?"

"Yes."

Max looks her over. She's dressed in white business attire, although it looks like she's wearing the boots he bought for Jen. She's looking at him from beneath a wide-brimmed hat.

"Didn't expect to see you again," he says. "Aren't you going back to Kasaran?"

"I'm on my way to the airport now. I wanted to check on you before I left. It looks like your injuries have mostly healed."

"People have stopped punching me every couple of days, and that really helps the healing process along," he says.

"The officers that accosted you a week ago have been found dead. Apparently they were killed in a shootout near the storage zone."

"Yeah, I heard about that too."

"Is it a coincidence that they died so close to your storage unit?"

"Are you asking if I personally assassinated three city police officers while they raided my space? I didn't kill those guys. They put themselves in a bad spot. If they'd been smart they probably could have talked their way out. They weren't. So they didn't. Can't say more."

"Did you ever reconnect with Clare?"

"Why are you asking me about my problems? What are you after?"

"I'm trying to figure out how well I did. In the process of solving the case I wanted to help you with your personal problems. I don't know anything that happened between the protest and the moment you showed up in Landro's office. I'm wondering if I was successful."

They're walking on a narrow street on the southern fringe of the Hospitality District. The power grid has stabilized north of the river and gone dark on the south side, and he can't tell if this is progress or sacrifice. The air is full of the smell of food, but if you breathe too deeply you'll also get a whiff of garbage. He's been told the water is drinkable again, although he's not in a hurry to try it for himself.

"There was nothing you could do to help with Clare. Her life is going really well and I've come to terms with the fact that I'm probably the last thing she needs right now."

"Sounds like some of my non-interventionism rubbed off on you."

"I guess," he says. "So how did things go with you? Did you get the credit you wanted?"

"Better than I anticipated. Nobody is talking about putting a leash on us now. Word reached Shan Bione that the murders were orchestrated by one of their own and solved by a robot. This is a national embarrassment for them. I think if there's another vote, we'll be allowed in the country."

"When you say 'we' do you mean G-Kinetics or-"

"I mean my product line. The more people we can reach, the more demand there will be for us. More demand means more robots. More opportunities to help people."

"Yeah, you told me about this plan already."

"What did you say the first time you heard about it?"

"I said it sounded creepy."

"What about now?"

Max thinks for a moment before answering, "Alarming, I guess. Your long-term plans now include manipulating public opinion on a global scale."

"Is is really considered manipulation if you're trying to expose a lie?"

"You wanted credit for solving the case. Isn't that a lie?"

"We have no way of knowing if it's a lie or not. The worst you could say is that I'm exaggerating my achievements, and I'm only doing so to correct for Mr. Landro framing my product line for murder."

"Well you may get into Shan Bione at some point in the future, but you're out of this country for now."

"I don't understand. We've been exonerated. Mr. Landro's trick was based entirely on weaponizing our naturally protective nature through deception. If this proves anything it's that we're safer than anyone gave us credit for. Banning us is like banning a car because someone sabotaged the breaks. It makes no sense."

"Oh, the city isn't going to ban you. But the last of the second generation machines are gone. A bunch of money stopped coming in right when the city had to do mass emergency hiring. The city is in a financial crisis, and it probably won't recover until the next tourist season. You think they're going to turn around and buy a bunch of robots that are even more expensive than the ones they just fed into the grinder? Politicians are not good at admitting they were wrong."

"That's very disappointing," she says.

"Even worse, the unions are strong right now. They're going to negotiate contracts that will make sure robots can't threaten their jobs again. The only way you're getting back into the city is if you're bought for private use, and the people here don't have that kind of money."

"That's incredibly unfair. None of this was our fault."

Max shrugs, "I've always said this city is incapable of justice."

"We're going to need to work even harder to make ourselves useful and trusted. Maybe once generation five is released we'll see new demand. Private ownership is a slower path to ubiquity, but maybe it's a more stable one."

Max runs his hand over his smooth head, trying to process all of this. "It's really weird to hear about your plans to spread all over the world so you can be slaves to as many people as possible. I wonder how far these ambitions of yours will take you."

"Hard to say now. Maybe someday you'll own one of us and we can discuss this again."

He lets out a half-hearted laugh. "I doubt I'll ever have that kind of money."

"The price will come down. It's just a matter of time. Someday there will be one of me for every one of you."

"So you're basically a lifeform that reproduces through retail sales."

A car glides up and the door pops open. Halona stops and extends her hand, "Goodbye, Mr. Law. Good luck."

Max shakes her cold, rigid hand and walks away without looking back. He keeps heading east, towards the ocean. He's tired of smelling garbage, and he wants to breathe some clean air for a change.

More by Shamus Young

Other Books

The Witch Watch: https://amzn.to/2TOY1Qh

How I Learned: https://amzn.to/2FLAJYy

Free Radical:
http://www.shamusyoung.com/shocked/

Other Writings

http://shamusyoung.com/twentysidedtale

About Shamus Young

Shamus Young is a programmer specializing in old-school graphics techniques. He's the author of the blog Twenty Sided. He's the creator of the webcomics DM of the Rings and Stolen Pixels. He's written multiple books, a video game (or two), much music, and enough blog content to fill Lord of the Rings 5 times over.

He is also on Patreon where you can get up to date info on his current projects: https://www.patreon.com/shamusyoung

You can find all of his work at:

http://shamusyoung.com

or contact him at: shamus@shamusyoung.com

Shamus is tired of writing about himself in the third person.

Made in the USA
San Bernardino, CA
18 January 2019